The Burial Chamber

Jeremy Cox

By the same author
The Stone Coffin
writing as Oliver Hogarth

The Burial Chamber

4526

Jeremy Cox

STROUD GREEN BOOKS

Published in 2012 by Stroud Green Books
14 Hanley Road, London. N4 3DR.
If you have enjoyed this book, please let us know.
Contact Roz Underwood
stroudgreenbooks@clara.co.uk

British Library C.I.P.

A CIP catalogue record for this title is available from the
British Library.

Printed and bound in the UK by the MPG Books Group,
Bodmin and King's Lynn.

With many thanks to my editor and mentor,
Sarah Litvinoff

For Rosie

Prologue
London January 1814

The chamber was to be built underground adjacent to the eastern side of the house. Access to it would be through a passageway to be dug through a wall in one of the rooms in the cellar. A gaunt-looking Englishman with a bald head engaged a house builder to carry out the work. A plan of the chamber, which was to be circular with a domed roof, had been drawn up by a man of Arabic appearance. He supervised the work, giving his instructions in his native language to the Englishman, who translated them for the builder. When the work was completed and the workmen had gone, the foreigner painted a large triangle in gold on the flagstone floor, its three points touching the base of the circular wall on which he drew a profusion of arcane symbols. A carpenter was then engaged. When his work was completed, the chamber was ready to receive its occupant.

Chapter One
London 1821

ROBERT MOUNTFORD

Laudanum used to afford me a whole night's respite, but it was beginning to fail me. As the St John's Chapel clock struck four, I listened to the rain, picturing Lizzie, twelve years old, lying on the operating table, her face merging with that of my sister as her lifeless eyes stared blindly up at me.

Through much of the autumn, London had been inundated with rain and buffeted by high winds. On that afternoon, rain drummed on the roof of the operating theatre at Barts Hospital and there was no light from its rattling windows to add to that of the gas lamp suspended from its ceiling. An assistant was wiping blood and splinters of bone from the operating table when Lizzie was brought in, lying in her father's arms. She had been employed as a cleaner in a newspaper print room where her father worked and had caught her hand in a printing press while it was in operation. Her hand and arm were in tatters and blood dripped through a makeshift bandage made out of a shirt. She was unconscious.

Her father was a large man whose physical strength belied a gentle nature and he stood, helpless as a child himself as he looked at his daughter's blood dripping on to the floor and took in the sight of saws, mallets, retractors, scalpels and tourniquets hanging on the walls or arranged on shelves.

I laid the girl down on the operating table with two assistants standing by and screwed a tourniquet on to her upper arm to stop the flow of blood. I had to work speedily as she would die from loss of blood in minutes. I marked the place where I would cut off her arm just above the elbow and prayed that the girl's unconscious state would free her from pain. It was not to be. The first incision awakened her and she screamed, her rain-soaked black hair flopping from side to side as she twisted her body to be free of the two assistants who were now holding her down, her unfocussed eyes bulging wide as she screamed. Moments later, she fell back limp, her eyes dull. I put an ear to her mouth to try to detect breathing while I felt for her pulse. I put a glass in front of her mouth and looked at it closely for the faintest fogging. There was none. When I looked up, I saw the stricken face of the girl's father looking back at me, not being able to take it all in.

***

Like all surgeons, I had to cope with the brutal nature of surgery but the strength of will I needed to shield myself from the suffering I was causing had never been quite sufficient. This time, my defences were shattered by the girl's unnerving likeness to my sister, Alice. After eight years, I believed I had learned to bear my devastation when she lost her young life but it was rushing back to me now as if it were yesterday. When St John's struck five I thought about taking another dose of laudanum but I dared not, lest I sleep too long. My increasing dependence on it worried me but the urge to obliterate the daily nightmare of the screams of my patients was becoming stronger.

The one hope that I held out for my future lay in something I had learned from a colleague at the hospital called Douglas Harvey. Harvey was more than a colleague.

He was also a friend, one of the few friendships I had formed since I had come to London, my natural reticence tending to deter people from getting to know me. One evening, when I was sitting in the tap room at the tavern down the road from the hospital, Harvey came up to me.

'My dear chap. You're looking even more disconsolate than usual, if I may say so.'

He put a hand on my shoulder and beckoned to a waiter.

'I think this man's in need of a brandy.'

When the drink arrived, he leant over to me, his elbows on the table, and peered into my eyes as if he were studying a specimen under a microscope.

'Tell me, Mountford. For once in your life, could you unlock your secretive old soul and tell me what the matter is?'

As always, I feared it would be shaming to admit my problems to a fellow member of a profession that demanded a show of fortitude and a robust attitude to the causing of pain. I could tell that some of my fellows had difficulty keeping up such a show but somehow managed to do so and toughen themselves to what they were doing. I took a swallow of brandy and decided that evening to confide in my friend.

'What are you going to do?' Harvey asked after he had listened to my troubles.

'I don't know.'

'Will you give up surgery?'

'Perhaps. I could become an apothecary.'

'That would be a pity.'

'Why?'

'Because you're such a skilled surgeon you can perform an amputation more quickly and cleanly than anyone else in the hospital. That includes me, and I know I'm good. And you show sympathy for your patients. You talk to them. That makes a difference, you know. I'm trying to follow your example.'

Harvey called to the waiter for another brandy. I knew I was a good surgeon and it would be discreditable to give up what was, with all its failings, a worthwhile occupation. I imagined myself being an apothecary, seeing my former colleagues walking past my dispensary, feeling ashamed that I wasn't with them.

***

A week later, Harvey came up to me in one of the wards and waved a copy of the *The Times* at me.

'You must read this, old chap,' he announced. 'A very interesting article. It's a piece about a surgeon at the Royal Infirmary in Edinburgh. James Carlyle. He attended a demonstration by a mesmerist and was persuaded that the man could control his subjects' sensory nerves. Now he's attempting to use the technique to relieve his patients' pain during his operations. With some success apparently, although I find it hard to believe. So do some of his colleagues, he says. They think him some sort of charlatan but he's certain he's on to something.'

He handed me the paper.

'Given the difficulties you're having, perhaps you should find out about it.'

I had read about Anton Mesmer, the Viennese physician who invented a medical treatment he called animal magnetism which was said to cure people of various ailments by having magnets passed over their bodies. I was also aware of travelling showmen calling themselves mesmerists who claimed to be able to put members of their audience into a trance and control their actions and thoughts. It was with some skepticism that I read the article about Carlyle's observation that they could also control their subjects' physical sensations but I couldn't help being genuinely interested in the possibility that the phenomenon really existed. I gripped Harvey's arm.

'Thank you, Harvey, you're a good friend.'

The following day I wrote to Carlyle asking if I could have a meeting with him to learn about his work.

***

Some weeks later I heard Harvey calling out to me as I came into the hospital.

'Any luck with that Edinburgh surgeon yet?'

'His wife wrote back to say that he is away in America and that he would write to me when he returned to Edinburgh later in the year'.

'Good. In the meantime, you should have a look at this.' He took a newspaper cutting from his pocket and handed it to me.

'An advertisement in yesterday's paper.'

Doctor Alphonse Pierot, the highly regarded physician from Paris, will give a lecture upon the subject of mesmerism and will conduct a series of the most extraordinary and entertaining experiments illustrating this newly discovered science at the Town Hall Oxford on Saturday evening at 7 o'clock. His three assistants and members of the audience will be experimented upon in a perfectly wakeful state. Their movements will be controlled, and their sight, hearing, memory and their sensibility to pain will be taken away and instantly restored at the instruction of Doctor Pierot. Single tickets, 2s.6d. A gentleman and two ladies, 5s.

When I had finished reading it, Harvey looked me in the eye.

'I can see what you're thinking' he remarked.

'You can?'

'You're afraid you'll be embarrassed about participating in something that turns out to be a trick.'

'You're right.'

'Well, Carlyle thinks the phenomenon's genuine and I think you should go.'

Chapter Two

The following week, I set off for the Golden Cross coaching office in the Strand on my way to attend Dr. Pierot's demonstration in Oxford. The city was bursting with activity, carriages and coaches going at breakneck speed as I pushed my way through the crowds, the cries of the street sellers coming from all directions. In Fleet Street I heard St Brides strike the quarter and realised I was late. The coach would be leaving in five minutes. I broke into a run, nearly knocking down a young crossing sweeper and narrowly avoided a hackney cab that raced past me an inch away from my nose. I was immediately overtaken by the thought of having run in front of it. Good God, I thought. Was life so difficult that I could picture myself putting an end to it? I shook the thought from my mind as I ran on. When I reached the Strand, I saw the Oxford coach pulling out from the Golden Cross stables and into the street. I waved my arms as I neared it, shouting up to the driver who pulled up and waited for me to buy my ticket and climb aboard.

I had slept so little the previous night that the movement of the coach and the clatter of horses' hooves soon sent me to sleep and I found myself in a dream theatre in which the dead girl, Lizzie, was inviting me to join an audience of corpses, waiting for the entrance of an illusionist who would reattach their severed limbs and bring them back to life by magic.

It was late afternoon when I was jolted awake by the coach pulling up in the courtyard of the George Inn in Oxford. I booked a room for the night and walked out into the square.

A large crowd surrounded the entrance to the town hall where Dr. Pierot was to put on his show. Posters pasted to the wall advertised his amazing powers.

Shortly before the Town Hall doors opened, a young man driving a phaeton at some speed turned a corner into the square, his hat nearly blowing off his head from the rapidity of his approach. As he began to pull up, I saw a boy of some six years running into the path of the horse. I was horrorstruck and ran towards the boy, knowing in the back of my mind that I and the child might both be trampled by the horses' hooves. I scooped up the boy and ran on to the other side of the road moments before we would have been hit. A cry went up from the women as the carriage came to a halt. I lifted the child and carried him back to his mother's arms. As soon as I had done so, I dropped down on to the steps of the town hall in a state of exhaustion, my heart pounding. I knew I had been close to death and recalled the hackney cab racing past me that morning.

'Sir, I am devastated,' a voice above me declared and I looked up to see the man I recognised as the driver of the phaeton; a good looking man in his thirties with long fair hair, dressed in a loose-fitting black velvet coat and a white silk neck cloth. A gentleman of leisure who fancies himself as an artist or poet, I thought with a hint of condescension.

'I cannot thank you enough,' the man said. 'Please excuse me for a moment. I must speak to the mother.'

He walked over to the woman holding the child.

'My dear lady, I am so sorry. The truth is I didn't see the child there, what with the press of people.'

The mother was holding the boy tight, her hand against the back of his head, his face pressed into the nape of her neck.

9

She was looking down not wanting to respond to the man's apology, fearful perhaps that it would confront her with the fact that she was partly to blame for the incident, not having held on to her child's hand in the crowd.

'Bless me, Jack, what a little scamp you are,' she muttered into the boy's ear and the man stooped to look at him.

'Are you alright, old chap?'

The boy nodded.

'I am most relieved.'

He looked at the woman's sullen face, offering her a disarming smile.

'Is there anything I can do for you, dear lady.'

'No thank you, sir.'

'Once again, please accept my humblest apologies.'

A man of the world, at ease in all manner of company, I thought as I got back on to my feet. Someone clearly belonging to a class above my own. The man came over to me, doffed his hat and bowed graciously.

'Fanshawe, sir. John Fanshawe.

I touched my hat.

'Robert Mountford, sir.'

'I'm most pleased to meet you, Mr. Mountford. Under the circumstances, more than you can imagine.'

For some reason, I resented the man's charm at the same time as being beguiled by it. A man with an easy life, I thought but with a glint in his pale gray eyes that I found disconcerting. Now, the man's face was full of concern.

'You must be feeling shocked. You've just averted a most horrible accident and risked your own life in doing so.'

'It's no more than anyone would have done,' I replied a little awkwardly.

'I don't think so, sir.'

He took a silver flask out of his pocket.

'Brandy? You must need a little of this. I'm sure I do.'

'Thank you.'

As we each took a gulp, another boy, about eleven years of age, came up to the mother.

'Where've you been,' she snapped.

'Just walking around.'

'Your other son?' Fanshawe asked, turning to her. 'Tell me, do you live nearby?'

'Just down the road.' The woman pointed with her eyes to a corner of the square. I watched Fanshawe employing his easy charm again.

'How would you feel if your boy were to look after my carriage for me while I go to Dr. Pierot's lecture and have a bite to eat at the George? There's a shilling in it for him.

'Yes please sir,' the boy interjected without waiting for the response of his mother who was looking at the man expectantly.

Fanshawe read its meaning correctly.

'And look. Here's a shilling for you and your little one, dear lady, for the distress I've caused you both.'

As he took a coin out of his pocket, the child lifted his head from his mother's nape, his hand held out to take it. The mother made a small curtsey.

'Thank you, sir'.

Fanshawe looked at the boy.

'What's your name, young fellow?'

'Tommy, sir.'

'Look, Tommy. You can sit in the carriage if you want to. My horse is called Chester if you want to pass the time of day with him.'

'Thank you, sir.'

Fanshawe and I rejoined the waiting crowd.

'Do you know anything about Dr. Pierot?' I asked.

'One of the old members of my club knows a bit about him. He is a real Frenchman. It's not just a stage name. His parents came over from France before the Revolution and made their home here. He went back to France when he came of age and learned about mesmerism in Paris from a disciple of Mesmer. When he came back here he set up as a travelling showman.'

As the town hall doors opened and the crowd made its way into the hall, I allowed Fanshawe to walk ahead of me. As soon as I had done so, I was struck by the realization that my standing back had been more than simple courtesy; it had been unthinking deference to someone I considered to be from a higher station in life than my own. The thought rankled. He's no more than a well-to-do man of leisure with Byronic pretensions, I told myself, dreaming up imagined faults in Fanshawe's character. I only just managed to stop myself slipping into the pietism that I hated in my Presbyterian family and judging the man to be unworthy of serious consideration.

The two of us paid our money and walked into a grand assembly room in which rows of chairs were set out for the audience. The room glowed pink, lit by candles in brass wall sconces with rose-tinted chimneys. On a table at the front of the room stood two candles and three voltaic batteries whose tall columns gave off the pungent smell of oxidizing acids. I

12

took a seat in the front row, wanting to be best placed to see any trickery, should any take place. Fanshawe came up to me, taking off his hat and motioning it towards the seat next to me.

'May I?' he asked.

'Of course,' I replied, a little tight-lipped. I was here on serious business and I feared that Fanshawe was going to be talkative and affect my concentration. Fanshawe turned to me with a raised eyebrow when he was settled in his seat.

'I'm looking forward to seeing what happens to those girls mentioned in his advertisement. What d'you think he's going to do to them?'

'I don't know,' I replied shortly.

I wasn't going to engage in the sort of banter the man was looking for and I made a show of studying the architecture of the grand hall. There was a hush as Pierot entered from a door at the back of the room wearing a long cape of maroon velvet. He strode purposefully up to the table on which the voltaic batteries were standing followed by three meek-looking girls wearing white mob caps, and dressed neatly in the clothes of household servants. Pierot motioned them to a row of chairs next to the table and turned to the audience. His neatly trimmed beard and jet-black hair, combed back from a widow's peak, made me think of Mephistopheles. Just a showman, I thought and prepared for a disappointing evening.

Pierot clapped his hands together with a flourish.

'Ladies and gentlemen, let me introduce myself. My name is Dr. Alphonse Pierot. I am a mesmerist and these are my 'patients' upon whom I shall conduct my experiments.'

13

He turned to the girls who sat modestly, their hands in their laps.

'I can assure you that they are of good character and that there will be no collusion between us.'

He let his gaze travel across the audience, holding a pointed finger in the air.

'Perhaps you know the work of Anton Mesmer, the Viennese physician.'

He waited for a response but the audience remained silent. I held my hand up.

'Very good, sir. Then you'll know what he did. Let me show the others. Mesmer passed magnets over the bodies of his patients like this.'

He held his hands close to the chest of one of the girls as if he were holding magnets in them and stroked them down her body several times.

'I wager he beds her,' Fanshawe murmured to me as an aside and I shushed him. Despite my irritation, I had guessed the same thing.

'Thank you, Jane,' Pierot said when he had finished. 'Mesmer's belief,' he continued, 'was that the magnets put his patients into a trance state during which he could manipulate invisible fluids inside their bodies and cure them of their ailments. We now know that the trance state was really brought about by Mesmer's powers of suggestion. It is this power that I am now going to demonstrate to you this evening. I will put the girls into trance states, talking to them quietly while passing this silver coin in front of them.'

He held up the coin for the audience to see.

'When I have done so, their consciousness will be under my control while their other functions remain unimpaired.

14

They will think or do or feel what I tell them to. Now please be quiet while I do this.'

He addressed the girls in slow measured tones.

'Listen to me. I want you all to keep your eyes fixed on the coin without raising your heads.'

He held the coin above their heads, waving it from side to side and moving it back slowly until the girls' pupils swiveled up to the point that they almost disappeared into the tops of their sockets in their effort to look at it.

As the girls sat demurely with their eyes raised, I wondered if there was truly no collusion with him. I concentrated my attention on their every move or change of expression. Pierot stood in silence for a few seconds, looking briefly at the audience, a finger to his lips. The showman again. There was a long hush after which he addressed the girls with exaggerated quietness.

'You are beginning to feel sleepy, your eyelids are becoming so heavy that it is only with great difficulty that you can keep them open.' He paused. 'Now they are becoming heavier still.' He continued this litany until their eyes closed.

'You are all now in a trance state. Can you hear me, Jane?'

'Yes sir,'

'Good. Open your eyes.'

Peirot pointed to the voltaic batteries on the table next to her.

'In a minute I am going to ask you to hold the two wires attached to these three batteries. They are linked together so that a powerful current will pass through you but you will feel nothing. Do you understand that?'

'Yes, sir.'

I wondered how I would know if the electric charge would be strong enough to give the girl anything more than a tingle. Pierot turned to the audience.

'Would one of you like to touch the wires to be sure that they are live?'

I raised my hand. Now was the time to find out.

'Please come forward, sir.'

Pierot put on a pair of leather gloves and held the two wires out to me.

'Would you please hold one wire in each hand, sir.'

I picked up the wires.

'Good God,' I gasped when I touched them. I let go of them instantly as the sudden shock of the current passed through my body. I felt as if I had been kicked by a mule. There was nervous laughter from the audience and I saw Fanshawe looking at me with a sympathetic expression before covering his mouth with his hand to hide a smile. Pierot handed me another pair of gloves.

'Please put these on, sir, and hand the wires to Jane.'

How will she be able to cope with this, I thought. It will be impossible. I held out the wires to the girl, not wanting to cause her pain, and looked at her calm expression for any sign of distress when she took them from me. There was none. She sat quite still without showing any reaction. There was no sudden movement in her hands or any expression of suppressed pain in her face.

'Can you feel anything, Jane?' Pierot asked.

'No, sir.'

I was totally mystified and shook my head as I went back to my seat.

'Extraordinary,' I said to Fanshawe. James Carlyle may well have been right in his belief in the power of this phenomenon. Pierot introduced the other two girls.

'Lucy and Emma,' he said, tapping the tops of the girl's heads in turn. Lucy appeared to be the oldest of the three and worldlier than the other two. Emma was the prettiest, fair-haired and wide-eyed with the guileless expression of a girl not yet aware of her looks.

Pierot picked up a flintlock pistol from the table and held it in the air above his head, his arm stretched out as if he were about to fire it. A murmur ran through the audience, thinking something dangerous was going to happen. I pictured William Tell shooting an apple off his son's head.

'Ladies and gentlemen, this is a powerful pistol that once belonged to Maximilien Robespierre. It was taken from him shortly before he went to the guillotine.'

'The pistol's English,' Fanshawe murmured behind his hand. 'It's a Brander & Potts dueling pistol. They only started making them ten years ago. I've got a pair.'

Showman again. I tried to suppress my frustration with Pierot. Why did he have to invent such a story? Surely it is sufficient for him to demonstrate what appeared to be an extraordinary gift.

'The pistol is charged,' Pierot announced, pointing it to the middle of the auditorium.

'Then point that thing away from us,' someone shouted and he put the pistol back on the table.

'However...' he continued, having injected a little fear into the audience, 'there is no ball in the barrel so it will do no harm when fired.' He held up a finger as he scanned the faces before him. 'It will nevertheless make a loud bang.

17

Watch carefully and you will see that the girls won't flinch when I discharge the gun three inches above their heads.'

He picked up the gun and turned to the girls.

'I want you to sit still, face forward with your eyes open.'

Kneeling down behind them, he pointed the pistol upwards just above their heads and fired.

There was a loud crack and a woman in the audience screamed. My ears rang but I kept my eyes steadily on the girls' faces. None of them flinched and they remained dead still as the smoke from the gunpowder drifted up above their heads. Jane was still holding the electric wires. There was more murmuring as members of the audience expressed their astonishment to one another.

'What do you make of all this?' Fanshawe asked. 'D'you know, I fancy it's genuine.'

'You may be right.' I replied, and waited for the next demonstration.

Pierot held up his hands to hush the audience and turned to Emma who stood up next to him close to the front row. He held his hand up and something glinted, held between his finger and thumb.

'A sewing needle, ladies and gentlemen,' he explained. 'Quite a thick one for sewing sacks. You are now going to see another demonstration of the power of mesmerism. Would another member of the audience care to step forward?'

'I'm rather taken by young Emma,' Fanshawe said, holding up his hand. I groaned inwardly.

'Please come forward, sir. Now I want you to press this needle lightly into Emma's arm. Not very far mind, just enough to break the skin and draw a drop of blood. It should

18

be just sufficient that it would make you flinch if it were done to you.'

I ignored Fanshawe winking at me when Pierot handed him the needle. This was another demonstration of someone being made to feel no pain in the trance state and it was important. I was shocked to see Fanshawe push the needle nearly a quarter of an inch into the girl's flesh. That was surely much further than the mesmerist had intended.

'That's enough,' commanded Pierot as a rivulet of blood coursed down her arm. 'Withdraw the needle now!'

I was repelled by Fanshawe's willingness to hurt the girl but amazed at seeing her seeming to feel no pain. At the same time, I was comparing the pain of the sewing needle to the infinitely greater pain of having a limb amputated. Could mesmerism be powerful enough to prevent that pain as well? Now I couldn't wait to meet James Carlyle.

'I'm impressed,' Fanshawe said when he returned to his seat, 'and she's a pretty thing isn't she? I wouldn't mind taking her home and giving her a prick that wouldn't hurt her at all.'

I ignored his grin when he turned to me. Pierot clapped his hands and opened his arms to the audience, a broad smile on his face.

'Ladies and gentlemen, I would like four volunteers to participate in
another series of experiments. Have no fear. I shan't be using voltaic batteries, needles or guns,'

A number of hands went up and Pierot selected three young men who were sitting together and a pretty young woman wearing a large yellow bonnet, decorated with feather plumes. They made their way to the front of the

19

room, the young men ribbing one another and eyeing the young woman who giggled and covered her mouth. Pierot stood in front of one of the men, talking softly as the man looked up at the silver coin above his head. When he had induced the man's trance state he asked him to lie on the floor on his back.

'Sir, I am going to put you into a state of cataleptic rigidity. It is a state in which your muscles will be unable to move.'

He whispered some words to him and clicked his fingers.

'Now lift him up,' he told his two friends. 'One of you lift him holding his ankles and the other holding his shoulders.'

As the two men did so, the man remained as stiff as a board, his body as straight as it had been when he was lying on the floor. Pierot looked at his watch, holding a hand in the air.

'Don't move until I drop my hand,' he commanded. The man remained stiff with not a muscle moving for nearly a minute.

'Now put him down.'

He released the man from his trance and there was a cheer as the three of them returned to their seats. He turned to the young woman in the yellow hat.

'Now madam, would you please come and sit over here.'

He drew up a chair for her and picked up a stick from his table.

'Can you tell me what this is,' he asked as he handed it to her.

'A stick of course' she replied, looking at him as if he were weak in the head.

'Quite right.' He put the stick on the table.

'Now, when I click my fingers, thus,' he did so, 'I am going to give you a snake to hold. He looked at the audience with a conspiratorial smile and picked up the stick. I was jolted by the sound of the woman's piercing scream when she saw the stick and I looked at her in bewilderment as she fell to the floor. What scientific explanation could there be for such an extraordinary occurrence. It was mind over matter. If I had not been a materialist, I would have been tempted to think the man was a magician. There was another shout from the audience.

'My old woman gets the vapours when I show her my stick.'

Peals of laughter ensued as Pierot lifted the woman back on to her chair.

***

The show came to an end with much applause, Pierot having taken his volunteers and his girls out of their trance states. The girls took a bow, Emma rubbing her arm, obviously in pain from where Fanshawe had stuck in the needle. I wondered what sort of a man Fanshawe was to have done that. My thoughts then returned to Pierot's extraordinary performance and my wonderment at the strange source of his power. I wanted to talk to him, to arrange to meet him if he were willing but I was hampered by the crowding of the departing audience and Pierot leaving the room promptly while his girls began to collect his paraphernalia. I decided that it would be more appropriate for me to write to him than to explain my interest in person. I sought out the official who had organized the performance and persuaded him to part with one of Pierot's ornate cards printed in black and gold.

***

My mind was racing as I left the town hall, inspired by what I had witnessed, at the same time as being unwilling to let go of my critical faculties. Could there have been a trick involved that I hadn't spotted? Could Pierot have found a way of secretly turning off the current before I had handed the electric wires to the girl? Could the girls have put wax plugs in their ears without it being noticed before the gun was discharged? Could the volunteers have been colluding with Pierot? I thought of Fanshawe sticking the sewing needle into the girl's arm and I couldn't explain how the girl's lack of pain could be produced by trickery. Fanshawe caught up with me.

'You looked as if you received quite a shock from those wires.'

'I did. And it looked as if you gave the girl quite a pricking with the sewing needle.'

I was unable to keep a tone of criticism out of my voice.

'You noticed. Well, yes I did. I'm sorry about that but I needed to feel sure that the trance was real. And it was. Most impressive. What do you make of what you saw?'

'I am astounded. I found it quite extraordinary. The girls' insensitivity to pain is what strikes me most forcibly.'

'A lecturer at Balliol told me about Mesmer,' Fanshawe said. 'He attended one of his experiments in Paris. It was all very odd. Patients sat with their feet in a large tub of water with powdered glass and iron filings in it, holding hands.

The tub had a lid with holes in it with bent iron rods pushed into them which could be moved around to touch the patients' bodies. The women, they were all women, started convulsing, laughing and crying, their bodies jerking back and forth in spasmodic fits. Apparently they all felt better afterwards and claimed to have been cured of whatever it was that ailed them.'

'I've heard about that. I imagine it would be something to do with states of hysteria from which some women suffer. What intrigued me this evening was what happening to the girl's sensory nerves. Could their brains be shutting them off in some way while they were wide awake and alert?'

'You sound like a medical man.

'I'm a surgeon.'

'Ah. A noble occupation.' Fanshawe's eyes twinkled. 'I wouldn't have the stamina to deal with the pain I was causing. A little light chastisement of a doxy with a riding crop would be as far as I would go.'

I winced and Fanshawe saw it.

'Forgive me. I didn't mean to make light of the matter. Perhaps mesmerism could be used to help your patients. I expect you've thought of that.'

Fanshawe was certainly quick off the mark.

'It's the reason I came. I've read about a Scottish surgeon who's experimenting with it in America and I wanted to find out about it myself. You can imagine the quite terrible pain that patients have to go through during an operation, so anything that could relieve that suffering…'

'Of course. What a valiant fellow you are.' Fanshawe put a hand on my shoulder and turned to give me a warm laudatory smile.

23

'Look, Mr. Mountford. I'm going over to the George for a bottle of claret and a lamb chop. Would you care to join me? It's no distance.'

Given Fanshawe's jocular talk of doxies and riding crops and sticking needles into girl's arms, I was unsure what an evening in his company would be like, but the man was clearly intelligent and I would be glad of some company.

'Thank you. In fact I'm staying at the George tonight.'

'Jolly good.'

Fanshawe beamed at me and tipped his hat to the young lad in his carriage.

The inn was as full and noisy as when I had arrived in the coach and when Fanshawe had given his order to a waiter, he led me into one of the upstairs rooms where we could dine in private. A waiter followed us with two bottles of claret and glasses.

'To think that mesmerism could alleviate your patient's suffering,' Fanshawe declared as he poured out the wine and dropped into an armchair, his arms draped over the sides.

'It would be astonishing,' I agreed.

I caught sight of his left hand for a moment and noticed that the top two joints of his little finger were missing. Fanshawe saw my glance and instinctively closed his hand. I walked to the window and looked down on the square, my mind full of contradictory thoughts; my amazement at the demonstration of the electric wires and the sewing needle and my irritation with the theatricality of Pierot's performance which undermined it. So what happens to the nervous system in such a trance state? And how could you compare the girls' resistance to pain with the ability to resist pain during a surgical operation? Did Carlyle have the answers?

Fanshawe took a swallow of wine.

'I once fancied the idea of becoming a physician, administering physic to the wealthy without having to deal with the gruesome side of things as you do.'

'Really?' I turned from the window and took a seat opposite him.

'The trouble is,' he continued, 'when I read classics at Balliol I discovered that I didn't have much of a gift for Latin and I did have a tremendous gift for drink and women. And that, I regret to say, led to my being sent down.'

A ladies' man and the black sheep of the family, no doubt, I told myself, but I had to admit that I liked the man and was embarrassed by the thoughts of social envy and moral condescension I had felt earlier in the town square.

'You don't look terribly regretful.' I said, offering Fanshawe a genuine smile. His eyes glinted.

'You've found me out, Mr. Mountford. I have to admit you're right. I expect you'll find me a bit indolent. I've enough money to get by without having to seek gainful employment. My grandfather was a wealthy man of business. When I was born, the old fellow put a good deal of money in trust for me so, when I turned twenty one, I became a chap of reasonably independent means.'

'A gentleman.'

'Indeed.'

I couldn't help smiling at my priggish use of the term.

'Is it such a comic condition in life?' Fanshawe enquired, seeking help.

'Not at all. Have you always lived here?'

'Yes. Oxford town and gown you might say. I grew up in Kidlington where my mother made too much of me as a first born and a boy. Anyway, I'm bored with Oxford now and I shall be moving to London next month. I'm organizing the purchase of a house in Lincoln's Inn Fields. Tell me, where do you live?'

'I've a lodging near to St Bartholomew's Hospital, where I work.'

'Is that near the East End?'

'Pretty near.'

A run down place, I believe.'

'A place of unimaginable poverty. You'd have to see it to believe it.'

'Yet you choose to live a stone's throw from such horror?'

'I suppose I hope I can do some good there.'

I was immediately embarrassed by my unintended expression of piety as Fanshawe looked down at his hands in his lap, nodding his head as if to show his appreciation of my fine philanthropic qualities.

The meal arrived and we took our seats at a table near the window. Fanshawe poured out more wine and we raised our glasses.

'Good health to you, Mr. Mountford. I say, may we drop the 'Mr.' I'm sure we shall be friends.'

'Of course,' I replied, forcing a smile and wondering where this friendship would take me.

'You are clearly a man of strong humanitarian principles. Religious principles perhaps?'

'No, I'm an atheist and a materialist.'

'I'm glad you told me that. So am I. All that religious mumbo jumbo. My mother, however, is very religious. She was born a catholic but converted to the Church of England when she married. The house is full of dreadful pictures of saints.' He raised his eyes to the ceiling. 'And she prays as much to the Virgin Mary as she does to Jesus. I can't bear all that. Why pray to the mother when you should be praying to the son, not that I want to do either. And those frightful paintings and statues of Christ on the Cross, dripping with blood and with spears sticking into him in churches all over France and Spain and Italy. Anyway, you can imagine how my opinion on all this upset my mother and my sister, Sarah, bless her heart. I am deeply despaired of by my mother. She sees me as a hopeless reprobate, rejected by God and beyond hope of salvation. Sarah isn't religious but she hates seeing my mother hurt. Nevertheless, they both still care for me after a fashion. Isn't that wonderful, Mountford? By the way, I say sister as that's how I think of her. In fact she's my cousin, the only child of my mother's sister. Her father was killed at the Battle of the Nile and sometime after that her mother took ill with glandular fever. In the end, she asked my mother to take the child on before she died. Sarah was only five. I was sixteen.'

His face warmed.

'She's the sweetest girl, you know, but single-minded and determined if she needs to be. She was something of a tomboy when she was younger. I taught her to shoot and she used to go out riding with me shooting rabbits. She would put on some of the old clothes I wore when I was younger so she could ride astride. She loved it. And she's a good companion to my mother. She has to look after her now, my mother's mind being feeble and not capable of clear thought.

'What about your father?'

The warmth fell from Fanshawe's face and he flexed the muscles of his hand before he spoke.

'He disappeared when I was five.'

'You've never heard from him since he left?'

'No.'

'And your mother had no idea why he left?'

'Not really.'

'Do you remember him at all?'

Fanshawe took a swallow of claret.

'Hardly.'

I could tell that Fanshawe was uncomfortable but I was intrigued and remained silent, hoping that he would continue.

'My mother told me he was a natural philosopher when I was old enough to know what the words meant. He had a laboratory at the back of the house and a tall, thin assistant who frightened me. He wore eyeglasses with thick lenses that made his eyes look small.'

'What d'you think happened to your father?'

'I've no idea but, for some time before he disappeared, I heard him going into great rages with my mother and hearing her crying. She never talked to me about it.'

'Did you ever see what was inside his laboratory?'

'No, I wasn't allowed in there. Not while he was living with us, anyway.'

There was a long silence in which he seemed to be lost in some memory. I felt he was uncertain about whether or not to continue.

'I do have a memory of going in there once after he left,' he said at length.

'Go on,' I prompted after a long pause. He looked across the room.

'It was when I started sleepwalking. I used to walk around with a candle and wake up to find myself in various parts of the house feeling petrified.'

He downed his glass of wine in one swallow.

'You're a disarming fellow, you know, Mountford. Maybe it's because you're such a serious chap. I've never told this to anyone before, apart from Sarah.'

He refilled his glass.

'On one occasion, I woke up standing in front of the door to the laboratory. From inside the room I could hear the sound of an animal whimpering and its feet scampering over the flagstones. My mother kept the key to the door on top of a cupboard in the corridor. I took it down, unlocked the door and went in. A small creature like a fox with long pointed ears was staring at me, bright eyed. It lifted its head and let out a long high pitched howl. I was terrified. I ran out of the room and started to scream. My mother came down. When I told her what had happened, she took my hand and led me back into the room. It was empty and the windows were fastened. She told me that I must have been in a sleepwalking dream.'

'Do you think it wasn't a dream?' I asked.

'It must have been,' Fanshawe retorted, sounding uncomfortable. 'I'm a materialist.'

Despite his professed rationalist view of the world, I could tell that the memory disturbed him more than he wanted to admit to and he looked at me, clearly wanting to change the subject.

'Come on Mountford. Tell me about you.'

'Scottish as I expect you can hear. I grew up in Aberdeen which is still the home of my parents and my younger brother.' I paused. Now I was finding it difficult to go on.

'I also had a sister. She died when she was twelve.'

'My dear fellow, forgive me for going on about Sarah.'

'Don't worry, Fanshawe. I like the sound of Sarah,' I replied, not wanting to speak about my sister. Fanshawe didn't press me and I went on to tell him about my slow-witted younger brother who would never be able to make his own way in life. I told him about my estrangement from my strict Presbyterian parents that came about when I took to the free-thinking philosophy introduced to me by my uncle, the surgeon to whom I was apprenticed when I was sixteen.

'I'm very sorry, Mountford. It seems that our libertarian views have estranged us both from our families. In my case, I'm luckier than you. My mother and sister haven't cast me out. They've just despaired of me.'

He looked at me with a quizzical expression.

'Tell me, do you consider yourself a broadminded man?'

I wondered what was coming.

'I'm not sure what meaning of the term you have in mind.'

'I'll take a chance in telling you something that I trust won't offend you. Do you know anything about Sir Francis Dashwood and the Friars of St Francis of Wycombe round about the middle of the last century?'

'You mean the Hellfire Club?'

'Yes.'

'I've read about it.'

I remembered being aroused when I read an account of it in a book in my uncle's library, its members indulging in all sorts of libertine excesses and satanic rituals. There were rumours of members of the nobility including royalty and government ministers being members. Fanshawe grinned, seeing my uneasiness.

'I expect you disapproved of it but you may imagine how such a club would appeal to me. I think the pagan and satanic rituals were just play-acting, by the way. It was just wine and women with the motto, 'Do As Thou Wilt.' Rabelais's phrase, I think.' He poured more wine. 'Anyway, you may wonder why I'm telling you all this. The reason is that a friend of mine has formed such a club of his own just outside Oxford. His name's Ashton, Knight of the Realm. Another free-thinker who can't stand religious mumbo jumbo. He inherited a fortune from his father who was in the shipping business and a wonderful Palladian mansion called Shadborough House. I met him at Balliol. He's some years older than me and was in his third year when I first went up. It was he who introduced me to wine, women and song. Well, not women in his case. He's an odd sort of fellow with rather eccentric tastes. After the death of his father, he discovered in the old chap's correspondence that he had belonged to Dashwood's club and he was so consumed with retrospective envy that he decided to start such a club of his own.'

I was beginning to feel uneasy.

'Ashton determined that it be as outrageous as anything Dashwood had conceived. It would be dedicated to Dionysus, Venus, Pan, Lucifer and Satan and anybody else who would be guaranteed to upset churchmen of any denomination. They're not much more than fancy dress parties with fellows dressed up in old-fashioned colourful coats, tricorne hats and so on, such that Dashwood's lot

31

would have worn. There's a bit of pagan ritual and sacrilege of various kinds to get the members excited. And the house is decorated somewhat idiosyncratically, Ashton's father being a rather eccentric lover of art. He made a tour of Egypt two or three years before he died. He came back with trophies from some of the tombs and started to have the house decorated with wall paintings in the Egyptian style. He returned to Egypt the following year and didn't come back. Ashton never found out what had happened to him.'

He took a swallow of wine.

'What makes Ashton's Hellfire festivities go with a bang is the abundance of dollymops. Real beauties too, some of them. All dressed up in their finery, their lips reddened and their eyes sparkling with belladonna powder. Some are dressed in nun's habits but you can still see the painted faces beneath. And they're all paid for. How about that? The servants are well paid to be discreet. Quite important that. I've seen some prominent gentlemen popping in and out of the bedchambers.' he grinned. 'You won't be surprised to know that I'm a member.'

He looked at me, his eyes narrowed.

'You're curious about it, are you not? I think you are.'

He was right. I was curious as well as apprehensive.

'I'm asking because they're having a meeting there tonight. I am going to it and I wondered if you'd like to come.'

He studied my face.

'I think I may have shocked you.'

'Not at all,' I replied untruthfully, knocking back some more wine and trying to sound at ease. I wondered if I should be courting the company of such a fellow and how I would feel amongst the upper classes in their libidinous abandonment. No doubt they would detect my modest station in life and I would be left feeling like an outsider. Not only that. The thought of them indulging, however frivolously, in satanic rituals made me feel deeply uncomfortable. I told myself I was a free-thinker but I couldn't help picturing my father glaring down at me. At that moment, there was a knock on the door.

'Say nothing yet,' Fanshawe said, 'but please share another bottle of claret with me.'

He shouted towards the door, summoning the waiter.

'Would you like anything else to eat, old chap?'

I shook my head.

'No more to eat, waiter, but bring us another bottle of claret and a pen and ink.'

He gave me a broad smile.'

'Mountford, would you please give me your address so that I can call on you when I move to London?'

'Of course.'

My reservations about a continuing friendship with Fanshawe were being submerged by the quantity of wine I had drunk. I had not met anybody like him before. As well as being something of a blade, he was intelligent and well educated, despite his time spent roistering at Balliol. And good company. I still felt uncertain about an evening of hellfire antics but decided that it would be better than drinking brandy on my own in the saloon bar of the George Inn. When the waiter returned with the wine and pen and ink, Fanshawe handed me a visiting card, its blank reverse side up and I wrote down my address. Fanshawe then brought the conversation to a close, raising his eyebrows and holding up his hand to invite my response to his proposal.

'Well, Mountford, how about it?' he asked, closing his hand quickly as he saw me noticing the missing finger.

'Would you like to come?'

'Thank you, I would.'

'Excellent. By the way, you don't need to go in fancy dress. Not everybody wears it. I shall go as I am.'

'But you already look the part with your long hair and your velvet coat,' I contended. 'You look like a poet.'

The wine was putting a silly grin on my face and Fanshawe burst out laughing.

'I do? I love that. I think I shall play the poet with the ladies. In fact, we may see some literary types there. Coleridge and de Quincey were at Ashton's last jollification. By the way, have you read de Quincey's *Confessions of an English Opium Eater,* in the *London Magazine*?'

'I haven't.'

'You must read it. His descriptions of his dreams while experimenting with laudanum are amazing. I could be tempted by that. It makes me think of Kublai Khan and all that sort of thing.'

'Really?' I remarked, and left it at that. It was not a topic of conversation I was inclined to pursue, not wanting to question my own use of laudanum as amounting to an addiction.

Chapter Three

Mellowed by drink, I was still pondering Pierot's extraordinary power over his girls as Fanshawe's phaeton sped along the lane to Sir Ralph Ashton's house and I tried to picture myself using Pierot's techniques to achieve such power over my patients.

The carriage made a sudden right turn and I was thrown to one side, holding on to my hat as the carriage swept past a gatehouse and into a driveway that curved up to a grand house in the neo-classical style. My speculations about mesmerism were eclipsed as I gazed about me in awe, taking in the spectacle of the landscaped grounds lit by marble torchères in the form of classical Greek goddesses holding flaming cups above their heads.

Fanshawe pulled up in front of the house and two footmen in green silk livery bowed to us. I climbed down on to the forecourt picturing myself as an 18th century aristocrat. One of the footmen climbed aboard the phaeton and drove it to the side of the house where the ranks of carriages were standing.

The sound of a string quartet came from behind the open doors of the entrance to the house where two more footmen bowed to us. Fanshawe gave his name to one of them who asked respectfully in a low tone for the name of his companion. A whispered conversation took place after which the footman walked into the hall and approached a man seated behind a Queen Anne desk. Fanshawe leant towards me.

'There's a certain amount of confidentiality required at these events, and the footman's checking with Atkinson, the household steward. The chap knows me well so your dependability will be accepted without question.'

At that moment, Atkinson looked up at Fanshawe, smiling and beckoning us in.

Fanshawe winked at me.

'You see?'

We walked across a huge colonnaded entrance hall past a chamber orchestra of bewigged musicians in colourful coats. Flickering torch flames from sconces illuminated the walls on which frescoes of Egyptian figures had been painted, their marching legs and animal heads in profile and their broad shoulders facing forwards.

'Ancient Egyptian gods, I imagine,' Fanshawe said.

As a footman took our coats, I caught sight of a life-size ebony statue with a human body and a dog-like head with long upward-pointed ears. The end of the entrance hall was framed by a broad arch under which stood a male figure carved in stone, wearing a crown and with a finger held to his lips.

'The god of secrets, that's what Ashton calls him. You can guess why they need him here.'

Beyond the arch, the expansive curves of a double staircase led up to a gallery whose walls were hung with paintings in ornate gold frames depicting lovers' trysts. I was overwhelmed by the magnificence of it all, gilding everywhere glittering in the candlelight. From behind me I heard the sound of horses' hooves clattering on the marble floor and turned to see a man dressed as an Arab in a long black tunic and headdress riding a tall chestnut stallion into the entrance hall. The rider nodded to Fanshawe as he passed us.

'Good evening, Fanshawe. You're well, I hope.'

'Indeed, Sir Ralph. And you?

'Best of spirits, old chap,' he replied, and rode the horse through an open doorway to the garden.

'Sir Ralph Ashton. Something of an eccentric like his father as I've told you,' Fanshawe remarked sotto voce. He led me down a corridor whose walls were also hung with paintings, this time explicitly depicting couples engaged in varieties of sexual congress and my eye was held by the detailed representations of acts of copulation. Fanshawe tapped my arm and pointed to a marble statue of a midget with a gargoyle face holding his erect member.

'How do you do, sir,' he announced, introducing himself to the midget and I felt my face flush as Fanshawe shook hands with its member and began to giggle to such an extent that he ended up crouching as if to stop himself pissing his breeches. He pulled himself together and smiled at my embarrassment.

'You're definitely in need of another drink, old chap'.

We walked into a room full of the sound of loud conversation and the smell of tobacco smoke mingling with that of flatulence, warm wine and cinnamon. Large bowls of punch were laid out on a long table around which sat a motley bunch of middle-aged men, wearing colourful coats and tricorne hats. Many of the men had half-dressed girls on their laps and in a corner of the room an old man in a stained yellow silk coat was urinating into a chamber pot. It was a living vision of my imaginings of Dashwood's gatherings. I tried to return Fanshawe's grin but it was made painfully false by the unwelcome presence in my mind of my mother voicing her outrage. When Fanshawe handed me a glass of punch I nearly emptied it in one swallow.

'Ashton got a Frenchie he picked up in Paris to do those,' Fanshawe said, pointing to a series of painted panels on one of the walls. 'Illustrations from some story by the Marquis de Sade.'

I peered through the smoke at a sequence of scenes in all of which a young girl was being unwillingly ravaged by a variety of men ending with a group of monks in a monastery. Fanshawe nudged me and looked up at the ceiling.

'The Frenchie didn't care for the catholic religion too much.'

I looked up to see a painting in a large gilt-edged oval panel in the middle of the ceiling. It was of a Pope on his knees being violated by Beelzebub in the form of a large black priapic devil with a huge grin on his face. Fanshawe looked at me, his face creased with laughter.

'Your countenance is a joy to behold, Mountford. Have another drink.'

We sat down at the table and Fanshawe waved to a short fat man further along who turned to him, looking at him through his eyeglass.

'Ah. Fanshawe. Good evening to you, sir.'

'And to you, Hodgson, I trust you are well.'

'Couldn't be better.'

From where I was sitting, I could see a girl kneeling under the table between the man's legs. I was shocked when I saw what she was doing and averted my eyes.

'I'll be with you in just a moment, Fanshawe,' the man said, letting his eyeglass fall and wriggling his haunches back and forth rapidly until he let out a great bellow and fell forward, banging his forehead on the table. A cheer went up around the room as he lifted his head and sat back, looking down at the girl with a sublime expression on his face.

'You're a wonder, Bessie. You must have a go with her, Fanshawe. She's a marvel.'

The girl crawled from under the table, the drawstrings of her white mob cap dangling down and Hodgson slid his hand into the opened front laces of her bodice as she sat on his lap.

'My new-found friend, Robert Mountford,' Fanshawe announced, putting an arm around my shoulder. 'We've been to a lecture on mesmerism. Very entertaining.'

'I can imagine.'

The man looked at me.

'Good evening to you sir.'

'And to you, sir.'

'It's all trickery, of course, wouldn't you say?'

My attention was caught by the sight of the girl licking Hodgson's ear.

'Wouldn't you say?' Hodgson repeated.

'I must say I thought it was genuine,' I replied but Hodgson was now fondling one of the girl's breasts and wasn't listening.

'There's life in the old dog yet, Bessie. I can feel it coming on. By George, I do believe you've mesmerised my stalk. I think it's time to retire.'

The two of them stood up, the girl a good foot taller than Hodgson who was looking wobbly as they made their way to the door.

'I'm feeling distinctly randy, old fellow,' Fanshawe said as he refilled our glasses. 'I'm going to have to find me a doxy before long. I expect you are too. Come on.'

For me, the prospect was very different from slipping quietly into a brothel at King's Cross. Here it was all going to be on a grand scale, out in the open and done with bravura. Along the corridor, the strong smell of hashish wafted towards us from an open door. Fanshawe stopped.

'I could do with a bit of that as well and I think you should have some too. You're looking a little uneasy if I may say so even if you are a bit soused. I think you need a pipe to settle you down. You've smoked hashish before I take it?'

'I have.'

I recalled the few times I had smoked it at the end of the day, to push thoughts of my work out of my mind. It offered me a temporary euphoria but it didn't help me sleep. Laudanum proved better for that.

I followed Fanshawe into a large conservatory full of exotic plants in tubs, its walls also decorated in the Egyptian style. The largest tubs held palm trees that rose up to a high ceiling. Through the tall windows that faced the garden, I could see a sweep of lawn leading down to a lake. In the middle of the lawn blazed a huge bonfire with an effigy of a fat pope on top of it. Men in fancy costumes, some wearing animal masks, and others masked as horned devils were strutting around the fire. Fanshawe drew me to the window and pointed out one of the revelers dressed as a catholic bishop in purple vestments.

'That's Valmont. Totally irredeemable pederast but he's good company when he's not on the look-out for boys. He loves France and he's been over there more than once to get away from the law when he's been shopped. He chose the name Valmont from 'Les Liaisons Dangereuses'. His real name's Birtwistle. Good fun, eh. I'll introduce you to him later.'

I strove to suppress the sound of my mother's voice expressing her outrage. Could her judgment also be my own, I wondered as I looked at Valmont. A footman invited us to a circle of cushions laid around a glass and copper hubble-bubble with four pipes snaking from it. Whispers and hushed laughter emanated from an unlit corner of the room. When the two of us had settled down, cross-legged, the footman held a taper over the bowl. After a few puffs, Fanshawe closed his eyes and took the mouthpiece from his mouth. I puffed on until my unease began to evaporate.

'I would like to remain in this state forever,' I declared at length. 'I feel released from all my troubles.'

'You mean cutting up your patients as they scream and bellow?'

'Indeed. And worrying about courting the company of a dangerous reprobate like you.' The words popped out of me unbidden. 'I'm sorry, I didn't mean that, Fanshawe. Forgive me.'

'Of course you did,' Fanshawe grinned. 'You know what you need now, my dear chap.'

I still felt unready for what was to come but I was reluctant to dampen Fanshawe's enthusiastic determination to make my visit enjoyable. He summoned the footman and smiled at him in a mood of tremendous geniality.

41

'There was a beautiful girl called Isabelle when I was last here; high cheekbones, brown eyes and very dark hair. Like a gypsy. I think she might remember me or remember my name at least. It's Fanshawe, John Fanshawe. I would be most obliged if you would look for her. If she's here and not otherwise engaged, would she care to join us? One more thing. Would you kindly put it her that if she has a friend of equal beauty and, equally important, of a sympathetic disposition, she should please bring her along to keep my friend company.'

The hashish was stronger than I'd smoked before and I was feeling somewhat disembodied as the footman bowed and left the room. Fanshawe lay on his back, puffing away silently with his eyes closed and I stared out of the window at the masked revelers who were now joined by a bevy of girls in various states of undress. I was beginning to contemplate the prospect of having a bedmate with some pleasure. A few minutes later the footman returned.

'I'm afraid that the lady is otherwise engaged at the moment, sir, but she will be along directly and she has spoken to a friend whom she trusts will prove sympathetic.'

We lay on our cushions in silence, sucking at our pipes from time to time. Some minutes later, a tall, shapely, dark-eyed woman came into the room and cast her eyes around regally in search of the man who sought her services. She was wearing a bright red dress tight around her body and with flounces down to the floor. With her black hair piled on top of her head she looked like a gypsy dancer. When she saw Fanshawe she drew herself up to her full height, her head tossed back and her hands on her hips.

'Jack, you dirty dog.'

'Isabelle.'

Fanshawe struggled to sit up. 'What a delight to see you again.'

The woman sashayed over to him.

'Look at you Jack. You don't look as if you've had a good time for quite a while.'

'I haven't, Isabelle.'

Isabelle sniffed the air.

'I hope you're capable after all the kif you've had.'

'Of course I am. And I'll soon prove it to you, Isabelle.'

'I'm sure you will. And you're still up to your horse riding tricks, are you?'

'And if I am?'

'It'll cost you three guineas on top of what Ashton pays me.'

I winced inwardly as I recalled Fanshawe's jocular comment about
chastising a doxy with a riding crop. Fanshawe grinned.

'Three guineas? You're a hard bargainer, Isabelle. I suppose I'll have to accept your punitive terms.'

'I know you will, dearie. Anyway, who's your friend?'

She looked at me, smiling sweetly.

'Robert Mountford, a fine upstanding gentleman,' Fanshawe informed her.

I began to stand up but Isabelle put a hand on top of my head and gently pushed me down again.

'Don't worry, dear, but it's nice to see that you're a real gentleman. You'll be the one looking for a little sympathy. Am I right?'

'That's what Fanshawe thinks I need and I'm sure he's well versed in these matters.'

'He's well versed in lots of things, sweetheart, but not many of them have much to do with sympathy. Anyway, I've got just the girl for you. Her name's Lavender. She'll be along in a minute.'

'Oh, the beautiful Lavender.' Fanshawe grinned. 'Let me know how you get on with her, Mountford.'

'Come on, Jack. Let's go and find somewhere private,' Isabelle commanded and they left the room. I lay back in the nest of cushions aroused at the prospect of my encounter with Lavender. After a few minutes, I heard the click of an opening door, and sat up to see a fair-haired woman in her twenties wearing a lavender dress of muslin, drawn in at the back, revealing her shoulders. She was more beautiful than any woman of pleasure I had ever encountered before.

'Could you be Lavender?' I asked dreamily.

'Yes, sir.'

'Beautiful Lavender in a beautiful lavender dress.'

The hashish was inspiring in me the illusion that I was being poetic.

'You're a true gentleman, sir.'

'Would you care to come and sit by me?

'Certainly, sir.'

She walked over to me a little unsteadily, holding her arms out to
keep her balance.

'Are you all right?' I asked, standing up to catch her in case she should fall.

'Of course, sir.'

She was wearing the same rouge and lip-reddener as the other girls but she had used it sparingly and underneath it I saw that her looks needed no enhancement. I noticed that the

44

pupils of her eyes were dilated and when I took her hand and led her to the cushions, I touched the underside of her wrist with an outstretched finger and felt the fast rate of her pulse. Belladonna. I was aware of it from my occasional visits to Kings Cross where some of the women dilated their pupils with it to make them appear aroused. It would belladonna that would have brought about Lavender's pulse rate and the blurring of her vision. I held her arm as she sat down and she looked at me with a soft-hearted expression.

'I've been told you need a little sympathy.'

'It's true but, hearing you say it, I realise I'm being unconscionably self-indulgent. I'm delighted simply to have your company.'

'I like the way you speak, sir. Are you a poet?'

'Indeed not. I hope you're not making fun of me, Lavender.'

'I wouldn't do that, sir.'

'I'm glad to hear it. May I offer you a glass of wine?'

'No thank you, sir, I'm already a little befuddled.'

Her accent was that of the East End of London but it didn't ring true.

'Would you like a go at my hubble-bubble?' I asked.

Lavender looked down at my breeches and fell on to the cushions, collapsed in laughter. Despite my discomfiture, the hashish made me join in her merriment. I looked at her long neck and her bare shoulders. I found her very alluring.

'No thank you, sir,' Lavender said coquettishly, 'and I hope you haven't been smoking too much if you know what I mean.'

'I'm sure I...'

'Don't worry, sir. I'm sure you can too.'

45

'I must say you are remarkably beautiful, Lavender, and I must tell you something else. I fancy your manner of speech is not your own. You must be an actress.'

'Oh no, sir, I'm not an actress.'

'So what are you? I'm sorry. I didn't mean 'what'. I didn't mean to be so rude. The question in my head is, "Who are you?" but perhaps you don't want to tell me.'

'I'm Lavender, sir.'

'Just Lavender.'

'Yes. That's all you need to know, sir.'

'A woman of mystery, indeed.'

She smiled and stroked my cheek with the back of her hand.

'My question to you is, 'Do you like me?' Do you find me pleasing?'

'I find you very pleasing'.

'Thank you. There's a little bedchamber at the top of the house where we won't be disturbed, sir. I imagine privacy is important to you, unlike some of the gentlemen around here.'

She turned her head to the sound of the groaning couple at the other end of the room.

'You're right, it is.'

'Come on then, sir.'

By now, I was in a state of considerable arousal. We stood up both wobbling a little and I took her hand. Nothing like this had ever happened to me before. Lavender was enchanting, even if she was a woman of pleasure and the prospect of our intimacy taking place in the lap of luxury was beginning to overwhelm me. Was this how the wealthy lived?

Despite the basis of what would be a brief liaison, I managed to persuade myself to invest it with the semblance of a romantic encounter and I squeezed her hand as we went up the stairs. She reciprocated by touching her cheek to my neck and sucking my earlobe. My erection was now hard against my breeches and she touched me there to confirm it. When we reached the first landing, we heard gales of laughter as an African footman emerged from an open door and passed us in the corridor. He was trying to hold his dignity, his coat and breeches being stained red all over and smelling of punch.

Lavender picked up a candle from a table and we went up into a little room on the next floor. I was dismayed to see the bedclothes of a four-poster in disarray and my attempt to sustain the illusion of a romantic encounter collapsed. It was to be a commonplace act of copulation with a prostitute and I had been foolish to invest it with any more importance than that.

'Lavender, do you mind if I ask if you've had a previous gentleman up here?'

'Oh no, sir, not me. I haven't been with anybody tonight.'

She looked at the sheets.

'I'm sorry, sir. I don't know who's been here but I can see how it would offend a gentleman like you.'

She took my hand and led me to an armchair by the window.

'Just sit here for a minute while I make the bed up.'

While she did so, I looked again at the line of her neck and shoulders. Whoever she is, I told myself, she is a beauty and I should put out of mind her love-making being her means of earning a living.

47

When she had finished, she sat on the floor next to me and slowly ran her hand around the hardness in my breeches. In a matter of moments, I was overtaken by carnal craving. The picture of the girl kneeling between Hodgson's legs in the saloon darted through my mind and I fumbled to undo my breeches and pull them down to my knees waiting for her to take me into her mouth. This she did, kneeling over me, moving her head gently up and down. Oh God, I thought. This is paradise. She lifted her head and kissed me on the mouth and I tasted my own saltiness on her lips.

'Come to bed sir.'

I clambered off the armchair and undressed with awkward haste before lying on the bed, feeling the pulse of my blood pressing through my member.

'Now tell me what you want to do to, sir,' Lavender asked coaxingly. 'There's many things gentlemen want to do.'

I was lost for words.

'Come on, sir. You've only got to say.'

'Will you come on top of me, please?'

Lavender smiled at me.

'What a shy thing you are.'

She undressed carefully, laying her clothes over a chair and climbed on to the bed, sitting astride me and moving her hips back and forth, riding me like a horse until I arched my hips and cried out, filled with joy and pain. I lay back, breathing heavily and looked up at Lavender still on top of me, her eyes closed. I felt my member being squeezed inside her, her hips trembling as she breathed in deep gulps of air. Suddenly a gush of wetness came out of her and she let out a cry as she fell on to the bed. While the afterglow of pleasure pervaded me, I was disconcerted. This wetness was new to me. I had never encountered it before.

'You have a fine body, sir. Do you want to wait a little while and do it again?' she enquired with a coquettish smile.'

She pinched one of my nipples with some force, making me wince, and I felt myself stiffen again.

'Come on, sir, come on top of me.'

I did so, pressing into her and running my lips along the length of her neck. Within moments, my ardour mounted to such an extent that what I intended as kisses on her neck became a succession of love bites and I feared I would draw blood. When I arrived at my climax, I was horror-struck to find myself in a state of frenzy, imagining that I was beating her ferociously with my mother's cane. My passion spent, I fell back onto the bed in a state of shock. How could the peak of my excitement lead me to imagine myself doing such a thing? Had Fanshawe's talk of riding crops awakened a demon inside me of the kind that Fanshawe appeared to have? Lavender looked at me as I stared at the ceiling.

'Are you alright sir?'

'Please forgive me, Lavender. I'm afraid I was beside myself.'

'With passion?'

'Yes, with passion.'

'A dark passion?'

'I'm afraid so. Please forgive me.'

'All men have the beast in them sometimes. What was in your mind, sir?' she asked gently but I was unable to speak about it. I wanted to blame Fanshawe's talk of riding crops for putting such cruel thoughts into my head but I knew that they were my own thoughts, not Fanshawe's. I ran my fingers through Lavender's hair, hoping it might help me put the atrocious thought out of mind.

'Would you be prepared to keep me company this evening?' I asked.

'You mean, in bed?'

'No, just to be together.'

'Have I not pleased you?'

'I was set on fire in a way I've never known before.'

'Is that not a good thing?'

I stroked her cheek, not knowing how to answer her.

'I just want you to stay with me for a while.'

'I would have to ask the steward, sir. Let me see what he says.'

We dressed and made our way downstairs, having agreed that I would wait in the garden outside the conservatory while she went to see the steward. I waited there, trying to justify my barbarous fantasy. Had my mother's beatings built up in me such a hornet's nest of hidden anger that, in a moment of carnal surrender, I had struck out in an imagined act of savagery against her. It didn't bear thinking about. After half an hour, I saw Lavender coming into the garden from a door at the side of the house and disappearing into the darkness. She clearly had no intention of joining me and I was more disappointed than I wanted to admit to.

Several bowls of punch were laid out on a long bench by the bonfire and there was much dancing to the sound of an Irish jig being played on a violin by a man wearing a bright green coat and long pointed shoes. I downed two glasses of punch with some speed. By this time, the scarecrow effigy of the Pope had collapsed into the flames and the dancers were passing round gas-filled bladders of nitrous oxide, taking turns to inhale their contents. Valmont, the man dressed as a bishop was now dancing with a boy with rouged lips, waving a bladder above his head as the two of them swirled around each other. The boy was dressed as an angel in a white muslin shift with wings made of white feathers attached to the back of it.

'Come sir, come and join us and be of good cheer,' Valmont called out to me. 'God loves you whatever wantonness may be hidden in your heart.'

He held the bladder out to me.

'Have a little puff, sir. It will cleanse you of all your sins.'

I bowed politely and declined the invitation. As I turned away, I noticed Sir Ralph Ashton in his Arab cloak sitting on the lawn. A book was lying open on his lap. Ashton looked up to see me and raised a hand in greeting.

'Good evening, sir. I think I've seen you before.'

'Robert Mountford, sir. You passed me in the house when you were riding your horse into the garden. I'm a friend of John Fanshawe.'

'Ah, yes. How interesting. I gather you met at a demonstration of mesmerism at the town hall earlier this evening.'

He bowed and spread out his arms.

'Sir Ralph Ashton, sir. Welcome to my home. As a friend of John, you may consider yourself an honoured guest. Come sit with me.

'Thank you, sir.'

'Tell me, Mr. Mountford, do you know anything about alchemy?'

'I fear not.'

Ashton picked up the book on his lap.

'This is a very interesting book. It's on alchemy and medieval magic.'

He cocked his head to one side and narrowed his eyes thoughtfully.

'Ah! Your being a friend of John, I suspect you consider yourself a materialist.'

'You are right, sir,' I replied, wondering if I would be led into a discussion on the subject, my intellectual faculties not being at their sharpest.

'I'm afraid I'm not a child of the Enlightenment, Mr. Mountford. I hope I won't upset you by telling you that I believe in God and the Devil.'

He grinned. 'And the Devil is more fun.'

'Then it is appropriate that you have a bishop here to represent the opposition,' I replied trying to emulate Ashton's jocularity.

'Indeed it is, sir.' Ashton beamed at me beatifically and beckoned a passing footman.

'Where's young Adam?'

'He's dancing with Mr. Valmont, sir.'

'What about Julian?'

The footman looked around again.

'I think he is over by the cupid statue, sir. He seems to be alone.'

'Go and fetch him,' Ashton ordered and turned to me.

'I hope you're enjoying yourself.'

'I am, sir,' I replied, persuading myself that I meant it and seeking a topic of conversation. 'I've been admiring the Egyptian murals in your house. John told me your father commissioned them after a visit to Egypt.'

'Indeed. He took two artists with him and they copied the paintings on the temple walls. They're wonderful aren't they? So mysterious, especially the hieroglyphics. We don't know what they mean but we soon will. Do you know about the Rosetta stone?'

I've heard about it. It is in the British museum, is it not?'

Ashton nodded.

'Napoleon's people found it on his Egyptian campaign and we took it from them when we defeated him. It contains what appears to be the same inscription written in three languages, one hieroglyphic, one hieratic and one in ancient Greek. Some bright chap called Thomas Young has already used the Greek to decode the hieratic. There's a Frenchman called Champollion working on it as well.'

He tapped the book on his lap.

'There are lots of references to ancient Egypt in this. You should read it. Do you travel to London at all?'

'I live there.'

'In that case you must go to the shop where I bought it. It's run by a fellow called John Denley in Catherine Street in Covent Garden. He specializes in books on occult matters and there's nothing about the subject that he doesn't seem to know. Despite your materialism, I think you'd find it fascinating.'

'I will definitely make an effort to do so, sir.' I replied with a smile to help maintain the white lie.

'Good. So what do you make of young John?'

'He's very good company, sir.' I didn't want to speak of my reservations about him. 'He told me you got to know each other at Balliol.'

'Indeed, and I expect he told you how I led him from the path of righteousness.'

'He told me you were both roisterers.'

'We certainly were. The only difference was that he chased women.'

The footman returned with a boy of some eighteen years dressed in a golden toga and with a wreath around his fair curly hair. He was carrying a bladder of laughing gas. He came up behind Ashton, putting his arm around him and puffed some gas into his mouth. 'You naughty boy,' Ashton admonished him as the youth sat down next to him.

Once again, I had to fight off my embarrassment and I was about to make my excuses when another footman approached.

'There's a gentleman at the door who wishes to meet Mr. Fanshawe, sir.'

'Really?'

'He says he was a friend of Mr. Fanshawe's father and he would appreciate the opportunity to talk to him.'

'How interesting. I suppose you'd better show him in so I can meet him. On second thoughts, let him in and find Mr. Fanshawe. I'll meet him later.

'Yes, sir.'

Let's go somewhere more comfortable' he said to Julian and turned to me as he and the boy stood up.

'I hope you will forgive me, Mr. Mountford. I look forward to continuing our conversation later.

As Ashton and the boy made their way to the house, a tall, bony man walked into the garden. He was advanced in years with a stooped frame and a bald head fringed with straggly grey hair. I walked over to the lake and sat at the top of the steps leading down to it, still unable to dismiss from mind the memory of imagining myself whipping Lavender with my mother's cane. Now, as I thought about the libidinous pleasure being sought by everyone around me, it was all beginning to lose its attraction. I was lost in these thoughts when I felt my hair being stroked and I turned to see the boy dressed as an angel who had been dancing with Valmont.

I pulled away from him with a jerk and the boy smiled saying, 'You don't have to be afraid. There's no one here to see us. Have a little of my elixir of life and love.'

The boy was in his cups and euphoric from the nitrous oxide. He held up the bladder and lunged forward, kissing me on the lips, while sliding his hand down to my breeches.

'Get off me!' I shouted, backing away, but the boy followed, holding a hand out so as to grasp my arm and bring me back.

'Please don't run away. You're the most handsome man I've seen here tonight.'

Rage and confusion burst out of me and I punched the boy on the jaw. The boy jumped back to avoid another blow and fell backwards, hitting his head against the plinth of a statue at the top of the steps down to the lake. His angel wings broke off in a flurry of white feathers.

'Oh my God,' I thought as I knelt beside the boy. It took half a minute for him to regain consciousness.

'You clouted me good and proper didn't you, sir?'

I helped him to sit up

'I did, and I'm very sorry.'

I dabbed my handkerchief on the back of the boy's head. There was no serious bleeding, thank God. The boy rubbed his head, wincing as he did so.

'I just wasn't what you wanted, was I? I'm sorry. It must have been the punch and the gas.'

He touched my lips with his forefinger.

'You'd better wipe your mouth.'

I wiped my lips with my handkerchief and was mortified to see rouge smeared it. At that point, I saw Fanshawe and Valmont making their way towards me.

'What a terrible thing,' I called out. 'I didn't mean to cause all this but the boy assaulted me, Fanshawe.'

'I know. I saw what happened. Are you all right, Adam?' he asked the boy.

'I think so. My head hurts a bit.'

Valmont put his arm around Adam to help him to stand up, and the two of them walked slowly towards the bonfire.

'I think he's alright,' I murmured to Fanshawe, watching Adam walk steadily and unaided.

'Forget about it now,' Fanshawe replied. 'Valmont will look after him.'

He picked up Adam's bag of nitrous oxide and puffed it into my face.

'Let's get something to drink.'

He put a hand on my back and tried to project me towards the bonfire but I resisted, still feeling terrible about what I had done.

'I'll just sit down here for a while.'

'Very well, but don't get downcast.'

After a while, feeling a little calmer, I walked back to the bonfire and saw Fanshawe looking at me as he lay down with his head resting on the lap of a girl wearing a tightly laced corset.

I bet you enjoyed Lavender,' he said. 'She's a lively creature, isn't she?'

'She is, as I'm sure you know.'

'Tell me what you got up to.'

'Really, Fanshawe, that's not the sort of thing...'

'My dear fellow, I quite understand but I'll wager you go hard as a rock when you think about it. I must tell you about her one day.'

I looked around me.

'Excuse me, Fanshawe, I'm going to have to relieve myself.'

I walked off to do so behind a statue in the shadow of the house. When I had finished, I saw a gaunt-looking man walking towards me. He was the man with the bald head fringed with straggly grey hair I had seen walking into the garden.

'Would you happen to know the whereabouts of Mr. Fanshawe?' the man asked.

'I do, sir.' I replied, pointing to Fanshawe lying by the fire.

'He's the man with long hair, his head resting on a girl's lap.'

The man squinted in an effort to make out the figure in the firelight.

'Ah, yes. Would you please ask him to come over to see me? I would like to have a word with him in private.'

'May I ask who's asking after him?'

'Gilchrist, Joseph Gilchrist.'

I went back to the fire, thinking the man's demeanor decidedly sinister and beckoned to Fanshawe.

'Yes?'

'There's a man standing over there who wants to speak to you in private.'

Fanshawe sat up and I pointed to the figure in the shadows.

'Who is he?'

'He says his name is Joseph Gilchrist.'

Fanshawe's benign expression collapsed and I watched him as he stood up unsteadily and walked towards the man, his arms stiff and his hands clenched. The two men were in conversation for some minutes. Eventually, Gilchrist walked off leaving Fanshawe with his arms wrapped tightly around himself as if seeking warmth or comfort. I walked over to him and looked at his ashen face in the light of the bonfire.

'Are you alright, Fanshawe?'

He turned away from me and walked towards the house without saying a word. What had been said that could have had such an effect on him? I was reluctant at first to pry into whatever it was that was distressing him, but when Fanshawe failed to return after half an hour, I walked to the house to talk to the steward.

'I'm looking for my friend, John Fanshawe. Would you know of his whereabouts?'

'He left in his carriage some time ago, sir.'

What had the man said that had caused such a sudden departure? I walked out past the footmen beside the open front doors and looked at the night sky. It wasn't long before I came to the conclusion that I would most probably never find out and, indeed, it was unlikely that I would see Fanshawe again even though my address was in his pocket. Perhaps it would be a good thing, I said to myself, given the effect that Fanshawe and his friends seemed to have on me.

In any event, I decided I had had enough of Shadborough House for one evening and asked the steward to arrange a cab to take me back to the George Inn.

Chapter Four

FANSHAWE

Three weeks after I moved to Lincoln's Inn in London, I received a letter from my father's old assistant, Joseph Gilchrist, telling me to come to his house in Clapham on the following Friday. I was haunted by my encounter with him at Shadborough House and by what he had told me was to happen to my father. That night, I dreamt about discovering the fox-like animal in my father's laboratory when I was sleep-walking as a child, and I awoke, covered in sweat and shivering with cold.

I thought about going to see Mountford to talk him about what Gilchrist had told me. Mountford was the most serious-minded man I had come across since I had been at Balliol and I liked him and respected him even though I teased him about his discomfort amongst the crowd at Shadborough House. However, I decided it would be too embarrassing to admit to him my deep disquiet about Gilchrist's hold over me. After all, he would most likely regard his claims as the imaginative creations of a fantasist. Nevertheless, Gilchrist's hold was so strong that I knew I had to go to see him even though I feared that it would change my life irrevocably.

***

The rain was drumming against the roof of my hackney cab as it made its way along Clapham High Road towards Gilchrist's house. The gutters were awash with detritus and the rain was illuminated by the gas lamps that threw the shadows of the tall plane trees lining the road on to the houses behind them. I breathed in the smell of damp

60

horsehair stuffing under my cracked leather seat as the cab clattered and jolted over the cobbles. Suddenly, the driver pulled up and I was nearly thrown out of my seat.

'Sorry about that, sir,' the cabbie called down. 'Nearly missed the house number.' He pointed to one of the town houses. There you are, sir. Number 42.'

I paid the cabbie and knocked on the door, hoping that it wouldn't be answered but as I was about to knock again it was opened by the gaunt figure of Gilchrist. I felt the hairs rise on the back of my neck.

'Good evening, sir,' I said, trying to sound confident.

'Good evening, Mr. Fanshawe.'

Gilchrist took me up a flight of stairs and into a study lined with shelves stacked with a higgledy-piggledy array of ancient-looking books. A roll-top desk stood in front of a rain-swept window. A gust of wind rattled the panes and made the two candles on the chimneypiece flicker. Next to the desk stood a glass case displaying a collection of bronze statuettes. I recognised the figures from the wall paintings in Ashton's house. Gilchrist noticed that I was looking at them.

'They are funerary sculptures from the tomb of Rameses II from the 19th dynasty. They represent gods in the ancient Egyptian underworld.

'They are very beautiful,' I remarked.

'Not so much beautiful as powerful, wouldn't you say?'

'Indeed,' I replied, feeling shaky. 'My friend, Sir Ralph Ashton, has similar figures painted on the walls inside his father's house.'

'Ashton's father was an interesting man. I got to know him when I was living in Egypt.'

Gilchrist allowed silence to fall and my palms were sweating as I tried to keep the conversation going.

'May I ask how you know what they represent if nobody yet understands hieroglyphics?'

'That's where you're wrong, Mr. Fanshawe. It's just that Christian scholars assumed that Egyptian culture disappeared when Egypt became part of the Islamic world. In fact, Muslim scholars always had a profound interest in it and deciphered hieroglyphic signs in the 7th century. What will prove of significance to you is the decoding of certain documents in the 10th century by a Persian scholar. The documents gave instructions for occult practices to be performed by Egyptian priests in a temple founded by a magician called Sobek during the reign of Rameses II. It is a temple that will be of great importance to you. It is called the Temple of Apep.'

He took out the statuette of a coiled snake from the cabinet and handed it to me.

'Apep is a demon in the form of a giant water snake that has lived in an endless cycle of combat with the Sun God Ra since the beginning of time. Each night he swallows the Sun, releasing the power of darkness and each morning Ra defeats him in turn. Sobek elevated the demon's status into that of a god and founded a temple dedicated to him. The documents were lost for seven hundred years, buried in the vaults of a library in Cairo. They were rediscovered in the 17th century by an Egyptian occultist who re-founded the temple. He gave himself the name Sobek and became the sixth incarnation of the magician. Since then, the knowledge contained in the documents has been handed down only to those who belong to the temple's order.'

Gilchrist held out his hand to take back the statuette and motioned me to an armchair.

You are a materialist are you not?

'I am.'

'It's of no importance. It is a philosophical concept that can deal only with the surface of reality. Without your being aware of it, I know your mind is open to that which exists below the surface. May I get you something to drink?'

'I'd like a brandy, sir.'

Gilchrist poured out a glass and handed it to me.

'Do you remember our conversation at Shadborough House?'

I took a gulp of brandy, trying to keep my hand from shaking as Gilchrist stood over me. I steeled myself to speak.

'I do, sir. You said my father became the magician's seventh incarnation.'

'That's right and his body is now lying in a burial chamber in London as he awaits his next incarnation at the entrance to the underworld.'

I felt icy cold as he spoke the words.

'Why do I have to be involved?'

'You are his son and great power will be bestowed upon you in order for you to carry out your father's wishes. For that you must undergo a period of initiation into the order of the Temple. During that time, you will acquire knowledge that you will never lose.'

I took another swallow of brandy.

'What kind of knowledge?'

'You will have to discover it for yourself, but I will give you an analogy. Stand up, please.'

63

As I stood up, I was overtaken by a sense of giddiness as if I were standing on the rolling deck of a ship at sea. I rested my hand against the chimneypiece to steady myself.

'Now, bring to mind a friend.'

I nodded as Mountford came to mind.

'Now think of his face. Then imagine yourself with me in a dark room. You can't see anything. You ask me to light a candle to find out where you are. I agree to do so.'

Gilchrist took a lit candle from the chimneypiece and held it close to my face.

'Now you can see.'

He stared into my eyes.

'You see in front of you a table and on it lies the severed head of your friend.'

I felt my heart thump as Gilchrist blew out the flame, filling my nostrils with waxy smoke.

'Now the room is in darkness again. You have seen your friend's severed head for only the briefest moment but the memory of it will remain with you to the end of your life. You cannot return to a state of not having seen it. In the same way, you will not be able to escape the knowledge that you will acquire but it will harm you only if you fail to complete the initiation.'

The picture of Mountford's severed head filled my mind as I made myself ask the next question.

'And what if I don't want to go through with this?

'Your father has considerable influence over you and he knows that you will carry out his wishes. Let me demonstrate your freedom of choice and the choice he knows you will make.'

He took a small piece parchment from a drawer and handed it to me. The symbolic depiction of a beetle was drawn upon it.

'It is an Egyptian hieroglyph of a scarab beetle, the symbol of spontaneous creation,' Gilchrist said and pointed to the candles on the mantelpiece.

'Set light to one end of the parchment and hold it in front of you. Immediately the flame reaches your fingers, say 'yes' or 'no' to doing your father's bidding.'

I did so and stared at the flame.

'Yes,' I cried out, feeling a strange rush of exhilaration as the flame touched my fingers and I dropped the burning parchment on to the floor. Gilchrist studied the incandescence in my eyes.

'You see?' he said. 'Your father has spoken through you,'

My exhilaration was replaced by a cold fear in the pit of my stomach. Was my father inside me?

'What kind of power will be bestowed on me?' I asked.

'The power to have others do your bidding, the power of sexual prowess, the power to destroy your enemies.'

Very slowly, like a change in the weather, a rising sense of dark excitement began to mingle with my fear as I waited to be told what to do.

'On the second Friday of next month you will come back here, arriving at eleven o'clock in the evening. Whatever other commitments you may have, you must come on that day and at that hour. The initiation will take twenty-one days. During that time you will have to stay in the house where it is to take place. Bring any clothes or nightwear that you want with you. In the meantime, I must remind you of what I told you at Shadborough House. You must not speak about this to a living soul. Do you have any servants?'

'I have a housekeeper.'

'Tell her you are going abroad and you don't know when you will return.'

'I understand.'

'Good. Then I'll bid you goodnight, Mr. Fanshawe.'

Is that all, I thought, putting out my hand. Gilchrist didn't take it. Instead he bowed slightly. I returned the bow and made my way down the stairs and out into the night, a storm of contrary emotions swirling around inside me.

Chapter Five

MOUNTFORD

Once again London was inundated with rain the following week when my friend Harvey came over to see me in the taproom of the Anchor.

'Mountford, old chap, how goes it? Has Campbell come back from America?

'No he hasn't and he's not coming back. I've had a letter from his wife. He's been expelled from the Royal College of Surgeons of Edinburgh for promoting the use of mesmerism and he's decided to stay in America. His wife's going to join him there.'

'What clots those people are. They would prefer to sit on their arses and dismiss the use of mesmerism as a conjouring trick rather than explore the possibility that science has more to teach us about the nature of the human mind. What about Dr. Pierot? Did you go to his performance?'

'I did and I was very impressed.'

I told him about Pierot's various demonstrations.

'Fascinating. Do you think you could acquire your skills from him?

'I don't know but I'm going to meet him tomorrow evening. I wrote to him telling him the reason for my interest in the subject and I asked if he would be willing to explain his methods to me. He's written back saying he's gratified by my interest and doesn't object in principle but he wants to have the opportunity to meet me first to find out more about my work'.

'To assess the cut of your jib, I suppose.'

'I'm sure you're right.'

***

Early on a Sunday evening, I knocked on the door of Pierot's large town house in Market Street, Oxford. I recognised the girl who opened the door for me. It was Lucy, the eldest of Pierot's three assistants.

'Good evening sir,' she said quietly with a little curtsy.

'I'm Robert Mountford, young lady. I believe Dr. Pierot is expecting me.'

'He is, sir.'

Pierot had explained in his answer to my letter that he had a busy schedule and that this evening offered a short respite from his travels, his having returned from Birmingham earlier in the day and having to be on the road again the following morning for a performance in Brighton.

I handed Lucy my hat and she helped me off with my overcoat.

'If you would care to come through to the drawing room, sir, he will be with you shortly.'

She led me into a large room, whose walls and ceiling were dramatically decorated with wallpaper blocked with a pattern of small silver stars against a dark blue background. The room was lit by candles in glass wall sconces. A portrait of Pierot hung over the chimneypiece, depicting him in his full glory with his cape of maroon velvet, his jet black hair and his Mephistophelian beard lit from below by unseen footlights. A collection of playbills was displayed in a large picture frame on the opposite wall, each announcement containing a wood-blocked silhouette of a top-hatted figure holding out his cloaked arms in a dramatic gesture. Clearly the home of a showman, I thought, but without condescension. I enjoyed the theatricality of it. Lucy motioned me to an armchair, curtsied and left the room.

As I turned to sit down, I was shocked to see by the window a bewigged man in a green coat and knee-length breeches staring at me, wide-eyed and holding out at arm's length a huge horseshoe magnet the size of a serving dish. I backed away instinctively but the man remained as still as death as if in a trance state. I then realised that, despite the disconcertingly realistic flesh tones of his face and his bright shining eyes, he was a life-size mannequin. At that moment, Pierot came into the room and held out a hand in greeting. I turned from the mannequin and we shook hands.

'You know who that is, don't you?' Pierot said, not waiting for an answer. 'Franz Mesmer himself. I bought him from Anna Tussaud when she brought her husband's collection of waxworks over from France. We came over on the ship together. He cost me a pretty penny but it was worth it, don't you think?'

'It gave me quite a shock,' I said. 'For a moment I thought he was real and you'd put him into a cataleptic trance.'

Pierot laughed. He looked older than he had done in the town hall, in his sixties, perhaps. His face was lined and the roots of his hair and beard were grey. He clearly dyed them for his performances. Pierot touched the mannequin's arm.

'I would have liked to bring him to my demonstrations so the audience could see who I am talking about in my introduction but he is too delicate. Sit down, Mr. Mountford, you're making me nervous looking at him as if he is about to move. And let me get you something to drink. Brandy? Sherry?'

'A sherry would be very acceptable.'

He rang a small bell on a side table and Lucy came back into the room.

'Two sherries, Lucy, if you please.'

He sat in an armchair and studied my face with an expression of amiable curiosity.

'I am delighted by your interest in mesmerism, Mr. Mountford. I have to say that I wouldn't know how much pain can be suppressed in your kind of work. I am an entertainer and I would never do anything that would cause more than a tiny fraction of such pain. The Scottish surgeon you mentioned in your letter could have taught you much more than I. It's so unfortunate that there are men of science who regard the phenomenon as some sort of chicanery when they have only to attend a demonstration to see that it's genuine.'

Lucy came in with the sherry and Pierot took a sip from his glass.

'As to money, I make a very good living as a professional mesmerist and you said in your letter that you're not in a position to pay me a large sum for teaching you my methods. I can well imagine that your salary as a young surgeon will be modest and, without wanting to be rude, you couldn't pay me the sort of sum I could command from anyone wanting to take up my profession as a public performer. However, I will be happy to teach you my skills. If they prove sufficient to relieve the pain of your patients, you will no doubt teach others and pass on the skill. I would regard it as a charitable gift.'

'You are most generous, sir.'

'As it happens, my performance in Brighton has been postponed so I could start teaching you tomorrow. Would you be free to spend the day here?'

'I would as long as I get the last coach back to London.'

'The overnight mail coach?'

'Yes. That would be fine.'

'I insist that you stay here tonight. Lucy will make up a bed for you.'

'Thank you very much for your hospitality, Dr. Pierot. I hope I prove a good student.'

Pierot turned to the door.

'Lucy!' A little more sherry, please.'

Lucy came in and poured the drinks.

'And make up a bed for Mr. Mountford.'

'I met a fellow called John Fanshawe at your performance in Oxford,' I remarked. 'He lives in Oxford and he told me he gathered from a member of his club who knows you that you learned about mesmerism in Paris from a disciple of Mesmer.'

'I did indeed. Might your friend be the son of Josiah Fanshawe?'

'I'm afraid I don't know.'

'I seem to recall the family living in Kidlington.'

'That was where John grew up.'

'Ah. I wonder if it's the same man. I never met the fellow but I remember a rumour spread around by a disgruntled servant who had lost her position in the household that he dabbled in some sort of black magic. Quite untrue, no doubt.'

71

Could Fanshawe's father be that man? I let the thought go, assuming I would never see him again.

***

By the end of the following day I was able to put the girls into trance states and it took me a while to come down to earth. My feeling of power was intoxicating and when the girls were subsequently unable to feel an electric shock from a voltaic battery or pain when I pushed a needle into them, I felt like a magician. A week later I paid my second visit to Dr Pierot. By then that fantasy had faded and was replaced by excitement at the possibility of operating on my patients without pain.

During the weeks that followed I made two further visits to Oxford to practice on the girls. Out of curiosity, during the second of those visits, I asked if I could try to put Lucy into a trance in which I was to make her believe that a box I was holding in my hand was a giant spider. Pierot agreed, having no concern that I would be a competing public performer. In her trance state, Lucy screamed in terror as she stared at the box, her face contorted into an open-mouthed expression of horror, her hands pressed to her cheeks. I tried to take her out of the trance without success and the girl began gasping for air. Suddenly she was silent, frozen to the spot, her body in a state of cataleptic rigidity. I was horrified and moved aside to let Pierot take over. Pierot stood before her, his hands on her shoulders and began speaking in soft tones saying he had turned the spider into a box and she had nothing to fear. He waited until her muscles began to relax and counted one to ten slowly, taking her out of her trance.

'This can happen sometimes if you're not experienced,' he told me, 'but it won't be a factor for you to worry about, given that your use of the trance is simply to remove pain. That's what you will have to practice. I suspect the trance will have to be much deeper than I need for my purposes.'

***

I began to use Pierot's techniques at Barts Hospital with some success, carrying out minor procedures on patients who needed to have wounds stitched up or goitres removed and, in one case, a finger amputated. During that time, I was pleased to receive a letter from James Carlyle in New York expressing his delight in what I was doing and giving me some guidance, describing the deep trance states required in order to carry out major amputations, the subjects needing to be mesmerised more than once in order to prepare them for it. It wasn't long before I felt that I would soon be ready to conduct my first major amputation.

Chapter Six

FANSHAWE

After my encounter with Gilchrist, my nights were filled with disturbing dreams about encountering my father by some supernatural means. I would try to erase my fears by telling myself that Gilchrist was clearly of unsound mind and the whole business was a figment of the man's fevered imagination. After all, I told myself, I'm a materialist and any sort of belief in the supernatural is absurd. Nevertheless, I didn't want to be alone with my fearful imaginings of what was to happen to me during my initiation and I became a member of the Fortune Club to which I had been introduced by a friend from Balliol called Carstairs. There I spent much of my time playing billiards or twenty-one and losing more money than I cared to think about.

One day at the club, Carstairs lent me a copy of Mary Shelley's, *Frankenstein*. Cairstairs was not burdened with great powers of imagination and when I had read the book he was highly amused by my horrified reaction to it. He then persuaded me to accompany him to a demonstration of galvanism that was to take place at the house of a surgeon called Ackerman. I found it difficult to believe Carstairs's description of what would happen there and he bet £10 that I would have to leave before the demonstration was over.

The sight of the naked corpse laid out on a table in Ackerman's operating theatre chilled me to the bone. I had never seen a dead body before and the smell of putrefying flesh from the remains of previous operations made me feel sick.

A crowd was standing around the corpse and three interlinked voltaic batteries stood on a table next to it. I wanted to get out of the room but I couldn't bear the idea of being humiliated in front of Carstairs and losing the bet, so I waited to see what was to happen.

'The man was a convict hanged a few hours ago at Newgate,' Ackerman announced pompously, 'and I'm completely confident that he is dead. His relatives hung on to his legs after the hanging to make sure he suffocated and was out of his misery. When he was brought here, his heart had stopped beating and he wasn't breathing.'

Having briefly surveyed the audience, he told us he would answer questions when he had completed the demonstration. He picked up the leads from the batteries with leather gloves and pointed to various parts of the corpse where he'd cut through the flesh to expose the nerves. One of the corpse's legs was in the bent position. The surgeon attached the leads to the heel of that leg and it shot out with such force that it nearly knocked over one of the onlookers. My heart was thumping and I turned to see the shock on the faces around the table. Ackerman attached the leads to the corpse's elbow causing its arm to lift and its fingers to open and clench, I feared I was going to faint.

'Oh, my God,' I muttered aloud when he pushed the leads into a cut in the corpse's neck and the creature's chest started heaving as if it were breathing. A man in the crowd collapsed and had to be taken out. The demonstration that drove me out of the room took place when Ackerman attached the leads to a cut in the man's forehead. Its face contorted into a grimace and its eyes opened. I was convinced that the corpse had come back to life and I pushed

75

my way out into the street and sat down on the pavement feeling deathly pale and dizzy. I had lost my £10. When Carstairs came out at the end of the demonstration, he grinned as he held out a hand for the money.

A week later after I had woken from a nightmare about the galvanized corpse, Mountford came to mind as a man trained in medical matters who might be able to give me a reassuring scientific view of the matter. I decided to write to him about it. I would also have liked to share my fears about what Gilchrist had told me but I was too frightened of the man to break his injunction that I speak to no one about it.

Chapter Seven

MOUNTFORD

The week after I had started using mesmerism when dealing with minor injuries I received a letter from a Dr. Villiers saying that he had been in conversation some time ago with an old friend, John Fanshawe, while on a visit to Oxford. John had told him that he and I had attended a demonstration of mesmerism in the Oxford Town Hall. He understood that I was a surgeon who was there to investigate the phenomenon to find out if it could be used during surgery. Dr. Villiers said he was a physician and a natural philosopher and he would be most interested to hear about the progress of my researches. He ended the letter inviting me to his club in London.

***

I felt my usual discomposure amongst the trappings of wealth when I arrived at Villiers's club in St James's Street a fortnight later. A waiter took me up to the grand drawing room whose walls were adorned with paintings of figures from classical antiquity and led me across the room to a corner in which Villiers was seated, reading a book with the aid of half-moon spectacles.

'Good evening sir,' I said with a bow when I was announced.

'Good evening to you, sir. I'm very pleased to meet you, young man, and thank you very much for coming to see me.'

'Thank you for the invitation, sir.'

A waiter came up and served us coffee.

'The use of mesmerism in surgery is a very interesting idea. Tell me what brought it to mind.'

'I read an article in *The Times* about a surgeon in Edinburgh who has been using it. He is working in America at the moment. I had hoped to meet him on his return to Scotland to see what I could learn from him but I regret to say that the article has caused him to be expelled from the Royal Society of Surgeons of Edinburgh. He is now going to continue his practice in America.'

'I'm not surprised. You will also encounter a deal of antagonism from most of your colleagues. As you know, most medical men strenuously avoid keeping an open mind on matters new to science, especially in this case, given the general view that the practice of mesmerism is intended for popular entertainment. They would be afraid their reputation would be undermined if they took it seriously. Now, tell me about Dr. Pierot' he said after a pause.

Villiers listened attentively to my description of the techniques I had learned from him and my use of them on my patients at Barts.

'There must be a scientific explanation,' Villiers declared when I had ended my account. 'Some years ago, I co-founded a scientific society for the discussion of recent discoveries and new ideas in natural philosophy and we send our papers to the Royal Society. Humphry Davy gave a lecture at one of our recent meetings.'

I was deeply impressed, Davy having been made President of the Royal Society the previous year.

'I don't know what you think of this but Davy believes that electricity controls the animation of everything in the universe and its investigation will eventually lead to an understanding of how creation works. Extraordinary. He's a great man, I'm convinced of it, and he'll be recognised as such in the pages of history.'

'I believe you're right, sir, but I admit to being somewhat alarmed by his expectation that the means by which creation takes place will eventually be discovered. I'm thinking of Mary Shelley's novel. I know it's a fanciful tale but it gives pause for thought.'

'It does. I understand that it was Davy's belief in the power of electricity that provided her with the inspiration for her story; that and seeing a demonstration of an electrical current causing a corpse to open its eyes. I met her once in Davy's laboratory. A sweet girl. It's difficult to think of her gruesome story coming out of such a young head.'

Villiers took a sip of coffee.

'Tell me, Mr. Mountford, would you be interested in joining our society and bringing the subject of mesmerism to our attention?'

I was overwhelmed by the idea that I could belong to a scientific society at which Davy had spoken and it took a moment for me to catch my breath.

'I would be honoured, sir, but I fear my contribution would not be sufficiently scholarly to meet your standards.'

'Don't worry, young man. What you've told me assures me that you will provide the members with a most interesting scientific subject that demands to be given serious attention. After all, it offers a completely new perspective on the workings of the brain and the nature of the human mind. I'll be most interested to see what the other members make of it.'

He smiled and shook his head at the thought.

'I expect you will have some persuading to do with one of them but I'm sure you will hold your own. It will be a very interesting meeting.'

My head was buzzing.

'We call our society the Wigmore Society as the meetings take place at the Wigmore Street home of Dr Wesley Fitzgibbon, one of the founder members and our President. We will be having our next meeting in a few weeks' time'.

Villiers went over to a writing desk and wrote down Fitzgibbons' address and the date and time of the meeting. He handed the note to me.

'May I ask how you came to know John Fanshawe, sir,' I asked.

'I knew him slightly when I was living in Oxford. He was something of a blade, as you can imagine. When he was at Balliol, he challenged a fellow student to a duel over some trivial matter and the two ended up shooting at each other with pistols in the botanical gardens opposite Magdalen College. Luckily, John was only grazed and his opponent was untouched. There was another incident at one of Sir Ralph Ashton's dreadful hellfire meetings, last year.'

I reddened and hoped Fanshawe hadn't told him I had been to one.

'Fanshawe and a couple of other members went up in a Montgolfier balloon and, apparently, John jumped out of it on the way down when the balloon was about fifty feet above a lake in Ashton's grounds. He was nearly drowned. He's something of a daredevil, you know.'

'And dangerous company?' I asked, wondering if Fanshawe would ever get in touch with me again.

'Not if you know how to deal with him.'

An attendant came up to Villiers and murmured, 'Your wife is waiting outside in her carriage, sir.'

'Thank you, Fletcher.'

'I hope you will excuse me, Mr. Mountford. I'm taking my wife to the theatre tonight to see Joe Grimaldi. Have you been to see him?'

'No, sir.'

'Not to your taste I expect, and possibly not to mine, but I know from what I've heard that Caroline will love it. In the meantime, I look forward to your joining our little society and learning more about this strange phenomenon.'

We made our way downstairs and were helped on with our coats. We shook hands out in the street and I looked up to see Villiers's wife waiting in an open carriage. The woman looked at me politely but coolly and I was rocked back on my feet, recognising her features as those of Lavender.

Chapter Eight

I had been surprised to receive Fanshawe's letter asking to meet me to talk about some scientific matter on which he wanted my medical knowledge. I hadn't expected to hear from him again and I was still furious about him encouraging me to bed Dr. Villiers's wife at the hellfire party. However, my thoughts were taken up by another letter I had received from my mother in Aberdeen. My brother Angus had been struck down with influenza. My mother was doing her best to look after him, but there was very little money to afford the attentions of a physician or physic from an apothecary as my father's stipend was so small. If I could help by arranging to send her a little money, she would be most grateful.

There was no question in my mind that I must do so and my salary being no more than sufficient to live on, I would have to move to cheaper lodgings to be able to offer any financial help. I felt conscience-stricken that I had only paid two visits to Aberdeen to see Angus since the brow-beating I had received from my father nearly ten years earlier when he found me reading the work of the freethinker, David Hume. I now determined to go to see Angus as soon as I could.

However, it was not the first time I had resolved to do so. I recalled with discomfort my postponing previous visits and in the end failing to carry out my pledge, telling myself that my work was making too many demands on me. I knew it was the prospect of seeing my parents that was at the heart of the matter. I replied to my mother's letter telling her that I would send some money to her each month. I then looked again at Fanshawe's letter, feeling unsure about continuing our friendship but wanting to find out more about Villiers's wife playing the tart. In the end, I replied, saying that I looked forward to his visit.

***

Fanshawe arrived at Calthorpe Street carrying a leather bag. I could tell that he was very unsettled and that he had had a lot to drink. We shook hands and I expressed my gratitude for the introduction to Dr. Villiers. When Fanshawe flopped down on my sofa I went on to say that I was rather put out about not having been told who Lavender really was. I had only discovered the truth after our meeting at Villiers's club, and she was waiting for him in her carriage. I was now in an embarrassing situation because of the friendship I had formed with Villiers and the invitation I had accepted to become a member of his scientific society.

'I'd never have laid a finger on her if I'd known who she was,' I declared, feeling hot under the collar.

'I'm dreadfully sorry, old chap. Of course I should have told you. The thing is that Caroline is half old George's age as you can see and she married him for security. Her father had a business that went bankrupt. Villiers knew the family and was besotted with her. After some persuasion by Caroline's father, she agreed to marry Villiers. Unknown to her father, it was to be on condition that she could indulge a certain proclivity for adventure without interference from her husband as long as she was discreet. Villiers had accepted her terms. As you've seen, she loves to play the strumpet, calling herself Lavender and Ashton's parties are the ideal setting, as you can imagine.'

'Nevertheless, I'm going to feel most embarrassed in his company.'

'There's no need to be. He won't know about it. She keeps the names of the gents she frolics with to herself. Tell me, did you like old Villiers?'

'I did, very much.'

'Good. I knew you would get on together, both being men with serious minds, unlike me.'

'You look a bit soused, Fanshawe. Is anything troubling you?'

No, no. I'm fine. So, apart from your unnecessary alarm about Villiers's wife, how's life treating you?'

'I'm well, thank you, but I've just heard from my mother that my brother Angus is very ill with influenza.'

'I'm very sorry to hear that.'

Fanshawe stood up unsteadily and took a bottle of brandy out of his bag.

'With all your worries, I think you could do with something to drink.'

'Thank you Fanshawe. Are you sure you want any more?'

I had never seen him so inebriated.

'Don't you worry yourself about me, old chap,' he replied as I took two glasses from a cupboard and poured out the drink.

'I hope you recovered from that bout of illness at Shadborough House,' I said.

'What illness?' Fanshawe asked abruptly.

'Don't you remember? You looked very pale and you had your arms wrapped around you.'

'Really?'

'It was after you were talking to that unpleasant-looking man with a bald head.'

Fanshawe's face tensed and he averted his eyes. I knew he was going to tell a lie.

'You're right. I'd forgotten. I had a bilious attack and I had to go home. I'm sorry I didn't have a chance to say goodbye to you. Luckily, it didn't last too long. Just a couple of days.'

He turned back to me, affecting a look of attentive enquiry.

'So what's going on in your investigations into mesmerism?'

I told him what I had learned from Dr. Pierot and that I was now using mesmerism on some patients at Barts.

'Were you able to mesmerise Pierot's girls into letting you bed them?'

'Trust you to think of that, Fanshawe.'

'And would you be prepared to teach me?'

'No, I wouldn't. God knows what you'd get up to if I did.'

'My dear fellow, what must you think of me? On second thoughts, don't answer that.'

He emptied his glass and held it up to be refilled.

'There's something more important I want to talk to you about.'

He tried to stand up and fell back down on the sofa with a bump.

'There are a couple of volumes in my bag. Would you mind taking them out and having a look at them.

I did so and looked at the title page of the first volume; *Frankenstein; or the Modern Prometheus, by Mary Shelley.*

'Have you read it?' Fanshawe asked.

'Yes, I have.'

'My friend Carstairs told me to read it. What do you make of it, a creature being brought to life by electricity?'

'It's a fanciful tale, of course, but it touches on the new thinking that electricity is in some way the key to life.'

'Exactly. Electricity being the key to life.'

Fanshawe leant forward pointing a finger at me to emphasise the importance of what he was about to say.

'I must tell you this, Mountford. The other day, Carstairs took me to a demonstration of galvanism on a corpse in the house of a surgeon called Ackerman.'

'Oh, Ackerman. He used to work at Barts. A rather pompous fellow.'

'I suppose you'll know all this, being a surgeon.'

'I do know about it but I don't think anybody fully understands it yet. I attended one of these experiments when I was a student.'

Fanshawe proceeded to give a dramatic description of what had happened, measuring his words slowly for effect and forgetting what part of the story he had got to a couple of times. When he had finished, he looked fixedly at me.

'Come on. Now tell me my medical friend. What do you make of all that?'

'Nobody yet knows enough about what's going on but electricity seems to play some part in activating the motor nerves. Nevertheless, it can't bring a dead man back to life. After all, the man had been asphyxiated by the noose when he was hanged and when his breathing stopped, his heart would have stopped and his body and brain would have begun to decay. What I was taught was that for a short while after death before rigor mortis sets in, the muscles are still supple and can react to an electrical charge in a similar way to a stimulus coming from the brain. The brain itself has nothing to do with it. It is dead and when the brain is dead the man is dead.'

'So is Frankenstein's creature is an impossibility?'

'Yes. That's my view anyway. Sir Humphry Davy may take a different view. He believes electricity drives the whole universe and that one day we may be able to control it. I'm rather uncomfortable with that idea, I must say.'

I put the two volumes back in Fanshawe's bag.

'I'm glad to have your explanation, Mountford, but I'm not sure it's put my mind at rest.'

He refilled his glass and drank it in one swallow before lying lay back against the cushions of the sofa and staring at the ceiling.

'What about reincarnation?' he asked after a long silence.

'Reincarnation? You mean the soul coming back after death in another body?'

I was bemused. It wasn't the sort of question I would have expected from Fanshawe.

'I can't help you there, old chap. That's not a question for science. It's a question for religion, Hinduism particularly. Anyway, why do you ask? After all, you don't believe the soul exists, do you?'

'Of course not. We are physical beings in a material universe. Nevertheless…,' he said sleepily.

'Nevertheless what, old chap?'

'I've got something very important to tell you.' There was a long pause. 'I'm going to meet my father'.

'What do you mean, Fanshawe?'

His father must have died years ago. There was no response and I saw that Fanshawe's eyes were closed.

'Tell me what you mean, old chap.'

Again, no reaction. I stood up and tapped him on the shoulder. He was completely unconscious. I laid him out on the sofa and checked that he was still breathing. Despite the amount of brandy he had drunk, Fanshawe's state didn't seem like sleep brought on by drunkenness. It was as if he were in a coma. I set about making a pot of coffee and then studied my notes for the address I was to give at the Wigmore Society. Half an hour later, I heard Fanshawe's voice.

'Where am I?'

I looked at his half-closed eyes.

'Yes it's me. Would you like some coffee?'

'Thank you. I would.'

I put the coffee pot on the coals of the fire.

'Do you remember coming here?' I asked. 'You'd had a fair bit to drink.'

'Of course I do.'

'Do you remember what we talking about?'

'Don't test me Mountford. Tell me.'

'About Frankenstein's creature and the corpse that opened its eyes.'

'Oh, yes.'

'You also said something rather strange and then immediately fell asleep.'

'What?'

'You told me you were going to meet your father.'

Fanshawe's eyes opened fully and he stared me.

'What did I say?'

''You told me you were going to meet your father.'

Fanshawe was now staring at the floor, his shoulders hunched.

'Are you alright?' I asked.

'Of course I am. I must have been dreaming.'

I poured some coffee and we sat drinking it in silence. After a while, Fanshawe took out his watch.

'I can feel the cards beckoning me to my club, Mountford.'

He stood up, looking a little wobbly and picked up his bag.

'By the way, about your brother. Look, if there's anything I can do to help ...'

We both knew he was referring to financial help.

'You're most kind, Fanshawe, but I can manage.'

I had never borrowed money before and it would make me beholden to Fanshawe while feeling uncertain whether it was a friendship I wanted to continue.

'Thank you for your company, Mountford.'

'And yours, Fanshawe.'

Fanshawe had changed since I had last been with him. He had lost his high spirits and he seemed to be drinking out of anxiety, wanting to allay his superstitious fears about electricity bringing corpses back to life. And what did he mean about meeting his father again?

Chapter Nine

FANSHAWE

There was a letter lying on the hall table when I arrived home from the Fortune Club at three o'clock the next morning. It was addressed to John Fanshawe Esquire and was meticulously written in a cursive script. I went cold as I recognised Gilchrist's hand. Since my meeting with Mountford that afternoon, I had been frightened at having told him that I was going to see my father. I had no recollection of having said it but I had obviously done so and I couldn't cast out of mind Gilchrist's injunction that I speak to no one about it. Although he wasn't with me at the time, my rationalism had become so frail that I had to stop myself imagining that he would know about it through supernatural means. I took the letter into my drawing room and opened it. He had written to remind me that the time had come for my initiation. I was to go to his house on the following Friday evening.

***

Now that Friday had come and I was on my way to Clapham, the materialism I had espoused at Balliol had deserted me completely.

When I stepped down from the cab outside Gilchrist's house, I saw a black closed carriage and horse standing on the other side of the road. Black curtains were drawn across its windows. Gilchrist answered my knock and led me into

90

his study. He motioned for me to sit down and handed me a tiny black lacquered box.

'Open it.'

I leant forward to be closer to the candle on the chimneypiece and lifted the lid. Inside the box was a small dark brown, organic object, lying in brown-stained cotton wool. A little over an inch long and jointed in the middle, it looked like the desiccated remains of a chicken's toe but without a claw at the end of it. I looked up at Gilchrist, waiting to be told what it was.

'It's the little finger of your left hand.'

I fainted. When I came to, I wanted to vomit. Gilchrist lifted me back into my chair.

'Your father cut that finger off when you were five years old. He took it with him to Egypt.'

I tried to think as I fought my nausea.

'My mother told me I lost it when my finger was crushed under a horse's hoof.'

'Your mother was staying with her sister at the time and your father put you into a trance state in order to remove your memory of what had happened.

'You mean he mesmerised me?'

'You may call it that but the power to induce a trance state was learned 3,000 years before Mesmer was born.'

I found myself holding the bottom joint of my little finger in my other hand.

'It's hurting,' I muttered.

'It will for a while.'

'Why do you want to show it to me?'

'It will be an important part of the ceremony in which you will be participating.'

Gilchrist picked the box up from the floor and took a thick piece of folded black cotton from his desk.

'A hood,' he said, holding it up. 'It is necessary that you don't know where you'll be initiated. From the moment I put it over your head to the end of your initiation in twenty one days' time you must say nothing unless you are asked to speak.'

He pulled the hood down over my head enveloping me in total darkness.

'Stand up,' he said, taking my arm, and led me out of the house.

I heard a carriage door being opened. It would be the carriage with the black curtains. Gilchrist helped me up the step and into a seat. The door was closed and the carriage rocked on its springs as I heard someone climbing into the driver's seat. There was the sound of a whip and the carriage lurched forward. I tried to calm myself by concentrating on the sounds coming from the streets in order to feel that I was still connected to ordinary reality. Soon I knew from the smells of the river that the docks were not far away.

The carriage stopped and, in the silence, I was terrified to hear the sound of breathing. My heart thumped as it came closer and I felt the soft weight of a hand on my head. A voice above me began speaking in a foreign tongue, intoning what sounded like an invocation. When it came to an end, the carriage door was opened. I was helped out and led up some steps, hearing the footfalls of two people apart from my own. A door opened and I was walking up a flight of stairs.

'Stand here,' Gilchrist ordered.

My hood was taken off and I noticed an animal smell as I looked around me. A candle standing on a block of wood on the floor was the only light in the room and it gave Gilchrist's face the appearance of a gargoyle. I could just make out a chimneypiece, a four-poster bed with a table next to it, a large wardrobe and a commode. Gilchrist pointed out a tall man dressed in a long Arab cloak standing in the shadows behind him.

'This is the priest who will be overseeing your initiation. His name is Amon. He invoked the spirit of Apep when you were in the carriage.

The man moved forward into the light of the candle and I felt a cold sweat on seeing a white mask covering the whole of his face with holes for the eyes and the mouth. He was holding a long-handled axe with a broad blade in one hand and, in the other, a rope tethered to a small fox-like animal with long, pointed ears standing at his side.

I was transfixed as a terrible memory came back to me from childhood. It looked exactly like the creature I had seen in my father's
laboratory.

'The Egyptian underworld is ruled by the god, Anubis who takes the form of a jackal,' Gilchrist explained. 'Because of Sobek's dark power, Anubis refused him entry into the underworld. If he had been an ordinary mortal, his heart would have been eaten by the crocodile-headed demon, Ammut, and he would have been committed to oblivion. Sobek's power prevented it but he has to continue his life through reincarnation. Anubis is a deadly enemy of Apep and this jackal from the Western Desert is to be sacrificed to facilitate your father's return.'

He took the candle off the block of wood and placed it on the floor. The priest handed me the axe and led the animal forward, using the lead to hold its neck over the block while intoning another litany. When it ended, Gilchrist drew breath and stared into my eyes. 'Behead the creature... Now!' he barked.

I lifted the axe, suddenly feeling like a colossus and brought it down with all my force on to the creature's neck. The jackal's head fell to the floor and an extraordinary sense of elation coursed through me as I stared at the blood spurting from its neck and splattering my breeches. Gilchrist came up to me and held out a hand.

'Please give me your watch. You will be experiencing a quite different sense of the passing of time.'

Bewildered by what was happening, I unhooked the chain from my waistcoat and handed him the watch.

'I have explained to you that we will be using the power of Apep in your initiation. This requires that you remain in this room for twenty-one days. The spirit of the serpent will be with you throughout that time.'

He looked at me and spoke with slow deliberation.

'As you know, the serpent is the god of darkness and I now have to give you the strongest warning. Should you see daylight before your initiation is complete, the spirit of the serpent will coil itself into your intestines and climb up to your head at which time you will lose your reason.'

I was overtaken by terror at the thought.

'You will not speak unless asked to do so. In the first week you will be taught some of the sacred language used in the temple. Your teacher will be the priestess, Shukura, your father's daughter by another woman. In your presence,

Shukura will always be masked as will Amon. No one going through the initiation may see their faces. Shukura will bring you food and water each day but without your watch and without daylight, you will soon lose the ability to tell whether it is night or day. When she comes into the room and kneels before you, you will kneel opposite her and she will speak sacred words that you must learn, although you won't know their meaning. When she speaks a word you must repeat it. Shukura will not know what you have said as she has no hearing. The fact of her deafness will be important to your struggle to attain a state of wisdom, so you must listen very carefully to make sure that you repeat the word correctly. You must say the word only once and when you have done so, touch Shukura's knee with your forefinger and she will speak the next word. That's all you need know for the present.'

Gilchrist put a small glass of amber liquid on the blood-soaked block.

'It contains the essence of the white lotus flower from the borders of the Nile at Luxor with a tincture of venom from the horned sand viper that lives in the Western Desert. It has the power to take you to places beyond the bounds of rational understanding and into the realm of magic. Drink it when you are ready.'

Amon unfolded a white sheet on the floor, wrapped the jackal's head and body in it and dragged it out of the room, its blood smearing the floor. Gilchrist picked up the candle.

'You will find a tinder box and candles on a shelf in the wardrobe,' he said as he left the room, blowing the candle out and locking the door behind him.

I was alone in total darkness. My mouth was dry and I felt my body trembling as I began to walk around the room, my hands held out before me, feeling for the wardrobe containing the candles. I felt the shape of a window frame in one wall. The window seemed to be boarded with wood with a thick velvet material nailed over it and I thought with horror of Gilchrist's warning about seeing daylight and losing my mind with a snake inside me. When I found the wardrobe, I ran my fingers over the glass inlays of its doors and opened them. It had shelves to the right and a hanging space to the left. A box of candles and two candle sticks were on one of the shelves. On another I found the tinder box. Having got a flame going, I lit a candle and carried it round the room to get my bearings. I saw the bloody block on which I had decapitated the jackal and tried to quell my fear of being in the hands of my father's acolytes. I summoned up my defiance and told myself I wasn't going to submit to it. I picked up the glass of lotus wine to welcome the power with which I was to be endowed and drank it in one swallow. A rush of excitement overwhelmed me and I felt a heightened awareness of all my senses; the sound of my breathing, the intoxicating smell of the jackal's blood on my breeches, the brilliance of the candle flame and the sharpness of the objects around me. Soon the objects started to change size and shadows began to move. The candle I was holding shone like the sun. I felt the wetness of jackal's blood soaking through my breeches and I squeezed the fabric between my fingers. I put them to my nose and the odour infused me with a bestial, primitive euphoria.

I looked at my reflection in the large, mirrored doors of the wardrobe, and I was horrified by the sight of the wild-eyed

frenzy in my eyes. Then,... *Dear God*... I saw the reflection
of the galvanized corpse from Ackerman's surgery standing
behind me. I screamed in fear as it approached me but no
sound came out of my mouth. The disgusting creature
touched my cheek with a cold hand, its putrid smell making
me nauseous. I climbed into the wardrobe and tried to shut
the door to keep the creature out. As soon as I had done so I
found myself rising up into the air and flying above a
cityscape of fantastic labyrinthine structures. Soon I was
descending on to a stairway in a vast, dungeon-like hall. I
recognised it from de Quincy's vision of such a place in his
Confessions. I looked up at stairways rising to incredible
heights and leading to arched galleries. Below me, huge
pieces of machinery lay silent, their wheels, cables, pulleys
and levers brown with rust. I was dumbfounded by the
immensity of it all. In one of the galleries above me I heard
the distant, echoing sound of a child calling out in distress.
Please don't let the snake kill me, Papa! I froze as a
recollection emerged from the depths of my memory. I held
on to the stairway's balustrade to steady myself but it gave
way and I fell into space, encircled by multiple reflections of
myself screaming silently.

***

It seemed that a hundred years had passed when I saw a lit
candle standing on the floor in the middle of the room.
Behind it I began to make out a kneeling figure wearing a
grey Arab cloak. I felt a moment of panic on seeing its white
mask but the figure was much smaller than Amon. Long,
lustrously black hair flowed down slim shoulders and the

97

hands were those of a girl. It was the priestess, Shukura. I climbed out of bed and knelt down in front of her. After a moment's silence, she spoke the word 'Askion.' Her voice was soft and it calmed me.

'Askion,' I repeated and touched my forefinger to her knee.

'Kataskion.'

'Kataskion.'

'Lix.'

'Lix.'

'Tetrax.'

'Tetrax.'

'Danameneus'

I had to be sure that I had heard it properly and I repeated it to myself in silence before I spoke.

'Danameneus'

'Aisi.'

'Aisi.'

The girl stood up and moved towards the door speaking the word 'Ambet.' The door was opened for her and locked behind her. I was alone again.

Chapter Ten

MOUNTFORD

The week before the Wigmore Society meeting, Villiers wrote to me to tell me that he had mentioned my account of Pierot's experiment with the voltaic batteries to Davy's assistant, Michael Faraday, who would be attending the next meeting. Faraday would be happy to be the subject of a demonstration of mesmerism on those lines. If I would care to conduct one, he would bring along some of Sir Humphry's batteries and a pair of leather gloves…

***

By the day of the meeting, my successful use of mesmerism with some of my patients sustained me up to a point but I was still apprehensive when I was ushered into Fitzgibbon's library where five men were seated round a long table, all looking at me. A large, broad-framed man with a big belly and mutton-chop moustaches stood up and held out a hand to me.

'Good day to you, sir. You are the mesmerist, are you not?'

'In a manner of speaking, sir.'

'I'm Wesley Fitzgibbon.'

'Robert Mountford, sir.'

We shook hands and Villiers came up to me.

'It's very good to see you here, Mr. Mountford,' he said.

'I am honoured to be here,' I replied, suppressing my disquiet at being in conversation with the man whose wife I had ravaged. Villiers invited me to the seat next to his at the table. Before he introduced me to the other members, he turned to me to murmur an aside.

'I would appreciate it if you would wait behind at the end of the meeting. I need to have a word with you about John Fanshawe.'

'Certainly, sir.'

Villiers introduced the other members and I nodded deferentially to each of them in turn. First came the anatomist, Charles Bell. I felt in awe of him, being aware of his celebrated and far reaching discovery of the separate systems through which the motor and sensory nerves operate and also his renowned skill in medical illustration. Villiers moved on, holding out a hand to the astronomer, Sir John Herschel, the son of Sir William Herschel who had made some of the greatest advances in astronomy since Copernicus. Then came Sir William Congreve, a leading expert in pyrotechnics who was developing the military use of rockets at the Woolwich Arsenal and Michael Faraday who was working as an assistant to the great Sir Humphry Davy. Finally, Villiers introduced the physician, Sir Wesley Fitzgibbon who was the President of the society and whose field of work was the medical treatment of lunatics. Fitzgibbon nodded to Villiers who addressed the meeting.

'Two papers will be delivered to the society today. The first will be from Sir Wesley who has recently been appointed to investigate current medical practice in lunatic asylums. That will be the subject of his address. The second will be delivered by Robert Mountford who will be addressing the subject of the use of mesmerism in surgery. I have asked Michael Faraday to bring some of Sir Humphry's voltaic batteries to the meeting in order for Mr. Mountford to perform a mesmerical experiment. We will all look forward to that.'

I was disconcerted by Fitzgibbon eying me with an expression of skepticism, his eyebrows raised as if he were waiting to see the performance of a stage illusionist. I was calmed a little when Faraday smiled at me and gave me an encouraging nod. He was clearly looking forward to the voltaic battery experiment in a spirit of genuine inquiry.

Villiers gave the floor to Fitzgibbon who stood up, clasping his hands behind his back and comfortably extending his stomach like the mainsail of a schooner.

'Gentlemen, the subject on which I shall speak touches on the philosophical and indeed the religious difference between the mind and the brain.'

I began to feel awkward, thinking I was going to be out of my depth.

'I think we would all accept that the shift from religious or demonological explanations of insanity towards a conception of it as an illness is due to the great advances in medical knowledge at the beginning of this century. Well-meaning though they were, some of the theories of treatment in the last century such as the purging of the bowels, blistering, and mortification of the extremities have not always proved effective. Nevertheless, I still believe that blood-letting and the emptying of the stomach through vomiting can still have a beneficial effect.'

Fitzgibbon described the new moral therapy that dispensed with restraints where possible and used kindness and patience in their treatment of inmates. He cited the example of the Retreat in York which was run by the Quakers and accepted that this was often proving beneficial to the patients as it rendered them mellower.

'Whether mellowing is curing is another matter,' he continued. 'As a Christian, I consider the mind to be an immortal, immaterial substance identical with the human soul and therefore lunacy cannot be a disease of the mind. It has to be that of the brain. As such, it will be medical advances that will bring about an understanding of insanity and new medical treatments for it in its various forms. Erasmus Darwin's rotating chair, for example. The chair spins the patient round at great speed so as to rearrange the contents of the brain into their right positions. The treatment also has the added benefit of bringing about subsequent vomiting.'

Fitzgibbon moved on to the subject of Franz Gall's theory concerning the workings of the organs in the human brain known as phrenology in which the examination of the outer surface of the head would enable the observer to recognise important elements in the character of that individual. I had read about phrenology in a book in my uncle's library and when I questioned my uncle about it I was told that its veracity was highly dubious.

Fitzgibbon expanded on his theme, describing the various regions of the brain, pointing out the markings that control amativeness, combativeness, destructiveness and secretiveness on a white phrenological head made of china that he took from a side table. He considered them very important in the investigation of diseases of the brain which result in the various forms of lunacy. When he sat down at the end of his presentation, Villiers asked for comments. I wanted to put forward my uncle's views of phrenology but I didn't dare. In the end, Michael Faraday started the discussion.

'Sir Wesley, I am intrigued by your correlation of the mind with the soul. You may know that I follow the religious teachings of the theologian, Robert Sandeman, and I share his belief that religion is independent of the physical laws of nature. As the rational mind is a reasoning machine I consider the soul to be independent of it.'

'In which case, Faraday,' Fitzgibbon countered, 'What do you consider to be the relation of the mind to the brain and, indeed, how does our consciousness relate to the physical object functioning inside our heads?'

'Would this analogy throw any light on the matter?' Charles Bell asked. 'Suppose we are standing on Richard Trevithick's steam locomotive running on its experimental tramway in Wales. We know how it works, how mechanics and the use of steam make the locomotive move. At the same time, we are also experiencing our movement along the tramway. Could the experience of movement be that of the mind and the machinery providing the experience be that of the brain?'

'Doesn't it all boil down to the problem of Descartes' dualism?' Congreve, the rocketeer added. 'How can an immaterial mind cause anything in a material body and vice versa?'

'Perhaps we should stay on the subject of the treatment of the insane,' Villiers suggested. 'This discussion regarding the mind and the brain will come about again when we consider the paper to be delivered by Mr. Mountford.'

There were nods of agreement and Fitzgibbon brought his address to a conclusion by describing the dreadful conditions that still existed in some of the pauper asylums. It reminded me of a visit I had made to a pauper asylum to operate on a lunatic shortly after I had qualified. I had been appalled and sickened to find my 'patient' chained in a dungeon-like cell, half starving and sitting in his own excrement. The recollection of the terrible experience occupied my mind to the extent that I failed to notice that Fitzgibbon's address had come to an end.

Suddenly, I was aware that Villiers was calling the room to order and was inviting me to share the results of my investigations into mesmerism.

Well, this is it, I thought as I picked up my sheaf of notes and rose from my chair. I saw that the notes were shaking in my hand and I put them back on the table, mortified that somebody might have noticed. I knew what I had to say, I told myself.

'First of all, gentlemen, I am honoured to be in your company and to have your attention regarding a subject about which we are still in considerable ignorance. I know that mesmerism works but I don't know how it works. A few surgeons are making use of it in this country as a means of annulling the pain felt by their patients during surgery but it is looked down upon by the majority who regard it as nothing more than entertainment performed by travelling showmen and the surgeons who use it as charlatans. I first became aware of the technique when I read in *The Times* about the Scottish surgeon James Carlyle who is experimenting with mesmerism in America. I wrote to his wife in Edinburgh, hoping to meet him on his return to Scotland but I regret to say that the senior members of the Royal Society of Surgeons of Edinburgh took a dim view of

Carlyle promoting its use and he was expelled from the society. He has now decided to stay in America and continue his practice there. In the meantime, I have been to see a demonstration of the phenomenon, albeit for popular entertainment, by the French mesmerist, Dr Alphonse Pierot. Although he put on a dramatic show of his skills, I was convinced that the trance states he induced were genuine.'

I went on to describe his demonstrations.

'I subsequently spent some time with Dr. Pierot at his home in Oxford during which he showed me various methods of inducing a trance state and he allowed me to practice them on his girls. I have now used Pierot's techniques with some success on patients at Barts Hospital needing to have wounds stitched up or goitres removed and in one case, a finger amputated. Since then, James Carlyle has written to me to give me some guidance as to the deep trance states needed in order to carry out a major amputation, the patient needing to be mesmerised more than once in order to achieve a sufficiently deep trance state when the operation takes place. If all goes well, I hope I will soon be ready to make my first use of it in such an operation. Thank you gentlemen.'

'Will you be willing to let the members of the society attend the operation?' Faraday asked. I hesitated for a moment and looked at Villiers who nodded at me encouragingly.

'Of course I will,' I said, trying not to appear anxious about the idea.

'Mr. Mountford will write to me to let me know when the operation is to take place,' Villiers announced to bypass my nervousness, 'and I will pass the information on to all of you. Now Gentlemen, Mr. Mountford would now like to demonstrate the phenomenon with the aid of three of Sir Humphry's voltaic batteries that Faraday has kindly brought to the meeting.'

He nodded to Faraday who left the room and returned wheeling a trolley on which stood three columns of zinc and copper discs connected to each other with wires. The odour of oxidizing acids filled the room.

'It goes without saying,' Villiers continued as the trolley wobbled along, 'that it is Volta's brilliant invention that has enabled Sir Humphry and Faraday to make such great strides in our understanding of electricity.'

There were murmurs of agreement and Villiers turned to me.

'Please go ahead, Mr. Mountford.'

'Gentlemen, I hope this will be a successful replication of Dr Pierot's experiment that I described earlier. The batteries here are sufficiently powerful to give a similarly painful shock. At the same time, no harm will have been done. Faraday, I gather you've generously offered to be the subject of the experiment.'

Faraday nodded.

'I hope I prove a suitable subject.'

'I'm sure you will and thank you for volunteering. I have to say that not everyone is susceptible and if you are not, I hope another of you gentlemen will be prepared to be the test subject.'

I looked at the reserved expressions on the faces around the table.

'I should also say that susceptibility to a mesmeric trance is very far from being a sign of weak-mindedness. Quite the reverse in fact, and your participation, Mr. Faraday could not be a better proof of that. Now sir, would you please take your chair and sit down next to the trolley.' As Faraday did so, I turned to the others.

'Gentlemen, while I'm attempting to put Mr. Faraday into a trance state, which might take a few minutes, I must ask you all to remain completely silent.'

I held a silver teaspoon in the air above Faraday's head.

'Mr. Faraday, would you please look at the spoon without raising your head.'

As Faraday did so, I moved the spoon a little further back until Faraday's pupils had nearly disappeared into the tops of his eye sockets.

'Please keep looking. It is essential that you don't lose sight of the spoon.'

I stood silently for a long moment before speaking slowly, my audience now hushed.

'Now sir, you are beginning to feel sleepy, your eyelids are becoming heavy and it is only with great difficulty that you can keep them open. Nevertheless, you must keep looking. You must not lose sight of the spoon. Your eyelids are now becoming heavier still.'

Faraday's lids dropped for a moment and opened again, continuing to stare at the spoon. I kept up a repetition of the phrases until, eventually, Faraday's lids closed again and did not open.

'Mr. Faraday, you are now in a trance state. Can you hear me?'

'Yes.'

'Good. Please open your eyes.'

Faraday's eyes opened.

'In a minute I am going to ask you to hold the two electric wires attached to Sir Humphry's batteries. The current will pass through you but you will feel nothing.'

Faraday nodded and looked across the room, his eyes unfocussed. I put on a pair of leather gloves and handed the two electric wires to him. He took one in each hand.

'Can you feel the current pass through you?'

'No.'

'Do you feel any pain?'

'No.'

'Good.'

I turned to the men sitting round the table.

'Would any of you care to touch the wires in Faraday's hands?'

'I will,' Bell offered. He walked over to the trolley and touched them with his forefingers.

'Good God,' he exclaimed, pulling his hands away with a jerk. I remembered feeling that I had been kicked by a mule when I had touched the wires in the hands of Pierot's girl. There was nervous laughter around the table as Bell rubbed his hands. For a moment nobody spoke. Villiers broke the silence.

'Mr. Bell, I believe that was a good demonstration of your understanding of the interaction of sensory and motor nerves.'

A little more laughter followed and Herschel, the astronomer, looked at me.

'That was an amazing demonstration, sir. What should we make of it?'

'I have to say I don't know what to make of it, sir,' I replied. 'But as you can see, it works.'

108

Faraday was still looking across the room.

'What about you, Mr. Faraday?' Herschel asked. 'Can you hear us?'

'I can,' Faraday replied, 'and the answer is I don't know. I feel as if I am outside myself in some way.'

'You can understand why churchmen think it the work of the devil.' Congreve said, attempting a laugh. 'What about you, Fitzgibbon?'

Fitzgibbon's eyes were closed and he appeared to be asleep. Villiers turned to me.

'I think you've mesmerised him.'

'Oh my God,' I thought, looking around the room. I had mesmerised the president of the society.

'I deeply regret this, gentlemen. It hasn't happened to me before but Dr. Pierot told me it can sometimes happen. I'll bring Mr. Faraday out of his trance and Sir Wesley should come out of his trance at the same time.

I knelt down in front of Faraday and held him in my gaze.

'Can you see me and hear me, Mr. Faraday?'

'Yes, of course.'

'Good. Now close your eyes. I'm going to count to ten and then clap my hands. When I do so you will awake from your trance state. Do you understand?'

'Yes.'

One...two...three...for...five...six...seven...eight...nine ...ten!'

I spoke the word 'ten' loudly and clapped his hands together. Faraday's eyes sprang open.

'What happened?' he asked.

'Do you remember holding the wires?'

'Yes.'

Fitzgibbon's voice came from the other side of the room.

'What's going on?' he asked.

Bell told him what had happened and all the others round the table tried to hide their smiles at his embarrassment.

During the subsequent discussion, a number of ideas about the possible nature of mesmerism passed back and forth. When Fitzgibbon had recovered some dignity, he addressed himself to me.

'Tell me, Mr. Mountford. Surely there is a great deal of difference between not feeling the electric current from a voltaic battery and not feeling your arm being cut off, wouldn't you say?'

'Indeed there is, sir, and not everyone can be put into a sufficiently deep trance state for that to be possible, but Mr. Carlyle has assured me that he has performed such operations in which the patient has felt no pain.'

Fitzgibbon turned to address the group.

'There's another question I have for us to consider. Is not pain a natural and intended consequence of primal sin? If this is the case, endeavours to do away with it would seem to be aimed at preventing us from passing through what God expects us to endure and through that endurance to acquire wisdom. What would your thoughts be on that, Mr. Mountford?'

I had to suppress the memory of my father having the same view.

'I'm afraid I don't know how to answer a religious question, sir, as I'm a materialist.'

There was an awkward silence which was ended by Faraday.

110

'As my faith is based on the belief that religion is independent of the natural world and as bodily pain exists in the natural world, I don't accept that it's God's will that we suffer it.'

'It's true that pain bravely borne is a mark of courage,' Bell joined in, 'and we hold in the highest esteem those who endure great suffering with stoicism.'

'There is also the vitalist view on the matter,' Faraday commented. 'It would claim that suffering is inseparable from the invisible life-force that makes our existence possible.'

'I don't hold with invisible life forces,' Bell remarked with a hint of contempt in his voice.

'Neither do I,' Faraday countered. I was just stating the case.'

As the discussion came to a close, Fitzgibbon conceded that there could be more than one view of the matter and Villiers announced that he hoped to bring Charles Babbage to the next meeting to talk about the calculating machine he had invented which he called his 'difference engine'.

'I'm sure you will all have heard of it. In mathematical terms it is effectively a thinking machine designed for the computation of astronomical and mathematical tables. It's a remarkable achievement'.

'I look forward to meeting him,' Fitzgibbon declared and the others concurred. Villiers and I sat in conversation when the other members left and Fitzgibbon had gone off to join his wife in the drawing room.

'That was a most interesting meeting, my boy. I'm so pleased that you're now a member of our little society. Now tell me, have you seen John Fanshawe since he moved to London?'

'Yes. He called on me the other day.'

'Really? The reason I ask is that we arranged to meet at his club. When I got there they told me he'd gone abroad. Did you know about that?'

'No. I didn't. I have to say he wasn't his usual self when he came to see me. He looked preoccupied and his face was strained. Something was bothering him. He seemed to have drunk quite a bit when he arrived and he continued drinking when he was with me. He talked about Mary Shelley's book and told me about attending a demonstration of galvanism on a corpse. By that time, he had drunk so much that he lay back on the sofa and began to drop off. Then he said something strange as if he were talking in his sleep.

Villiers's expression darkened.

'What did he say?'

'"I'm going to meet my father." When he eventually woke up I asked him what he meant. He couldn't tell me. He had no memory of saying the words.'

Villiers appeared disconcerted as he looked at the puzzled expression on my face.

'Very strange, I don't know what to think of it,' he said.

I looked at him and I knew he was holding something back.

Chapter Eleven

When the long-cased clock in my bedchamber struck the hour, I awoke instantly and wondered, as I often did, how my sleeping brain could ignore the clock's bell chiming the half and the hour through the night but bring me to consciousness only when the hour for my rising was struck. I would be performing my first major amputation using mesmerism that morning and I felt nervous about it. Villiers had written to me to say that he would be attending along with Charles Bell. Sir Humphry Davy was also going to come. I felt honoured that Davy would be there but the prospect of his presence added to my nervousness.

I had to be up particularly early on that day as I had to go to the medical school to deal with the Clerke brothers. When I had dressed, I put a wooden club and one of my pair of percussion cap dueling pistols in my overcoat pockets as I always did on the days I needed to walk through the city in the hours of darkness. I had kept the pistols loaded ever since I had bought them in a street market when I was a student, but I had never yet had to fire one of them.

My route to Barts Hospital was through gas lit streets. It would be more than my life's worth to take any shortcuts through the labyrinths of unlit alleys, scarcely wide enough for two men to pass one another. As I made my way down Saffron Hill thinking about the operation I was to perform, I heard the sound of grunting and turned to see a night watchman stumbling out of the darkness of an alleyway, his lamp swinging from side to side. The old man's feet slid on a pile of horse dung and he fell into a heap on the ground. I lifted him up. It was Albert, the night watchman I had seen many times in his early morning journeys. I had sometimes given him a coin or two and had listened to his troubles. Fortunately, the lantern had fallen on its base and the candle was still alight.

'Hello, Albert. What are you running from?' I asked.

'A man been murdered in the alley down there, sir. His body's covered in blood. You don't want to go down there. I couldn't do nothing for him and nor could you. He was dead alright. And two ruffians had just run off.'

Albert was long in the tooth, blind in one eye and his gait suggested some arthritis in his old bones.

'How goes it, old chap?' I enquired.

'Not well, sir. My wife's got the quinsy.'

'I'm sorry to hear that. Which wife would that be?' Albert had told me about his colourful life on one or two occasions.

'Only one at a time, sir, them not being as strong in their constitution as I am.'

'I hope she recovers soon. Are you going to be alright?'

'I'll be fine, sir, thank you.'

'Good. I hope the rest of your night is quiet.'

I put a hand on his shoulder and continued on my way down Saffron Hill. Before my brother's illness, I would have given the man a shilling but my financial circumstances now meant that I had to hoard every penny.

Dawn was about to break when I arrived at the medical school and stood waiting outside the main entrance. After a few minutes I heard the sound of horses' hooves and the rumble of cartwheels. A horse and cart with two men in it emerged into the light of a gas lamp on the other side of the road. The two men humped a sack off the cart, each taking one end of it. I let them into the entrance and they carried their load into the anatomy room. One of them returned to the cart for the second, lighter sack. They carefully emptied them onto a table. One of the bodies was a heavily built man in his forties and the other a child, a girl of about seven years.

'A hanged man from Newgate,' the older brother said, 'and the child died of croup. Both fresh, the man hanged only yesterday afternoon and the child buried only last evening.'

I had become used to the need for dead bodies for the anatomy lessons since I had been a student. They didn't bother me in the way that living patients in agony did. I handed over eight guineas and the two men left. The job was paid for by the senior consultant surgeon who felt it beneath him to deal with the deliveries himself. An assistant came into the anatomy room and the two of us cut the clothes off the bodies with large pairs of scissors. I worked on the girl. When I had finished I laid the child out on the anatomy table and walked to one of the surgical wards where the smell of rotting cadavers was replaced by that of infected wounds. The patient on whom I was going to operate that morning was lying in one of the beds. I held up a hand in greeting.

'Good day to you Mr. Garnett. You know we're going to deal with that leg this morning.'

The man was of middle years, gaunt and with a sallow complexion and receding sandy hair. He looked at me nervously.

'Yes sir.'

'I'm confident we're going to be able to remove it without too much pain.'

The man nodded obediently.

'I'm going to do one more test. Are you in pain now?'

'Yes, I am.'

I put Garnett into a trance with the teaspoon.

'Are you in pain now?'

'No, sir.'

'Now I'm going to prick your arm with a needle once again as I did yesterday and let's see how we get on.'

I picked up a needle from a kidney dish by the bed and pushed into the man's arm.

'Can you feel that?'

'No.'

'And has the pain in your leg still gone away?'

'Yes, sir.'

'Good. I'm going to take you out of your trance state now.'

When I had done so I looked for someone who was responsible enough to wake me in two hours. There were two nurses asleep on benches smelling of gin. They would be no use. Through the open door of the ward I saw another nurse walking along the corridor.

'Good morning, Betty,' I called out, catching up with her.

'Good morning, sir.'

Betty used to be a prostitute but syphilis had put a stop to that. I had seen her attending to Garnett's needs and knew her to be kind-hearted and reliable.

'Betty, can you tell the time?' I asked when he had caught up with her.

'Yes, sir.'

I took my watch from my waistcoat pocket and handed it to her. I was confident she wouldn't run off with it.

'I am going to sleep for a while in one of the empty beds in Mr. Garnett's ward. I would be grateful if you would wake me at half past nine. I have to operate on him at ten.'

'Certainly, sir.'

'Thank you.'

Back in the ward, I removed my shoes and lay down on an empty bed hoping for an hour's sleep. In fact I hardly slept, being restless and wakeful and my nerves were on edge. It was to be a very important day for me. Half an hour before Betty returned to rouse me I was wide-awake. Despite my lack of sleep I was impatient to get on with the task that awaited me.

***

I entered the theatre followed by two young assistants carrying a stretcher bearing Mr. Garnett in a thin cotton nightshirt. We were all in our shirtsleeves and wearing white, blood-specked aprons, tied at the back. I saw Villiers and Bell seated among his senior colleagues in the stepped rows of benches that lined three sides of the room and looked around, doing my best to calm my nerves as I tried to guess the identity of Humphry Davy among the faces I didn't know. The assistants placed the stretcher next to the operating table in the middle of the room and lifted the patient on to it. I went over to greet Bell and Villiers who introduced me to a well-dressed man with a cantankerous expression seated next to him.

'Robert, this is Sir Humphry Davy. Robert is the friend I've spoken of, Sir Humphry.'

I reminded myself that this was not a time to let myself be overawed by such a celebrated figure.

'Thank you for coming, sir,' I said with a gracious nod. The renowned man looked very different from the handsome young man in the portrait I had seen in the Royal Academy some years earlier. Davy returned my nod.

'I'm afraid Faraday is unable to come because of some work he is doing for me. I gather he was the subject of your experiment with my voltaic batteries,' he added with a certain haughtiness.

'Indeed, sir,' I replied as the great man fell silent. It was only later that I learned that Davy had become unaccountably envious of Faraday's growing reputation and he frequently kept him out of the limelight by giving him menial tasks to perform.

I stepped back to address the assembled onlookers.

'Gentlemen I hope to be able to demonstrate to you the use of mesmerism to render the patient free from pain while undergoing an amputation. You would be right to be skeptical of Mesmer's belief that his ability to produce a trance state in his subjects was the result of animal magnetism, the body's response to being in close proximity to magnetic forces. Since then, experiments by others have led to the view that the trance state is based on the function of the human imagination and the power of suggestion on the unconscious mind. This is the view that I hold. I know that many of you will remain to be convinced, partly because mesmerism has become such a popular entertainment and partly because it's difficult to believe that the power of suggestion alone can make a patient feel no pain during an amputation.'

By now, I was sweating but I was determined to appear confident.

'I've undertaken minor procedures with the use of mesmerism and I've been very pleased with the results. This will be my first operation using the technique while amputating a limb. I've tested my patient, Mr. Garnett to be sure that he is susceptible to mesmerism as not everyone is. I have followed the guidelines given to me by James Carlyle an Edinburgh surgeon who is using the technique in America. These include mesmerizing the patient at least three times before surgery as this enables each successive trance state to become deeper. I'll be talking to Mr. Garnett while I'm operating to let him know what I'm doing. Mr. Carlyle believes that the patient's conscious awareness of the surgeon's actions facilitates his unconscious maintenance of his trance state. I've explained all this to Mr. Garnett who comes here as a willing subject. His injury is a serious one. his lower right leg and knee joint were crushed when he fell under the wheels of a hansom cab. I shall amputate his leg at the lower end of the thigh. As you know it's important to save as much of the leg as possible as this will give him the best use of prosthesis. I will be aided by my two assistants, Mr. Jones and Mr. Marsden.'

I took out my silver teaspoon and began the induction, holding it above Garnett's head. After two or three minutes Garnett's fluttering eyes closed.

'You are now beginning to go into a deep trance in which you will feel no sensation in your body. You will just be aware of my speaking to you and of your breathing which will remain calm at all times whatever is happening to you. Can you hear me, Mr. Garnett?'

'Yes sir.'

'And you understand what I've told you?'

'Yes.'

'Good. I am now going to operate. The tourniquet, Mr. Jones.'

The assistant buckled the leather strap around Garnett's upper thigh, turned the metal screw tightly to block off the femoral artery and pulled up the skin below the tourniquet as forcefully as he could while Marsden held the lower leg. It was the moment of truth.

'I am now going to cut through the skin and the soft tissue.'

As the two assistants held Garnett's leg, I ran my scalpel around his lower thigh cutting deep down to the muscle in one quick sweep. Spurts of blood escaped from the wound, some hitting my apron and Jones's face. To my great relief, Garnett didn't scream, and I felt, not for the first time, that there was something uncanny about my ability to control my patient's pain during such a devastating surgical procedure.

'Can you still hear me, Mr. Garnett?'

'Yes, sir.'

'Good. I am now going to separate the muscles and detach the tendons.'

I worked quickly and smoothly until a good few inches of bone became exposed.

'The retractor, Mr. Marsden.'

Marsden took a broad piece of linen, tore it down the middle at one end and put the exposed bone in the slit holding both ends of the linen strip. Then he pulled up all the loose muscle, soft tissue and skin to expose as much bone as possible. I cut through it lightly and carefully with a surgical saw.

'Sutures, Mr. Jones.'

Jones handed me lengths of cat gut and I tied off arteries and veins. I then drew down the skin, soft tissue and loose muscle, gathered it together until it covered the end of the bone and sutured the skin below it in a neat stump.

'You do the bandaging, Mr. Marsden.'

As Marsden did so, I looked at Garnett.

'How are you doing, sir? Feeling all right?'

'Just a little soreness around my knee. That's all.'

'Excellent.'

There was applause from a little group of medical students which quickly faded as one of the senior surgeons sitting in the front row turned and scowled at them before addressing himself to Mountford.

'You are to be congratulated, sir,' he announced. 'Tell me, when will his bodily sensations return?'

'I will extend the trance state with further use of suggestion in half an hour or so and he will be given some laudanum to help him sleep. When he awakes, his sensations will have returned. He can go back to the ward now, Mr. Marsden.'

My assistants held the stretcher next to the operating table. I eased Garnett carefully on to it and they carried him out of the theatre.

Bell and Davy came up to me, followed by Villiers in conversation with an elegant and smartly dressed man of some sixty years with a full head of silvery hair. Davy spoke first.

'Most impressive,' Mr. Mountford. How can it be that the psychological power of suggestion can enable the subject to switch off the electrical current that activates his sensory nervous system?'

'I don't know, sir.' I shrank a little before the great man.

'We will discover how it works in the course of time, will we not?' Davy went on.

'No doubt, greater minds than mine will do so, sir.'

'Indeed.' Davy smiled confidently as Villiers drew forward his silver-haired companion and introduced him to me.

'I would like you to meet Monsieur Auguste Devereux who is also making a very interesting clinical use of mesmerism. He is using the technique to unlock the hidden causes of mental disturbance in those whose minds are bedeviled by melancholy or anxiety.'

Devereux and I nodded formally to one another.

'I found your operating technique most impressive.' Devereux spoke in French accented tones.

'Dr Devereux has to return to Norwich tomorrow,' Villiers continued,' but he will be coming back to London in a week or two. I would like the two of you to get together. I think you will be interested in each others' ideas.'

'Thank you, sir. I look forward to it, Dr. Devereux'

Chapter Twelve

FANSHAWE

I had lost all sense of time, the long intervals between Shukura's visits to my room providing my only sense of its passing. My patches of fitful sleep were filled with dreams. In some, I experienced a strange sense of elation when repeating Shukura's words, listening to the soft sound of her voice and wanting to take off her mask. In others I was in state of terror, being followed by the galvanised corpse. The dreams usually ended with my falling into space in darkness crying out for help but no sound coming from my mouth. By now, darkness has become a thing of terror.

Shukura was in charge of my needs, bringing me food and water and emptying my chamber pot. As always, on leaving the room she spoke the word 'Ambet.' The door was opened for her and locked behind her. As well as becoming overpoweringly airless, the room had taken on the smell of the sewers and Shukura brought me some incense sticks of the kind that are sold in the Chinese shops around the docks.

***

Eventually, I learned to repeat the sequence of all twenty one words and on occasion felt the same strange euphoria that I experienced in some of my dreams. In one dream, I was stroking Shukura's long, black hair and I longed to see her face. In the end, I was driven to pull off her mask and found nothing behind it but empty darkness. I awoke to see Gilchrist and Amon in the room, Amon wearing his mask.

'Do you remember the words that Shukura taught you?' Gilchrist asked.

'Yes.'

'You will now need to speak them in the order they were taught you. This is going to be the next stage of your initiation. Remember, you must make no mistakes.'

Amon left the room and returned with Shukura in her mask with a white cloak wrapped around her. Gilchrist pointed to where the beheading block had stood. In its place, the Egyptian symbol of the eye had been painted in gold on the floor.

'Take off your clothes,' Gilchrist said, 'and stand on this spot.'

As I undressed, Gilchrist took a piece of rope from his pocket and tied my hands behind my back. Amon moved Shukura towards me. When she was some inches away, he lifted off her cloak. She was naked. I was deeply aroused but also disturbed by the dead stare of her mask.

'Speak the words now,' Gilchrist said.

As I began, Shukura lowered her head and moved it from side to side allowing her long hair to brush against my erect member, her hands cupped just below it. My excitement was beginning to overwhelm me and I was twisting my wrists to be free of rope holding them. When my litany came to an end, I succumbed to a climax more powerful than any I had experienced in my life. I let out a great groan and my legs began to buckle as I watched my semen falling into Shukura's cupped hands. Gilchrist stepped behind me and held me upright while Shukura dipped a forefinger into the semen in the palm of her hand and drew a circle with a vertical line and a cross bar below it on my chest.

'That is the Egyptian sign of life,' Gilchrest explained as Amon put the cloak over Shukura and left the room with her. Gilchrist undid the rope around my wrists.

'Get dressed,' he commanded.

I was trembling as I put on my clothes and sat down on the side of the bed.

'Do your dreams usually end with your falling into space in darkness?' he asked.

'Yes.'

'That is important. It means that you're preparing yourself for the final part of your initiation. It is called the Abyss. For the next fourteen days you will remain alone in this room in complete darkness. There will be no candles. After a short while you will experience a state of falling of the kind you've had in your dreams. You must learn to control the fear it may induce in you. When you have done so, you will find the experience of falling becoming one of flying and you will be filled with elation. In a moment Shukura will bring in another glass of lotus wine which you may drink when you have learned to fly. But only then. And remember this. By the fourteenth day in the Abyss you will have acquired tremendous power, including the power to bring your father back from the entrance to the underworld where he awaits his next incarnation.

Was I to have such a crucial role in bringing my father back? Gilchrist had never made it so explicit before. The realization then struck me that I was to be in total darkness for fourteen days. Gilchrist was staring at me.

'I can see the fear in your eyes but you must complete the initiation. Although you don't yet know it, you have already acquired too much knowledge to return to a state of

125

'unknowing.' We will bring you bread and cheese and spring water to drink. Then we will take away the candles and the tinder box when we leave. From that moment on you will be in the Abyss. You will be given a bucket into which you can empty your chamber pot as no one will come into the room from now on for fourteen days. And remember. Should you chance to see daylight during that time, the spirit of the serpent will coil itself into you and it will cause you to lose your reason.'

I stood up and instinctively made for the door, but Gilchrist pushed me back.

'You must learn to control the fear,' he said and left the room. Shukura brought in water and provisions, a bucket and a glass of lotus wine which she put on the chimneypiece. She took the candles and tinder box from the cupboard and picked up the one lit candle from the table. When she reached the door she blew out the candle. The door was opened for her and locked behind her, leaving me in total darkness. I was in a desperate panic. How could I make myself think that I could see? I ran my hands along the walls and felt the now familiar objects, painting a mental picture of the room, imagining it in bright sunlight. But it didn't work. I was falling into space enveloped in darkness, darker than the blackest night.

**

Before long, I had no idea how many days I had been there. The rhythm of time passing was created only by the experience of waking and sleeping. In my dreams I could see. The house was completely silent and I was sure I had been left there alone. The room stank and I was constantly retching but nothing came out of me. *When am I going to fly, father?* I would shout. Sometimes, a song would roll round my head and I would bellow it out between bouts of hysterical laughter.

On yonder hill there stands a creature. Who she is I do not know. I will court her for her beauty. She must answer yes or no. Oh no John, no John, no John, no! My husband was a Spanish captain, went to sea a month ago. The very last time we kissed and parted, he bid me always answer no. Oh no John, No John, No John, No! Madam shall I tie your garter? Tie it a little above your knee. If my hand should slip a little farther, would you think it amiss of me? Oh no John, no John, no John, no!"

My laughter would be followed by weeping.

I dreamt about being in bed as a child and hearing the sound of my father's footsteps ascending the stairs and crying out, '*Please don't let the snake kill me, Papa!* I dreamt that the galvanized corpse picked up the axe and broke open the boards nailed over the window. I woke up with a start, fearful of Gilchrist's warning.

***

How much longer before the nightmare of this initiation was to come to an end? If I was unable to fly, what would my father do to me? Would he reach out in rage from the entrance to the underworld that was barred against him? I thought about the lotus wine. I knew I was supposed to drink only when I could fly but perhaps it would help me to do so.

What had I got to lose? I remembered the delusions it produced in me when I had first drunk it but nothing could be worse than what I was experiencing now. I recalled the moment I had jumped from the Montgolfier balloon into Ashton's lake. The memory triggered the same sense of bravado. I felt my way towards the chimneypiece and drank the wine in one swallow.

What exhilaration! I focused on the sound of my breathing, the smell of the jackal's blood on my breeches. Then it happened. I floated up into the air.

'I'm flying! I'm flying! Thank you, father!'...

It felt more like swimming than flying. It reminded me how I had learned to swim, extending my arms and sweeping them back while kicking my legs out like a frog. Soon I was swimming round the room feeling euphoric and curiously never encountering a wall, no matter how far I swim in any direction. Then I heard a voice whispering inside my chest.

'You are not flying. This is just an illusion. You should have waited.'

At that moment, I found myself standing on the floor again, holding the empty glass. The voice whispered, 'You haven't woken up yet.'

'Get out of me,' I shouted, pounding my chest.

'I can't. I am you. Now look at the grate.'

'How can I see it in the dark?

The empty grate abruptly burst into flame, adding the smell of burning coal to the other smells in the room. I dropped to my knees and stared at the flames. Now that I could see, I started to walk around the room, looking at the familiar objects in the firelight. But when I touched them, my hand passed through them. A figure emerged from the shadows. *Oh, God, please, no!* It was the galvanised corpse coming towards me. The creature touched my cheek with its cold dead hand and I was sickened by the foul smell of its rotting flesh. I watched it as it turned from me and walked to the block on which I had beheaded the jackal. It knelt down and placed its neck on the block. It was waiting for me to behead it. I picked up the axe and brought it down on the creature's neck with massive force.

Instantly, the illusion was gone. The room was in darkness and I was alone again. In a state between waking and dreaming, I pictured myself taking the axe to the window and breaking open the boards nailed over it. I picked up the axe and lay down on the bed, cradling the blade and running my forefinger along its edge. Once again, I brought to mind my fearless jump from the Montgolfier balloon and felt an immense surge of power. I told myself that Gilchrist had lost his hold over me and he could no longer do me harm.

I carried the axe to the window, my power over Gilchrist suffusing me and the hairs rising all over my body. I swung the axe through the felt covering and into the wooden boarding beneath it. The wood was thick and, at first, the blade failed to pierce it. I swung it again, this time spurred on by a triumphant rage in which I imagined myself beheading Gilchrist. Through the torn black velvet, a tenuous slice of light appeared, as thin as a thread. I looked around the room. My eyes were so accustomed to darkness that it was sufficient for me to make out the gray forms of walls and furniture. I lifted the axe and swing it again. This time the thread of light opened to the width of a tallow candle and the room was suffused with a dim half-light. I put my eye to the gash and I saw a derelict factory standing amongst demolished tenements. In the distance, I made out the winding snake of the Thames curling round the Isle of Dogs. I kept my eye there for what felt like hours, excited by the glorious validation of my triumph over Gilchrist. As the light faded, I lay my bedclothes under the window, ready to fall asleep and dream of victory. Instead I began to feel an agonising pain in my stomach. Something was coiling around inside me.

Oh, father, no, please no.

Chapter Thirteen

MOUNTFORD

I was exhausted after a long day, my last patient not being susceptible to mesmerism and my financial worries were claiming my attention. I had been sending my mother money each month and the time had come to move to cheaper lodgings. I would need laudanum again to sleep that night.

A letter awaited me when I arrived home. It was a note from Dr Villiers inviting me to join Dr Devereux and himself for coffee at Boodles the following afternoon at four o'clock. There would be no patients for me on that afternoon and I gave my maid's son, Charlie, a note to take to Villiers, thanking him for the invitation and saying I would be pleased to come.

***

The same waiter at Boodles led me to Villiers's corner in the drawing room where he and Devereux were drinking coffee. We exchanged greetings and Devereux repeated his congratulations on my surgical use of mesmerism. He suggested that we begin our exchange of ideas with my telling him about my work. When I began, Devereux listened intently, his eyes sometimes closed in concentration. I could see that he was something of a charmer. He was good-looking and well-spoken with an engagingly Gallic quality in his speech and demeanour. I could imagine the effect he would have on his female patients, especially English ones.

'Your work is to be applauded,' Devereux declared when I had finished and Villiers invited Devereux to speak about his work.

'For several years now, I've been using mesmerism in an attempt to heal the troubled minds of patients who suffer from nervous disorders. The technique was discovered by the French mesmerist, Armand de Chastenet, the Marquis de Puysegur. Do you know of him?'

'I don't, I'm afraid.'

'He was a man of considerable importance in the understanding of the human mind. He was already something of a natural philosopher when he began to take an interest in Mesmer's work and he experimented with his methods to cure various disorders of workers on his estate by waving magnets over them. Of course, the use of magnets seems so naive now, doesn't it, but you have to bear in mind that this was nearly fifty years ago. During that time he came across a very interesting case; a farm worker who had come to him with a respiratory problem. After the man had gone into a trance, he began to talk quite openly about his distress due to a falling-out that had taken place with his sister. The Marquis found it perplexing as the man would normally have been too cowed to talk at all in his presence. During their conversation the Marquis came up with a way of resolving the dispute and suggested it to him. When the man came out of his trance he had no memory of anything that had happened during it. What is fascinating is that he resolved the quarrel with his sister by taking the action the Marquis had put to him without his being aware that it had been suggested to him in his trance state.'

Devereux leant forward and clasped his hands together.

'Isn't that amazing? It means that the mind keeps secrets from itself.

'The Marquis recounted similar experiments he had conducted successfully with other members of his household and workers on his estate. There were some cases he treated in which the subject seemed not to be aware of being troubled at all but was behaving strangely and often destructively. Having mesmerised one such man who was subject to bouts of violent anger, the Marquis found out that he was acting out a disturbance in his childhood. Somehow the Marquis managed to suggest to him a way of coming to terms with the memory and his subsequent behaviour became less destructive. You can see the implications can't you?'

I nodded, fascinated that mesmerism could be a gateway to yet another undiscovered aspect of the human mind. It put me in mind of Fanshawe's taste for wenches and riding crops and always courting danger.

'There's another extraordinary aspect to all this,' Devereux continued. 'I've read about a German physician who gave an account of a case of what he called 'exchanged personality'. It sounds hard to believe but, in the trance state, the personality of one of his patients, a bourgeois German woman regularly changed to that of a French aristocrat. In her changed state she spoke perfect French, adopted French aristocratic manners, described events in her life as a French woman with total conviction and was unable to speak German. When her personality reverted back, she had no recollection of what had taken place and had no awareness of this secondary personality. I read subsequently that Erasmus Darwin had come across a similar case. Don't you find it baffling that the unconscious mind can be inhabited by completely independent identities? Difficult to believe isn't it? I don't know what to make of it but the German physician and Erasmus Darwin were men of the highest probity.'

'Quite extraordinary,' I remarked, completely baffled. It seemed supernatural but it was not for men of science to indulge in such idle ideas.

'How did you come to know about the Marquis' work?' I asked.

'He wrote a book about his ideas and he set up an Institute for students to learn how to use his techniques. I spent two years studying there. It was disbanded during the Revolution and the Marquis was imprisoned. My parents were less fortunate. They went to the guillotine. I managed to escape to England and was taken in by a family in Norwich. That's where I've set up my practice. I'm not going back to France. I'm happy here, although I'm sorry that mesmerism seems not to be taken seriously as it should be in England. At the moment I'm doing some work at the Bethel Asylum in Norwich where they are using the new moral treatment. I want to see if the Marquis' methods can be applied to lunatics.'

'Fascinating, eh, Mountford,' Villiers said. 'I've asked Devereux if he'd talk about his work at the Wigmore Society next week but he needs to return to Norwich.'

Devereux turned to me.

'Would you care to share what I've told you with the other members? I imagine it could lead to an interesting discussion on all sorts of levels.'

I was taken by surprise and felt unexpectedly honoured.

'I would be delighted to do so, sir.'

***

I was nearing my home that evening, imagining myself giving up my career as a surgeon and setting up a practice on similar lines to Devereux's when I saw a cab drawn up outside my house and a young woman in a blue cloak and bonnet walking down the steps from my front door. She was about to climb into the cab when she saw me coming up to her.

'Excuse me, sir. Are you Mr. Mountford?'

'I am, young lady.'

'I am Sarah Fanshawe, sir, John's cousin.'

'I am very pleased to meet you, Miss Fanshawe. How can I help you?'

'I've just left a note with your housekeeper's son. I've been looking for John without success.'

'So have I, Miss Fanshawe. Please come up and take some tea with me. I will call another cab for you later.'

'Thank you,' she said and paid off the cabbie. I was taken aback by her confident bearing, travelling alone after dark in such a dangerous city. I took the note from the hall table and led her up to my rooms. When she had settled on the sofa, I picked up a pair of fire tongs.

'Excuse me for a moment,' I said and took the tongs to the lodger next door to me, returning with a burning coal. I set about lighting a fire and Sarah's face, radiant and dark-eyed, soon became clear in the glow of burning kindling wood. I warmed to her.

'How long have you been in London?' I asked.

135

'For two days.'

'I hope you won't mind me saying this, Miss Fanshawe, but London is a dangerous place for a woman to be about, especially at this time of night, even travelling in a cab.'

'Thank you for your concern, Mr. Mountford. I've had to learn to look after myself since John left home and I do have some means of protection.'

She opened her cape and showed me a large pocket sown inside it. She put her hand into it and heaved out a double-barreled percussion cap pistol.

'Good God,' I exclaimed with a jolt and immediately coloured. 'Please forgive my language, Miss Fanshawe.'

'Think nothing of it, Mr. Mountford. This is what I used when I went out with John to shoot rabbits.'

'I'm relieved to hear it. May I ask how you found me?'

'John has sometimes spoken of you, telling me that you work at St Bartholomew's Hospital. I was hoping you might know of his whereabouts so I went there and found somebody who gave me your address. I've left a note with John's housekeeper. She told me he's gone abroad and she doesn't know where he's gone or when he'll be back.'

'I'm afraid I don't know where he is either. I also heard he'd gone abroad.'

'Did John tell you that I grew up with him and his mother?'

'He did.'

'I feel very close to them both. My aunt gave me their family name and I think of them as my mother and brother.'

I lit two candles on the chimneypiece and the burner in the cradle of my kettle to make tea. I waited for her to go on.

'The reason I'm looking for John is that my aunt has become ill with croup and she has taken to her bed. The physician is prescribing blood-letting and leeches and he has performed a surgical incision into her neck which has eased her breathing a little. But she is 81 years old and physically weak. I don't know how long she'll live. She asks after John and I think he should go to see her even if she has difficulty knowing who he is. Her mental faculties are feeble, I'm afraid. I wrote to John but he didn't reply. Perhaps he never received my letter.'

'I'm so sorry. John told me she sometimes has imaginary conversations with his father.'

'For some time, now, I find it most distressing.'

'When did John last see her?'

'Some months ago. She's seen nothing of him since he came to London. I'm afraid his materialism set her against him. She's a devout woman.'

'I'm afraid I have to tell you that I'm a materialist too.'

She didn't respond to the comment and I felt awkward as it hung in the air for a long moment.

'Forgive me, Miss Fanshawe, I hope I haven't offended you.'

'Far from it, Mr. Mountford. I was hesitating because it is not supposed to be a woman's place to have views on such matters. I hope I won't shock you by saying that I read all the books John brought home when he was at Balliol and I am a materialist myself. Of course, my aunt knows nothing of this.'

I was disconcerted and gave myself a moment to gather my thoughts.

'It has not been my lot to come across independently minded women, Miss Fanshawe. Let me say that I am delighted now to have
met one.'

I hoped her sharp-eyed smile indicated that she took my remark as a compliment.

'What do you think might have happened to John?' Sarah asked, returning the conversation to the reason for her visit.

'I wish I could tell you. He's rather impetuous as you know.'

'The trouble is that I can't stay in London to keep looking for him. I've got to go back home to be with my aunt.'

'I understand. If I see him I'll tell him to go to Oxford without delay.'

I handed her a cup of tea and saw her looking at a framed drawing of Loch Lomond on the wall next to the fireplace.

'My sister Alice drew it when she was a child,' I said.

'She's very talented,' Sarah said with a smile.

She was. I regret to say that she died when she was twelve.'

'I'm so sorry, Mr. Mountford.'

I didn't want to talk about it and Sarah didn't press me. We sat in silence for a while as she sipped her tea, huddled in her cloak.

'I think I'd better go now,' she said when she had finished it.

'Where are you staying?'

'At a boarding house in Tavistock Square. It was recommended by a friend. It's quite respectable and I feel safe there. Mrs. Bradley who runs it only takes in women.'

'I'm glad to hear it. Nevertheless, I would be pleased if you would let me accompany you there, Miss Fanshawe. There's a cab rank in Rosebery Avenue. You're a brave young woman and well armed, but I still fear for you being alone at night in London.'

I tried not to think of the cost of the cab to take us there and to take me back to Calthorpe Street.

'I'll be glad of your company, Mr. Mountford.'

'I too have to protect myself,' I said as I put on my greatcoat and put a pistol and a club into my pockets. 'By the bye, I'll be in Oxford myself next Thursday morning to see a surgeon at the Radcliffe Hospital.'

'John told me you were a surgeon.'

'I work at St Bartholomew's Hospital. The senior consultant there wants me to talk to a former colleague at the Radcliffe Hospital about a surgical technique I'm using. May I call on you while I'm in Oxford? It would be in the early afternoon.'

'I'd be pleased if you would, Mr. Mountford.'

***

When I had returned to my lodging, I looked at Alice's drawing and drank a glass of laudanum. Once again, the memory of the accident flooded my mind. Three years younger than me, Alice had been the only source of real joy for me in my God-fearing family. In her, I was to find a soul mate. She was a clever child and a joyous spirit with none of her parents' austere religiosity. She warmed my heart and we shared our love for our slow-witted younger brother

Angus, a sweet child who would never be able to make a life of his own.

One summer, the family visited our mother's cousin in a little village in the Cairngorms. Alice and I went for walks together up into the hills along drovers' paths. Alice had discovered a talent for drawing and she took her sketch book and pencils with her.

During one of these walks on a windy day, I twisted my ankle and I had to sit down and wait for the pain to pass. Alice went on ahead, pointing out a crag that she wanted to draw and was soon out of sight. After half an hour had passed, I became anxious and I set off to look for her, calling out her name as I limped up the track towards the crag. A gust of wind suddenly knocked me sideways and, as I steadied myself, I heard the sound of water. I walked on and came to a deep ravine with a waterfall at its head. I climbed up a small outcrop of rock that overlooked it and from where there was a clear view of the crag that Alice wanted to draw. A pencil was lying on the grass next to the rock and I looked down into the ravine. Small trees grew out of its sides and, directly below me, some forty feet down, swaying in the wind, I saw Alice's sketch book caught on a branch. I became hysterical, screaming out her name again and again, my voice drowned by the wind as I looked around for a way down to the bottom of the ravine but I could find none.

It was evening when I accompanied my father and a party of men from the village holding flaming torches and found Alice's broken body in the stream at the bottom of the ravine flickering in the torchlight. Her white face was under the water, drained of blood, her eyes were open and her long black hair trailed downstream. Her sketch book had fallen from the branch and was lying in the grass beside the stream.

We were all devastated and my home became a desolate place. Neither I nor my parents could erase from our minds the thought that Alice might not have fallen if I had been with her.

Chapter Fourteen

My meeting with the surgeon at the Radcliffe Hospital had not been a success and I was glad that it was over. I hired a horse at the Oxford coaching inn and set off along the Woodstock Road to Sarah's aunt's house in Kidlington. I was attracted by Sarah's strength of spirit and her determination in making use of her cousin's books to educate herself. During the previous few days I had sometimes pictured her as someone to whom I could imagine myself happily attached. However, I was unable to entertain such feelings for long and they soon slipped from my grasp.

The house was in shade when it came into view, set amongst beech trees at the bottom of a steep valley. As I gazed at it, I felt a chill as I pictured Sarah's aunt engaging in demented conversation with the apparition of her dead husband.

A housekeeper opened the door to me and I saw Sarah standing behind her in the hall. Her face broke into a smile and she stepped quickly up to the door.

'I'm so pleased to see you, Mr. Mountford. Do come in. Have you come from the Radcliffe?'

'I have.'

'How long are you able to stay?'

'For an hour or two. I must catch the London coach at five o'clock.' I paused. 'I regret to say I've no news of John.'

Sarah looked away and I could see the depth of her disappointment.

'I'm sure his mother will die before he comes to see her.'

'How is she?'

'She had another attack of croup yesterday but she's a little better today.'

I followed Sarah into the drawing room, a little overawed by its elegant furnishings. The walls were hung with landscape paintings and a clavichord inlaid with pearl stood under one of the windows. On one wall, there was a framed pen and ink portrait of Fanshawe.

I looked at it closely.

'I like that very much. It captures John perfectly.'

Sarah waited for a long moment before responding.

'I drew it,' she said quietly.

'You have a talent, Miss Fanshawe.'

'Thank you.'

There was a silence, Sarah clearly feeling reticent about her work. In that moment I felt a lump in my throat as I thought of my sister, Alice. One day, perhaps I would tell Sarah what had happened. I looked up at a large portrait of a portly periwigged gentleman in his finery hung over the chimneypiece.

'That's John's grandfather. He was a director of the East India Company. He made his fortune while others lost theirs at the time of the South Sea Bubble.'

She motioned me to a sofa.

'Did the meeting at the Radcliffe Hospital go well?'

'Not altogether, I'm afraid. I was there to tell him about my use of mesmerism in surgery.

'Mesmerism. Tell me about it, Mr. Mountford. It sounds fascinating.'

I did so and she looked at me in amazement.

'What an extraordinary thing,' she remarked.

143

'It is, but I don't think the surgeon at the Radcliffe will take it up even though he's prepared to consider the phenomenon may be genuine. Although he didn't say so, I'm sure he fears it would get him into difficulties with his colleagues. Most surgeons who've heard of it are against it or don't believe in it.'

'But *you* could get into difficulties with *your* colleagues.

'I know, but it's too late now.'

Sarah nodded thoughtfully.

'I sometimes used to think that I would have trained to be a physician if I'd been a man. Instead, my only accomplishments are drawing, dancing and music and a little knowledge of French, all taught me by a very dull governess.'

I was taken aback by the strength of her feeling.

'But you've taught yourself the tenets of materialism and much more, I imagine, from reading John's books.'

'I know, but I have to say I think it unfortunate that women are not allowed the same education as men.'

She picked up a book from a shelf and handed it to me. *A Vindication of the Rights of Women,* by Mary Wollstonecraft.

'She makes a very strong case against the denial of education for women,' she said, going a little pink. 'She believes that young women should have the opportunity to learn about the world instead of devoting their endeavours to making themselves decorative and pleasing to marriageable men, especially as it usually necessitates a show of endearing ignorance of worldly matters.'

I felt awkward as I saw the effort she was making to moderate the passion in her voice and, for a moment, I was lost for words. Sarah put her hand to her mouth.

'Oh dear. I can see that I've shocked you.'

'Not at all, Miss Fanshawe.'

I didn't know what to say next. Sarah's unassuming manner had left me unprepared for her forthright expression of her views. The housekeeper came in with a taper to light the candles and Sarah took it from her.

'I'll do this, Jenny,' she said.

'Very good, miss.'

'Don't most men think it unseemly for a woman to be free to express her opinion on serious matters?' Sarah asked as she walked round, lighting the candles.

'*I* don't think that,' I insisted but fell silent, not knowing how to expand on my response. Sarah looked disappointed as she waited for me to say something more.

'To be honest with you,' I admitted at length. 'I haven't given sufficient consideration to the opinion of most men on the matter. Now that you make me think about it, I agree with you. Such men are wrong to hold those views.'

'I'm gratified to hear you say that.'

Sarah returned to her seat and smiled at me with an expression that teased me as to whether I really meant it.

'Now I want to talk about something else. I want to talk about John.'

She paused for a moment, choosing her words carefully.

'I know you may think he's just a charmer and something of a black sheep as most people who come across him probably do. I want you to know that there's more to him than that. I believe he's deeply troubled. He would have

145

been an only child until I came along and his father's disappearance and the manner of his leaving must have been very disturbing. My aunt said his father was a good Christian until the year before he left when he began spending more and more time in his laboratory. He told her he was studying books about natural philosophy but she thought that whatever it was that he was reading was darkening his soul and sucking his faith out of him. John told me he used to lie awake at night during that time, hearing the sound of his father's enraged voice and his mother's tears coming from downstairs. It terrified him'. She paused. 'The reason I'm saying all this is that I believe John's devil-may-care attitude is something of a mask and those early years of his life before his father left are hidden behind it. And now I'm deeply concerned about his whereabouts. I know that he could have gone off to France or Italy or Greece to spend time with one of his friends but I can't help feeling that something untoward has happened to him.'

I recalled Fanshawe's reaction to the sinister man at Shadborough House but I didn't want to admit to having been at Ashton's Hellfire party.

'I share your worries, Miss Fanshawe and I'll keep asking after him in London.

'I know you're a good friend to him, Mr. Mountford.'

The housekeeper came in with a tray of tea.

'Do you have any idea what might have happened to his father? I asked.

'Not really. The only clue we have is a book that my aunt found lying in a bottom drawer in his laboratory after he left. He must have forgotten to take it. Do you want to see it?'

'If it's not too much trouble.'

Sarah left the room and returned with a large tome bound in leather.

'John showed it to a tutor a Balliol who has an interest in the study of ancient Egypt. Apparently, it's a very rare book written by a 16th century German scholar. It was published in Munich in 1610. Have a look.'

She handed it to me and sat next to me as I turned the pages full of finely detailed engravings depicting Egyptian ceremonial figures. They reminded me of the Egyptian wall paintings in Ashton's house that I had found so mysterious. I would have mentioned it to Sarah but again, I didn't want to admit to being there. I turned to the plates containing hieroglyphic symbols.

'They are tantalizing,' I remarked.

'Aren't they? They make you want to find out what they mean.'

Sarah pointed to a page of simpler symbols.

'John's tutor believes that is an abridged form of the language called hieratics used by the priests in their records. Apparently, a scholar in London has deciphered such a text on a tablet called the Rosetta stone that Napoleon's people found in Egypt.'

'Thomas Young?' I asked, recalling what Ashton had told me.

'I think that was his name.'

I put the book down and Sarah caught sight of me looking at a large wooden doll on a chest under one of the windows.

'It was a birthday present that my aunt's father gave her when she was a child. Go and have a look. It's very beautiful.'

147

It was a boy with tousled fair hair, dressed in a red velvet coat, sitting at a writing table and holding a pen over a piece of paper. It had delicately painted flesh tones and unnervingly realistic eyes.

'It's exquisite,' I remarked, looking at it closely.

'It's much more than a doll, you know,' Sarah said, taking a bottle of ink from an escritoire and pouring a little of it into the inkwell next to the doll's pen.

'There's a key in the side of the figure. Wind it up and see what happens.'

I wound the key but nothing happened.

'Oh, dear. Perhaps the mechanism's become rusty. I can't remember when it was last wound up. John used to keep it in his bedchamber. It's an automaton that can write. It was made by a famous French clockmaker called Jacquet-Droz.'

'You mean it can actually write words?'

'Yes. Well, it could once. You could adjust the mechanism to make it write any sentence of up to forty characters.'

'What an extraordinary toy.' I also thought it somewhat macabre.

There was a distant sound of coughing.

'My aunt's awake. If you'll excuse me, I'll just go up to see if she needs anything.'

When she had left the room, I touched the doll's arm. There was a sudden whirring noise and a clicking metallic sound coming from inside its chest as it came to life. I stared at its writing hand as it began to move. It turned its head, dipped the pen into the ink well, and started to write, its eyes following the text. I was transfixed. When Sarah came back into the room, the two of us watched as it completed the

148

sequence of letters. On the page was written *'please don't let the snake kill me papa'.*

Sarah looked at me.

'What a sinister thing. Could John have made it write that before his father left?'

There was the sound of more coughing and Sarah began to excuse herself again.

'Would you object to my meeting your aunt?' I asked as she began to make her way to the door. 'I would like to put her into the picture of John's life.'

'Not at all, but I'm afraid she won't be able to understand who you are.'

'I'm prepared for that. What's her name?'

'Catherine. And John's father's name was Josiah. Before we go up, you remember John telling you that she has imaginary conversations with her husband. Well, now they've grown more disturbing.'

She led me upstairs and tapped lightly on an open door.

'Hello mother. I've a visitor for you.'

She took my arm and led me into the room. It was dark and had the odour of sickness. The woman was sitting up against a pile of cushions in a heavily curtained four-poster bed, her breathing, hoarse and rasping. Her emaciated face was the colour of parchment and dark eyes stared bleakly out of shadowy sockets that emphasized her high cheek bones. I looked for her tracheostomy and saw the incision in the base of her neck. A fire was lit and above the chimneypiece hung a painting of the Virgin Mary at prayer. A bath chair stood in a corner.

Sarah began an introduction, but before two words were out, her aunt reached out and grasped my coat sleeve.

'Josiah, what have you done?' she demanded, her breath wheezing through the hole in her neck.

'Mother...,' Sarah began but she took no notice.

'Josiah...you will burn in hell if you don't seek forgiveness and absolution.'

I was considerably unnerved as she tugged away at my sleeve. Was she simply demented or did she know something about her husband that terrified her? She began coughing again and Sarah broke open a small glass pearl of amyl nitrite in a handkerchief and held it under her aunt's nose. After a while, she breathed a little more easily and she pushed it away. She looked at me again.

'We used to be happy, Josiah. Do you remember?'

I looked at her in silence, as she stared at me, breathing heavily with the rattle of phlegm in her chest. Soon, she closed her eyes and the rattle became a snore as she fell asleep. Sarah and I looked at one another and I wondered what kind of person Josiah Fanshawe had become.

Chapter Fifteen

By the following week, I could no longer put off going to Aberdeen to see my brother. I managed to find a seat on a stagecoach that took me to Edinburgh in two days and another that took me from there to Aberdeen within a day. The frostiness I expected from my parents had been softened a little by the financial help I was providing. I spent much of the time by Angus's sickbed, asking about his work which consisted of simple tasks in the cowsheds of a local farmer. I reminded him of the games we used to play and the stories I used to tell him. It was a difficult time for me as the fevered state my brother frequently suffered was added to by his limited intellect and our conversations often had little meaningful content. Nevertheless, it was a time in which I realised how much I loved my young brother. I thought about the local physician who seemed to me to have a limited grasp of medical matters and I was weighed down by the thought that the efficacy of his remedies might well do him no good. The chances were that he wouldn't survive his illness.

***

When I was back in London, my spirits were raised by my exposition of Devereux's work to the members of the Wigmore Society. It had gone down well with all the members except Fitzgibbon, as was to be expected. I was pleased with my performance and was continuing to play with the possibility of giving up surgery and acquiring the skills to do Devereux's kind of work. However, the occasion was marred for me by Villiers who seemed to be in a troubled state of mind. He had looked distracted throughout the meeting and had said very little.

The following Sunday, my landlord came to see me. I was late in the payment of my rent and he threatened me with eviction if I didn't pay up within the month. I was preparing to go out to look for cheaper lodgings when I heard someone knocking on the street door. Maggie was at church so I answered the knock myself. A cabbie stood there awkwardly and recited a clearly prepared speech.

'Mrs. Villiers asks you to forgive her, sir, for presenting herself without prior arrangement and asks if you would be prepared to receive her.'

'Yes, of course,' I replied after a moment. I was flabbergasted. I had guessed that we might come across one another since I had seen her in Villiers's carriage but the thought of her visiting me had never crossed my mind.

The driver returned to his cab and she emerged from it wearing a grey walking dress trimmed with ruby velvet and a matching bonnet. Her delicate features were undisguised by Lavender's make-up and the sight of her rekindled the arousal I had felt at Shadborough House.

'Good morning, Mr. Mountford. I'm Dr. Villiers's wife, Caroline. It is most forbearing of you to receive me at such short notice. May I take it that you recognise me after seeing me in George's carriage?'

'I do, Mrs. Villiers.' I bowed as she held out a white-gloved hand and I kissed it, pink-faced, stirred by the low velvet tones of her voice and her bold disregard of the usual proprieties.

'Please come in. I'm afraid you have to negotiate these rickety stairs as my lodgings are on the second floor.'

Caroline gave me a smile as she picked up the front of her dress and followed me up to my rooms with great daintiness. When she had settled herself in my dusty arm chair, she put her hands in her lap and looked at me with a confident directness.

'One of my reasons for coming here is that Johnny Fanshawe seems to have disappeared and I understand he's a friend of yours. D'you have any idea where he is?'

'I'm afraid not. I've been looking for him too. His housekeeper says he's gone abroad.'

'I know.'

I was bowled over by Caroline's self-assurance. She seemed completely unperturbed about conducting a formal conversation with a man she had so recently ravished in the guise of a tart. She was much more radiant without her dollymop makeup and when she smiled at me, it put butterflies in my stomach.

'Do you have any idea of what might have happened to him?' she asked.

'I don't, but the last time I saw him, he looked very strained. There's something wrong with him, I'm sure of that.'

'Will you send me a note if you hear from him?'

'You have my word.'

'Thank you, Mr. Mountford. Now tell me,' she asked coyly after a pause. 'Do you remember your encounter with Lavender at Shadburgh House?'

My face was burning.

'Forgive me, Mrs. Villiers. I regret to say that I'm most embarrassed by what happened between us.'

'Not between us, Mr. Mountford. Between you and Lavender. And I can tell you, she very much enjoyed your company.'

'My dear lady…' I was floundering and Caroline began to laugh.

'You're such an innocent and very sweet. May I call you Robert?'

'Please do.'

'And please call me Caroline.'

'I shall. May I ask if your husband knows about Lavender?'

'Did Johnny not tell you? My husband chooses not to know. And he doesn't know I'm here, by the way.' She gave me a brief coquettish look.

'Now let's move on to the other reason I'm here. George sometimes tells me about the discussions at the Wigmore Society. I want to ask you about the last meeting. George mentioned the talk you gave describing your use mesmerism to open up someone's mind to discover the secret person hidden in there.'

'That's not me, I'm afraid. I'm a surgeon. Your husband was referring to a French mesmerist to whom he kindly introduced me. I was simply reporting on his work.'

'But no doubt you could do what the Frenchman does?'

'I've never tried.'

'That's a pity. The idea of being mesmerised and having my secrets discovered by a clever man like you rather appeals to me. You might find out who Lavender is.'

I knew she was playing with me.

'Would you be prepared to experiment on me sometime using the Frenchman's methods? I'd find it all most interesting.'

'I promise to give it some thought, Mrs. Villiers,' I replied, not knowing how to refuse her request politely or perhaps to accept it. Caroline put on an expression of mock formality.

'I'm glad that you will. I'll write to you to request a consultation. You can give me your answer then and let me know the fee you'll charge. I can see your eyes lighting up, Robert. I do hope you'll grant me an appointment.'

When she left, I tried to return my thoughts to the business of finding cheaper lodgings but I was unable to prevent myself from picturing my use of Devereux's technique to delve into the secret world of Caroline's unconscious mind. I had been aroused by her visit and I thought about what I might find there, assuming that she was susceptible to mesmerism. By then I knew I would agree to see her but I told myself that I wouldn't make any advances to her, now that I knew who she was. At the same time, I put out of mind the question of my resistance to any that came from her.

Chapter Sixteen

That evening, Fanshawe came back into my life when a boy arrived at Calthorpe Street with a note from him asking if he could pay me a visit at a time of my choosing in the next day or two. After Fanshawe's strange behaviour when we had last met, I was curious to know what was happening to him and, despite my ambivalence about continuing the friendship, I felt some concern for his welfare. I gave the boy a note to take back to him suggesting the following Sunday morning at 11 o'clock.

***

When Sunday came around, I looked down from my window to see Fanshawe arriving in his phaeton. A large woman of middle years in drab grey clothes and bonnet was sitting next to him. She stayed in the carriage when Fanshawe came to the door and Maggie brought him up to my rooms.

'Good to see you, Mountford,' Fanshawe said with attempted joviality but he looked as strained as he had done before and I noticed the smell of brandy on his breath as he sank into an armchair.

'I've been worried about you, old chap,' I began, 'You don't look well.'

'I have been poorly but I'm on the mend. I had a bout of influenza while I was in Paris.'

'I'm sorry to hear that. Your housekeeper told me you'd gone abroad when I called by the other day.'

'Forgive me. I should've let you know. I've been staying with a friend from Balliol who's gone to live there.'

I felt duty-bound to bring up the subject of his mother.

'Listen, old chap. I must ask if you've seen your cousin since you've been back.'

'Not yet. Why?'

'She came to see me to find out where you were. She told me about your mother's ill health.'

'I know. She left a note for me telling me about it but I only got back from France a couple of days ago.'

'She was very worried and she'll be mightily relieved to see you.'

Fanshawe nodded absently, looking distracted.

'I was in Oxford last week,' I continued. 'I went to see a surgeon at the Radcliffe Hospital and I paid her a visit afterwards.

Fanshawe looked bewildered.

'So you've been to my childhood home.'

'Yes.'

'Did you see my mother?'

'I did.'

'Listen, Mountford, I'll go to Oxford as soon as I can, not that my mother will want to see me. I don't suppose she'll even recognise me.' He paused. 'Now tell me about my sister. Are you by any chance courting her?'

'My dear fellow, she'll make some lucky man a wonderful wife but I'm afraid I don't think I'm cut out for married life.'

'A pity. Tell me, how is your brother?'

'No better, I'm afraid.'

'I'm sorry to hear that.'

Fanshawe looked out of the window, seeming to find it difficult to gather his thoughts.

'Forgive me for being forward, old chap, but I cannot but think that you must be pretty hard-pressed at the moment. Your brother's illness must be putting your finances under considerable strain.'

'It's true, I regret to say.'

'What are you going to do?'

'I'm going to move to cheaper lodgings.'

'But even so, how long will you be able to look after him financially?'

'I don't know. That's the truth.'

Fanshawe was about to speak when he started coughing and his hand trembled as he put a handkerchief to his face.

'Sorry about that. The thing is...' he coughed and started again.

'The thing is...I'd like to help you out, old friend.'

He held up a hand to stave off any attempt to refuse the offer he was about to make. Again, I noticed the missing little finger.

'Now, bear with me, Mountford, before you say anything. First of all, there's a great service that you could do for me. It's a request on behalf the woman in my carriage. Her name is Mrs. Burrows. Her husband's in Newgate for the crime of murder, a crime he didn't commit. He's to hang in two weeks' time. I regret to say that the woman's daughter, Jenny was with child because of me. To add to my shame she nearly died in childbirth and she's still quite ill. The child was stillborn.'

He screwed up his eyes, looking pained.

'Please don't say it', he went on. 'I can read your face. The fact is I now feel honour-bound to do something to help her and her mother. I've paid for the services of a physician but there's also something else. Her mother is convinced of her husband's innocence.'

Fanshawe cleared his throat nervously.

'Now to the nub of the matter. During her visits to Newgate to see her husband, Mrs. Burrows has come to know Mr. Fawcett, the chief turnkey.'

'I know him too. I've sometimes operated there. A rather dubious character.'

'Indeed so. Now, at my suggestion, Mrs. Burrows has asked Fawcett if he'd be prepared to spring her husband from the gaol if he were paid an appropriate sum, a sum that I'd provide. I've offered the right money and he's agreed. The idea is to take Burrows from the gaol to a house in Rotherhithe where his wife is now installed as housekeeper. The master and mistress are abroad. Mrs. Burrows will then spirit him up to her aunt's home in Yorkshire where he'll be able to live in anonymity.'

I was becoming increasingly apprehensive as I wondered what all this had to do with me.

'The problem is, you see, that Fawcett couldn't spring him alone. The man is strong and, although innocent of this crime, he's capable of being rough if he senses danger. He's not a man of great intelligence and Fawcett fears that whatever he's told about being freed, he'll most likely think he's being taken to the gallows. If that happens, he'll cut up rough. I'd be there to help but I'm not strong and I'm ashamed to say I'm not very brave in such situations.'

159

Oh God, what's he going to ask of me, I wondered as Fanshawe tried to look encouragingly at me.

'If you could mesmerise him, as you did Dr Pierot's servant girls, you could make him leave the prison quietly and take him to the house in Rotherhithe.'

'I'm really not sure, old chap...'

'Fawcett would organise it all.'

I looked out of the window at Mrs. Burrows sitting in the carriage in her grey bonnet. I didn't like the idea of this at all.

'Surely there'll be some danger involved.'

'Fawcett says they're a bribable lot in charge of the prison at the moment from the governor down and I don't have a problem with the necessary resources. Listen, Mountford, I realise what a great service you'd be rendering me and I'd like to do you a favour in return. I'd like to cover the cost of your rent and the finance required for the best medical attention your brother can have for as long as it takes.'

I stood looking out of the window in silence for a long time, feeling very uncomfortable.

'You're being most kind to me, Fanshawe, I don't want to be lily-livered about it but I'm not used to having these kinds of dealings with people like Fawcett. It's all so underhand. And against the law. I suppose the nearest I get to this kind of thing is paying the resurrectionists for the corpses they bring to the medical school.'

Despite my qualms, I found myself thinking that the ministrations of a better physician than I had been able to afford might save my brother's life. I paced the room in silence, talking myself through all the reasons why I shouldn't agree to the undertaking and the one reason why I should. I stoked the embers of the fire, wondering what kind of woman Mrs. Burrows was. I thought about her daughter, her brutish husband and the egregious Fawcett. Once again, my thoughts returned to my brother. Eventually, I sat down, staring at the fire before turning to my sickly companion.

You're sure of Fawcett are you?'

'I'm sure,' Fanshawe replied.

'Very well. I'll do it.'

'Thank you, dear friend. I can't tell you how much it'll mean to both mother and daughter to have him back.'

Chapter Seventeen

A thick fog, yellow with chimney smoke had descended on the city on the evening that I hailed a hackney cab outside my lodgings to go to Newgate Prison. It muffled the sound of the city's traffic making me feel as if I were hard of hearing and my nose and throat were filled with its musty smell and acrid taste. I was carrying a large Bukhara carpet bag containing a lantern, an old discarded greatcoat and hat and my dueling pistols.

Throughout the previous night and the day that followed, I had become increasingly anxious about the clandestine nature of the evening's undertaking and my stomach churned as the cab crossed over Newgate Circus and made its way up the Old Bailey past the Sessions Court and the looming windowless east wall of the prison before stopping at the entrance to the prison governor's house. The late hour of my arrival had been chosen by Fawcett as the governor would be at dinner with the mayor. The cabbie coughed up phlegm from deep in his chest and spat it into the road.

'This is the place you want, sir?'

'Yes.'

I paid him, picked up my bag and knocked on the door of the governor's house. A servant answered, and when I gave my name, he led me to a small office in which two clerks were bent over their desks, reading piles of documents and making notes on them.

'I'll go and fetch Mr. Fawcett for you, sir.'

The servant returned accompanied by a small, wiry man in his middle years, dressed in a shabby black coat. I remembered him from the time when I had performed two operations at the prison. The man waited for the servant to leave the room before putting out his hand to me.

'Good evening, Dr Mountford.'

Fawcett had always called me doctor even though I was a surgeon.

I tapped my hat.

'Good evening to you, Mr. Fawcett.'

'Come with me, sir.'

Fawcett unlocked a heavy oak door at the back of the room and led me into a cold, stone-walled passage which had a rotting smell of dampness mixed with that of the sewer. The walls were high with small windows at the top of them making me feel as if I were at the bottom of a chasm.

No more words were spoken by either of us, both knowing the nature of the task in hand. I heard the distant sounds of a shouting match between two women and a baby crying, its bellowing infant voice denoting neediness turned to rage. We passed steel-gated entrances to other passages, guarded by turnkeys. Fawcett instructed one of them to open the gate he was guarding and we climbed up a flight of stone stairs to one of the men's wards. Before opening the door, Fawcett came up to me and spoke quietly to me in the manner of one who has been entrusted with an important and confidential undertaking.

'I understand that you're asking me to release Burrows because you have reason to believe that he's innocent of the crime he's been convicted of. That's right, isn't it?'

'His wife is convinced of it.'

I didn't want to be involved in the matter. Fawcett stood in silence looking at the floor until I realised why and I took a purse, heavy with coins, from my pocket and handed it to him. Fawcett nodded his thanks.

'As instructed, I've told Burrows nothing other than that he'll be receiving a visitor. He's a strong man, simple-minded and with something of a temper and I don't want him to get him agitated. He might think he's going to be taken to the gallows, whatever I say to him about being freed. It might get him flared up and I don't want to have to deal with that. He's a lucky man. He was sentenced yesterday and the hanging's due next week. The reason he's in here and not in a condemned cell is they're all full. It'll take a few days to clear them all. Seven at a time, starting next Sunday. Quite a show. I can offer you the best viewing if you'd care to come. Complimentary of course.'

'No, thank you.' I winced at the thought of it. I was shocked at the insatiable public appetite for hangings and reading lurid accounts of murders, suicides and executions in the papers. I'd once tried to walk down the Old Bailey on a hanging day on my way to visit a friend. The crush was so great that I had to go by another route.

Fawcett looked at me questioningly.

'I understand you've a means of calming the prisoner.'

I nodded.

'That's important. He may seem calm but you have to watch out for his temper. I'll be having a word with the prisoner in charge of the ward when we go in. He's an accommodating fellow, a clerk. He's only here 'cause he cooked the books for a probate lawyer. I'm going to say the prisoner's got something wrong with his stomach. It's been giving him some pain. I'll be saying you're taking him to the prison hospital.'

164

I nodded and Fawcett stood back.

'All right. In we go.'

When we entered the ward, Fawcett approached a nervous looking man who looked like a clerk standing next to a large fireplace in which dying embers glowed. I guessed that he must be the warder and I looked around me, wondering where Burrows might be. It was a large room lit only by the embers and a guttering tallow candle on a table in front of it. Three men sat around the table on wooden forms, staring into the fire; a servant whose livery was ingrained with dirt from prison life, an old man in a threadbare great-coat and a shaggy-haired man who looked like a farm worker.

A dozen or so recumbent forms lay on the floor under their blankets. Most were as still as death but underneath one of the blankets a tousling was going on and the blanket fell away for a moment revealing the figure of a girl with her skirt hitched high and a scrawny arm around her waist. She looked no older that twelve. How much would she get for her services, I wondered. Sixpence? Another man was standing against a wall, rocking his body from side to side, dribbling and uttering indecipherable words in a low moaning voice. I thought he should be in Bethlehem not Newgate.

Fawcett came up to me with the candle from the table.

'This way, sir.'

He led me to the other end of the room where the candle illuminated a hunched figure in shirtsleeves and torn trousers sitting on the floor with his back against the wall. He was a burly man, his shaved head showing a week's growth of stubble. He was staring across the room, a look of

165

resignation in his eyes. My apprehension grew as I looked at his ankles shackled to iron rings fixed to the floor.

'Why does he have to be shackled,' I asked.

'As I said, he's got a temper.'

The man looked up suspiciously and flinched when I put a hand on his shoulder.

'Your wife has asked me to come here. She says you're innocent of the crime of murdering your son and she's asked me get you out of here and to take you to her.'

'What? I don't believe you.'

'Did you murder your son?'

'I was set up. Nobody could prove it. The jury just didn't like my face.'

I didn't want to push him on the matter. Burrows looked at me, his eyes narrowed.

'Is this some kind of trick?'

He stood up and grabbed me by the lapels.

Fawcett tried to pull him away but he didn't have the strength.

'If you're playing games with me I'll break your neck.'

I smelled the man's foul breath and tried not to show my nerves. Using the look I had learned when mesmerizing Dr. Pierot's girls, I held Burrows' gaze steadily until the man let go of me.

'Do you want me to take you out of here?' I asked quietly in the tone of voice I had learned from Dr. Pierot. 'If you do, you'll have to do exactly as I say. Do you agree to come quietly with me?'

I continued to stare at him until the man's eyes dulled. He was already approaching the beginning of a trance state.

'I agree.'

'Now kneel on the floor.'

When he had done so, I knelt opposite him so that our knees were touching and tried to ignore the smell of his body.

'Now press the palm of your hand against mine.'

I presented my palm to Burrows who placed his palm against it.

'Press hard.'

Burrows put his weight into it.

'And harder.'

I was now using all my strength to match Burrows's.

'Now look into my eyes. Think of sleep, and keep pressing.'

I could see the tension in Burrows's face and I suddenly pulled my hand away, letting Burrows fall forward onto my lap.

'Go to sleep, go to sleep this very instant!' I shouted.

The men round the table turned to look as I took Burrows's head and pressed it into my lap, saying more quietly, 'Sleep, sleep,' again and again, trying not to think of the smell of the man. After a while, I lifted Burrows' shoulders until his back was upright, his eyes closed.

'Can you hear me?'

'Yes.'

'Now open your eyes.'

Burrows opened them.

'Good. Now stand up.'

Burrows stood up and I saw that he would just about be able to get into my greatcoat and wear my hat although he would most probably appear a somewhat risible figure.

'Would you please unlock his shackles, Mr. Fawcett?'

Fawcett was agog with wonder. When he had removed them, I took the greatcoat out of my carpet bag and helped Burrows into it. Burrows went along with this compliantly, saying nothing.

'Now listen, Burrows. If at any time, I see you looking agitated or you seem to be coming out of your waking sleep, I will say these words to you. "Rest in peace". You will return to the state in which you are now. Do you understand?'

'Yes.'

'What are the words I will say to return you to the sleeping state?'

'Rest in peace.'

'Good. Now we're going on a journey to see your wife.'

Fawcett took us through another labyrinth of passageways and locked gates and eventually to a small door opening on to a yard off Newgate Street.

'Burrows, stay by my side and match my pace,' I commanded as I put the top hat on Burrows's head. We started off down Newgate Street with Burrows beside me and I looked around for a cab. Burrows kept looking down at my feet, trying to match my strides and when I raised his arm to hail a cab, Burrows did the same. A cab drew up and I looked up at the driver, my hand on Burrows's shoulder

'I need to take this gentleman to Rotherhithe. I'll be with him there for a few minutes. I'd like you to wait for me and then take me to Calthorpe Street.

'That's out of my way, sir, and I'm about to go home.'

'I realise it's a long journey, cabbie, but I can pay you well for it. Two sovereigns to go to Rotherhithe, and a further sovereign to take me on to Calthorpe Street.'

The cabbie frowned as he looked at Burrows whose well-made but undersized coat and top hat were in comic contrast to his grizzled face and dumb expression.

'Two sovereigns now, and another two after I've taken you to Calthorpe Street. That's my price.'

'Very well. Come on Burrows, in you get.'

The two of us made a tight fit as we squashed together side by side. The cab set off down Cheapside and crossed the river at London Bridge. Once again, I wondered what kind of mischief I had become involved in as I looked at the pale shapes of the fishing boats tied up alongside the Billingsgate waterfront and breathed in the stench of fish. The cab turned left south of the river along Tooley Street and Jamaica Road, the smell of fish now replaced by that of the Bermondsey tanneries, the surroundings growing ever darker as the gaslights became fewer and farther between.

'Where exactly is it that you want to get to?' the cabbie asked.

'It's somewhere along Rotherhithe Street near the junction with Swan Road. I'm afraid I don't know the area.'

'Neither do you want to, sir. It's full of thieves and press gangs and smugglers and all manner of vice. I'll take you to the Angel at Bermondsey Wall which I think is pretty much nearby and I'll wait for you there. No longer than an hour, mind. You take your life in your hands beyond there if you don't mind my saying so. Still, your friend looks as if he can look after himself and you as well I don't wonder.'

By the time the cab arrived at the Angel, the fog had lifted a little. The cabbie pointed to a narrow court, the only light in it coming from the windows of the inn. I paid him and entered the inn's tap room to light my lantern while Burrows

169

stood outside the door awaiting his instructions. I rejoined him and took a sheet of paper from my pocket, held up the lantern and studied the directions to the house that Fanshawe had written on it. It was called Albion House.

As we set off, I hoped fervently that Burrows wouldn't come out of his trance and that he wouldn't need to bring him back into it by intoning a phrase that might or might not work. I kept to the waterfront as much as possible where the road was wide enough to see people at a distance as far as the thinning fog would allow. I turned right at Swan Road with Burrows following and into another side turning. Now we were in a maze of narrow alleys always to be feared at night and I held one of my pistols at the ready. It occurred to me that if we were attacked I could instruct Burrows in his trance state to take on the attackers rather in the manner of instructing a guard dog.

Soon we were in open ground, a mist hanging in the air. I held up the lantern to look again at Fanshawe's directions. The ground ahead of us was strewn with the flattened remains of tenements, no doubt making way for warehouses like the many others that had sprung up along both sides of the river. In the distance, I made out the nebulous contours of a large house standing in gloomily splendid isolation. As we made our way towards it across the debris, I soon saw that it was a three-storey house with bow windows. The gray ethereal shapes of trees stood behind it in grounds bordered by heavy iron railings. A faint light came from a downstairs window. I imagined the house having been built in open countryside some hundred years earlier for a man of substance and his genteel family. Now its brickwork would be blackened by factory smoke. When we reached it, I saw the name Albion House carved into the lintel above the portico. I knocked the lion's head door knocker and waited. The door opened and I recognised Mrs. Burrows, recalling her morose features as she sat in Fanshawe's phaeton. She took a step towards me.

'Is he still mesmerised?' she whispered, glancing for a moment at Burrows's dumb features.'

'Yes he is.'

Burrows looked confused so I reminded him that this was his wife as his trance state might have made it difficult for him to recognise her. I stood aside to allow her to go to him and she put her hands on his shoulders.

'It's good to have you back, Henry,' she said in a flat tone and led us into a book-lined study where she settled Burrows into an armchair. He was still looking confused as if he didn't know where he was.

'Would you please come with me for a moment, Mr. Mountford?' she asked.

I followed her out of the room and we stood together in the corridor.

'Tell me, is it only you who can take him out of his trance?'

'No, I think you could do it if you speak with the right force.'

I explained that she was to tell Burrows, speaking in a low voice that he was to come out of his trance after a count to ten. She was to do so slowly saying 'ten' loudly and clapping her hands.

'Thank you,' she said. 'I'll leave him as he is for the moment. I'm expecting his brother to come and see him within the hour and I want him to be here when Henry comes out of his trance. Would he remain mesmerised for that long?'

'I think so.' I answered, not being sure if he would or not.

'Then I'll bid you goodnight.'

I felt uncomfortable about leaving the man in his trance state but I wanted to get away from the house and leave the grim Mrs. Burrows to her own devices. As I descended the steps, I felt a great relief at being on my own again despite the dangers of Rotherhithe after dark. I turned to look back at the house. A small figure in a white shift with long dark hair approached an upstairs window lit by a candle standing on the windowsill. The figure was wearing a white mask.

I vowed never to undertake such an assignment again as I walked through the alleyways back to the inn. The journey was considerably more dangerous without the company of a man of such strength as Burrows to do my bidding and I held my lantern high, both to see my way and to illuminate the pistol I was holding in my other hand. One likely assailant ducked out of the shadows and disappeared back into the gloom when he saw the gun. After that, I readied myself to fire at what turned out to be empty shadows. When I reached the Angel at Bermondsey Wall, I found the cabbie drunk in the tap room. I eventually persuaded him to take me home.

I retired for the night, trying to convince myself of my good fortune and that of my brother. Fanshawe had placed a substantial sum of money in a bank in Lombard Street and had opened an account for me. I had written to my mother telling her that I was going to send her a larger monthly sum and she was to obtain the services of a senior physician at the Aberdeen Royal Infirmary to attend Angus.

At five o'clock the next morning, I got up having slept fitfully, dreaming of Burrows and his wife and the figure in the white mask at the upstairs window of Albion House. I opened the curtains in my bedchamber and stared at the smoky roofs of Calthorpe Street's huddled dwellings made pink by the dawning sun. Then I wrote a note to tell Fanshawe that I had carried out my assignment without any misadventure and Burrows had been safely installed in Albion House. When the maid came to collect my chamber pot, I handed her the note.

'I'd be obliged if you'd ask your son to take this to Mr. Fanshawe in Lincoln's Inn.

'Very good, sir.'

When I returned home that evening I met Maggie on the landing.

'Charlie delivered your note to Mr. Fanshawe, sir, but there's no answer. His housemaid said he was unwell and was not receiving visitors.'

'Thank you Maggie.'

So the illness was still with him.

***

The next day I went to Lincoln's Inn as soon as I had finished at the hospital. Fanshawe's housekeeper, Mrs. Jenks, opened the door and curtsied politely but she didn't invite me in. Instead she repeated the message she had given to young Charlie. Her master was ill and was not receiving visitors.

'Mrs. Jenks, I am a friend of Mr. Fanshawe and a medical man, not just a visitor. I must find out how he is. Please tell him that Mr. Mountford is waiting at his door.'

The housekeeper nodded and went off, returning to lead me up to Fanshawe's room. She knocked quietly and held her head close to the door. She dipped her head to acknowledge a response and let me into the room. It was large and sparsely furnished, its walls dark maroon with dark blue curtains half drawn across the windows that looked over Lincoln's Inn Fields. Opposite stood a four-poster bed whose tapestry curtains were closed. I smelled hashish.

'Fanshawe, old chap, are you in there?'

There was a grunt from within and I drew one of the curtains back a little. A fug of marijuana smoke floated out through the gap.

'Mountford, old fellow.' Fanshawe spoke in a faint voice, his breathing wheezy and his face, pale and sweaty. He winced at the sunlight coming through a gap in the curtains.

'I'm sorry, I seem to have an aversion to bright light at the moment.'

I closed the gap and sat on the edge of the bed.

'Did you receive my note about Burrows? I delivered him to Albion House and his wife took him in.'

'I did receive it, Mountford. And thank you. You are a good man.'

'Let me thank you again for the funds you've provided for me.'

'Think nothing of it.'

In the gloom, I made out Fanshawe's hand holding a clay pipe with a twist of smoke coming from it.

'Would you like a puff?' Fanshawe asked, holding it out to me.

'No thanks, Fanshawe, not now.'

'Dashed inconveniencing, this illness.'

'And this is the result of influenza?'

'So my physician tells me.'

'And the marijuana helps?'

Fanshawe's body suddenly convulsed and he turned on to his side, curling up into a ball.

'What is it, Fanshawe?'

Fanshawe began to mouth words, his face contorted, but he couldn't speak. Eventually, his body uncurled and he lay on his back.

'I get these spasms of pain in my stomach. The hashish seems to ease them. You are a good friend, Mountford, but there is nothing you can do'.

He began to sit up.

'Another pipe perhaps and I'll sleep. Thank you for coming but please go now. I'll be well again soon.'

'Are you sure you want me to go?'

'Yes, I'm sure, and thank you again.'

'I'll call on you again tomorrow.'

Fanshawe seemed not to hear as I stood up and looked at the brown scorch marks on the pillow and the bed sheet.

Chapter Eighteen

That evening there was a letter for me on the hall table. I carried it up to my rooms, poured myself a brandy and opened it.

Dear Robert,

I would be much obliged if it were possible to arrange a consultation with you at your lodgings on the afternoon of Sunday next. Three o'clock would suit me well if you have no prior engagements at that time. I look forward to hearing from you and I very much hope that I will be able to see you.

Yours truly,
Caroline Villiers

I found its tone unexpectedly formal, given Caroline's playful mood when she had visited me. I also detected a note of urgency. I wrote a reply for Charlie to deliver the next morning, agreeing to the appointment and expressing my pleasure in seeing her again.

***

Caroline's expression was serious as she sat on the sofa, looking at me earnestly.

'I expect you remember that the appointment was to do with the idea of your mesmerizing me. I have to say I've come with a more serious request.'

I waited for her to continue.

'It's a medical matter that I have some difficulty in talking about.'

I drew up a chair opposite her.

'Some time ago I was in the company of a young man who had been studying medicine at St. Thomas's Hospital and was living with his aunt and uncle in London. They were friends of that pompous Fitzgibbon who's a member of your Wigmore Society. The young man had just passed his medical exams and was to set off to Glasgow the following morning to take up a position at the Royal Infirmary there. He was in high spirits and we spent an enjoyable evening together while his aunt and uncle were at the Vauxhall Gardens. Anyway...' she paused. 'To cut a long story short, the upshot was that he noticed a lump.'

She touched her left breast.

'Here. He told me I shouldn't worry about it if didn't get any bigger. He said it seriously but we were both in an elevated mood having taken a little nitrous oxide and I put it out of my mind. Now it's worrying me and I wonder what I should make of it?'

'Has it grown bigger?'

'Yes. Is that important?'

'It could be, but I've no great knowledge of tumours. I only know that some can be harmful while others are perfectly benign.'

'And if it's not benign?'

'The truth is, Caroline, I don't know enough to give you a professional answer.'

'Would you know by examining it whether it's benign or not?'

'I'm afraid not.'

'I suspect you know more than you're telling me. So if it's not benign, I'll die? Before you answer, Robert, I want an honest medical opinion. D'you understand?'

I hesitated.

'Well, the prevailing medical opinion is that they're difficult to cure except, possibly, with surgery. Even if that were possible, there would be a problem about loss of blood. The amputation of a limb is quick but this would have to be done very carefully so there's a greater problem about the loss of blood and the pain involved.' I felt deeply anguished about telling her all this.

'You could operate using mesmerism.'

'That's true if you are susceptible. But I've never performed such an operation on a breast before.'

Caroline looked tearful and I took hold of her hand.

'May I ask if you've told your husband?'

'Not yet. I wanted to talk to you first.'

Her cheeks were wet and I handed her my handkerchief.

'Caroline, I'll tell you what I want to do. Professor Campbell, one of the senior surgeons at Bart's, has some knowledge of this area of surgery. I'll talk to him tomorrow and then I'll be in a position to tell you more.'

'Would you please examine me anyway?'

'You really want me to?'

'Yes. I don't want to be alone, knowing what's there. You'll have to help me undress.' She stood up. 'Everything is tied at the back and my maid ties my corset very tight.'

I tried not to think about the time I had seen her undress at Ashton's hellfire celebration as I stood behind her undoing the upper laces in her tunic dress and the chemise beneath it. I carefully folded both garments down to her waist before

178

unlacing her corset. When that was done, Caroline lifted the corset away from her and turned to face me.

'I'm afraid,' she said quietly.

I warmed my hands by the fire and gently pressed my forefinger and middle finger into her left breast, moving them around to find the tumour. I nodded to myself when I found it, noticing that I was able to move it slightly by pressing my fingers on either side of it. Caroline looked at me as I examined her other breast.

'Is there anything there?'

'No.'

Neither of us spoke as I helped Caroline to dress, smoothing out the wrinkles on the back of her dress.

'The tumour seems to be moveable, Caroline. That may be helpful.'

'I see. Could you find out if I can be mesmerised now?'

'I don't think so. You're too unsettled at the moment. In any event, before we go any further, I think you should talk to your husband. Then I'd like to talk to him myself.' I paused. 'There's another matter I need to be clear about, Caroline. Would you mind telling me if your husband knows what happened between us at Ashton's revelry?'

'You mean between you and Lavender?' Caroline attempted a smile.

'Not Lavender, Caroline. We must be serious now. Between you and me.'

'I'm sorry. I'm being silly because I'm frightened. No, he doesn't know.'

'Thank you. I need to be careful, that's all. I also think he would find it improper if he knew that I'd examined you without his knowledge. He might take that as an indication

179

of an intimacy between us. I know he accepts your dalliances but he would surely dislike the suspicion of your liaison, however brief, with a member of his society and, in all truth, a friend. At least I would like him to consider me a friend.'

'I know he does.'

'In that case you should tell him you've felt the lump and you want him to examine it. He should know enough to say if he thinks it'll require surgery but he'll want a second opinion. Someone like Fitzgibbon, I expect. If there's to be surgery, say you want it to be performed under mesmerism and you want him to talk to me about it.'

'Alright. I'll do that,' she replied simply, biting her lip and dabbing her eyes with the handkerchief before handing it back to me.

'You're being very brave about this, Caroline.'

'Really? I don't feel it. Anyway, I suppose I'd better go home now.'

'Please get your husband to send me a note tomorrow.'

'I will. On another matter, may I ask if you've seen Johnny since we last met?'

'I'm afraid not.' It was an uncomfortable lie but I didn't want to add Fanshawe's wretched state of mind to the worries she now had. I helped her on with her cloak and walked her to her cab. She kissed me on the cheek and we parted.

'Please ask him to come to see me if you come across him, Robert.'

'I will.'

I climbed up the stairs to my rooms, weighed down by my knowledge of the significance of Caroline's tumour and

180

deeply affected by her bravery in asking me to examine her. The memory of her playing the tart with me had faded and my embarrassment about her being Villiers's wife was now eclipsed by my fear that her condition was more than likely to be a death sentence.

Chapter Nineteen

'We don't need another opinion,' Villiers told me when, a week later, we were seated in his library. 'I'm enough of a physician to know that this is a matter for surgery.'

He had written to me about the tumor and I had talked to Professor Campbell about it.

'Now tell me what your colleague said.'

I told him about my meeting with Campbell and described his techniques for breast surgery, both lumpectomy and mastectomy. His view was that lumpectomy could be carried out if the tumor was moveable. I asked Villiers if it was moveable.

'I am afraid to say, I couldn't be certain. My medical skills in that area leave something to be desired'.

I couldn't tell Villiers that in Caroline's case, it was. I went on to say that Campbell reluctantly agreed to allow me to put Caroline into a trance state for the duration of the operation if she was susceptible to mesmerism. If not, she would be suffering pain for a considerable time. In the case of mastectomy, it could take up to twenty minutes to complete.'

Villiers looked at me, his expression pained.

'Of course, there's also the question of the loss of blood.'

'And the problem of subsequent infection.'

'Yes.'

'How many of his patients have survived?'

I steeled myself to give Villiers his answer.

'So far, three out of seventeen after lumpectomy and one out of twenty after mastectomy.'

'What a dreadful business,' Villiers muttered to himself, staring out of the window. 'I'll be devastated if she dies, you know.'

After a while, he turned to me and held him in a steady gaze.

'I have another question, Mountford, and I want an honest answer.'

'Of course.'

'Have you already examined Caroline?'

I felt my face flush and I averted my eyes.

'Yes I have, sir. I regret that it was done without your knowledge or consent. Please accept my apologies.'

'I know my Caroline very well and I could tell that there was more than the wish for professional expertise when she asked you to be here today.'

'I am deeply sorry, sir.'

I prepared myself to be banished from the house.

'Do you wish me to leave?'

'No, don't leave, Mountford. Tell me, have you met Caroline before in the guise of Lavender?'

'Yes.'

'Was your relationship with her entirely proper when you examined her and does it continue to be so now?'

'My answer is yes to both questions.'

I put as much conviction as I could muster into the reply, knowing that if Caroline had not been ill, the nature of her second visit would likely have been quite different.

'Very well. Let's get down to the important question. What did you discover in your examination?'

'The tumour was moveable and was still not big enough to be visible but Caroline told me that it had grown since she'd first noticed it so I have to assume it may be malignant.'

'And what is your advice?'

'My description of the tumour made the professor consider it small enough to be removed with a lumpectomy. I think you should ask him to carry out the operation. Prior to that, he would need to examine Caroline himself.

'And what about the use of mesmerism?'

'I can keep Caroline in a trance state while the professor operates. He's agreed to it although he's of a conservative cast of mind like Fitzgibbon and thinks God meant us to feel pain. Anyway, before that, I'll need to find out if Caroline is susceptible.'

'Have you not mesmerised her before?'

'I felt the sting of Villiers's barbed remark, with its suggestion that the playful use of mesmerism would go hand in hand with intimacy.

'No, sir.'

'Can you find out if she's susceptible now? She's in her bedchamber at the moment waiting to hear the outcome of our discussion. I have to say she's distraught, poor creature, as you can imagine.'

'Yes, I can.'

'Good. One more question. Caroline has told me that if there's to be an operation, she would like it to take place here rather than at Professor Campbell's surgery. Would you or Professor Campbell have any objection to that?'

'None. She'll be calmer if it takes place here and it'll be easier to mesmerise her. The professor will need to have two assistants with him, partly, I regret to say, to hold her down

184

if, for some reason, she comes out of the trance during the operation. I should say that's never happened during my operations so far.'

'I'm relieved to hear it.'

I hesitated before coming out with my next question.

'May I ask, sir, if you've told her about your suspicion of impropriety between us?'

'No I haven't. You'll have to tell her that I now know about it.'

Villiers looked down at his hands.

'I expect you'll think it ridiculous for a man of my age to be married to Caroline. The fact is that I was infatuated with her, an embarrassing condition now that I am middle-aged and my potency on the wane. She wanted security and I gave her that. And she cares for me. She listens to my troubles with a sympathetic ear and I love to see her around the house, not that she spends a great deal of time here.'

His voice trailed off.

'She sometimes tells me about her adventures but she didn't tell me about you. I expect that was a kindness to you because of our friendship and your belonging to the Wigmore Society. You know who she's in love with now, I suppose?'

'Tell me.'

'Young Fanshawe. With him it seems to have gone a little deeper than the others. Nevertheless, she doesn't want to leave me. I'm still important to her and she's happy the way things are. She doesn't want to change anything.'

Villiers stood up and I followed.

'Let me take you to her room. I'll leave you there with her to tell her what we've discussed. The decision as to whether or not to go ahead with surgery will be hers.'

I felt Villiers's pain in his devotion to Caroline and his acceptance of her wayward affections. Villiers's awareness of my own intimacy with Caroline had transformed my embarrassment into self-reproach. I had been no more than one of her many admirers and I had easily obtained carnal satisfaction from her playing the part of a courtesan. Now her life was to change forever and she would need a devoted husband's presence in it for as long as it was to last.

***

A mist had descended on London the following Tuesday morning when the operation was to take place. Janet, Caroline's lady's maid brought bowls and jugs of hot water and a pile of towels into her bedchamber. I had arranged for an operating table from Barts to be placed in the middle of the room. An array of surgical instruments was laid out on a table beside it.

While her room was being prepared, Caroline was lying in the four-poster in her husband's bedchamber. She had spent a sleepless night fighting her terror and now I was sitting next to her, holding her hand. Villiers sat in an armchair by the window, sunk in thought. He had told me he wouldn't attend the operation. He didn't want his anxiety to get in the way. Caroline looked at me.

'If I don't come out of this, please remember me to Johnny.'

'You'll come out of it, Caroline.'

186

I squeezed her hand.

'We're ready to start now so let your thoughts go.'

I took my silver spoon out of my coat pocket and held it above her head, intoning the words that would bring about her trance. I had tested her susceptibility to mesmerism three times during the previous week and she had proved a good subject. When she had descended into a deep trance state, her eyes closed, I carried her to her bedchamber and laid her carefully on the operating table. Janet was standing by the window, awaiting further instructions. I could see that she was deeply fond of her mistress and the thought of the operation was acutely distressing to her.

'Janet, please stand by Mrs. Villiers to stop her falling if she moves.'

'Very good, sir.'

I went off to summon Professor Campbell and his two assistants in Villiers's breakfast room. The professor was smoking his pipe and describing a difficult but successful breast operation he had undertaken some years ago. A man of middle years, Campbell cut a good figure as an authoritarian medical man. He was tall and straight-backed with an imperious bearing, a hooked nose and long white hair brushed back from the broad dome of his forehead. Remembering my student days, I saw his two assistants giving what I imagined to be well-practiced impressions of listening to him, while nursing headaches that had resulted from their previous evening's drinking. I came up to Campbell.

'Mrs. Villiers is ready, sir.'

Although Campbell felt morally uncomfortable about operating using mesmerism, the advantage of the patient not writhing around and having to be held down was not lost on him. Caroline lay with her eyes closed as I told her, what his colleague was about to do. Campbell began to work slowly and carefully, feeling where the lump was and making a three-inch incision through the skin and subcutaneous tissue over the site of the tumor.

'Can you feel any pain?' I asked.

'No, I can't,' she murmured.

One of the assistants held the incision open with two retractors while Campbell cut around the edge of the lump, some of the surrounding tissue and the lymph nodes, avoiding the mammary arteries and veins. One more cut and it would all come free. At that point, to his and my horror, he inadvertently cut through an axillary artery and Caroline began to bleed profusely. Within moments her body was soaked and blood was dripping on to the floor. There was a tremor in the professor's fingers as he prepared two ligatures to tie off both ends of the artery and staunch the flow that was gushing out at a frightening rate.

When they had been tied off, Campbell looked at the pallor in Caroline's face. It looked as if she had gone into haemorrhagic shock. I couldn't help empathising with Campbell who would have to speed up the operation without risking a further mistake. This he did and Caroline's incision was sewn up within a minute.

I laid a towel on Caroline's bed and carried her to it. Campbell took her pulse, inviting me to do the same. I could barely feel it. The two assistants left the room leaving

Campbell and me alone with the unconscious Caroline. Campbell was slumped in an armchair.

'My God, Mountford, that's never happened to me before.'

'You rectified it very quickly, sir.'

'I'm going to Guy's Hospital to ask Blundell to bring his gravitator. I only hope he's there and he can come straight away'.

I knew of it as a blood transfusion apparatus Blundell had invented for severe haemorrhaging in childbirth.

'I'll tell Dr. Villiers what's happened. You will stay in here with Mrs. Villiers, will you not?'

'Of course.'

It felt strange for me to see my self-assured senior colleague in such a state of agitation. Shortly after Campbell left, Villiers came into the room and knelt on the floor next to Caroline's bed. He ran his fingers gently across her cheek and looked at the pallor in her face.

'Campbell told me what happened,' he said.

'I feel very bad about it, sir, especially as I'd recommended him to you.'

'I understand this Blundell's got some means of transfusing blood into Caroline.'

His tone was skeptical and he looked at me, seeking reassurance that it might work.

'It's been successful in at least half of the occasions in which he's used it in post-partum haemorrhages when the loss of blood in the mother could be at least as great as Caroline's.'

'Let's hope.'

***

When Campbell made his next entrance, a man of my age with fair curly hair followed him into the room carrying a wooden box.

'How is she,' Campbell asked.

'Unchanged,' I replied.

Campbell turned to his companion.

'Gentlemen, James Blundell.'

Blundell bowed in greeting and went up to the unconscious Caroline without further ado.

'Take my blood,' Campbell said, taking off his coat, and rolling up one of his shirtsleeves. Blundell opened his box and took out the various parts of his gravitator; glass funnels, lengths of flexible tubing, syringes and lancets. When he had put it all together, he attached a tube coming from one end of the apparatus to a syringe inserted into a vein in Campbell's arm. The tube coming from the other end he attached to a syringe in a vein in Caroline's arm. Campbell kept his arm in the air, enabling gravitation to bring about the transfusion.

After a considerable length of time, Caroline's face began to regain a little colour but she was still deeply unconscious and her loss of blood was such that she still might well die.

Chapter Twenty

After further transfusions of Campbell's blood during the next two days, more colour came back into her cheeks and she slowly regained consciousness. She was still very pale and weak and she lay flat on her bed, Blundell having advised that it would facilitate the circulation of blood to her head. During my third visit, a week later, she seemed to be getting a little of her strength back and asked about Fanshawe. I told her with honesty that I didn't know where he was. I had been trying to find him ever since Caroline's last visit to my lodgings. I had gone more than once to his home and his club, and, on one occasion, the house in Rotherhithe. All without success. I told this to Caroline, leaving out the part about Rotherhithe. I still wanted to keep that from her. We had both had been silent for a while when Caroline looked at me and touched my arm.

'Something's occurred to me.'

Her eyes opened and she looked at the ceiling. 'Johnny's a strange man, as you know, but no stranger than me, I suppose. He's intrigued by my dressing up and mixing with the dollymops and sometimes he likes to court the company of the street people in the public houses in the city. He says he does it when he's bored being himself, like me, I suppose. He dresses up in old work clothes and calls himself Jack Tyler. I've never been with him on any of these expeditions but he's told me his favourite haunt for mixing with what he calls the hoi polloi when the evening's warmed up is a tavern in Newgate Street. I'm trying to think of its name.'

She stared at the ceiling as if the name might be written there for her.

'Perhaps somebody there may know where he is. I hesitate to ask you to demean yourself, Robert going to such a place but you might find out if there's any news of him there.' She squeezed my hand.

'I have it,' she said. 'The Cross Keys. It's called The Cross Keys.'

***

It was raining that evening when I pushed my way through the bustling crowd on my way to The Cross Keys. The gutters were overflowing with sewage from the day-long rainfall and the soot-filled raindrops looked black as tar in the light from the gas lamps. A small, barrel-shaped mongrel with a large ugly head waddled across my path and snapped at my legs. I kicked it away and looked up to see its owner, a toothless vagabond who held it on a string and shouted obscenities at no one in particular. Was this the city I had described to Fanshawe as feeling 'like home?' To my constant bemusement, it did.

I reached the inn shortly after nine o'clock and entered the smoke-filled tap room where a coal fire glowed in a little fireplace. A gust of wind blew down the chimney, wafting smoke into the room where it mingled with the fug of warm, smelly bodies, wet clothes and tobacco. The room was peopled with the usual crowd for such a place, an assorted gathering of costermongers, dockers, clerks, lodging-house keepers and prostitutes. I approached a portly man with extravagant side-whiskers and a jolly countenance who was carrying a tray of drinks with the bearing of an innkeeper.

'I'm looking for a man named Jack Tyler. Might he be here?' I asked.

'Jack Tyler?'

'A friend of mine says he sometimes drinks here. Would you know of him, by any chance?'

'Jack Tyler.' he thought for a moment.

'Yeah. I haven't seen him for a while. Ask that woman over there. She knows him.'

He pointed with his eyes to the back of a large woman in a black cape and bonnet.

'Thank you.'

I went up to the woman who was in deep discussion with somebody. I leant towards her.

'Excuse me for interrupting. I wonder if…'

She turned round.

'Good Lord…Mrs. Burrows.' I lifted my hat. 'Robert Mountford. Forgive me for intruding.'

The woman looked stunned and said nothing. I ploughed on.

'The inn keeper thought you might know of John Fanshawe's whereabouts.

'I don't know where he is,' she answered curtly.

I glanced at the man she'd been talking to. It was Fawcett, the Newgate turnkey. Fawcett turned away from me as soon as he saw me and disappeared into the crowd.

'Thank you all the same,' I said. 'I hope your husband's safe in Yorkshire.'

'Yes he is. Thank you.'

With that, she walked out through the tap-room door without saying another word. I heard a voice behind me.

'I'll tell you something. That woman ain't got no husband, nor sister, nor daughter and she ain't called Mrs. Burrows.'

I looked around me and saw a man with a white stick sitting next to the fire. A pot of porter stood on a table beside him.

'I got sharp ears y'know. I know what goes on even if I can't see.'

'What do you mean?' I snapped in bewilderment. 'Are you telling me she isn't Mrs. Burrows?

'No need to shout at me. You a thief-taker?'

'No, I'm not. So who is she?'

The man put his hand on the glass.

'How about a drink, sir?'

'What do you want?' I asked brusquely.

'A brandy would suit me well.'

I beckoned to a waiter.

'What can you tell me anything about the woman?' I asked when the drink arrived.

'Audrey Clegg? She runs a brothel in Bermondsey. Hard as nails. She's a sharp creature. Not someone to mess with.'

What in God's name was going on? I tried to gather my thoughts.

'Have you heard of somebody called Jack Tyler coming here?'

'Yes. I believe his real name's John Fanshawe. Tyler's the name he likes to use when he wants to hobnob with people like us. Am I right?'

'You are.'

'I've heard him talking to the Clegg woman. Him and Fawcett who you would have seen just now. They were talking about springing a convict from Newgate. Fawcett's the head turnkey there.'

My head was reeling.

'What was the convict's name?'

'Burrows. Very nasty man, done for murdering his son. Vicious man he is.'

'What happened to him?'

'I don't know. I'd tell you if I did. By the way, Burrows ain't the first one they've sprung. The one before was easy, mind. Just a kid, a dipper trying to get away from a constable. Tripped him up and the constable fell in the river. He couldn't swim and drowned. The kid was done for murder. It's funny though. Why should your friend and the turnkey and the Clegg woman want to spring 'em? And why was it so important to them Fawcett being certain when the murders'd been done? Had to be a particular month. Odd, isn't? I couldn't make no sense of it.'

'Neither can I. May I ask your name?'

'Tom Abbott.'

'Robert Mountford. Listen, Tom, Thank you for your help. I'd be very grateful if you'd keep an ear cocked for anything more you hear from these people. Here's a sovereign.'

'Thank you, sir.'

'What time are you normally here?'

'From sunset to eleven o'clock every night. It's my nephew's inn. He looks after me.'

'Good. I'm glad he does. Good evening to you, Tom. I'll call by again soon.'

Chapter Twenty One

I had been tricked. That scoundrel Fanshawe had tricked me. Even though I had been well paid for my assignment, by the time I got back to Calthorpe Street, I was boiling with rage at Fanshawe's deceit and his willingness to put me in danger. And all the while, the unanswered question kept repeating itself in my head. Why did they want to get that abhorrent murderer out of prison? I determined to go to Rotherhithe the next day as soon as I finished work.

***

It turned out that the last two operations on that day were to be particularly taxing, neither patient being susceptible to mesmerism and both operations taking longer than usual. By the time I left the hospital and hailed a cab, the sun was low in the sky.

'The Angel Inn, Bermondsey,' I called up to the driver as I climbed in, shading my eyes from the sunlight coming through the cab window. My thoughts had been racing the previous night as I tried to make sense of what Tom Abbott had told me. At least I had Fanshawe's money, I told myself, so I could afford to take cab rides to try to find out what was going on.

'You a surgeon, sir?' the cabbie asked in a friendly way, slurring his words.

'Yes I am.'

'Very fine profession. My brother lost a leg at Waterloo. Surgeon did a fine job on him...very fine.'

At that point he seemed to have lost his stream of thought. He was silent for a few moments before starting afresh.

'Forgive me if I seem a little intoxicated, sir. I was having a bit of a ding-dong with my wife earlier today and too much gin passed our lips.'

'I'll forgive you if you get me to the Angel without getting lost.'

The cabbie burst out laughing.

'Without getting lost! I've been drivin' a cab for twenty three years.'

'I'm very pleased to hear it.'

In fact he did get lost twice but managed eventually to arrive at the Angel Inn. I paid my fare and agreed a price for waiting for me, saying I would be back within the hour. Once again, armed with my pistol and club, I set off for Albion House, winding my way through the maze of alleys and treading carefully across the demolished slum tenements where scavengers, their backs bent double like fruit pickers, poked through the debris for anything they could sell.

When I reached the house its heavy outside shutters were closed. I knocked on the door and shouted out all the names that I now associated with the place. After half an hour, I gave up and made my way back to the Angel Inn where I found the driver asleep in his cab. I went into the inn, ordered a pint of porter and looked around. Three or four men were sat in their chairs with their drinks, each silent and alone.

'May I ask if anybody by the name of Jack Tyler or John Fanshawe has spent any time in here?' I asked the innkeeper. 'A man with long fair hair?'

'Can't say as I've heard either of those names and I don't recognise the description.'

'Thank you all the same.'

I took my drink and asked the same question of the men slumped in their chairs. No one knew either name. I sat at a table under a window and looked out at the darkening sky as the inn began to fill with its riverside customers. A character looking like a waterman came in, bought his pint, and sat down opposite me. I asked him the same question.

'Sorry. Can't help you there,' the waterman replied as he filled his pipe with tobacco and lit it from a candle on the table. Something about the man's coat caught my eye and I examined it in the candlelight. Although it was filthy, it reminded me of the one I had given to Burrows. There was a tear in one of the cuffs just like the one in my own coat and the lining was of the same colour. The man puffed away, staring blankly at me with brutish incuriosity as I inspected the coat's sleeves and collar. There was a burn mark on one side of the collar, the same as the one on the collar of my own coat where someone had dropped a cigar on it. I was looking at my own coat.

'Excuse me sir, may I ask where you acquired that coat?'

'What's it to you?' The man gave me a surly look.

'I seem to recognise it. Would you mind if I looked inside the collar? My initials would be sown in it. RM for Robert Mountford.'

'Look mister, I got this coat off someone else.'

'If you'll let me have a look, I'll buy you a pint.'

'You can buy the pint first.'

'Alright.'

'Come on then,' I said when the porter was brought to the table. I stood behind the waterman and lifted the collar away from his back.

'There, you see. My initials, RM. I told you it was mine.'

'And I told you I got it off someone else.'

'Look, I don't want the coat. I just want to know who you got it from.'

'Difficult to say as he was dead at the time. I fished him out the river a couple of weeks ago.'

I felt a sense of dread and waited before asking my next question.

'Do you remember what he looked like?'

'I can't say as I do on account of his head being cut off.'

Oh, my God, I thought, beginning to feel nauseous. The man grinned at me.

'Blimey. That seems to have taken you a bit sudden.'

My rage at Fanshawe's duplicity had now been turned to a sickening sense of foreboding.

'I fish all sorts out the river, y'know,' the man continued in a conversational way. 'I found a child's arm floating in the water the other day down near the Regents canal. Not that I pick up much that's worth selling.'

He put his hand on the collar of the coat.

'I couldn't sell this, f'rinstance. It took me a week to dry it out and it'll always smell of the river as you'd expect.'

He took a swig of his porter and looked me in the eye.

'Anyway, how come your coat should end up on a headless man?'

I didn't know what to say.

'You look like you're thinkin' about it. You look like your mind's tickin' away like a fob watch. Tickety-tick. Care to tell me about it?'

'What did you do with the body?' I asked.

'Well, it weren't much use to me. There was nothin' in the pockets and the clothes underneath weren't much more than rags so I kept the coat and handed the body over to the river police.'

As I stared at my coat, horrified by the waterman's story, a group of men in seaman's sailcloth dungarees came in and sat down at a table next to us.

'I hope I get your attention soon, landlord,' one of them called to the innkeeper. He was a large, swarthy man wearing a red neck cloth, his black hair pulled back into a pigtail. He grinned at me.

'This don't look like your sort of place, squire. I don't s'pose you're from around these parts.'

I didn't like the look of him but felt I must continue with my enquiry.

'I'm looking for a man who sometimes calls himself Jack Tyler and sometimes, John Fanshawe.'

'What does he look like?'

'He's in his thirties. He's got long fair hair.'

The seaman grinned.

'Don't mean nothin' to me. Special friend, is he? Keeps you warm in bed at night?'

Before I could respond, one of the seamen spoke up in broken English.

'I see man like that.'

The pigtail turned to the innkeeper.

'First things first. I think we'd each like a pint of porter, landlord.'

He glanced back at his friends.

'That not so?' They mumbled assent.

'And as you know me well, landlord, I think we should start a new tally and wipe the old one off the slate. I'd consider that very generous of you.'

I could see that none of the seamen would pay for their drinks in this place. The pigtail turned to the man who had recognised Fanshawe's description.

'Come on, Loopy. Tell the gentleman what you know. He's Portuguese,' he added as an aside to me, 'name of Lopez.'

'I see man like that before we sail to Lisbon. He's looking for opium. He's very, how you say, agitado.' Lopez put on a performance of shaking and pulling crazy faces to get his point across.

'I say to him, "Go to the gin shop in Stone-Cutter Lane. They got it."'

'Sound like him?' the pigtail asked.

'It could be,' I replied and looked at Lopez. 'Have you seen him any other time in here or in the neighbourhood?'

The man shook his head.

'Thank you for your help. Get yourself another drink,' I said to the waterman, putting a coin on the table.

'Very kind sir.'

I got up to leave and saw the pigtail looking at me.

'On your way are you, squire?'

'Indeed I am. Thank you for your help, Mr. Lopez.'

When I was outside the inn, I heard footsteps behind me. Moments later, I felt a massive whack on the back of my

201

head and an excruciating pain as I fell to the ground on my back in a state of semi-consciousness. I looked up to see the pigtail fumble inside my pockets until he found my purse. Lopez took my watch and my pistol.

'Give it here. Let's finish him off,' the pigtail said, taking the gun from Lopez.

I watched him aim it at my head, too dazed to take in the thought that my life was about to end. He tried to pull the trigger.

'This thing's no bloody good. It's all rusted up.'

He threw the gun to the ground where it discharged with a mighty bang.

'Blimey. Oh, well. I suppose we'd better leg it.'

'What about the others?'

'Sod 'em. They'll only want some of the money. Come on, let's go.'

After some minutes, I regained full consciousness and I sat up, my ears ringing and my head in excruciating pain as if a cathedral bell was tolling inside my skull. No one came out of the inn to find out what had happened and I wasn't surprised. It was not a part of London in which people indulged their curiosity about such things. When I felt able to get to my feet, I picked up the pistol and stumbled along the alley to the road, my greatcoat smeared with mud from the fall and the side of my face bruised from its impact on the cobbles. The cab was still there and the driver was inside it, fast asleep. I shook him awake and asked to go to Calthorpe Street. When he noticed the bruise on my face, I explained that I had tripped and fallen. I didn't mention anything about being attacked and robbed as the cabbie would assume I wouldn't be able to pay my fare. As it was, I hoped I had enough money in my lodging to pay him.

Chapter Twenty Two

I was feeling dizzy and sick from concussion as I made my way to Barts on the morning after the attack. I couldn't stop thinking about Fanshawe and the headless body in the river, haunted by the fact that in freeing Burrows I had committed a crime that had subsequently made me an accessory to murder. Walking down Saffron Hill, I missed my footing and fell heavily on to the pavement. It was a while before I could stand up, the concussion making me feel as if I were on a ship at sea. It took half an hour to get back to Calthorpe Street, leaning against walls and railings to keep myself upright. For the next few days I was unable to go to work. I got Charlie to take a note to Barts and sat around in my lodgings. All I wished for now was to be well enough to confront Fanshawe.

***

By the end of the week I had recovered sufficiently to take a cab to Lincoln's Inn Fields. I banged the door knocker and called out, 'Are you there, Fanshawe?' There was no response. I called out again, banging repeatedly on the knocker. Silence. I looked around and noticed steps next to the front door leading down to a stairwell with a basement door that stood slightly ajar. I descended the steps and walked through a passageway to a small courtyard at the back of the house where Fanshawe's phaeton stood in a stable. I tried the door of a tradesman's entrance which was locked and peered through a sash window next to it, making out a servant's room in the gloom. The window latch was open and I managed to lift up the lower window sufficiently to climb into the room. I stood still, listening for any sound. The house was completely silent. I climbed a staircase up to the entrance hall and on up to Fanshawe's bedchamber. I opened the door and took a pace into the room.

The curtains were half drawn and the room was a shambles. Gin and brandy bottles lay around on the floor with bits of clothing and the air was filled with the sweet, pungent smell of opium. A dirty copper saucepan and a tin box stood next to the fireplace in which the embers of a fire were still glowing. The tapestry curtain to the four-poster bed had been pulled away at one end. Behind it Fanshawe was lying asleep on his back and breathing heavily.

I was shocked by his wretched state, his clothes were soiled and his hair matted as if it had been stuck down with fish glue. A small book lay in one hand and, next to it, a bamboo opium pipe. He stirred in his sleep, half sitting up with his eyes closed and threw the book across the room, letting out a terrible groan before falling back on to the bed. The book landed at my feet and I picked it up. The pages were covered in the same Egyptian hieratic script I had seen in the Josiah's book that Sarah had shown me in Kidlington and the ancient Egyptian image of an eye was blind-embossed on the cover of its calf binding. The first few pages were stuck together with what looked like dried blood. I turned as a floorboard creaked behind me and was jolted by the sight of a girl with long black hair standing in the open doorway, wearing a white mask. It was the girl I had seen at the upper window of Albion House.

Fanshawe stirred again, mumbling to himself. The girl took a glass of amber liquid to the bed and touched Fanshawe's arm. He pulled himself up, bleary-eyed as she handed him the glass and tossed back the liquid in one draught.

'Why are you wearing your mask, Shukura?' he asked. 'It's only me here.'

He lay down again and the girl left the room.

'You're wrong, Fanshawe. I'm in here too.'

'My God. Who are you?'

Fanshawe sat up, his eyes still unfocussed, and saw me standing before him.

'Who are you?' he asked again, his eyes straining to see who it was.

'Don't you know me?' I asked.

'Good, God! Mountford! How did you get in here?'

'The door to the courtyard was open. So was the catch on the window at the back of the house.'

'You shouldn't be here.'

'I must know why you asked me to bring Burrows to the house in Rotherhithe.'

'I told you why.'

His eyes focused and he saw the book in my hand.

'You mustn't touch that! Drop it. Straight away, Mountford. Drop it on the floor.'

I dropped it and stood looking at Fanshawe's wasted features, wondering how he would react to what I was about to tell him. I drew up a chair next to the bed and sat down.

'I spoke to Mrs. Burrows in The Crossed Keys, except that she wasn't Mrs. Burrows. Then I happened upon a waterman in Rotherhithe who fished Burrows's headless body out of the river. He was wearing my coat.'

'Oh no,' Fanshawe whispered to himself falling back on to the bed. ' Mountford, I don't know what to say to you. I can't tell you what it's about. It may be difficult for you to understand but I've no choice in the matter. You have to believe me. I'm sworn to secrecy. It's inculcated into me. I don't have the mental power to overcome it.'

He lifted himself up and put a blanket around his shoulders before picking up the pipe and climbing off the bed. He knelt in front of the fire and held out his hands to warm them.

'I hope you'll forgive me if I take a little opium, Mountford. I need to calm down. I welcome your company even if it can only be for a while. Amon and Gilchrist will be back in an hour or so. I'm not supposed to be in the company of anybody but Shukura. And please don't ask me who they all are.'

I looked on in dismay as Fanshawe picked up a metal bodkin from the fireplace, his hand trembling, and poked it into the treacly substance in the tin box. When there was a good lump on the end of it he held it over the glowing coals until it began to sizzle and quickly pushed it into the metal bowl of the pipe. Sucking furiously, he inhaled the vapour continuously as he climbed on to the bed. After a while he dropped the pipe to his side and rested his back against the bed head. his expression now was one of serenity, his eyes closed and his mouth a little open, like the face of a praying Virgin Mary in a Catholic church. After ten minutes, the reverie came to an end. He opened his eyes and sat up.

207

'I must say, it's good to have your company, Mountford. I think one more pipe would be good.'

I guessed he would do anything to escape the agony he was going through and at that moment I knew what I was going to do.

'Instead of a pipe, Fanshawe, why not try a little experiment. If you'd let me put you into a trance state, I could give you a sense of peace that would last longer than a pipe dream.'

'That so?'

'Indeed. It's a technique I learned from Dr Pierot. Do you remember him?

Fanshawe searched his mind.

'The mesmerist?'

'That's right.'

I talked about Dr Pierot's experiments with his girls, although it was Dr Devereux's ability to unlock the secrets of the unconscious mind that I was thinking about. This would be the first time I had ever used mesmerism for that purpose and I was feeling deeply apprehensive about attempting to discover the secrets concealed in Fanshawe's mind. Would he be susceptible to mesmerism and if he was, what would I find there, given that he seemed to be on the edge of lunacy? Nevertheless, I was determined to try to find out what he was hiding from me. I decided to use a technique that Dr. Pierot had described as being effective when dealing with subjects who might be difficult to mesmerise.

'Are you willing to go ahead?' I asked.

'I'm in your hands.'

'Good. Now lie down.'

As Fanshawe did so, I began to speak slowly and quietly.

'I'm going to count from one to twenty. As I do, a pleasant feeling is going to spread through your right hand and into your right arm. As I continue counting, the feeling will grow stronger and stronger. Don't try to resist it.'

I began to count, speaking very slowly.

'One...the first light, easy sensation is moving into the fingertips of your right hand.'

I waited to allow Fanshawe to respond.

'Two...the feeling is spreading through your fingers.'

I paused between each instruction.

'Three...it's moving up towards the palm of your hand. Four...it's spreading across the back of your hand. Five...you're beginning to feel the first slight movements of the fingers. Six...the light sensation spreads into your wrist. Seven...your hand is feeling lighter. Eight...the light sensation is spreading up your arm. Nine...think of your left hand now. You'll see by comparison, your left hand is beginning to feel very, very heavy. Ten...your right hand is growing lighter still and with each number I count it wants to float up into the air like a Montgolpfier balloon. By the time I reach the count of twenty, your right hand will be above your head.'

I continued counting while making suggestions about the lightness of Fanshawe's left hand and the heaviness of his right. I lingered over each phrase and by the count of sixteen Fanshawe's arm began to rise. By the count of nineteen, it was suspended above his head.

'When I say the next number, your hand will drop on to your chest and your eyelids will lock tightly closed...twenty!'

Fanshawe's hand dropped on to his chest.

'Now your eyelids are firmly closed and the more you try to open them, the more you cannot do so.'

I waited nervously to see if Fanshawe had gone into a trance state. He lifted his eyebrows, trying to open his eyes but he was unable to do so. It had worked. Despite myself, I felt a momentary thrill of power as I had when I first mesmerised Dr. Pierot's girls.

'Now stop trying to open them and allow yourself go down deeper into your trance state. Can you hear me, Fanshawe?'

'Yes.'

'Are you feeling calm and composed?'

'Yes.'

I decided to be circumspect in my attempt to get him to tell me the truth about Burrows in case his being pressed too soon to reveal a deadly secret might shock him out of his trance while he still had deeper to go.

'Can you tell me why you're so disquieted,' I asked.

Fanshawe was silent to the point that I was about to set aside the question and then he spoke.

'I'm going to meet my father.'

I felt the hairs rise on the back of my neck as I remembered Fanshawe having spoken the words before going into a coma at my lodging. It disconcerted me and I had to hide it. If Fanshawe were to pick up some disquiet in my voice, the trance could be broken.

'Is he alive?' I asked.

'In a manner of speaking.'

'What you mean, "in a manner of speaking"?'

'He's at the entrance to the underworld, waiting to come back to life in a new incarnation. That's when I'll meet him.'

I could make no rational sense of what he was talking about.

'When will the meeting take place?'

'When the sacrifices have been made.'

I was chilled by the words.

'What sacrifices?'

Fanshawe spoke like a child trying to recall a poem learnt by rote.

'The first must be in the month of Payni, the second in the month of Epiphi and the third in the month of Mesore, all in the time of harvest.'

'What language are the words in?'

'They come from the ancient Egyptian calendar.'

'You mean they're acts of supplication to an Egyptian god?'

Fanshawe nodded.

'What god?'

'Apep, the god of darkness.'

'How do you come to know of Apep?'

'I can't tell you.'

I was silent for a while, wondering how to proceed. I tried another tack.

'What was happening to you when I last saw you? D'you remember? You kept doubling up in pain. That wasn't the aftereffects of influenza, was it?'

Fanshawe began shaking.

'I can't tell you,' he whispered.

I put my hand on his forehead and stroked my thumb along the ridge of his nose, another technique I had learned from Dr Pierot.

'You're gently falling into a deeper trance.'

On hearing those words, Fanshawe grabbed my arm, his breath panicky.

'You won't let me fall into darkness, will you?'

I tried to keep the nervousness out of my voice as I ransacked my mind for something that would draw Fanshawe back from the edge.

'No I won't. Now listen to me. I want you to imagine you're lying on warm grass next to a river on a sunny afternoon.'

We sat in silence for nearly a minute before Fanshawe spoke.

'Let me tell you, Mountford...I need to tell you...the reason I was in pain was that...inside me...inside me is....' he doubled up in pain.

'What was inside you...?'

'The snake.'

Keep calm, I kept telling myself, horrified by the thought. Fanshawe fell on to his side and curled up into a ball, his face contorted. He opened his mouth but he couldn't speak.

Although I felt justified in my attempt to find out why I had been tricked into committing a crime that led to a vile act of murder, I felt bad about subjecting Fanshawe to such a painful ordeal. I had to come up with something else that would bring him back to a benign state of mind. I lifted him up and laid him against the pillows piled up against the bed head, Fanshawe wincing with pain.

'Listen to me, I said quietly. I had to improvise.

'When I place my hand on your stomach, the pain will go. Do you understand?'

'Yes.'

I lowered my hand slowly on to Fanshawe's stomach. To my great relief, Fanshawe's face relaxed.

'Your trance state is now deepening further as you lie on the grass on the bank of the river, your face warmed by the afternoon sun.'

Would Fanshawe now be ready to speak about the dark heart of the matter?

'I have another question for you, Fanshawe.'

'What is it?' Fanshawe's voice sounded remote.

The horror inside me grew as he answered each question.

'Are the sacrifices needed to bring your father back human sacrifices?'

After a long pause, he gave his answer.

'Yes they are.'

'Who chooses the victims?'

'The priest from the Temple of Apep.'

'How are they chosen?'

'Each victim must have committed a murder during one of those three months in the Egyptian calendar.'

I paused before asking the next question, glad that he couldn't see the tremble in my hands.

'Was Burrows one of the sacrifices?'

'Yes. He was the second one.'

I felt sick.

'Why did you need me?'

'He was the only murderer we could find who'd committed his crime in the right month. We knew he was

213

violent so I thought you could mesmerise him in order to get him out of Newgate.'

'And they all need to be decapitated?'

'Yes. I had to put Burrows's body in the river afterwards '

Beads of sweat were forming on my brow as I thought of what I had done to get Burrows out of Newgate and what then happened to him. My nausea was increasing but I had to keep going.

'Why did you make me drop that book on the floor?'

'It's an ancient Egyptian book of spells that belongs to my father. No one who is not initiated is allowed to touch it.'

'Is that dried blood on some of the pages?'

Yes. It's Burrows's blood. The priest was holding the book when he beheaded him.'

'Where are the heads of the first two?'

'In the burial chamber.'

'How many in all?'

'Three. One more to go.'

'Who will that be?'

'A woman due for transportation'

'Where is the burial chamber?'

'It's in...'

Fanshawe's sentence was broken off as he sprang up on to his knees and started retching. Strings of saliva dropped from his mouth and a strange noise came out of him, a deep, snarling voice that wasn't his own.

'No, you don't!' the voice barked. I was terror-stricken. Fanshawe climbed off the bed and pulled me up from my chair, seizing the collars of my coat and pulling the ends together, blocking my windpipe.

214

'What's the matter?' I spluttered, trying to push him away. Fanshawe picked up the little book from the floor, his eyes blazing, and held it in front of me like a cross used to stave off a vampire.

'Keep away from my son,' the voice barked, 'He's not yours, he's mine!'

My eyes were fixed on the book and my blood ran cold. A moment later Fanshawe collapsed on to the floor, falling on to his back where he lay quivering as if he were in a fit of the falling sickness. My heart was beating fast, my rationalism overwhelmed by the thought that Fanshawe was possessed by the spirit of his father. I was afraid to go near him and I sat on the bed, waiting for him to come round. Eventually he opened his eyes.

'What happened?' he asked. I felt mightily relieved that he was speaking in his normal voice. He sat up and looked about him.

'Why am I on the floor?'

I hastily invented an answer.

'When you were in the trance, I suggested you imagine yourself lying on the grassy bank of a river in the warm sunshine. The only problem was that you decided to go for a swim and you jumped into the water. Unfortunately, the water was the floor. I'm sorry. I hope you haven't hurt yourself.'

Fanshawe picked up the little book and crawled towards the fire.

'What's in the book, Fanshawe?'

'I can't tell you. I'm sorry.'

He picked up the bodkin and pushed it into the tin of opium.

'I don't think the mesmerism has calmed me down much, Mountford. I hate to say this but I don't want you to come to see me anymore. It won't do you any good and it will put me in danger.'

We heard the sound of the front door opening and footsteps coming into the house.

'You've got to go,' Fanshawe said and led me out of the room, down to the servant's quarters and opened the door of the tradesman's entrance.

'Go out the same way you came in. Look, Mountford I don't want you to come back. There's nothing you can do. Go quickly before the others start looking for me.'

I slipped out into the street in a state of turmoil, unable to drive out of my mind the chilling voice that had spoken through Fanshawe or the ghoulish account of an ancient Egyptian god and sacrificial killings.

My rationalism having returned, I tried to think of the voice as having to do with the phenomenon of exchanged personality that Devereux had described, although that too was a mystery. The freezing sensation I had felt when I looked at the book that Fanshawe held in front of me, I put down to an overactive imagination.

By now, my anger with Fanshawe had been overtaken by alarm at the horrifying business in which he had become embroiled. I had to help him, but how? I needed to find out more about the people with whom he had become involved. I thought about The Temple of Apep that he had mentioned and Sir Ralph Ashton came to mind. I recalled Ashton talking about a London bookshop specializing in occult literature where he had bought a book on alchemy. I recalled the owner's name, John Denley. Ashton had said that Denley knew everything there was to know about the occult. It took a while to remember the whereabouts of the shop. It was in Catherine Street in Covent Garden.

Chapter Twenty Three

It was market day in Covent Garden when I pressed past wagons, donkey-drawn barrows and columns of baskets, my boots squelching over the detritus of vegetables that covered the ground. I pushed my way through the throng of street hawkers and costermongers, shouting their wares behind their market stalls. At the corner of Catherine Street I passed the entrance of the Theatre Royal with its posters advertising Joe Grimaldi in Mother Goose and I thought about Caroline on her way to an evening's entertainment. Very soon I saw the sign for Denley's bookshop. A bell jangled above my head when I opened the door and entered a small room whose walls were lined with books from floor to ceiling. It was a dim interior, not much light percolating through the shop's bottle-glass bow window. At the back of the shop a small man in a green velvet coat sat behind a writing desk reading a large leather-bound book.

'John Denley?' I asked.

'I am, sir. Can I help you?'

'I hope so. Robert Mountford, sir.' I tapped my hat.

I felt uneasy, wanting to find out about the Temple of Apep while withholding my reason for doing so. As I didn't know who might belong to it, I wanted to avoid saying anything that might put Fanshawe further into harm's way without my knowing it.

'I am trying to find out about an Ancient Egyptian god called Apep and a temple dedicated to him.'

'A temple dedicated to Apep?' Denley looked surprised. 'I'm intrigued as to how you heard about such a temple. Can you tell me where you came across it?'

'I regret that that would mean breaking a confidence.'

'Really?'

'I'm sorry I can't be more forthcoming.'

'I see. Come upstairs with me, if you would.'

I followed him up a narrow staircase to another book-lined room, a little lighter than the shop below, with two desks under windows facing the street. At one of them sat a boy of eighteen years or so, pen in hand, bent over a manuscript.

'This is Mr. Hockley who, amongst other things, copies manuscripts for me. He knows a great deal about occult matters, more than you would guess from his years. Mr. Hockley, this is Mr. Mountford.'

We nodded to one another.

'And this is Mr. Barrett.' Denley held his arm out to a middle-aged man sitting at the other desk. 'He's a man of great learning, having spent many years translating Cabbalistic and other ancient texts on occult lore. He's the author of *The Magus,* a very important book on esoteric knowledge.'

He turned to the two men in turn.

'Gentlemen, I have a question for you both. Mr. Mountford here is seeking information about an ancient Egyptian temple called The Temple of Apep. Unfortunately, he isn't at liberty to tell us where he heard about it.'

Barrett crossed the room and picked up a folder from one of the shelves.

'We don't have any evidence of Apep being a god or having a temple dedicated to him,' he said as he flicked

219

through sheaves of notes. 'Most of what we know about him comes from the period of Hellenistic rule when the stories of a few Egyptian gods and demons went into circulation. Apep is one of them, translated into Greek as Apophis. He was a demon in the form of a water snake. We should know more when Thomas Young and Champollion have decoded the hieroglyphs on the Rosetta stone.'

He paused as he looked at a page of his notes.

'There are a few records citing a Persian alchemist who is said to have deciphered hieroglyphics in the seventh century. He is supposed to have translated a number of ancient Egyptian documents into Arabic including a grimoire called *The Book of Apophis,* written by a magician during the reign of Rameses II. The book has never been found.

'A grimoire?' I asked.

'A manual for gaining magical powers.'

Barrett looked back at his notes.

'There are also references to a satanic church in the 16th century France that worshiped Apophis. That's as much as I know, I'm afraid.'

I thanked him for his help and Denley led me down to the shop.

'If you'd care to give me your address and I hear any more about the subject, I'll write to you. I'm fascinated to know the reason for your interest in it. I hope one day you'll feel free to tell us.'

I wrote down my address and left the shop feeling highly disturbed. The fact that Apep was prayed against as a force for evil and that a satanic church worshiped him was enough to add more horror to my picture of the terrible events that had been going on.

***

After another sleepless night, I desperately needed to share my worries with Sarah and I wrote to her asking when she could come to London to see me about her brother. I didn't spell out what had happened to Fanshawe or what I had learned at Denley's bookshop. I wanted to be with her when I told her.

Chapter Twenty Four

It took a catastrophe to push my troubled thoughts to the back of my mind. Such a catastrophe took place as I was walking along Hatton Garden on my way to Barts. The air was rocked by the sound of a huge explosion coming from the direction of the river and I saw a thick black cloud of smoke rising above the horizon. When I arrived at the hospital, two dilapidated former mail coaches stood outside the entrance. Surgeons and their assistants were climbing on board along with those nurses who were able-bodied and not too drunk to be of any use.

'What's happening?' I asked Professor Gibson, a senior colleague who was sitting in one of the coaches.

'Didn't you hear it? Forty kegs of gunpowder blew up at the Woolwich armoury just outside a room where the women were making paper cartridges. It's a massacre. They're getting the injured to the Naval Hospital at Greenwich. It's the nearest one but there aren't enough surgeons and nurses to cope. We've just commandeered these. Come on!'

I climbed on to the roof of the coach, the inside being full and found myself sitting next to my friend Harvey.

'Hello Mountford. Terrible business, isn't it?'

'Do you know what the facilities are like at the hospital?'

I remembered the place being not much more than a nursing home for retired sailors mostly wounded in the Napoleonic Wars. Harvey pointed to a large leather case in front of him.

'I don't know, but we're bringing our own instruments. Most of the people on board will be going to the hospital but I'm going on to Woolwich to see if I can help there. We'll have to do some of the surgery on the spot.'

'I'll come with you.'

The driver's whip cracked and the carriage jolted forward. Conversation was constrained as everyone was deeply affected by the scale of the disaster and the gravity of the scene we were all going to encounter. Added to that was the distressing knowledge that the dead and injured were nearly all going to be women and girls, some no older than twelve.

We were numbed with shock by the scene of carnage that met us when we arrived. Limbs were scattered about and the acrid smell of sulphur and burnt flesh filled the air. There were terrible cries and moans and calls for help and people were poking through the collapsed outer wall of the building, heaving up pieces of rubble in an effort to find those whose agonized calls were coming from beneath them. A lighterman who had delivered his cargo to one of the docks downriver earlier in the day had moored his empty barge at the Arsenal dockside and injured women were being carried on board. Harvey went off to talk to the man.

'The lighter's going to take them to Greenwich,' he said when he came back. 'There's a fast rising tide and the journey should be smooth. Poor creatures. It's worse than dealing with soldiers, eh?'

A man was carrying a sack and wheeling a brandy barrel up to the docks. He set it down and took a load of tin mugs out of a bag. Soon they were being filled and taken to the injured, their moans beginning to mingle with the sound of coughing as the liquid was tipped into their mouths.

Harvey and I went up to a row of women and girls who had been laid out on the waterfront. They were lying as still as death and we started to sort out the dead from those that were alive but unconscious. Given the state of some of their injuries, I thought that those that were dead were fortunate. A surgeon was operating on a table that had been taken out of the wreckage of the armoury. Professor Gibson came up to us.

'Harvey, you go to work here. Mountford, help people on to the lighter and go to the hospital with them.'

I looked at the agony and bewilderment on the faces of the injured as I helped to carry them on to the barge. My heart bled for them. There were more than forty on board when the lighter began its journey upstream driven by the incoming tide, the lighterman maneuvering the boat through the currents of the river. The few nurses who had any nursing skills wrapped bandages round the injuries while I did the rounds, trying to assess their wounds so as to decide those who would need the most immediate attention on our arrival. They included a young woman whose stomach had been lacerated by large splinter of wood from one of the exploded barrels. The gash was nine inches long. The splinter was still in there and her entrails were coming out of the opening. She had lost a great deal of blood, her face was deathly pale and her eyes were half closed. Suddenly they opened wide. She lifted an arm and pointed a finger. I turned to see that she was pointing at a decrepit-looking ship at anchor looming over us. Its name was painted on the bough. *The Narcissus.*

'Please don't send me back there,' she whispered.

'You mean the hulk?

224

'It's a prison ship. I've been on it for three years.'

'And you get taken out to make cartridges?'

She nodded faintly. I stroked her forehead gently with my thumb as she looked at me. It was the trance-inducing technique I had used on Fanshawe and was the only comfort I could give her. A few moments later she stopped breathing and I felt her wrist, seeking her pulse. There was none.

'You won't have to go back there now,' I whispered and closed her eyes.

The tide carried the barge round the Isle of Dogs and soon after that the grand edifice of the Royal Naval Hospital at Greenwich came into view.

***

I was hard pressed to shut out the agonized cries as I concentrated on carrying out amputations and stitching wounds. I had no time to make use of mesmerism and I had to work at the fastest possible speed. In most cases an amputation took less than a minute.

The retired sailors for whom the hospital was home took the sight and sounds of the injured in their stride, having lived through the Napoleonic Wars, and those of them who were sufficiently able-bodied helped with fetching and carrying.

During one operation in which I had no assistants to help me I failed to tie a tourniquet sufficiently tightly on the upper arm of an unconscious woman whose lower arm I was about to remove and on the first incision, blood spurted from an artery in a spray that showered all those around her. A young surgeon ran to me and screwed the tourniquet down

225

tighter before continuing to assist me until I had completed the amputation and sutured the wound.

'To whom do I owe my thanks?' I asked.

'Palmer. Stephen Palmer.'

'Robert Mountford. Where do you work?'

'I'm based on *The Narcissus*.

'I saw it on our way here. A prison ship.

'A prison ship for women. Some of the prisoners were making cartridges at the arsenal when the explosion took place.'

'I attended one of them on the barge. She died before we arrived here.'

'Where do you practice?' Palmer asked.

'Barts.'

Harvey had come to the hospital on the next barge and he came up to us, seeking the company of fellow surgeons for a few moments before going back into the fray. After a brief introduction, Palmer turned to me.

'I think I've heard your name, Mr. Mountford. Are you the surgeon who uses mesmerism?'

'Yes.'

'Your reputation precedes you. My colleagues and I have been thinking about experimenting with it. You must tell us about your technique one day.'

At that point, two assistants called for Palmer's help and he went off with them. Harvey put a hand on my shoulder.

'Back to work, eh? No time for mesmerism here.'

Before turning away, he leaned towards me and said quietly, 'Have you heard there's rumoured to be a meeting of the Fellows of the College of Surgeons to discuss whether surgeons using mesmerism should be allowed to continue as members?'

I felt my heart thud.

'I hadn't, but I suppose it was bound to happen in the end.'

'Maybe you should lay off it for a bit.'

'No, I'll take my chances.'

'I thought you'd say that. You're a good man.'

***

After operating almost continuously all day with hardly a break, I returned to Calthorpe Street in a state of exhaustion, worrying what would happen at the College of Surgeons meeting, but when I climbed into bed my disquiet didn't stop me sleeping for twelve unbroken hours. When I awoke, I noticed that a letter had been slipped under my door.

Dear Robert,

Thank you for your letter. John hasn't come to see his mother and I am worried that you want to talk to me about him without giving me an indication as to what the matter is that concerns you. It must be news of him that you want to give me in person. His mother's condition remains unaltered. Her cousin, Emily, has been staying with us and she will be here for another week. That will allow me to come to London this coming Sunday, but it will be only for a short stay, I'm afraid. I am hoping, I'm sure unrealistically, that I may find John while I am there and I will be able to bring him back with me to Oxford. Foolish, I know. In any event, it will be good to see you again.

With warmest regards,
Sarah

***

What would have otherwise been a pleasurable anticipation of Sarah's visit on that Sunday was overshadowed by the distress I knew I was to cause her. When she arrived at Calthorpe Street, we greeted each other warmly, but briefly and Sarah sat down on the sofa, her face serious and her hands in her lap. She drew breath.

'So, Robert, tell me what news you have of John.'

Her eyes widened as I told her the whole story from the beginning with my assignment to spring Burrows and my discovery from the blind man at the Cross Keys that Fanshawe had tricked me. When I came to Fanshawe's account of the human sacrifices and the hideous voice that came out of his mouth, she was thunderstruck.

'What's been happening, Robert?'

I told her about my visit to Denley's bookshop.

'I think he's been drawn into something monstrous, Robert. We have to rescue him. We must get him out of this dreadful business. We can't leave him to flounder around in it all. We must go to Lincoln's Inn tomorrow.'

'Listen, Sarah. I think I'd prefer to go alone. It may well prove dangerous and I don't want to put you in harm's way. After all, we don't know who'll be there.'

'*You* listen, Robert. I love John, wastrel or not. I insist you take me with you.'

I was continuing to learn about Sarah's strength of mind.

'Very well. I'll pick you up at your lodgings at five o'clock after I've finished work at the hospital.'

We were silent for a while as I prepared some tea.

228

'You look very tired,' Sarah said. 'You need more sleep. This dreadful business about John must be telling on you. And all the strains of your work as well, I expect.'

'It's both.'

I hesitated and then told her about the massacre at the Woolwich arsenal. My hands were bunched up as I described what had happened and I stared at the wall before me as if the scene were painted upon it. When I'd finished, she came up to me and laid her hands on my clenched fists. I looked at her and my hands relaxed.

'What a terrible thing.'

We drank our tea in silence and Sarah stood up to leave.

'I'll see you tomorrow, Robert. The house number in Tavistock Square is 53. Now you must get some more sleep.'

Chapter Twenty Five

Fanshawe's house was shuttered when Sarah and I arrived, and no one answered my knock on the door. The basement door to the courtyard was open and the door of the tradesman's entrance was unlocked. Sarah followed me into the house and up to Fanshawe's bedchamber. A grunting sound came from inside the room.

I went in, holding my pistol and was shocked to see a fat man in Fanshawe's bed, wearing only his shirt, his buttocks sunk into the thighs of a plump girl who had pulled her dress up to her chin and was staring up at the canopy of the bed. Bottles and clothes were lying around on the floor as they had been before and the room still smelled of opium.

'What are you doing here?' I snapped. 'And where's John Fanshawe?'

'The room's taken,' the girl replied in a bored voice when she saw me, 'and I don't know no John Fanshawe.' The man rolled off her saying 'What the devil...?'

He looked at my pistol and started shaking as he climbed off the bed and tried to pull on his breeches.

'Give me my money first,' the girl called out to him, taking no notice of the gun. The man took some coins out of his pocket and threw them on to the bed. He tried to leave the room, his breeches half down and his coat and boots held to his chest, but Sarah blocked his path pointing her own gun at him. He backed into the room again, Sarah following.

'This is John Fanshawe's house,' she said, 'He's my brother and you're both trespassers.'

Sarah must have judged that being Fanshawe's sister gave her more authority than being his cousin.

'What's the problem?' the girl replied. 'We're not doing no harm. The owner, if that's your brother, left a couple of weeks ago and a friend of his said we could use the place. If you don't believe me you can ask him.'

The fat man chose his moment to run out.

'What friend?' I asked.

'He calls himself "Valmont." He's down in the cellar with his little blackamoor flunky. You'll find the cellar door underneath the stairs,' she added, tidying her hair and paying no further attention to me. I pocketed my pistol and took Sarah's arm.

'Come on, let's go and find him.'

The cellar door was open and candlelight came from below.

'I'm looking for Valmont,' I called down.

'In that case, you've found him, sir. Take care on the steps. They're rather steep.'

Sarah and I walked cautiously down into a cold, damp room with unrendered walls, wine racks stacked against one of them. In the middle of the room stood an oak table covered with valuables of all kinds, clocks, dishes, chargers, tureens, decanters, all sparkling in the light of a candle. A man of about forty years was standing behind the table, a large ormolu clock in front of him, his hair was frizzed up at the front and he was wearing a flamboyant but threadbare green silk coat with a high collar that looked as if it'd been pulled out of one of David Garrick's costume baskets. He bade us good day.

231

'Would you mind telling us what you're doing here?' I asked.

'I might ask the same of you, sir,' the man replied, moving from behind the clock to reveal a flint lock pistol in his hand which he aimed at each of us in turn until he noticed the guns in our hands. Sarah looked at him with gimlet eyes.

'Let me tell you, Mr. Valmont, I'm John Fanshawe's sister so you can put that gun away.

'Very pleased to meet you, Miss Fanshawe,' he replied, putting the gun on the table.

'We've been told that you're a friend of John's.'

'Indeed I am.'

'And we understand he invited you and your friends to make use of the place while he was away. Is that right?'

'Yes he did. Just a couple of friends and my servant.'

'When did he leave?' I asked.

'Two weeks ago.'

'Where did he go?

'I don't know. '

'How did you get into the house?'

'I've always come in through the tradesman's entrance. I have a key. I used to bring opium for him.'

'Oh, yes? How do we know you're not just a bunch of trespassers and thieves?' I retorted although I knew that the man might well have been telling the truth. Valmont put on an actorly expression of shock.

'I may not be able to speak for everybody here but I can assure you I'm not.'

'When did you last see my brother?' Sarah asked.

'As I've told you, about two weeks ago. He left with two shuddersome gentlemen who used to come here from time to time. He didn't want them to see me when I was here.'

I looked at the valuables on the table.

'Why are all these down here?'

'Ah...well...right. Since I've been here, the matter's got a bit out of hand. Friends of friends, you know, if you see what I mean, all very proper, I can assure you, but to be on the safe side I've been locking up the valuables down here.'

There were footsteps on the staircase and I looked up to see a dark-skinned boy, about sixteen years old, coming down the stairs, holding two crystal decanters to his chest. He was dressed as a footman and wearing a wig. His colourful outfit looked as threadbare as his master's.

'Christophe, my one and only servant in the entire world,' Valmont announced as the boy put the decanters on the table. He stroked the boy's cheek and handed him a silver salt cellar.

'Please take this to Mr. Westcott, Christophe. It should fetch five shillings, and buy some food; bread, cheese, chicken. You know what I like. Oh...and some wine.'

'Yes, sir.' The boy bowed to the three of us and climbed back up the stairs. Valmont looked at me with a pitiful expression.

'Isn't he beautiful? And he's very reliable. I found him in Paris. Unfortunately, my circumstances are somewhat straitened at the moment so I've had to hock the odd small item in order to survive. Of course I'll make sure they're all retrieved when Mr. Fanshawe comes back.'

'D'you think my brother will be happy about that?' Sarah asked.

'I can't think why not. He's always been very generous to me.'

He wrapped his arms around himself.

'Would you mind if we continued our conversation upstairs? I'm a little cold.'

I nodded my agreement and we climbed the steps out of the cellar and made our way to the drawing room where Valmont turned to Sarah.

'I think I can satisfy you as to my honesty in claiming a friendship with your brother, Miss Fanshawe.'

He looked at me.

'The cellar's so dark with only one candle to light it. I thought I recognised you, Mr. Mountford and I thought I remembered your name, but I wanted the chance of seeing you in daylight to be sure. D'you know, we've met before? It was at Sir Ralph's last celebration. Fanshawe brought you. He told me about the mesmerism demonstration you'd been to. Of course you won't recognise me. I was dressed as a bishop, an archbishop in fact.'

I blanched as the memory came back to me.

'I was dancing with Adam. What a sweet boy and what a tragedy that evening was to lead to.'

'What tragedy?'

'Did your friend tell not you about Sir Ralph's celebrations at Shadbrough House?' Valmont asked Sarah.

She didn't answer.

'It was very unfortunate. 'While your friend was there, Adam approached him in a friendly way. He most probably just wanted to dance with him. Anyway, your friend took offence for some reason and he hit him. Adam fell down and knocked his head against the pedestal of a stone statue and was knocked unconscious for a while. He kept on getting headaches after that and he died suddenly a month ago while swimming in Sir Ralph's lake. Sir Ralph is convinced it was due to a brain tumor caused by the fall.'

I stared at Valmont, the blood drained from my face, unable to take in what I had heard. I began to feel giddy. Had his death been brought about by the fall? Could I be accused of murder? I was devastated by the thought. Valmont was looking solemnly down at the floor, his hands cupped together over his chest like a parson listening to a recently bereaved parishioner. Sarah was counting some coins from her purse.

'If my brother comes back, will you kindly get your boy to bring me a note to let me know? I'm staying at 53 Tavistock Square. Do you think you could remember that?' She handed him the coins and looked at me.

'Please let's go, Robert. I don't want to be here anymore.'

We were both silent when we left the house and looked for a cab, my knowing that Sarah must be wondering what sort of a man I was, going to one of Ashton's hellfire parties and consorting with corrupted boys and pederasts like Valmont. I felt terrible about what had happened and was haunted by the thought that Valmont might be spreading a rumour that I had attacked the boy who had simply approached me in a perfectly friendly way. I hailed a cab and looked at Sarah when we had climbed on board.

'May I explain what happened that night?'

'Not now, Robert, please.'

'Very well.'

I eventually broke a long silence.

'I promised I would call on a patient in Russell Square this afternoon. Would you mind if we were to go there and you take the cab on to Tavistock Square?'

'Of course not,' Sarah answered coolly and I instructed the cabbie.

'I attended an operation on the woman and the wound's become infected,' I continued, endeavouring to push out of mind the picture of the boy lying on the ground amidst the scattered feathers of his wings and the thought of Sarah knowing that I had been to such a gathering. What she would think if she were to know about Lavender?

'I want to know how she's faring. Her husband, George Villiers, knew John when he lived in Oxford. You may have met him, although you would have been no more than twelve years old I suppose.'

Sarah didn't respond and there was another long silence.

'May I tell you what actually happened at Shadborough House?' I asked again. 'I'd be most grateful if you would after what Valmont told you.'

Sarah looked at the passing traffic.

'Please tell me some other time, if you don't mind, Robert.'

'Very well.'

Neither of us spoke further until the cab pulled up at Villiers's house. Sarah turned to me, a determined expression on her face.

'I want to go to the house in Rotherhithe, Robert, and please don't tell me it may be dangerous.'

'If you insist.' I had learned to accept her determination.

'Could we go tomorrow?'

'It would have to be at the end of the day. I'll be working until five o'clock for the next week. It'll be dusk by the time we get there. Not an ideal time to be somewhere like that.'

'All the better to see if there are candles alight in the house.'

'I suppose so.'

'That's settled then. I'll wait for you at the hospital entrance at five o'clock. You'll have your pistols with you?'

'Yes.'

'I'll have mine,' she said.

Her expression softened.

'Listen, I've been thinking. Wouldn't it be safer in Rotherhithe if we were to wear clothes that don't stand out? There's an old clothes market in Gordon Street near my lodging. I think I can guess what would fit you.'

Her forwardness made her blush.

'Thank you. Sarah. You're very resourceful.'

'Forgive me for asking, but are your finances sufficient to cope with all this traveling around?'

'Just about. It's ironic that it's John's money that's enabling me to find out what's happened to him.'

'That's the best use it can be put to.'

We parted, Sarah taking the cab on to Tavistock Square. I stood in the street feeling like a murderer. Might the boy's death have had another cause? Even if it had, would my friendship with Sarah survive all this? I knocked on Villiers's door.

Mrs. Harvey, the housekeeper answered.

'Caroline has taken a turn for the worse, Mr. Mountford, and Dr. Villiers is at his club. I've sent an errand boy to call at the club and to get him to fetch Professor Campbell.'

237

She took me up to Caroline's bedchamber which was pervaded by the smell of infection, masked a little by quantities of eau de cologne. Janet, Caroline's lady's maid, was bending over her, the bedclothes drawn down.

'How long has she been in this state?' I asked Janet quietly.

'For most of the day, sir. The wound's been weeping and I've tried to clean it up from time to time.'

'I see.'

'Janet, come with me and allow Mr. Mountford to examine Mrs. Villiers,' Mrs. Harvey ordered and the two of them left the room. Caroline was staring up at the ceiling, her face white and her eyes half-closed and unfocused.

The stitched surgical incision in her breast was inflamed and pus was oozing out of it.

'Hello, Robert,' she whispered.

'Hello, Caroline. How are you feeling?'

'Not well. I feel hot and nauseous and the wound hurts.'

'Professor Campbell will be here soon.'

I put my palm on her forehead. She had a fever.

'Before you go, Robert, tell me what's happening to John. I keep having dreams about him. Is he alright?'

'I'm afraid I still haven't seen him. If I have any news of him I'll let you know, I promise.'

I hated lying but she wasn't well enough for me to tell her what I had found out. There was a knock on the door and Professor Campbell came in followed by Villiers. I took Caroline's hand.

'The professor's here now. I'll come and see you again soon.'

Chapter Twenty Six

The afternoon sun was low in the sky on the following day when I came out of the hospital and looked around for Sarah, still preoccupied by Adam's death and the opinion I imagined Sarah had of me. A scruffy youth in a fustian jacket and mole-skin trousers came up to me, his dirty face was half covered by a brimmed cloth cap pulled down over his ears. He was carrying a large carpet bag in one hand and a lantern in the other. It wasn't until he was quite close that I realised who it was.

'Sarah. What an amazing disguise.

'Thank you.'

I was becoming used to Sarah's self-confidence but I was still taken aback to see her dressed in the clothes of a ragamuffin. She handed me the carpet bag.

'It's your turn now.'

I changed my clothes in a washroom and came back wearing a cloth hat, a shabby black overcoat with pewter buttons, the shoulders spotted with dandruff, and a grey waistcoat and trousers. I pulled a face as I breathed in the odour of them and Sarah restrained a smile as she looked at me.

'Did you bring a pistol?' she asked.

'I did. And a truncheon and a couple of spare candles.'

I tapped the pockets of my overcoat and Sarah opened her jacket. Her gun was stuck into the belt of her trousers. All in all, she was an impressive sight and I nodded my approval. We hailed a cab.

'The Angel Inn, Bermondsey,' I called up to the driver and delivered a carefully prepared speech, playing the part of a thief-taker so the driver would know that, despite my appearance, I had the money to pay the fare. 'I'm doing some business for the Bow Street Magistrates Court, establishing the whereabouts of a felon. I have his son with me. I'd like you to wait at the inn for an hour while I make my enquiries. That alright with you? You'll be well paid.'

'I'll not get a fare from there if you bugger off and I don't like hanging around there. It more than my life's worth.'

'How much is that? Three sovereigns each way, the first three paid when we arrive?'

'I have to keep a loaded pistol by my side, these days, you know. There's more villains in Rotherhithe than anywhere else in London.'

'I don't blame you. I have one in my coat. So do you agree the fare?'

'Three sovereigns now, four for the return and I won't wait longer than an hour.'

'Very well.'

Sarah and I sat in silence for most of the journey. In the end, I felt compelled to bring up the conversation of the previous evening.

'Sarah, I have to tell you why that boy was hurt.'

'Very well,' she agreed, looking out at the street as I gave my account of what happened, ending with the boy falling as he backed away from me and hit his head against the pedestal of the statue. Sarah turned to me, her expression cool.

'I think you could regard it as an accident, Robert. You did demean yourself going to that debauched revelry but John is a very seductive man and I can well imagine how he could persuade you.'

I winced inwardly on hearing the words.

'I'm sure many men are attracted by the idea but don't have the opportunity to find out what it's like. Well, you found out. I'm sorry about the boy but nothing can be done about that.'

I was amazed by her matter-of-factness.

'Can we still be friends?'

'Yes.' We looked at one another and her voice was softer.

'Our friendship isn't based on any of that. You are being a sterling friend to John and me in trying to find him. That's what counts.'

I was overcome with relief.

'Thank you Sarah.'

***

When we arrived at the inn, I got a light for the lantern in the taproom, relieved not to see the pigtailed sailor in there, and we set off for Albion House. As before, we kept to the waterfront as much as possible so that I could see around me and I held my truncheon and pistol on open display. The light was fading by the time we turned into Swan Road and entered the rabbit warren of narrow alleyways. Sarah held the lantern up high and we trod carefully to avoid tripping over vagrants slumped against the walls, or barefoot children playing outside their doorways.

When we reached the house, the shutters were closed and no light came from behind them. I led the way up the steps to the front door and banged the knocker with all my might,

241

my anger about what was going on giving me strength and courage.

'I'm looking for John Fanshawe,' I shouted. 'Are you there, Fanshawe? Whoever's there, open the door.'

I knocked again and we waited for any sound of life. There was none. I led Sarah round to the back of the house and banged on the shutters with the club.

'Are you there, Fanshawe?'

Sarah touched my arm as a tapping sound came from above them.

'Did you hear that?'

'Hear what?'

'Listen.'

We looked up. It turned out to be the branch of a tree, swaying slightly in a gust of wind and knocking against the shutters of an upstairs window.

'Well, that's that,' I concluded. 'There's nothing we can do except wait. Perhaps John's captors are lying low until they think we've gone.'

'But we didn't see any light in the house before you knocked on the door.'

'I know.'

We returned to the front of the house and I noticed a small object on one of the steps. I picked it up and called Sarah to bring over the lantern. It was a little book in a calf binding, similar to the one in Fanshawe's room. I opened it, noticing that the first few pages were stuck together with what appeared to be dried blood. It was the same book.

'I found this book on the floor of John's bedchamber. When he saw me holding it he became wildly agitated and told me to drop it. He said I shouldn't have touched it. It's a book of ancient Egyptian spells that belonged to his father.'

I held out the book to Sarah who backed away, not wanting to touch it herself.

'Dear God,' she said. 'Something terrible has been happening here. Leave the book where you found it, Robert, please.'

I put it back on the step, surprised by Sarah's apparent acceptance that it might have some supernatural power. I took the lantern and walked around, looking for any other clues as to what was going on there. I picked up a tarpaulin lying on the ground some yards from the side of the house. Underneath it was a circular grating about a foot and a half in diameter, set into a flagstone. I knelt down and held the lantern above the grating, moving it around, trying without success to see if it would illuminate whatever was beneath it. Sarah knelt down next to me. I lowered my head over the grating and called out, 'Fanshawe?' The sound echoed.

I crumpled some dried leaves into a ball and set fire to it with the candle from the lantern. Then I pushed it through the grating and we watched it land on a large, brightly coloured object. For the few moments that the flame flickered before it died, we saw that it was an Egyptian anthropomorphic coffin. We sat up and stared at each other.

'John's father,' Sarah said. 'Robert, I have to admit I'm finding all this very disturbing.'

'That's understandable,' I said soothingly and touching her arm, not wanting to admit to my own unease.

'Anyway, there's nothing more we can do here. Let's go back to the Angel.'

When we had reached the alleys, we stayed close to one another, Sarah carrying the lantern and each holding our pistols in front of us. Although I had made the journey twice before, the alleys looked so similar that I became unsure of one of the turnings. A minute later, we came to a wooden bridge over an open sewer.

'I'm sorry, Sarah, I've made a wrong turning. We'll have to go back.'

That was when Sarah stumbled and fell. The lantern fell on its side and the candle went out.

'Oh, God. I'm sorry, Robert.'

It was a dark night and neither of us could make out more than dim shadows. I tried to locate Sarah from the sound of her voice.

'Speak again, Sarah, I'm trying to find you.'

'I'm here. I'm here.'

I held out my hands and our fingers met. Sarah fumbled about on the ground and picked up the lantern.

'Stupid of me,' I said. I meant to bring a tinder box and I forgot.'

'Don't blame yourself. I'm the lamp carrier and I should have thought of it.'

I took her hand and we walked back along the alley, making out the way ahead by a pool of light some fifty yards ahead of us. When we reached it, we saw that it was coming from a tallow candle on the sill of an open upstairs window. Moments later, the candle was gone.

'Can you help us?' I called up. Our lantern's blown out.'

The light returned and a thin, dark figure appeared, holding the candle out of the window.

'Who's down there?' a gruff male voice asked.

'Me and my son.'

The man looked down at us.

'I don't like the look of either of you. Especially him.'

He pointed at me but directed his remark to Sarah.

'What you going to give me for it?'

'I'll give you a tanner.' Sarah tried to sound like a street-seller.

'Tanner's not much. It'll be a long way home in the dark.'

'A shilling then,' I said irritably.

The man kept looking at Sarah.

'You come up here without him, sonny and give me a shilling and I'll light your lantern. I don't want him up here. Too many thieves round these parts. The door's down the side alley.'

'You're not going up there,' I said forcibly, but Sarah was already walking away from me.

'Where are you for God's sake?' I shouted.

'Don't worry, Pa,' Sarah called out to me, keeping her voice in the low register.

'Let me in,' she called up to the man.

I stood in the darkness telling myself that she had made a terrible mistake. When half a minute had passed I heard her scream.

'Sarah!' I bellowed, no longer thinking about identifying her sex. I felt my way along the front of the house and turned the corner, running my hands along the alley wall until I found a paneled door. As I turned the door handle, I heard Sarah scream again. The door was locked.

'Sarah, I'm coming,' I roared and started throwing myself against the door until the rotten wood around the lock gave way and I found myself in a long narrow passage, candlelight coming from an open doorway some yards ahead. I heard the report of a discharged pistol.

'Sarah,' I shouted again, running to the doorway and into a small room smelling of gunpowder. A candle stood on a tea chest next to a straw mattress and a pile of clothes and blankets. It took me a few moments to realise that one of the piles of clothes was Sarah, lying face down. The lantern was on its side next to her.

'Oh, my God,' I muttered, kneeling down and gently lifting her on to her back. Her eyes were closed and her face looked as white as marble in the candlelight. Her hat had come off, and her hair was spread around on the straw of the mattress. She was holding her pistol. I lifted it out of her hand, smelling the discharge from it and felt her pulse. She was alive.

'Robert,' she mumbled and opened her eyes. 'I must have fainted. He ran off when I fired at him. I don't think I hit him.'

'Are you hurt?'

'Just bruised. You can guess what happened.'

'He assaulted you.'

'He tried to but he didn't get very far. My hat got caught on a hook in the corridor. When it came off, he saw my hair and realised I wasn't a boy.'

She tried to sit up but I eased her down again and put my hand on her forehead.

'You should lie a little longer until the blood's got back to your head.'

As I pocketed the pistol, I heard a woman shouting from down the corridor and turned to see a two year-old baby tottering into the room carrying something in its hand.

'Where've you gone, you little bleeder?' the woman shouted.

The baby grinned at me and held out a little hard lump of faeces as the woman appeared in the doorway. She swept the child up and looked at me.

'What's been going on,' she asked, sniffing the air. 'Where's Bert? You shot him? Fuckin' good thing if you have.'

She sniffed the air again and stalked off down the passageway, throwing the child over her shoulder and holding it by its feet. Sarah sat up.

'I think I'm feeling better now, Robert.'

'I helped her to her feet, feeling her body trembling.

'Robert?'

'Yes?'

'I'm sorry. It was stupid of me.'

I lit the lantern and put my arm round her to steady her as we walked slowly along the passage. Sarah saw her hat on the floor and put it on. Then we made our way out into the alley.

When we reached the Angel Inn, I told the cab driver that the felon had moved on so I wasn't able to bring him to court. I looked at Sarah as the cab set off.

'Wasn't I right, not wanting to take you to that dreadful place?'

'No you weren't. I'm going to be with you when we find John.'

A mist had settled on the river when we crossed London Bridge and Sarah stared out at the ghostly forest of masts and rigging and the halos of light from the gas lamps.

'What can we do to save him, Robert?'

247

'First we have to find him. You remember me telling you about Tom Abbott, the blind man at The Cross Keys. I gave him a guinea to keep his ears open for me. I'm going to pay him a visit tomorrow after I've finished work. Do you want to come with me?'

'Of course I do,' she answered with defiance.

***

'I like the sound of your voice, girlie,' Tom Abbott said, as Sarah asked him about her cousin. He was about to start on a plate of pork pie and potatoes.

'I want to help you if I can, but I need to eat first so I'll be able to remember clearly.'

I had ordered the supper and a bottle of brandy in a private room upstairs in The Cross Keys. That was the deal agreed in the tap room when Abbott told me he had some news to impart. Sarah and I sat waiting for him to finish, filling his glass from time to time.

'The truth is I can't tell you where your cousin is, my dear,' he said at length and broke off for a loud belch. 'However, I've heard his name come up in conversation between this Gilchrist man and Fawcett, the turnkey. He's definitely part of it all, whatever it is they're up to and I know who the next one is they're going to spring. A woman called Rosie Carswell. She was in Newgate and going to hang but her sentence got commuted to transportation and she's been put on a hulk at Woolwich while they're waiting for the next ship to go to Australia. Fawcett'll get her off the hulk next Wednesday when a turnkey called Jenkins is going to be on duty.'

'Which hulk is she on?' I asked.

248

'*The Narcissus*, if I rightly recall.'

'I know it,' I said. 'I treated a woman from it after the explosion at the arsenal.'

'You a medical man?'

'I'm a surgeon at Barts hospital.'

'What was she convicted of?' Sarah asked.

'Some toff tried to pick her up, thinkin' she was a judy. She kicked him into the road. He fell under the wheels of a growler and she got done for murder. And the funny thing was, just like before, Gilchrist had to be sure when the murder'd been done. Had to be a particular month again.'

I thought about the months in the ancient Egyptian calendar that Fanshawe had mentioned.

'Did they say what was going to happen to her?' Sarah asked.

'They talked about it but I didn't understand what they were on about. Anyway, this Fanshawe fella's part of it.'

'Did they say anything about her being killed?'

'Nothin' I could hear, but I couldn't hear everything, what with the noise in the taproom. Sounds like she's in a bit of trouble.'

'You don't have any clue as to where Fanshawe might be from what these men said?' I asked.

'Afraid not.'

He reached across the table and found Sarah's hand.

'Nice soft skin you've got, girlie. I hope I've been some help. I'll keep my ears open for you.'

'Thank you.'

I pressed a coin into Abbott's palm.

'There's another guinea for your trouble, Tom, and do keep an ear cocked.'

'No question of it, sir.'

Abbott picked up the brandy bottle with one hand and skillfully lifted his glass towards its neck with the other.

'Do you want some help getting back down to the taproom,' Sarah asked.

'Don't worry, girlie, I know my way around here pretty well.'

***

'What are we going to do?' Sarah asked as we sat in a cab headed for Tavistock Square. I can't believe John's capable of getting involved with such a thing.'

'Perhaps he's not but his father could be.'

'Do you believe the voice that came out of him was his father's?'

'I'm a materialist and I don't believe in the supernatural.'

'You mean ghosts and spirits? The spirit of John's father, for instance?'

I didn't know what to say.

'You're not sure of your rationalism are you?'

'I don't know how to answer you, Sarah. All I can say is I was terrified when I heard that voice coming out of John's mouth.'

'I was terrified just from you telling me about it.'

We sat in silence waiting to see who would bring up the inevitable dilemma of what to do about Rosie Carswell. Sarah spoke first.

'What day is it today, Robert?'

'Thursday.'

'Did Tom say they're going to get the woman off the ship next Wednesday?'

'Yes, they did.'

'Should we try to save her? You managed to spring Burrows from Newgate.'

'I don't know if I'm up to doing anything like that again. I could have ended up in prison. Anyway, there's no one to set it up as Fawcett did in Newgate and…'

'And what?'

'If we did, I suppose they'd just find somebody else.'

As soon as I had said it, I wished I hadn't.

'Is that a reason for not trying to save her?'

'No, it's not.'

'And remember, it's not as if she's going to be hanged like the first two victims. Who knows? Maybe she could make a good life for herself in Australia.'

I looked out of the cab window. It had started raining.

'There's another thing,' I said. 'It was the surgeon from the *Narcissus* who helped me out at the Naval Hospital after the Woolwich explosion. If he recognised me and these murderers found out that it was me who'd messed up their plans, I'd be done for. I'm not sure if I have the courage to take that risk.'

'I know how you feel, Robert, and you *are* brave, whether or not it's sensible to take that risk. It's just that we're in a dilemma, aren't we? Maybe it would be possible to find a way to save a woman from being murdered and we have to decide whether or not we're going to do anything about it. What you are thinking?' she added after a pause.

'If we were to try and save her, I'm trying to think how we would do it.'

Chapter Twenty Seven

It was dark along the waterfront at Woolwich when Sarah and I climbed into the cab that was to take us to the *Narcissus*. The shops full of jumble and cheap household goods were shut and the business of the night had come into play. Pools of light from the windows of public houses and brothels illuminated the tired faces of the prostitutes waiting in the street and the wizened faces of the sailors, dock workers and watermen passing by, looking for a good time or oblivion.

Further along the waterfront stood the wall that surrounded the Royal Arsenal's armaments factories, churning out their ordnance night and day. The orange glow of smelting iron was under lit by the smoke from its factory chimneys. After the cab had passed the Arsenal, my eyes had to adjust to the darkness before I could make out the dockyard ahead of us and the shadowy bulk of the *Narcissus*, a seventy-four gun ship-of-the-line that had last seen active service forty years earlier. In the distance behind it lay the flat expanse of the Essex marshes. The ship was moored with her bow facing towards London, her gun ports battened down with wooden planks. A guard armed with a musket stood next to a gangway leading to an iron barred gate under the ship's forecastle.

I had needed to screw up my courage to the sticking point to undertake this rescue. Sarah's appeal to my conscience had persuaded me that it was the right thing to do and her presence next to me helped to bolster my confidence. In my pocket was a letter purporting to be from Mr. Trimble, the

Newgate Governor, addressed to Mr. Dobson, the Governor of the *Narcissus*. Sarah had talked to a clerk in the Magistrate's Court to find out their names and I had bought a pair of handcuffs at a gun shop in Holborn. I was wearing the clothes I had worn when I had taken Sarah to Albion House and the handcuffs hung at my side, attached to a chain. As the cab drew up, Sarah produced a bottle of linseed oil from under her cloak, poured a little of it into her hand and spread it over my face.

'Good luck,' she whispered and I climbed down from the cab, suffused with a terrible rush of nerves. I approached the guard, saying I had an urgent message for the governor, and was led along the gangway to the iron-grilled gate. I said the same thing to a warder who let me on board and led me into the Governor's quarters at the stern of the ship. I removed my hat and looked at the very portly figure of Dobson who was slumped in an armchair in a comfortably furnished saloon. He and his deputy were drinking port.

'Excuse me, sir. I'm employed by Mr. Trimble, the Governor of Newgate, and he's instructed me to give you this letter for your urgent attention.'

I handed the letter to Dobson and began coughing.

'Forgive me,' I muttered between coughs, putting a handkerchief to my mouth to stifle the noise. The handkerchief was spotted with blood that Sarah had splashed on to it at a meat stall. Although coughing up blood was not an early symptom of smallpox, I had guessed that Dobson wouldn't know that and, combined with my face seeming to be in a heavy sweat, which was an early symptom, I hoped that the governor would want to get rid of me as soon as possible.

253

'Rosie Carswell.' Dobson turned to his deputy. 'What's her number?' The deputy took a sheet of paper from a drawer in a roll top desk.

'497.'

Dobson handed him the letter and looked at me with an expression of distaste as he prised himself out of his chair and opened the door.

'Come here, Morgan,' he called out and a warder appeared in the doorway.

'Yessir.'

'Apparently 497 may be infected with smallpox. There's been an outbreak in Newgate and she's to be taken to a hospital ship.'

He pointed to me.

'This man's going to take her there.'

'Very good, sir.'

Dobson made shooing gestures at me with his hands.

'You go with him Mr. whatever your name is.'

'Harris, sir.'

'Harris. Right. Off you go.'

I followed the warder along the deck and down a hatchway. On the deck below I found myself in a corridor running the full length of the ship, lit by tallow candles in tin holders and bounded on either side by iron bars from roof to deck like those in a zoo. Behind them, the prisoners lay in their hammocks slung in long rows. There must have over seventy of them on each side, packed tight, some noisily asleep, others holding murmured conversations with those next to them or mumbling to themselves. Several of them had bandaged heads, victims of the Woolwich explosion. The smell and the heat coming from unwashed bodies mixed with that of the latrines was suffocating. We passed a turnkey dozing at the end of the corridor and the warder pointed down to another hatchway.

'497's on the bottom deck. It's for newcomers and the ones intended for transportation.'

I was led down to the next deck, identically laid out, and down again to the cold bottom deck where the mixture of smells was added to by damp seeping through the rotting timbers of the hull.

'497,' the warder called to the turnkey who unlocked an iron-barred gate and led us along the cage until we reached a hammock that seemed to be empty apart from a blanket lying inside it. When the warder pulled the blanket away, I was shocked to see a skinny girl of no more than eleven years lying asleep, her arms wrapped round her against the cold. I was shaken to come across so young a girl in such a dreadful place and it was with difficulty that I managed to show no surprise that she wasn't a grown woman. I tapped the girl's shoulder.

'You Rosie Carswell?' I asked, displaying no interest in her. She opened her eyes.

'Yes, sir.'

'Get up.' She climbed out of the hammock and stood on the floor, wobbly from sleep.

'You're going to a hospital ship, Carswell. Has she got a coat?' I asked the turnkey who picked one up from under the hammock and handed it to the girl.

'Why am I going there?' the girl asked sleepily.

'Never mind about that. Put your coat on.'

I unfastened the handcuffs from my belt, worrying that they might not have a setting tight enough for her slender wrists. I cuffed the girl's hands in front of her using the tightest ratchets and held on to the chain as I led her out of the cage and up the two hatchways to the top deck. As we approached the door to the saloon, I decided to start coughing again, this time quite violently. I held my handkerchief to my face and between coughs I asked the warder if the governor wanted me to sign anything. The warder knocked on the saloon door and went in as I resumed my coughing. The warder returned within seconds.

'No, he doesn't. Just get the girl out of here.'

The plan had gone well until I reached the entrance gate to the ship. Despite the gloom, I recognised Stephen Palmer, the ship's surgeon standing on the gangway, waiting to be let on board. He must have wanted to check on the women injured in the explosion. I started coughing again and put my handkerchief to my mouth but not before Palmer had seen my face in the light of a candle in a tin holder nailed to a beam next to the gate.

'What's the problem with the girl,' Palmer asked.

I pointed to the warder who answered the question as I continued coughing.

'She may have been infected with smallpox when she was in Newgate. There's been an outbreak in one of the women's wards and they're all being taken to a hospital ship.'

'Which one?'

'I dunno. Ask him.'

He pointed to me. I held the handkerchief to my mouth as I spoke.

'*The Hestia.*'

'Wasn't that abandoned years ago?'

I had rehearsed my answer.

'It was, but they can't find anywhere else to keep the women in isolation.'

'The poor creatures.'

Palmer stood to one side and the warder opened the gate to allow us out. Could he have recognised me I wondered as we crossed over to the jetty? Surely not. How could he imagine a surgeon having turned into a prison warder? Nevertheless…

Sarah was clearly disconcerted to see the child as we approached the cab but said nothing as we climbed in. I sat Rosie in the middle next to Sarah and squeezed in beside her.

'That surgeon, Palmer, was on the gangway,' I murmured. 'I hope he didn't recognise me.'

'How could he with those old clothes on?'

'Am I goin' to die of the pox?' Rosie asked.

'No, you won't because you're not infected.'

Then why're you takin' me to the 'ospital ship?

'We're not. We had to make up a story to get you off the *Narcissus*.'

'Why?'

'I can't tell you.'

'Why're you lookin' so ill coughin' and that? You got the pox?'

'No, I was just pretending.'

'Pretendin'?'

She screwed up her face into a grimace of disbelief.

'You a lunatic?'

'No.'

'Who are you?'

Sarah and I had decided not to spell out the reason she was in danger and to stick to fictional names in case Rosie was recaptured.'

'The name's Dick Harris and this is my sister, Nellie.'

'And you're the governor's clerk at Newgate?' Rosie asked.

'Not exactly.'

'And you're not goin' to tell me the reason for all this business?'

'You don't need to know.'

'I don't geddit. You're not goin' to make me a slave, are you?

'No, we're not. You're going to stay at Nellie's lodgings for the time being. Tell me, are your parents still alive?'

'No.'

'I'm sorry. Where've you been living?'

With me nan in Houndsditch.'

'Have you got any brothers or sisters?'

'No.' She lifted up her manacled hands.

'Hey, d'you mind takin' these things off of me.'

'I will, but I don't want you to run away. You need to stick with us for the time being at least.'

I took off the handcuffs and Rosie sucked at the contusions around her wrists.

'I'm sorry we had to do that.'

'Oh yeah? There's men who like doin' that sort a thing and, anyway, how do I know you two don't want to do me in?'

'I guess you'll have to trust us.'

'I've learned not to trust anybody.'

She looked at Sarah.

'What kind of place you live in?'

'It's only small. A bedchamber and a parlour. We'll be there in a minute. You were lucky not to have been at the arsenal when the explosion happened.'

'I was going to be on the next shift.'

The cab became stuck in traffic in Limehouse and I looked out through the window at a fight going on outside a public house. A pistol shot rang out and Sarah looked out to see what was happening. In that moment, Rosie was out of the door on the other side of the cab. I jumped out and ran through the throng of people making their way through the stationary traffic. My head was spinning as I looked this way and that in a desperate attempt to find the girl, but it was no good. She had gone and I wouldn't find her.

When I rejoined Sarah in the cab we talked about what might happen to her. Would she be able to look after herself? It seemed she had done so up to the time she had been taken into custody. Perhaps a magistrate would try to get a thief-taker to look for her but who would be interested in looking for an eleven-year-old girl amongst thousands in the metropolis and would the magistrate care? At least, we tried to reassure ourselves, she was out of the clutches of Josiah Fanshawe's murderous followers.

Chapter Twenty Eight

I answered Maggie's knock on my door at six o'clock the next morning and she handed me a letter.

'This came this morning, sir. Also, sir, Miss Fanshawe is at the door asking after you.'

She must have been worrying about Rosie Carswell just as I was.

'Show her up, please, Maggie.'

Sarah came into the room out of breath and pink in the face.

'I'm sorry to be coming so early, Robert, but I wanted to catch you before you left for work. There was a letter from my aunt's sister when I got back to Tavistock Square. My aunt has had a severe attack of croup and her sister says she seems determined that she's close to death. She now keeps asking after John and me, wanting to see us before she dies. She doesn't like being looked after by her sister and it may be her way of obligating me to come back. Nevertheless, I feel I must see her. I'm so sorry about this, Robert. I expect you've been thinking about Rosie Carswell. I have too. I hate leaving this business about John to you, but it'll just be for a few days if her condition's stable. You do understand, don't you?'

'Of course I do,' I replied stoutly but feeling deeply disappointed not to have her around to share the burden of finding her cousin and rescuing him.

'I'll come back as soon as I can.'

When she left, I opened the letter.

Dear Mr. Mountford,

I don't know if this will help you at all but yesterday evening, I met an old friend, a Russian scholar called Victor Abramov who had recently come back from Egypt. He was one of the savants who accompanied Napoleon on his Egyptian campaign. He is fluent in the Coptic language and his mind is a repository of esoteric knowledge. When I asked him if he knew anything about the Temple of Apep, he said he had come across a French Egyptologist called Giradot who was travelling with him in Napoleon's cortege. Giradot had visited the temple and had heard stories of a man called Sobek who was one of the priests there. Abramov would like to meet you. Would you be able to come to the coffee house opposite the shop at six o'clock tomorrow?

Yours sincerely,
John Denley

***

Victor Abramov was a large man in his sixties with lively brown eyes under bushy eyebrows, a full head of grey, grizzled hair and a beard to match. While I was greeting Denley, Abramov was sitting at the table, taking small fingers of finely cut pipe tobacco from a leather pouch and putting them carefully on a small square of thin yellow paper. He rolled the paper up and looked up at me as he licked the length of it to make a tube. He lit it from a candle on the table and started puffing. It was an activity I had never seen before.

'I can't think clearly without my cigaritos,' the man said, holding out his hand in greeting.

'Victor Abramov, sir, and you're Robert Mountford with a tale from the Temple of Apep, I believe.'

'I am indeed.'

'Tell me about it.'

Abramov puffed away as I told the whole story from its beginning. I finished with a description of Devereux's use of mesmerism to unlock a subject's hidden thoughts and my own use of the technique to try to find out what had been happening to my friend. I then told him what Fanshawe had said in his trance state and the horrifying voice that came out of him.

Abramov stared intently at me as if he might learn more from looking at me. I asked him about Sobek, the magician that Denley had mentioned in his letter.

'Could Josiah Fanshawe and Sobek be one and the same?'

'They could. Giradot had heard a number of stories about him. He claimed to be the seventh incarnation of a magician who had lived in ancient Egypt where he had founded a temple built in the far south of Upper Egypt dedicated to the worship of the demon, serpent, Apep. They kept the object of their worship secret. There were no statues outside the temple and there were no hieroglyphs on the outer walls. Those who built it and adorned it inside with hieroglyphs, statues and wall paintings were sworn to secrecy. The most important among them became priests of the temple and the others were slaughtered. The temple was half buried under sand when Napoleon's expedition and his savants found it. The man who claimed to be the seventh incarnation of the magician was rumoured to have been an Englishman who went to France sometime during the Revolution. When he returned, he raped one of the priestesses in the temple who subsequently gave birth to a deaf daughter called Shukura. The assault was witnessed by an English aristocrat called Ashton and Sobek murdered him.'

Ashton's father, I told myself. I was chilled by the thought.

'Apparently, shortly after the girl was born, Sobek left the temple with another Englishman. Nobody there knew where he had gone.'

'What about the voice coming out of Fanshawe? D'you think he could be possessed?'

'You mean, demonically possessed?' Abramov asked.

'I don't know. I'm a materialist and I'm swimming in strange waters using such terms.'

'That may be so but it is most important that you try to make yourself allow for the possibility of a supernatural element in all this, the reason being that if Sobek is John Fanshawe's father, I believe your friend was fathered by a monstrous creature who will continue to bring evil into the world in each of his incarnations. And it will not only be evil of his own doing, but also of those who have fallen under his maleficent influence.'

I was stunned.

'Is there any way that he could be stopped?'

'I imagine there were rituals to try to stop an enemy being reincarnated but I doubt whether they would have much power over a magician.'

'And what about my friend? Is there any way that he can be rescued?'

'I'm afraid I don't know. It makes me think of souls that have been stolen by evil spirits. The nomadic tribes in Siberia and Mongolia have healers called shamans who put themselves into a trance state and plead with the spirit or do battle with it in order to bring the soul back to the person from whom it's been stolen. It's a dangerous business. The shamans risk their sanity in doing so.

Chapter Twenty Nine

CAROLINE

The wind drumming at my bedchamber window woke me up early as usual, bringing back the pain in my breast. I had dreamt again about making love to Johnny. They were good dreams in which I didn't feel the pain. Now I was cold and I wanted company. George had been in a dark mood for weeks, spending his time locked up in his study and refusing to be drawn when I asked him what was wrong. Now he had left for Norwich where he was to visit Auguste Devereux. It was the cook's day off and the housekeeper and housemaid were carrying out errands. Janet was now alone in looking after me. I put on my peignoir and tugged the bell-pull beside the bed. Janet hurried in.

'A cup of tea, please, Janet, and would you please light the fire?'

'Yes, ma'm.'

Janet was a plucky girl with a sense of fun and I'd often taken her into my confidence in my romantic adventures when I needed a go-between. It was a role she greatly enjoyed.

'D'you remember Roger Ainsworth?' I asked her when she returned with the tea and a burning rush candle. 'He used to be one of George's friends. I think their friendship came to an end when they fell out about something. I can't remember what. Anyway, he was a friend of Johnny's so I thought I would write to him. Perhaps he will know his whereabouts. Roger's address will be in George's address book but that's not much use with his study locked up.'

'I think I can help you there, ma'am,' Janet offered as she knelt before the grate and lit the fire. She turned to me and smiled conspiratorially.

'About a month ago before your operation, I'd been dusting a table in the morning room. The door was open and, from where I was standing, I could see the master's reflection in the looking-glass on the wall opposite the staircase. He was locking the door to his study and when he'd done it, he put the key under the second step of the stair carpet. I thought no more of it at the time.'

'What a resourceful girl you are, Janet.'

'Would you like me to bring the address book up to you ma'm?'

'Let me come with you. It's bound in red leather.'

I was still weak, but I could walk slowly to the other rooms on the same floor.

'I'm worried about the stairs, ma'm. Are you sure you'll be able to cope with them?'

'Yes, I'm sure I will.'

I was bored and I wanted something to do.

'Very well, ma'am.'

Janet helped me off the bed and held my arm as we descended the stairs one at a time. When we reached the bottom, she took the key from under the stair carpet and unlocked the study door. We walked in and I looked at her. We were like naughty children sharing a frisson of excitement at being in the master's private study without his knowledge or consent. I sat in an alcove while Janet looked around for the address book. Having searched the book cases, she tried the drawers of the desk. All but one of the drawers was unlocked and it wasn't in any of them.

'I bet it'll be in the locked drawer, ma'm. I wonder where he keeps the key.'

She looked around the top of the desk and then searched the room.

'I'm not having any luck.'

'What about the carriage clock on the chimney piece?'

Janet lifted it up and heard a rattle.

'Ah!' she said. She turned a ring on the back of the casing and opened it up. She took out a silver-coloured winding key and another small key made of brass. She held it up for me to see.

'Let's see if it does the trick.'

It did. Janet opened the drawer and took out a red leather-bound
book.

'Well done, Janet,' I said admiringly.

I tried to stand up but I missed my footing and fell. Janet rushed to me.

'What happened, ma'm?'

'I slipped, that's all.'

Janet helped me up and sat me down in a armchair.

'Oh, dear,' she murmured.

'What's the matter, Janet?'

She leant over me and touched my peignoir with her finger. She held it up for me to see.

'It's blood. It must have been because of the fall.'

'Oh, no.'

'Let me have a look at the wound, ma'am.'

Janet untied the peignoir and lifted my chemise.

'There's a little tear in the skin where the wound was sewn up, ma'am. It's nothing, it'll heal up in no time.'

I felt a stab of fear as she took a handkerchief from her apron and dabbed the blood from the wound.

'You'll be alright, ma'm, but I must get you back to bed.'

Slowly, step by step, she helped me up the stairs and into bed. She had another look at the wound.

'It's beginning to dry up,' she said.

'Thank God.'

'Now I'll get you Roger Ainsworth's address.'

She returned with the address book and another book with a vellum cover bound with leather ties. It looked very old.

'This was in the drawer under the address book, ma'm,' she said, sounding agitated.

She handed the book to me.

'Please forgive me, ma'm. I'm afraid I looked inside it and I thought you'd want to see it.'

She curtsied and left the room.

Chapter Thirty

MOUNTFORD

At ten o'clock in the evening when the wind was high again, Maggie tapped on my door. It had been two weeks since Sarah had gone back to Kidlington and I was missing her. It was too early for me to go to bed. I would need at least two glasses of laudanum before I retired and I was about to drink my first glass before reading de Quincy's *Confessions of an English Opium Eater,* in the London Magazine, wondering if I could become so addicted myself.

'Yes, Maggie?'

'There's a gentleman knocking at the front door, sir. I asked who he was without opening it. He called out, saying his name is Dr. Evans and he would be obliged if he could come up to see you.'

'Dr. Evans?' I didn't know anybody of that name and I thought it a little late for visiting.

'Thank you, Maggie. You must be in your night clothes. Go back to bed. I'll show him up.'

I went downstairs and opened the front door to a thin, wiry man in his sixties.

'Dr. Evans, sir.'

The man took off his hat and bowed, revealing a bald head and hair long at the sides.

'Thank you for seeing me at this late hour. I'm trying to discover the whereabouts of John Fanshawe.'

I showed him up to my rooms.

'I used to work at the Royal Chelsea hospital with John's uncle,' he continued, 'and I came to know John quite well,

The reason for my visit is that I'm worried about what's happened to him. John wrote to me saying he wanted to see me urgently. Unfortunately, I was abroad at the time so I only read the note yesterday. I went to his house and found a motley crew of people living there. They told me John had left the house some weeks earlier and hadn't been back since. Nobody seemed to mind me looking around the house and I found a letter addressed to a Robert Mountford, presumably yourself, in one of the bedchambers saying he wanted to see you urgently. Anyway, I think he's in some danger. That's why I'm here.'

'May I see the letter?'

'Certainly.'

The man handed it to me. I sat down in my armchair, opened it and looked at the handwriting. This wasn't Fanshawe's hand. A moment later, I felt a handkerchief soaked in ether being held over my nose and mouth. The effect was instantaneous.

The letter fell to the floor and I sank into my chair, my head falling back, my eyes still open. My vision was blurred, my tongue numb and I was unable to move my limbs. I stared up in dread at the unfocussed image of the man looking down at me.

'Powerful stuff, isn't it?' he said. 'Cooked up some years ago by a surgeon in Liverpool. You will know about it being a medical man. My name's Joseph Gilchrist, by the way.'

He took a pair of handcuffs from his coat pockets and bent down to cuff my wrists as I lay sprawled in my armchair in a state of paralysis. As he did so, my memory of his bald head returned. I had seen him at Shadborough House in

270

conversation with Fanshawe, leaving him in a state of shock. The man drew up a chair.

'Last week, Mr. Fawcett was in the Cross Keys in conversation with a turnkey from The *Narcissus* called Mr. Carter who had been helping him to bring us a girl called Rosie Carswell.'

Oh God, I thought. Palmer, the ship's surgeon had recognised me.

'Listen carefully, Mr. Mountford. Mr. Carter was explaining that he hadn't been able to get Carswell off the ship as she'd already been taken off being suspected of having smallpox. One of the waiters overheard them talking and recognised the name, Rosie Carswell. He suggested they talk to Tom Abbott who might have something to tell them. Abbott must have been a bit of a gossip with the waiters. Fawcett asked him what he knew. It took a while to get the story out of him. In the end, he did, having put the fear of God into him. The old man told him you worked at Barts so it wasn't a problem to get your address. I'm afraid your friend Blind Tom won't be drinking at The Cross Keys anymore.'

I was utterly horrified to think that my actions could have brought about Tom Abbott's death.

'A while ago', Gilchrist went on, 'a friend of Sir Ralph Ashton paid him a visit. He found the man distraught. Adam, his most favoured catamite had died of a brain tumour caused by your having knocked him down at his last bacchanal. He was enraged, as you can imagine. His friend tried to calm him but Sir Ralph couldn't stop thinking of you as a murderer.'

Please, God, no,' I said to myself. Gilchrist leant over me.

271

'Let me tell you about the importance of the Egyptian calendar in selecting those who are to become our sacrificial offerings. One of them must have committed his murder in the month of Mesore at the time of harvest. Adam died on the 15th of June. The 15th of June is in the month of Mesore at the time of harvest. Do you understand what that means, Mr. Mountford?'

I stared at him, feeling sick to my stomach with fear, unable to move or speak. I pictured my own headless body floating in the river.

Eventually, I began to be able to move and to focus my eyes. Gilchrist took my arm and I stumbled down the stairs and out into the street. A black carriage with black curtains drawn across the windows was standing at the side of the road. A tall dark-skinned man wearing an Arab cloak and headscarf was standing by the horses.

'Put the hood on him,' Gilchrist ordered, and the man came over to me.

'This is the priest Amon who will be in charge of the ceremony.'

The man pulled a black hood down on to my head with a hard jerk.

'Apep is the god of night,' Gilchrist went on, 'and he demands that
you spend the final hours of your life before the ceremony in darkness.'

He helped me up into the carriage and I sat I down in darkness. I was covered in sweat and breathing rapidly. My clothes were sticking to me. I could smell my own panic. The carriage lurched into motion and I saw my life unraveling before me, listening to the sound of the wind and the wheels rattling over the cobbles. After three quarters of an hour, the carriage made a turn. From the sounds of the branches of trees scraping its sides and the horse's hooves on soft ground, I guessed we were in a narrow muddy lane. We came to a stop and I was led out of the carriage and down some stone steps. The cold, damp air and the echoing of our footsteps told me we were in the cellar of a house. Albion House I told myself. A door was opened in front of me and locked behind me.

Chapter Thirty One

CAROLINE

I couldn't get that horrible, leather bound book in my dressing table drawer out of my mind. Having opened it once, I was not going to do so again. What would George want with such a dreadful thing and what would I say to him when he returned from Norwich? I heard the distant sound of a knock on the front door and Janet's footsteps on the stairs.

'Come in Janet,' I called out. 'Who is it?'

'A young lady called Sarah Fanshawe. She's looking for Mr. .Mountford.'

'Really?'

I knew she was Johnny's cousin. Would she know where he was?

'Tell her I'd like to talk to her. Put her in the morning room and help me get tidied up. Then bring up some tea. I'll receive her in here.'

'Yes, ma'am.'

Janet brought Sarah up to my bedchamber and the girl gave me a shy smile.

'Good day to you, Mrs. Villiers. I am Sarah Fanshawe.'

She had a pretty face, a pale complexion and dark, honest eyes.

'Good day to you, Miss Fanshawe. I am pleased to make your acquaintance. Come and sit by the bed.'

I waited for her to begin.

'You may know that I am John Fanshawe's cousin and a friend of Robert Mountford. I have just come down from

274

Oxford where my aunt has been ill. I have been looking for Robert. I have called at his lodgings and I have been to Barts Hospital and he wasn't at either place. Would you have any idea of his whereabouts?'

'I'm afraid not. Johnny has disappeared too and I am very worried about him as well.'

I decided to draw her out.

'I gather you've been spending some time in London with Robert. Tell me, is he courting you?'

Sarah blushed.

'Oh, no. We're just friends.'

'What a pity. You seem to me to be a sweet girl. May I call you Sarah?'

'Please do.'

'And please call me Caroline. By the way, please forgive me for receiving you up here. I'm afraid I had a fall and it tore the stitching after an operation on my chest. Robert attended it and put me into a trance to stop the pain. He's a wonderful man. You should snap him up.'

Sarah blushed again as I studied her face. I could see that she was having difficulty holding something back. I stretched out my hand and touched hers as she sat beside the bed.

'Sarah, let me tell you something. I'm a very good judge of character, especially that of women, and I can easily spot a woman who has an honest nature.'

Sarah sat in silence as her colour deepened.

'I think you know more than you're telling me and I can see you don't want to cause me any distress. Now that I know, it will cause me greater distress to have news of Johnny kept from me. You're holding back, aren't you?'

275

Sarah sat looking at the floor for a long time, waiting for me to press her further. I decided not to do so. Instead I waited until the silence was too much for her.

'It's only what I know from Robert,' she said eventually. 'He didn't want you to know what he's been finding out while you were recuperating.'

'He's a kind man. Sarah, but when you know me better, you'll discover that I've a strong constitution. Tell me what's been happening.'

I have been confident in the strength of my character and I have not easily been shocked but I was astounded at what Sarah told me. It took the best part of an hour for her to finish her account of what had been happening with long pauses in which she looked down, biting her lip. The full horror of her story hit me when she told me about Johnny mentioning The Temple of Apep in his trance state. I felt the colour drain from my face and Sarah stopped. I pointed to the drawer in my dressing table containing the vellum-covered book.

'Take out the book in the top drawer. My maid found it in my husband's desk drawer, this morning. Then look at the first page.'

Sarah did so and read.

The Book of Apep

Here is a translation from the Hebrew into Latin and English of the Manual of Magic that has been Vouchsafed to Sobek, the Magician by the Priests of the Temple of Apep in order that he should acquire the Power to invoke Spirits and

Demons in the name of the Serpent God who releases the power of Darkness and Chaos.

I watched Sarah's face as she looked at it in disbelief and rang the bell at my bedside. Janet came into the room.

'Janet, please put the book back into George's desk drawer and lock it.'

When she had left the room I looked at Sarah.

'I'm frightened, Sarah,' I said.

Chapter Thirty Two

MOUNTFORD

I was in a waking and sleeping nightmare, staring into the blackness of the hood, my hands cuffed in front of me and a constant dread churning in the pit of my stomach. After what seemed like an eternity, I heard the door being unlocked and the sound of footsteps. It was Gilchrist.

'The time has now come, Mr. Mountford,' he said as he took off my hood and led me along a passageway to a large circular chamber smelling of rotting flesh and burning resin from three torches in sconces set into a circular wall. Their smoke drifted up through a grating in the middle of a domed ceiling. I was soaked with sweat as I looked around me at depictions of animal-headed Egyptian gods and hieroglyphics covering the wall and a painting of a serpent coiled around the top of the dome.

On a plinth in the centre of the chamber stood an Egyptian anthropomorphic coffin, its sides covered with hieroglyphs and a painting of a recumbent figure on its lid. It was the coffin Sarah and I had seen through the grating. There was a large triangle, painted in gold on the flagstone floor, its three points touching the base of the circular wall. A putrefying human head had been placed on each of two of the points. Despite its decomposed state, I recognised one of them as being the head of Burrows. I felt sick with fear.

Six heavy, wooden chairs, high-backed like clergy chairs, were placed around the wall. Fanshawe was slumped in one of them, his chest tied to its back and his wrists tied to its arms. His head was flopped forward and his mouth hung open. There were blood streaks in his hair and his face was scratched. To his right, the cloaked figure of a girl with long black hair sat cross-legged on the floor, wearing a white mask. She was the girl I had seen at the window of Albion House and in Fanshawe's bedchamber. On the chair next to her sat a tall male cloaked figure, also wearing a white mask. He was the man who had pulled the hood over my head. A large axe leant against the wall next to him. In front of it stood a wooden block with what looked like the rotting head of a small fox on it. Fanshawe raised his head a little and squinted at me for a moment before recognising me.

'Oh, God! What are you doing here, Mountford? You don't want to see this.'

He pointed with his eyes to Burrows's head.

'You know who that is, don't you? And next it'll be the head of a child. I'll have to behead her, you know. My father has told me it's the only way to bring back my sanity after what happened in the Abyss.'

He fell silent and Gilchrist motioned me to an empty chair. As I turned to sit down, I saw Villiers in the chair next to me. My God, I thought. I couldn't believe it.

'Why in God's name are you here?'

'This is a fearful thing, Mountford, but it has to happen. I wish I could explain it all to you but I can't.'

He was huddled inside the folds of a greatcoat that looked two sizes too large for him. A vellum covered book bound with leather ties lay in his lap. I turned away from him as I sat down, outrage now added to my paralysing state of shock and fear. Fanshawe lifted his head again and looked around him.

'Where's the girl from the prison hulk?'

Gilchrist looked at me.

'Tell him, Mr. Mountford.'

My body was shaking and I found that I was unable to speak.

'Alright, I will tell you, Fanshawe,' Gilchrist continued. 'Mr. Mountford and your cousin, Sarah, took her away from us.'

'And that's why he's here?'

'Yes, he is to replace her.'

'What do you mean?'

'It seems that his knocking the boy down at Ashton's celebration

led to his death.'

'I know. We've spoken of it.'

'The boy died in the month of Mesore at the time of harvest.'

'Oh, my God.' Fanshawe groaned.

He closed his eyes and started mumbling, his mind drifting. Gilchrist turned to me.

'Your friend's reason has been slipping away, Mr. Mountford. We had to take him from Lincoln's Inn and bring him here to stop him wandering off. He's been scratching himself with his fingernails. He thinks that if he scratches hard enough, he will be able to get the snake out of his head.'

I recalled Fanshawe, curled up in pain on his bed, saying that there was a snake inside him.

'You cannot believe the darkness of the Abyss, Mountford,' he said. Then he started mumbling again and I heard the words, "Please don't let the snake kill me, Papa."

At that moment, Fanshawe's body jerked violently and the dark snarling voice I had heard in his bedchamber came out of him again.

'I was looking forward to seeing the little girl, Mr. Mountford,' it grunted and my terror caused my bladder to give way. I felt my urine soaking into my breeches.

'It would have been stimulating to see the slaughter of one so young. No matter, you will be well remembered for your part in this. I expect you are wondering when the ceremony will begin. Look up at the grating. It will begin when the moon appears through it and it will end when it is eclipsed.'

Fanshawe's head was drooping and the words seemed to have to force their way out of him. I was unable to shift my gaze from his upturned eyes, possessed by the spirit of his father, staring malevolently at me. He turned to the man in the white mask next to him and then back to me, his head seeming to swivel round mechanically, moving like the head of a ventriloquist's doll.

'Gilchrist will have told you that this is the priest Amon who will preside over the ceremony. It took him five years to prepare this chamber and the coffin and my mummification. He used great astrological knowledge to have it built in the exact position to see the eclipse of the moon through the top of the dome on this night and he called up the spirit of the serpent to ensure that the sky would be clear.'

He turned to the girl.

'This is Shukura. She is a priestess in the temple, having spent five years as an acolyte, serving Amon. She is my daughter.'

Somewhere in the back of my mind was a distant memory of Abramov recounting the story of Sobek having fathered a deaf child called Shukura as a result of raping a priestess in the temple and his murdering an English scholar called Ashton who had witnessed the rape. The malignant eyes turned to Villiers.

'You should have stayed in Paris, Villiers. It was an extraordinary time to be there and you could have shared in the fortune I accumulated.'

What was the voice talking about? Had Villiers been an accomplice to Josiah? I felt I was losing my reason. The voice ordered Gilchrist and the priest to lift the lid off the coffin. They did so and put it on the floor. The mummified body inside was tightly wrapped in strips of linen, brown with age, bound with leather straps. The head was covered with a mask, its face painted gold with large white eyes outlined in black. Above it was a headdress that took the form of four red serpents. Beside the mummy were four earthenware jars. Gilchrist lifted off the mask and headdress and the priest carefully cut through the strips of linen wrapped around the head with a surgeon's scalpel until it was exposed, brown and shiny, its skeletal open jaw revealing dark yellow ochre teeth.

'Put my book of spells on my chest,' the voice ordered. Gilchrist took a little book from his pocket and put it on the mummy's chest. I recognised it as the book of hieroglyphics that I had picked up in Fanshawe's bedchamber.

'The finger!' the voice grunted. Amon put a small brown object into the mummy's mouth. And where is the moon, Villiers?'

'Not visible yet.'

Fanshawe's head fell back, his eyes closed, and the grating voice muttered, 'John, I thought you were strong enough to be my son. The animal spirit had entered you and you could have been endowed with such power. But you were weak'.

There was a long silence.

'Where is the moon, Gilchrist?' the voice grunted. 'Can you see it yet? I am ready.'

'It's beginning to appear.'

'Now speak the words, Villiers.'

Villiers opened the book on his lap and spoke some words in Latin. At that point I fainted and collapsed on to the floor. When I came to, I sat up and found myself silently mouthing the Lord's Prayer. I looked at Shukura who seemed to be reading my lips and mouthing the words. She signed to Fanshawe.

'A Christian prayer, Mr. Mountford?' the voice grunted. 'Where is your materialism now?'

Gilchrist knelt down in front of me and I saw him looking at the wet patch under my breeches where I was sitting on the floor. He uncuffed my wrists and cuffed them behind me. I knew it was to prepare me for the beheading. My terror had rendered my sweat-soaked body limp, my muscles trembling. Gilchrist and Amon then dragged me to the block. Amon removed the jackal's rotting head from it and Gilchrist placed my neck on the block.

There was the sound of a gunshot and I was knocked sideways. I had been shot. I lay still, waiting to feel the injury. I felt none. Was it because I was in shock? And why had they decided to shoot me instead of beheading me? The voice inside Fanshawe was making a grunting noise as if unable to form words and I heard Villiers's saying, 'The gun's double-barreled.'

Of all people, it was Villiers who was trying to shoot me. I couldn't believe it. And he was going to try again. He would succeed this time. Then I turned to see Gilchrist's prone body lying on the floor, blood oozing out of the back of his coat. It was Gilchrist who had been shot, knocking me sideways in his fall. Gilchrist groaned as Villiers lifted the keys and a pistol from Gilchrist's pocket while pointing a gun at the priest. He unlocked my cuffs, put the pistol in my coat pocket and handed me a note.

'Do as I say quickly, Mountford. Take one of the torches and get out of the house. Then wait under the portico and read the note.'

I lifted a torch from its sconce and stumbled into the corridor.

Chapter Thirty Three

VILLIERS

Would I now be able to bring this horror to an end forever? I had to get John out of the house but not before the ceremony was completed. For that to happen, John had to carry out the third sacrifice while he was still possessed by the spirit of his father. Only then would I be able to cast Josiah into eternal oblivion. Would John be able to do the deed and cast the memory of it from his mind when this horror was all over? I had planned that the victim should be Gilchrist and I hoped that would reassure him that he had done the right thing.

I glanced up at the grating, keeping my gun trained on Amon.

'Josiah,' I say, 'the moon is beginning to be eclipsed.'

The grunting noise coming out of Fanshawe's mouth found words to speak.

'Address me as Sobek.'

'Very well.' I kept my eye on Amon and made my suggestion.

'You need a third beheading, Sobek. Take Gilchrist. He murdered people every day during the Terror so one of the murders will fit the month of Mesore in The Time of Harvest.'

A wordless, grunting sound came out of John's mouth. It was the sound of demonic laughter.

'I wonder why you haven't shot Amon. Is it because you must allow the ceremony to be completed? Are you trying to use a ritual that will cast me into oblivion? It's such a pity that we didn't go on working together.'

The voice laughed again and gave an order to Amon. Gilchrist groaned in pain as Amon dragged him by the head to the wooden block and laid his neck it. Then he untied John from his chair and handed him the axe. Forgive me, John, I said to myself. May you not be haunted by this act. Despite myself, the words in my head were a prayer to a god in what I used to believe was a godless universe.

'Behead him,' the voice barked and I watched John walking towards Gilchrist in somnambulant torpor. I closed my eyes as he lifted the axe above his head. Then, as if he had woken from a dream, his own voice came out of him.

'No,' he shouted. I watched him staggering, letting the axe drop and falling backwards on to the floor. He looked unconscious. Then whispered words began to come out of his open mouth.

'You cursèd creature. You're no son of mine. The serpent will live inside you for all time. And you are of no further use to me, Gilchrist. Behead him, Amon.'

Amon picked up the axe, lifted it high above Gilchrist's neck and brought it down with great force. There was a sound of cracked bone and the thud of the axe striking the block. Gilchrist's head dropped on to the flagstones and rolled forward while his heart pumped deep red arterial blood out of the severed arteries in his neck.

'It is done,' the voice whispered.

This was the moment of truth. The ceremony has come to an end and I thought of my friend Jeannot and our philosophical society in Paris. Now I could carry out the instructions Jeannot sent me for casting the soul of an evil man into oblivion. Still keeping my pistol trained on Amon, I took a piece of papyrus from one the pockets of my oversized greatcoat. On it was the depiction of the serpent, Apep being decapitated by the sacred cat, Bastet. I pushed it into the mouth of the mummy and took out a bottle of surgical spirit, a bag of gunpowder and a small tinder pistol. I emptied the bottle of spirit over the corpse, sprinkled the gunpowder on to it and discharged the tinder pistol close to the spirit-soaked binding. There was a bright flash as the gunpowder ignited the spirit and the linen binding went up in flames. When the corpse was alight, its insides beginning to glow orange, I was horrified to hear Sobek's voice coming out of the mummy's mouth. It is screaming in pain. Then it stopped.

For a moment, I was transfixed by the silence and the thought of Sobek being annihilated. Too late, I realised that Amon had seen his chance and was running at me with his knife. He stabbed it into my stomach and I fired my pistol into his chest at point blank range, knocking him to the floor. I called out to John as he lay on his back, semiconscious. I had to get him out of the chamber.

'Wake up John, your father has gone.'

He began to sit up, bleary-eyed and looked at the floor of the chamber, awash with blood.

'Your father has gone,' I shouted again. 'Now get out of the house. Robert will be waiting for you. Please go. Time is running out.'

John got to his feet and staggered out into the corridor. Now Shukura was standing up and walking to the coffin. She took off her mask and dropped it into the flames. Her face was beautiful, her olive skin as smooth as that of a child

287

and her almond eyes like those of the women in Egyptian wall paintings. I held out my arm towards the open door, inviting her to follow John but she shook her head and sat down again, cross-legged against the wall, her eyes staring blankly as if she had left her body.

I had to act quickly. Blood was leaking from my stomach and the time had come for this horror to be brought to an end. I took two metal canisters containing nitroglycerine and silica from pockets I have sown inside my overcoat. It was an explosive many times more powerful than gunpowder that William Congreve had learned about from the Italian chemist, Ascanio Sobrero. Each of the canisters had a fuse going into it. I bring an end to my story, dropping them into the flaming coffin to atomise Sobek's corpse and bring a welcome end to my life.

Chapter Thirty Four

MOUNTFORD

I read Villiers's note by the light of the torch as I sat on the portico steps and the blind fear I had felt earlier had now changed to stupefaction.

My dear Mountford,

I am mortified that you should have become embroiled in this terrible affair and my shame at my part in it knows no bounds. John should be out of the chamber soon after you have read this. Please don't come to help me. I am bent on the destruction of Josiah in body and spirit. It is of the utmost importance and it will have to happen in a particular way. If you come back down you might unwittingly prevent it. When you walk out of the house you will see a round grating to the right some yards away. It is the grating in the ceiling of the burial chamber. Don't go near it. Wait for John. When he arrives, leave at once.

There will be a letter from my solicitor, awaiting you tomorrow morning proposing a time and date for the two of you to meet at my house. I hope you will learn everything you need to know from him. He will have told the magistrate what has happened and I would be grateful if you would go to see him after you have seen Caroline. My dear friend I am thinking of you and Caroline and Sarah as well as John and I hope you will be able, between you, to give John some of the help he will need to be free of his demented state.

289

Your dear friend,
George

Fanshawe came through the front door and sat down opposite me his back against one of its pillars, his legs splayed out and his head flopped forward. At that moment there was a massive explosion. A brilliant flash of white light came from under the grating, illuminating the surrounding trees for a split second, like lightning. The house reverberated from the impact and the grating fell into the chamber. Smoke poured out of the hole and, brick by brick, the roof of the chamber began to cave in. Soon, larger chunks of brickwork were falling and it wasn't long before the domed ceiling had completely collapsed into the room below. I was shattered by the sound and my ears rang. In a state of shock and confusion I went to the crater and looked down into the pile of earth and masonry that covered the floor, illuminated by one remaining torch, still alight in its sconce. I saw Amon half buried, missing a leg and his blood-soaked brown cloak in tatters. I sat down, feeling nauseous and put my head in my hands.

It took some minutes for my fragmented thoughts to coalesce. When they did, I looked into the crater again, knowing that there would be nobody left alive down there. I reread Villiers's note wondering what I would learn from Villiers's solicitor. What possible explanation could I be given for Villiers's collusion with these terrible people, only to turn on them in the end and throw away his own life in doing so?

I walked back to Fanshawe and bent down to see his eyes. They were closed. He was unconscious. I entered the house and found a jug of water in a laboratory full of chemical paraphernalia. I poured some into a glass beaker and brought it to Fanshawe. I touched it to his lips.

'Wake up, old chap. Here's some water.'

Very slowly, Fanshawe lifted his head and opened his eyes, staring ahead of him, glassy eyed.

'It must happen on the night of the winter solstice when the body of Osiris was entombed,' he murmured as if committing the words to memory. I could make no sense of what he was saying but, to my massive relief, it wasn't spoken in his father's voice.

'Drink some water, Fanshawe. We have to leave this terrible place.'

As I edged the water into Fanshawe's mouth, I thought about getting him to Lincoln's Inn, most probably still peopled with hangers-on and I decided we should aim for Calthorpe Street. I felt in my pockets for a few coins and looked at my watch. It was a quarter past one in the morning. I recalled it being market day in Covent Garden. If we could get to the Jamaica Road, there would be hawkers on their way to the market with their vegetables, some on horse-drawn carts. With the few coins I had, I should be able to persuade one of them to give us a ride as far as Holborn and we could walk the rest of the way to my lodgings.

'Come on,' I said as I helped Fanshawe to his feet. We set off in silence, me at the front, holding the torch and the pistol that Villiers had taken from Gilchrist. I walked slowly so as not to outpace Fanshawe's shambling progress and, every so often, I retraced my steps, seeing Fanshawe some way behind, leaning against a wall and mumbling to himself.

I concentrated hard on the route. I didn't want to lose my way again, but I couldn't stop thinking about the night's events, fighting my fear that the voice of Fanshawe's father might come out of him again. I pictured Villiers's body under the rubble. How could a man of science allow himself to become involved with these terrible people? Someone would have to dig it out in order to give it a proper burial. And the others, too. I tried to think of Fanshawe's state of mind in the burial chamber as a case of insanity and not possession but that too was a bleak prospect for him. Fanshawe was sufficiently wealthy to avoid the horrors of a pauper madhouse but even the dubious benefits of a private asylum would be a devastating blow to him. Would it be possible for him to remain in his own home, looked after by Sarah? In any event, he would need someone to look after him.

*****

As dawn began to break above the roofs in Calthorpe Street, we made our way through the flocks of silent, shadowy figures on their way to work. I led Fanshawe into my lodgings, pushed him up the stairs and laid him out on my bed where he fell into a deep, mumbling sleep. I took a cushion from my armchair, poured a quantity of laudanum for myself and fell asleep on the floor without drinking it.

I awoke in the early afternoon. For a brief moment I had forgotten the events of the previous night and then the horror of it hit me again. I drank the laudanum and heard the sound of Fanshawe groaning. I knew I should see if there was anything I could do to help him. I struggled with a tinder box and managed to light a candle. With faltering steps, I entered the bedchamber. Fanshawe was sitting on the side on the bed holding what looked like a piece of parchment.

'Take that candle away,' he said, turning to me and hurriedly pushing the parchment into his pocket. I winced to see new scratch marks added to the dried lacerations on his face, and his hair, clotted with dried blood, now had fresh red streaks running through it. Gilchrist's words came to me. "He thinks that if he scratches hard enough, he will be able to get the snake out of him." I blew out the candle and began to draw back the curtains.

'Don't do that. We must have darkness.' Fanshawe shouted.

'Who is with you?' I asked.

'The snake. We are now one.'

I felt my heart thud and my skin prickled. Once again, I was I suffused with the same fear that I had experienced in the burial chamber. The nightmare hadn't ended. Once again, I tried to persuade myself that Fanshawe's delusional ramblings were the result of his being temporarily of unsound mind because of the horror he had been through and nothing more. Nevertheless, I avoided asking him about the snake.

'Fanshawe?' I asked quietly, 'Is there anything I can bring you? Do you want some more laudanum?'

He was now curled up on his side, mumbling to himself,

'It must happen on the night of the winter solstice when the body of Osiris was entombed.'

'How do you know this?' I prompted.

'Amon told me.'

'Amon is dead.'

'No, he's not. He came here to see me.'

'I haven't seen him here.'

'You wouldn't,' he said dismissively.

Could there be any clue as to Fanshawe's condition in that note he didn't want me to see?

There was a knock on my door.

'Yes, Maggie.'

'I thought I should let you know that Miss Fanshawe called by this morning, sir. She's been looking for you here and at the hospital for the last three days. She said she will come back this afternoon.'

'Thank you, Maggie.'

I felt a huge sense of relief at having her back but it was quickly replaced by alarm at the thought of her discovering Fanshawe's dreadful state of mind and body before I was able to forewarn her. I put a bottle of laudanum into Fanshawe's hand as he lay on the bed in the hope it would send him to sleep. That it did just in time for Sarah's arrival.

***

'My dear Sarah, it's so good to see you'.

I wanted to hug her.

'Robert, you poor man. You look worn out. And where's John? Have you found him?'

'I have, but I need to explain what's happened to him. He's alive and safe but it's a long story and you need to hear it before you see him. First, please tell me about your aunt.'

'Her condition is unchanged. I'm sorry I stayed there for so long but she kept putting such pressure on me to be with her. She let me go in the end when I told her I had to go to

London to find John. I'm afraid I'll have to go back to her soon.'

She dropped down on to the sofa.

'So tell me where you have been for the last three days.'

'I will explain everything, Sarah.'

I was hoping desperately that Fanshawe wouldn't wake up.

'I've something very important to tell you too, Robert.' Her face was full of concern. 'I have made a terrible discovery about Dr. Villiers. I went to see Mrs. Villiers to find out if she knew where you were. She showed me an abhorrent book that her maid had found in her husband's desk drawer, an ancient volume called *The Book of Apep*. It described itself as a manual of magic. It said something about bestowing the power to invoke spirits and demons in the name of Apep, the god of darkness. Wasn't Apep the name of the Egyptian demon that John mentioned during his trance?'

'Yes.'

'You don't look surprised.'

'I'm not any longer.'

'Oh my God, Robert. What's been happening?'

I didn't know how to begin, imagining the effect on her of what I had to say.

'I must warn you, it will shock you, Sarah.'

'Go on.'

I was right. Sarah stared at me horrified as she heard what had happened. When I told her about Fanshawe's demented state, strapped to a chair, her face drained of colour.

'Are you sure you want me to go on, Sarah?'

She nodded and I told her about the presence of Villiers in the burial chamber and Josiah's words coming out of his son's mouth. I recounted the moment at which I had been seconds away from being beheaded myself and Villiers' saving the lives of Fanshawe and me before the chamber exploded. By now, Sarah was staring down at the floor, rocking back and forth with her eyes closed. When I told her about the explosion and seeing the priest lying in the rubble, Sarah covered her mouth and held up a hand towards me, palm outwards as if to push me away.

'I'm going to be sick.'

I should have known. I rushed to get my washbowl and put it on her lap. I turned away, as Sarah vomited, retching again and again. When she had finished, her head still hanging over the bowl, I gave her a face cloth and took the bowl into the corridor, calling for Maggie to take it away. When I came back, her head was resting on the back of the armchair and she looked at me, her eyes half closed.

'I don't know if I can take any more of this, Robert.'

I fetched a glass of water and she drank it down.

'Forgive me, Robert. Please go on.'

'Are you sure?'

'Yes.'

I gave her the note that Villiers had given me. When she had read it, she threw it to the floor.

'How could such a man get involved with these evil people? He may have tried to rescue you both but he clearly participated in dragging you into their clutches in the first place. Are you sure those dreadful people are dead?'

'Yes.'

'And Dr. Villiers, also?'

'Yes.'

'And Dr. Villiers intended to kill himself as well as the others?'

'I'm sure of it.'

'Where is John now?'

'He's asleep in my bedchamber.'

'Robert!' she exclaimed. 'How could you have held that back?'

'Dear Sarah, I felt you had to know what…'

She unlocked the door and stared open mouthed at Fanshawe's lacerated face in the semi-darkness.

'Oh, my God! What have you done to yourself, John?'

Fanshawe looked up at her, curled up and half asleep, heavily dosed with laudanum. He didn't answer.

'How could he have got into such a state, Robert!'

'Let him rest, Sarah and don't pull back the curtains. He's plagued with delusions, including having to live in the dark.'

Back in the living room, she saw me shivering and brought my overcoat from the wardrobe. I huddled inside it.

'What do you think you will learn from Dr. Villiers's solicitor?' she asked.

'I don't know.'

She lay down on the sofa as I paced the room and stared out of the window.

'What shall we do about John?' she asked.

It took me a while to answer.

'He's too deranged for you to look after him in Kidlington.'

'Do you think that dreadful manifestation of his father may still be inside him?'

'I don't know. It frightens me to think about it. I suppose it's best if he stays here. There's nobody to look after him at his own house apart from Mrs. Jenks if she's still around and God knows who else will be there.'

'But you must get back to work.'

'I know. Listen, Sarah. I've got to see Villiers's solicitor tomorrow morning. After that, I've got to go to the magistrate. Could you come here before I set off and stay with John until I come back?

'Of course.'

Chapter Thirty Five

I knocked on Villiers's door, dazed with fatigue, having spent the night listening to Fanshawe's groaning.

'Good morning, Mrs. Harvey. What an unhappy occasion this is. Do you know if Dr. Villiers's solicitor is here? I had a note to come here to see him this morning.'

'Yes, he's in the drawing room.'

She was holding back tears.

'Do you know if Mrs. Villiers would be prepared to see me while I'm here?'

'Not straightaway, sir, if you don't mind, it's been terrible shock.'

I nodded my acceptance. When I entered the drawing room, a dark-haired man in his forties rose from his chair and held out a hand.

'Anthony Chapman, sir. I'm Dr. Villiers's solicitor. I'm sorry to be meeting you on such a sad occasion. It is all most regrettable.'

'Indeed.'

'Last week, Dr. Villiers arranged for an amended copy of his will and some letters to be sent to me along with another document, one copy for Mrs. Villiers and two for you and Mr. Fanshawe. I was instructed to bring them here this morning. I've informed the magistrate, who wants to see you. You'll understand that the matter obviously needs to be cleared up from the legal point of view.'

'I know. I am going to see him this afternoon.'

Chapman sat down and took two sealed documents out of his case. He handed them to me.

'I would be grateful if you would keep Mr. Fanshawe's copy in your safe-keeping for the time being. Mrs. Villiers has her own copy. At Dr. Villiers's request I have had my clerks make copies for those friends and colleagues he wished to receive it. And there's also a letter for you.'

He rummaged again in his bag and handed it to me.

I offered my thanks, adding, 'I would be indebted to you if you would do something for me in this matter. The members of the Wigmore Society to which Dr. Villiers and I belonged may feel they should know that I was present in the burial chamber that night. Would you be kind enough to add a brief note to their copies of Dr. Villiers's testimony, telling them so and asking them to write to me if they want to know more about the affair?'

'Of course I'll be happy to do that.'

'I just need to give you their names.'

'No need. Dr. Villiers has already indicated which of his colleagues belong to it.'

He picked up his bag.

'I'm afraid I have to go now, sir. Please let me know if there is any further clarification that you require.'

We shook hands. It was a long time after he had left before I was ready to break the seal on the document and to read what turned out to be a confession.

My dear Caroline,

I am beginning this letter to you in my study, hearing the sound of the rain against the windows. The sound seems so clear, my knowing that soon I won't hear it again.

The letter is also addressed to you, Robert, to ask your forgiveness for entangling you in such a terrible business in which you nearly lost your life. Most of all, it is addressed to you, John. To my shame, you have experienced terrible suffering at the hands of your father, an unspeakably malevolent man to whom I was once in thrall.

I was living in Paris in the autumn of 1788, having been commissioned by my publisher to write a book on the experiments in chemistry being undertaken in Paris. I was a twenty-four-year-old seeking adventure and I was roused by the political and social ferment in the city. I joined a philosophical society run by a friend called Michel Jeannot. The meetings took place in Jeannot's home and were held in secret as all of the members including myself supported the growing republican movement.

By the Spring of '89, there were riots in the streets and in May, the Bastille was stormed. Nevertheless, we kept up the meetings, feeling the invulnerability of youth and not seeing ourselves as targets for the violence.

At one of the meetings, Jeannot introduced us to an English scholar, a rather sinister man unusually dressed in an Arab cloak and headdress. A gold amulet in the form of a coiled serpent hung from a chain around his neck. He had lived for some years in Egypt and his skin was deeply bronzed to the point that he had the appearance of an Arab. He gave himself the Egyptian name, Sobek.

The man said little at the meeting but at the next one he asked to make a contribution to our discussion about Jean-Jacques Rousseau. He then proceeded to undermine Rousseau's ideas, claiming that the notion of a "general will" was ridiculous, as people are weak-minded and need

301

strong leaders to hold their loyalty through a combination of admiration, devotion and fear. It would be such leaders that would bring about the birth of the French republic. He then embarked on a discourse about occult knowledge that could imbue a man with great power, power that could be put to revolutionary use. He went on to claim that he was endowed with a power and he had the ability to bring about events by means that were outside the laws of nature.

A commotion followed with everybody talking at once. We were affronted by his claim and shocked that such a person should be invited to speak at our society. We were freethinking materialists. The man was obviously a charlatan. He should be thrown out. Sobek sat quietly while this was going on and, when the clamour ceased, I asked him how he had acquired his power. He told us he was the seventh incarnation of a magician who founded the ancient Egyptian Temple of Apep in the Nineteenth Dynasty.

A member called Chartier, wanting to disprove Sobek's claims, challenged him to perform a piece of magic in front of us. Sobek offered a spell in which Chartier would have a heart attack when the longcase clock in the corner of the room struck the hour which it was about to do. When the clock struck, Chartier clutched his chest and fell to the floor. I rushed over to him and checked his pulse. He was still conscious but his face was white as death. I looked up into Sobek's eyes. Always the palest blue, they burned like ice.

We were horror-struck. Sobek sat in silence, looking out of the window. Someone said he should be accused of attempted murder, but it was pointed out that there would be no evidence for it. Jeannot put Chartier into his father's old bath chair and wheeled him out of the room to recover.

Sobek thanked us for allowing him to participate in our discussions and said that he was shortly going to return to Egypt.

That is how it all started. Sobek's seemingly supernatural act, however atrocious, had kindled in me a dark exhilaration at the idea of the laws of nature being usurped by forces beyond scientific understanding. However, with Sobek gone, I soon became ashamed to have allowed my rationalism to be subverted. When my book was finished, I returned to London and continued my work with Sir William Congreve, the rocketeer. I was happy to be back in the world of free thinkers. If only I had remained so.

This morning, the rain has stopped and there is a high wind that echoes the turbulence inside me as I recall what was to come. While I was in London, I dreamt about Sobek and wondered if I would see him again.

Daumier wrote to me telling me what was going on in Paris. My heart missed a beat when he went on and to say that Sobek had returned and he wanted to see me. Despite Daumier's account of the city now being highly dangerous, I determined to see Sobek again. I kept the reason for my visit from you, Caroline. You had your own life to lead and you knew little of what was happening in the Revolution. As I recall, you were happy for me to go.

When I met Sobek, I asked him why he had come back and he answered, saying that the city was now of more interest to him because of the destructive power that was being unleashed in it. I was stunned when he went on to tell me why he wanted to see me. He said a day would come when I was to participate in the ceremony that would bring about his next incarnation. When I asked him why, he said it was because of a dream in which I took on the form of the god, Ammet and I had the power to allow him to move on to his next life. He then insisted that we establish our friendship by sharing the drink of priests, lotus wine with snake venom. Within moments of drinking the wine I started to hallucinate. Sobek's body seemed to glow and his voice deepened when he spoke as if it were coming from the pit of hell. He demanding that I make an oath of allegiance to him. I did so without question as if someone else were speaking the words, my own will being in suspension.

It is so difficult to put this terrible confession on paper, Caroline, thinking of you lying upstairs in your bedchamber in pain. Nevertheless I have to write it even though I know I cannot be forgiven for what I have done. You are going to think I should have got away from Sobek as soon as I could and return to England. But I didn't. I was in his thrall. I met his assistant, Joseph Gilchrist, a cadaverous man with a bald head who looked like an undertaker in his dark coat and breeches. Sobek then told me that he was going to found a temple dedicated to Apep in the grand house of a wealthy shipping merchant on the banks of the Seine. He had acquired the house by falsely denouncing the merchant to a member of the National Assembly as a royalist, causing him and his family to flee the city. There were to be twelve acolytes in the temple. He had already gathered the other eleven, including Jeannot. I was to be the twelfth.

The streets of Paris were becoming increasingly dangerous for the bourgeoisie and Sobek instructed us to buy old clothes, leave our homes and move into the

*merchant's house. He hung a tricolor flag from an upper
window to show that it was occupied by friends of the sans-
culottes. I was overtaken by curiosity about whatever was to
take place there.*

*During the first week, I saw the other followers being
transformed into murderous louts and I experienced the
most terrible change in myself. I discovered that I had an
appetite for watching scenes of depravity. In one of their
orgiastic ceremonies, one of the followers suffocated a
prostitute. Sobek instructed them to cut her body open,
leaving the drawing room awash with blood, and showed
them how to use its entrails to commune with the dead.*

I must stop now, Caroline.

*It is morning. I must finish this appalling story. One
Sunday, Sobek wanted to amuse us by turning a priest into a
murderer. Priests were not easy to find in Paris as most of
them were either dead or in hiding. However, one of the
followers managed to find one called Père Lescot in a
lunatic asylum. When the priest was presented to Sobek, he
was dressed in rags and his body was in a constant tremor.*

*That evening, Sobek invoked a demon to make the man do
his bidding. Within moments, the priest's tremor left him and
his countenance began to take on the uncouth appearance of
the other followers. By morning, he was gone.*

*In the days that followed, some of the followers reported
that the priest was inciting mobs to appalling atrocities. He
called himself Citizen Lescot and he became one of the
leaders of the mobs that carried out the September
massacres in 1792. One day, I followed him around the city
and I watched transfixed as he ordered a woman who was a*

member of the nobility to be stripped and raped and her body dismembered.

Some weeks later, Sobek left Paris for a time with his assistant and his hold over me began to weaken. There were moments when my addiction to barbarity was overtaken by the unspeakable horror that had been suppressed beneath it. I decided I must get out of Paris and make my way back to England as soon as I could. There was plenty of money lying around the house, stolen by the followers during their murderous escapades, and on the night I planned to leave, I took as much as I could find, taking comfort from the thought of being rid of these terrible people. However, when I walked out of the house, I was thrown into a state of panic, seeing the cloaked figure of Sobek walking towards me. 'So you've decided to leave me and go back to England,' he said, looking at my packed bag. I tried to form a reply but he held up a hand to stop me, telling me he had been to Marseilles to arrange a passage to Egypt in a month's time. He said there was something he wanted to give me before I left. He led me to his bedchamber and handed me a manuscript bound in vellum. He explained that it was a medieval translation into Hebrew, Latin and English of an ancient Egyptian manual for the casting of spells and summoning demons. I should guard the book with my life as I would be using it at the ceremony that was to bring about his next incarnation. It would take place on the 15th of October, 1821 in London. 'You will be there, Dr. Villiers,' he said.

Back in the street, I sat down, my head in my hands and the dreadful grimoire on my lap. I wanted to throw it away but I couldn't. I could hear gunshots a few streets away and I looked up to see a red glow above some distant houses, no doubt the homes of aristocrats that had been torched.

I set off for a café near my old apartment in Montparnasse where I drank half a bottle of brandy, reassuring myself with the thought that 1821 was nearly three decades away and anything might happen in the intervening years to give the lie to Sobek's prediction. In the meantime, I had to leave Paris. A diligence took me to Calais in three days and when I arrived, a packet boat from Dover had just docked and the wind was set fair for it to take me back to England that day.

In London, I stayed indoors for a week reading the daily papers to bring me back to reality and to stave off my nightmares about Sobek. I knew that I needed to get back to work and eventually I went to see Congreve who was happy for me to work with him again. Shortly after that, Wesley Fitzgibbon asked me if I would like to join him in co-founding the Wigmore Society.

It is late now. I am remembering you at that time, Caroline. You were still a joy to my eye if not always to my heart and my nightmares faded somewhat.

In the summer of this year I started wondering if anything was to happen on the 15th of October. The date became horribly alive when I received a letter from Michel Jeannot a month ago. Its tone was disturbingly urgent. He said he was a husk of his former self, still fearing Sobek, convinced that he was a magician. He recalled my telling him that Sobek had summoned me to participate in his reincarnation in London and he was writing to say that he had recently met a hermeticist called Ducasse who was one of the

307

scholars who had accompanied Napoleon on his Egyptian campaign. Jeannot told him of Sobek's murderous activities and about his next incarnation and asked if he knew of any way in which it could be stopped. Ducasse spent some time investigating the matter and came back to Jeannot with a Coptic translation of an Egyptian set of instructions for casting the soul of an evil man into eternal oblivion. It would make use of the depiction on a piece of papyrus of the serpent, Apep being decapitated with a knife by the sacred cat, Bastet. The papyrus had to be placed in the mouth of the man's mummified body immediately after the reincarnation ritual had come to an end. The body had then to be burned, but this must not happen before the end of the ceremony, otherwise the reincarnation would take place unaffected. He added the caveat that he was unsure if it would work on a magician. Jeannot ended the letter saying that if I could bring about Sobek's annihilation, he implored me to do so. The letter contained a piece of papyrus with the hieroglyph of the snake and the cat on it.

Yesterday, Gilchrist came to my house and I was filled with the horror, seeing him again. He told me that Sobek had come to live in London with his daughter, a priestess of the temple. He had died seven years ago having given Gilchrist instructions to arrange for his mummification and burial in a chamber under his house. For the reincarnation to take place, the sacrificial beheading of three murderers had to be carried out. I was to be present at the third beheading to read one of the spells from The Book of Apep. Gilchrist asked to see my copy of the grimoire and pointed out the spell I was to read, reminding me of my oath of allegiance to Sobek. Gilchrist then told me who Sobek was *before he had acquired the power of a magician. I was devastated to hear that he was your father, John, and that you had been chosen to execute the third murderer.*

I began writing this account the day after Gilchrist paid his visit to me and it has become clear to me what I have to do. I shall follow Ducasse's instructions for casting Sobek into eternal oblivion. I have packed two grenades with the explosive on which I have been experimenting at Woolwich and I will have them with me when Gilchrist calls on me on the evening of the 15th. If my plan succeeds, the explosive will atomise Josiah's remains and bring my own life to a welcome conclusion.

My dearest Caroline, John and Robert, I beg your forgiveness for having allowed myself to be drawn into such depths of depravity and for the horrors you have suffered, John, at the hands of this terrible man. The truth is that my mind has been poisoned by Josiah to such an extent that I no longer wish to keep my own company. My greatest hope is that you will recover, John, from the devastating experience you have been through and that you, Caroline, will find a better man than I to love you and look after you. I hope that you will understand the reason for what I am going to do.

George Villiers The 16th of October, 1821

I was stunned. I thought about the suffering that Fanshawe had been through and might well continue to do so, devastating his own life and Sarah's. And what effect would it have on Caroline? Despite the odd arrangement of their marriage and Caroline's amorous adventures, Villiers was always there for her, a tolerant and loving figure so far as she was concerned, given that she chose not to think about the pain he felt in not having her as a devoted wife. And what about the members of the Wigmore Society? What would they think? I was also deeply disturbed by Villiers's belief in the supernatural, given that my own rationality had already become unsettled by what I had experienced.

There was a quiet knock on the door.

'Come in,' I called out and Janet stood in the doorway.

'Mrs. Villiers has asked to see you, sir.'

'Show me up, Janet.'

'She's in a bad way, sir.'

'I can imagine. How's the suture. Is it healing?'

'It's healing fine, sir.'

Janet showed me into Caroline's bedchamber and I sat down next to the bed, taking her hand in mine. Her face was white and there were dark rings under her eyes.

'Are you in pain?' I asked.

'It's nearly gone now.'

I could see from her face that it hadn't gone. She was being stoical about it and I admired her for it.

'I'm desolated by what's happened, Caroline. No words can express it.'

Caroline spoke slowly.

'It's strange to notice for the first time how much I've needed George here. I feel quite bereft. Poor George. How could he have become involved with all this magic nonsense? Have you read his ...I don't know what to call it...

'His confession?'

'Yes.'

'I have. And you?'

310

'Not all of it, Robert. It was too much to take in. I'm going to get Janet to read it to me tomorrow. I want her to be with me. Do you understand? I'm so frightened of being alone.'

Very quietly, almost inaudibly, she began to cry, then dried her eyes with a handkerchief and squeezed my hand.

'Now, what about Johnny?'

I felt it best to say as little as possible.

'It's going to take some time for him to recover from what's happened to him. He's at my lodgings at the moment. Sarah's looking after him. I'm afraid he's in such a febrile state that he has difficulty knowing who we are.'

'You're telling me nothing, Robert. I can see you think I'm not ready for it. Sarah told me what happened to Johnny when you mesmerised him. Anyway, I'm glad she is there for him. And for you. This question will make you think unfavourably of me, Robert, but please answer it honestly. Should I visit him or is he so changed that I'll be repelled by him?'

'You would find it extremely distressing and I think you should wait until he's recovered somewhat. And he will recover, I'm sure.'

It was a statement made more to comfort her than an expression of my true opinion and I guessed she realised that.

'Thank God I have Janet to look after me. She's been dosing me up with laudanum in case you didn't know. I'm trying to keep the shock at bay but it knocks me flat as soon as the intoxication wears off.'

She closed her eyes.

'I think I'm going to go to sleep for a while. You will keep coming to see me, won't you? Do you promise?'

311

'I do.'

'And soon you must tell me what this terrible business is all about.'

***

The sceptical expression on the magistrate's face that afternoon made me nervous as I gave my account of the strange events that had taken place in Rotherhithe. When I handed him Villiers's testimony, he read it with his eyebrows raised. Then he questioned me for nearly an hour, trying to decide whether I was telling the truth or was myself implicated in the gruesome and seemingly demonic events that had taken place. He even considered having me questioned by a man of the Church. However, it was all too much trouble and, in the end, he let me go, saying he had ordered some workmen to unearth the bodies in the burial chamber the following day and I was to accompany them there and identify the remains. I would subsequently have to attend the inquest. I left the court feeling shaky.

I returned to Calthorpe Street carrying the two copies of the confession, wondering if Fanshawe would ever be well enough for me to give him his copy. When I entered my lodging, I was shocked to see Sarah sitting on the sofa, a dark bruise on her cheek and a jagged red line where the skin had been broken. Maggie was kneeling in front of her, wiping her cheek with a face cloth, a bowl of water tinged pink beside her. The kettle was lying on its side near the door.

'Sarah, you poor thing. What happened?'

'Oh God, Robert. About an hour ago, John came out of your bedchamber while I'd been lighting the candles and he shouted at me to blow them out. He looked delirious. I asked him why but he wouldn't say anything. He just stared. When I tried to comfort him he bellowed at me to keep away and threw the kettle at me. Luckily, it was empty. He went back into the bedchamber and slammed the door shut. I know you told me he wanted to stay in the dark but how could he do a thing like this?'

I was chilled. After all the horror that Fanshawe had been through, was he now really turning into a violent lunatic? Maggie caught my eye.

'I heard the shouting and Miss Fanshawe crying out. I started knocking at the door but she must have been too dazed to answer. In the end I came in and saw her lying there. She asked me to lock the bedchamber door which I did and I got some water to clean her up.'

'What are we going to do with him, Robert?'

'I'd better go in and see him.'

I tried to keep my apprehension out of my voice but there was a tremor in my hand when I picked up a candle from the chimneypiece and the flame danced as I did my best to hold it steady.

'Be careful. He's going to attack you if you take a candle in there!' Sarah warned.

'I'll have to take my chances. I need to see him.'

I unlocked the door of my bedchamber. The curtains were closed and there was the sound of moaning as I let myself into the room and closed the door behind me.

'Who's that?' Fanshawe's voice sounded croaky.

'It's me, Fanshawe. It's Mountford.'

313

Fanshawe was lying on his back, staring at the ceiling.

'We don't know you. Go away and take the candle with you.'

I put the candle on a chest of drawers and tried to adopt a bedside manner.

'Look, old friend. I need to see how you are.'

I felt a jolt of panic as Fanshawe leapt from the bed and pushed me against a looking-glass on the wall behind me. Fanshawe caught sight of his own image in the candlelight and looked horror-struck as he stared at the lacerations in his face, and his hair, clotted with dried blood.

'No!' he howled and slammed his fist into the glass, cracking it down the middle. I pushed him away as hard as I could and he fell back onto the bed.

'Take away the light,' he gasped.

I blew out the candle.

'Why did you throw the kettle at your cousin?'

'Because she'll try to use the power of light to destroy us. What she doesn't know is that we can use the power of night to destroy *her*.' he shouted the word *her* and I felt another stab of panic.

'You mean you and the serpent?'

'Yes.'

When I returned to the living room, Sarah asked what had happened. I kept my voice low.

'He attacked me because of the candlelight.'

'I knew he would.'

'Shall I go now, sir?' Maggie asked.

'No, please stay. We may need you.'

'Very well, sir.'

She sat in a corner so as not to intrude and I spoke quietly.

'Sarah, I regret having to say this but you were right when you thought John was delirious. He has completely lost his mind. Do you remember me telling you about the serpent he believed was in his stomach?'

'Yes.'

'He told me it has now moved into his head and the two of them have become joined together like Siamese twins and must live in darkness. He said the priest called Amon who was one of the people killed in the burial chamber had come to see him here and told him about something that must happen on the day of the winter solstice when the body of Osiris was entombed. Sarah, you can't look after him now that he's become violent as well as demented. We'll have to commit him to a madhouse.'

Sarah stared at the floor, unable to speak. Maggie broke the silence.

'Excuse me for overhearing what you said, sir. My uncle Henry's in a small private asylum quite nearby. He's paid for by a Christian charity. It's run by Dr. Berry and his wife at their home in Frederick Street. He's a decent man. They've only got a few inmates, but they're all very placid so it may not be suitable for Mr. Fanshawe but Dr. Berry may know of somewhere suitable.'

Sarah lifted her head looking deathly pale.

'Thank you for the thought, Maggie. I'll go and see him first thing tomorrow morning.'

'The problem is,' I said, 'I can't be here to take care of John. The magistrate told me to accompany the workmen to the burial chamber so I can identify the bodies when they dig them out. They will be picking me up here at 10 o'clock tomorrow morning.'

315

'I could bring my brother Sam round before you set off, sir,' Maggie offered. 'He lives up the road in Wicklow Street. He's a strong man, sir; he was a medical orderly in the infantry. He's just been doing odd jobs since he was discharged after Waterloo.

'Thank you, Maggie. You are being most helpful, I must say.'

Maggie reddened.

'Thank you, sir. When I bring Sam round, would it help if I were to buy some laudanum from the apothecary in Gray's Inn Road to calm the gentleman?'

'It would indeed.'

I had my own supply and it was running low but I didn't want to talk about my use of it. I handed Maggie some coins and turned to Sarah.

'I'm going to talk to John again.'

I went into the bedchamber leaving the door open so that a little light percolated through. I sat on the side of his bed. Fanshawe was curled up, his eyes closed.

'It's me again, Fanshawe.'

'Should we know you?'

'Don't you recognise my voice?'

'No.'

'D'you remember what your father said in the burial chamber? You were tied down in a chair, waiting to be told to cut my head off.'

There was a long silence before Fanshawe spoke again, his voice darker.

'Are you trying to trick us?'

'How d'you mean, trick you?'

316

'Trick us into seeing *burning candles*!' he shouted, jumping off the bed and slamming the door shut. When he found me in the dark, he made a grab for my neck and pressed his thumbs into my throat. I felt my head swell, my lungs bursting. The door opened and Sarah ran in, trying to pull Fanshawe away from me. Fanshawe turned to her with a snarl and I jabbed my knee into his groin and pushed him back. Fanshawe cried out in pain and fell to the floor. I grabbed Sarah by the arm, pulled her out of the room and locked the door. There was no way it could be avoided. Fanshawe was destined for the madhouse.

As I was getting my breath back, Sarah picked up one of the copies of Villiers's confession on my sideboard, still sealed and with Fanshawe's name on it. Fanshawe's maniacal condition had knocked the thought of telling her about it out of my mind. The content of the confession came flooding back to me. How was Sarah going to react?

'Is there more to learn about this dreadful business?' she asked, her expression clouded as she waited for me to reveal yet more about the gruesome events that her cousin had been drawn into.

'I'm afraid so. It's a confession from Dr. Villiers about his becoming involved with a terrible man while he was living in Paris during the Revolution.'

'Do you think I should I read it?'

Not now, Sarah. You're weighed down with more than enough worries about John.'

'I'm glad you said that. I'm going to go back to Tavistock Square, Robert. I need to sleep. I'll come back early tomorrow morning. When Sam arrives, I'll go to see Dr. Berry and you can go to Albion House with the workmen.

The sky was heavy with dense cloud the following morning when I put on my overcoat and hat and waited for the arrival of the workmen, dreading the prospect of seeing Villiers's mutilated body. I heard the sound of horses' hooves outside my window and looked down to see a cart with a canvas roof drawing up outside the house. I went down to the street and climbed aboard, tipping my hat to a constable and three labourers, sitting on benches. The cart was loaded up with pickaxes, mattocks, shovels, ropes and torches that smelled of coal tar, ready to be lit when we arrived. The workmen would need the extra light on that dark morning. As we set off for Rotherhithe I gave my fellow travellers a description of the people who were buried in the chamber, the constable looking suspicious as he listened. Perhaps it was an expression adopted by all those in authority in such circumstances to show that they were not easily to be taken in.

The burial chamber and its door to the corridor were two feet deep in rubble and the labourers had to climb down a rope tethered to a tree to get into it. They then moved enough of the rubble to open the chamber door so that they could get the bodies out of the house through the front door.

I stood next to the constable looking down at them, their long shadows cast against the chamber wall by the torches as they shoveled the rubble from place to place, trying to find where the bodies were buried. Shukura hadn't lost any limbs but Villiers had lost an arm. The burnt remains of their clothes were permeated with dried blood. It took a while to find Villiers's arm and longer still to find Gilchrist's head. I had to turn away when Villiers's body was loaded on to the cart. Meanwhile, the men carried on looking for Amon.

'What's going on?' the constable called down after an hour.

'We can't find any more bodies, sir. There's no one else down here. I'm sure of it.'

I looked into the pit.

'He has to be there,' I remonstrated. 'I saw him in the rubble. He was a tall, dark-skinned man wearing a brown cloak. He was half buried but I could see his head covered in blood and one of his legs had been blown off by the explosion.'

'We'll keep looking, sir.'

'Well?' the constable shouted down after half an hour.

'Nothing sir.'

The constable turned to me.

'A bit of a rum do if you don't mind my saying so, sir.'

At first, I was mystified, and then a cold sensation began to pervade me as I remembered telling Fanshawe in my bedchamber that Amon was dead. 'No he's not', Fanshawe had replied, 'He's been here with me.'

Chapter Thirty Six

SARAH

I warmed to Dr. Berry, the proprietor of the asylum in Frederick Street. He was a small man whose white beard gave him a friendly elfin appearance and I found him a thoughtful listener when I explained the problem of my cousin to him. I made it clear that John's family would cover the cost of a private establishment and I went on to ask him if he could think of anywhere suitable.

'There are such establishments around London, Miss Fanshawe. They have well-appointed rooms and individual attendants for private clients. Nearly all of them also have separate parts of their establishments for pauper lunatics, paid for by the public purse. Overcrowding and mistreatment of the pauper lunatics are rife in most of them but the private clients are looked after reasonably well.'

'Could you recommend one that would be suitable for John?'

Dr. Berry pulled at his beard.

'I am trying to think. Mr. Warburton's establishments, for example. His most select establishment is Whitmore House in Hoxton. The residents are all exclusively from the classes that can afford the fees. I gather that residency there costs 1500 guineas a year. A rather large sum even for a man of independent means, I would have thought.'

The sum took me aback.

'Warburton's keepers attended the late King during his periods of insanity. His pauper houses, however, were severely criticized in a committee report. Then there's Fisher

House in Islington, quiet, in country surroundings, run by a mother and daughter but again I fear they might not be able to accommodate a lunatic with a tendency to violence.'

His descriptions of unsuitable places were beginning to ruffle my nerves and I looked at him sternly.

'I'm sorry to press you, Dr. Berry, but we'll have to find somewhere for John quickly. He's being looked after at the moment by a friend and what with his violent outbursts, he's having to be kept locked in my friend's bedchamber.'

'Of course I understand, Miss Fanshawe. Ah.' he tapped his chin. 'The other one that comes to mind is Stepney House. It's a large manor house on the Mile End Road that includes a sizeable residence for those paying fees as well as a wing that houses pauper inmates and criminal lunatics from Newgate. I would imagine the fees there wouldn't be as high as those for Whitmore House.'

'Thank you, Dr. Berry, you have been very helpful. I think I shall pay a visit there.'

'I'm glad to be of service, Miss Fanshawe. Oh, before you go, I have something that may be of use to you.

He left the room and returned with a canvas jacket with strings dangling from its sleeves.

'A few of these strait-waistcoats came my way some time ago. I have no need of them and I hope your cousin won't either, but please take this one just in case.'

***

I returned to Calthorpe Street, horrified by the thought of what was to happen to John. Maggie opened the door to me and I peered through a fog of tobacco smoke at a stocky man dressed in fustian trousers and a dirt engrained cotton shirt seated by the grate, smoking a stubby pipe. Maggie curtsied.

'Good day, miss. This is my brother, Sam.'

I smiled at the man.

'Thank you for keeping an eye on my cousin, Sam.'

'Sam and I will stay until Mr. Mountford returns, if you are happy for us to do so, miss, in case the gentleman should have another of his turns.'

'Yes. Thank you.'

I turned to Sam.

'Have you needed to restrain him?'

'No, miss. He's been no trouble but his head's troubled isn't it, mumbling all those queer words all the time.'

'It is, I'm afraid.'

'I've seen such madness on the battlefield, miss.'

I remembered Robert telling me about John looking at a piece of parchment which he had quickly pocketed when he came into the bedchamber. Could there be a clue there as to what was happening to him? I opened the bedchamber door and peered into the darkness. John appeared to be in a deep sleep, lying supine on the bed. Could I prise the note from his pocket without waking him? I knelt by the bed and felt my face flush as I slid my hand slowly into one of his breeches pockets. I felt the note and slowly drew it out. I crept out of the room and looked at it by the light of a candle. The parchment was covered in symbols I recognised from the illustrations in the book that I had shown Robert in Kidlington. John had told me they were thought to be hieratic symbols used by Ancient Egyptian priests in their records.

322

I found a pen and paper on Robert's sideboard and used my skill in drawing to copy all the symbols, praying that John wouldn't wake up. The task took most of an hour and I had just finished when I heard him grunt. I hurried to him as quietly as I could and began to slip the note back into his pocket. With my hand still there, he woke up.

'Get off me,' he shouted, grasping the sleeve of my dress. Sam hurried into the room and released my arm. Then he pushed John down on to the bed.

'Steady now,' he said, holding him down until his ranting died down and he lay still. He looked at me standing in the doorway.

'I think it might help if I gave him a glass of laudanum, Miss Fanshawe.'

I poured a glass and Sam edged it into John's slack mouth and laid him down on to the bed, where he curled up into his foetal position.

At that point, Robert arrived looking distracted. I told him what had happened after I had copied the script. By then, John had descended into a lethargic stupor.

'Do you need us any more, sir?' Maggie asked. 'It's just that Sam's got to go to Clerkenwell to clear out a lodging for a landlord and I want to give him some supper before he goes.'

'No, Maggie,' Robert said, 'and thank you both for your help.'

He shook Sam's hand.

'It's been invaluable.'

When they had left, Robert poured himself a brandy and sat down on the sofa looking totally distraught. I had expected him to ask me about Dr. Berry but he remained silent.

'Sam's done a good job, keeping an eye on John,' I said to draw him out but he didn't respond.

'What's the matter, Robert? Is it seeing Dr. Villiers's body? It must have been grueling.

'There's more to it than that.'

'What do you mean?'

'One of them was missing.'

'I don't understand.'

'One of the people who were killed in the chamber, the priest called Amon has disappeared.'

'Go on.'

'After the explosion, I saw his body in the rubble. One of his legs had been blown off and the remains of the cloak he was wearing was blood-stained and in tatters. When the workmen dug the other bodies out of the rubble his body wasn't there. It doesn't make sense. And yesterday, John told me that Amon had visited him here. That was when he talked about the night of the winter solstice.'

'Could he have got out of the chamber before the explosion and you mistook another body for his?'

'I'm sure I didn't. I don't know what to make of it.'

He rubbed his forehead and stared out of the window.

'I must say, I can't help feeling profoundly uncomfortable about it all.'

He picked up the copy of the hieratic script on the sideboard.

'What's this, he asked.

'It's a copy of what was written on the parchment in John's pocket. It's hieratic script, isn't it? You remember that book I showed you in Kiddlington?'

Robert nodded.

'It was while he was asleep but he woke up when I put it back. Sam had to hold him down.'

'You've done well, Sarah. Maybe it's got something to do with John going on about that phrase to do with something happening on the day of the winter solstice.'

He softened his voice.

'Tell me, how did it go with Dr. Berry?'

'He suggested a place in Bethnal Green. It's a large manor house in open parkland called Stepney House. It takes in private residents and has the facilities to constrain John when necessary. It also takes in pauper lunatics paid for by the parish, domiciled in a separate part of the house. He believes the private residents are looked after reasonably well.'

I paused to gather my thoughts.

'We mustn't waste any time, Robert. I'll get Maggie's boy to take a note to the proprietor of the place this afternoon and I'll go and have a look at it tomorrow morning. Can you stay with John?'

'Yes. I don't have any operations scheduled for tomorrow. I'll send a note to the hospital to let them know I won't be coming in.'

Chapter Thirty Seven

I was surprised how impressive Stepney House looked from a distance, a grand manor house that must once have belonged to a wealthy aristocratic family. But as I approached the front door, I noticed the peeling paint and dirty windows, some broken. I was let in by a heavy-faced housekeeper who showed me into a large room full of long, refectory tables and benches. She invited me to take a seat at an oval table under one of the windows and left the room saying she would fetch Dr. Logan.

I looked around the room. All the tables were unoccupied except for one at which two men and a woman were seated in silence, dressed in the clothes of 18th century aristocrats. The woman was wearing a billowing silk dress frayed at its edges, her hair piled up in the pre-revolutionary French manner. The men wore greasy, powdered periwigs and colourful coats begrimed with food and drink stains. The faces of all three were whitened and their lips reddened. One of the men looked at me with bulging eyes and raised a finger as if to start a conversation but he lost the thread of his thought and looked out of the window.

After a few minutes, the tall, lean figure of Dr. Logan came into the room. He sat opposite me, his hands clasped on the table, and listened with sad eyes to my account of John's condition. He seemed unperturbed by John's delusion that he had been possessed by the spirit of his dead father, and was now inhabited by a demonic Egyptian serpent that demanded that he live in darkness.

'Forgive me for asking an indelicate question, Miss Fanshawe,' Logan interjected politely, 'but do you happen to know if your cousin indulges in self-abuse?'

'I've no idea,' I answered, feeling pink in the face.

'Nor would I expect you to know, Miss Fanshawe. Forgive me, but for clinical reasons if felt I had to ask. We have two residents who've been driven to lunacy from having indulged in the practice and they're both now doing well as a result of medical treatment. Please continue.'

'It is something quite different in John's case,' I retorted with annoyance in my voice and gave as brief a description as I could of what had happened in the burial chamber and the circumstances that had led to it. When I had ended my story, I gave Dr. Logan a determined look.

'In case you're concerned about this, I'm not inclined to believe that there's anything supernatural about my cousin's affliction. I'm sure that his delusions have arisen from the balance of his mind being disturbed by his treatment at the hands of these terrible people.'

Dr. Logan nodded knowingly.

'An extraordinary story, Miss Fanshawe, and I entirely agree with you that what he is suffering from is a medical condition. It seems clear that he's showing all the symptoms of monomania brought on by these recent events. I'm sure we can treat it successfully.' He drew breath. 'Now let me explain how we work here. The men in the private wing are housed on the first floor and the women on the ground floor. We avoid mixing the sexes except at meal times when they are under supervision.'

'What about those people.'

'How do you mean?'

'Those two men with a woman.'

I nodded towards the aristocratic threesome.

'Ah. Well they've been here so long and they're so quiet that they have a special dispensation. Actually,' he added quietly, 'the one dressed as a woman is a man. They used to be on the stage.' He returned to his theme. 'Those who are harmlessly deranged and imbeciles are free to walk about on their floor. Of course, lunatics with a tendency to violence have to have restraints and I regret to say that it seems this will be the case with your cousin. Along with all the other residents, he will eat in this room unless there are any particular difficulties in that regard. Tell me, can he eat normally?'

'I don't know. His dementia only came on yesterday.'

'Sometimes, those who refuse food may have to be force fed. It's for their own good as you'll understand.'

I tried not to imagine what that would entail.

'Your cousin will have a room of his own with a small writing desk, a bedside table and an armchair. He will have his own keeper and his confinement at Stepney House will be treated in the strictest confidence. We have dispensed with some of the old fashioned treatments such as blistering and purging, but we do find cold baths and vomiting quite successful. To calm a patient when necessary, we make use of opium, henbane, hyoscyamus, camphor, hashish and digitalis and, for anyone in a highly disturbed state, we make use of the latest medical devices. The patients are given porter if they wish it and, for a small extra fee, they can have claret and brandy.'

'And the cost of all this?'

'Four hundred guineas a year. Would that be acceptable?'

'Yes. Could he be admitted tomorrow?'

'Certainly.'

'How will you find a keeper so quickly?'

'We'll take one of the more experienced attendants from the pauper wing.'

'I see. May I see the room he will occupy?'

'Of course. If you'd kindly wait a moment, I'll fetch the keeper who'll attend your cousin. His name is Bennett.'

He was about to get up when a thought struck him.

'One other thing, Miss Fanshawe. As you've said, there's no need to consider there being anything outside the natural order in your cousin's delusions, but I don't intend to tell Mr. Bennett about the events which seemed to have brought them on. You'll understand that the keepers and the other people I employ here are not from the educated classes and are usually superstitious. The story of what happened to Mr. Fanshawe could lead some of them to foolish imaginings.'

'Of course.'

Dr. Logan smiled his thanks and left through a door at the back of the refectory. I heard the door lock behind him. The pauper's wing, I thought. After a few moments, he came back and invited me to follow him upstairs.

'Mr. Bennett will be with us in a moment or two.'

He led me up to the first floor, our footsteps echoing against the bare floorboards and wood-paneled walls. Suddenly, I was brought to a stop by a military order being shouted from an open door next to me.

'Halt! Who goes there?'

I turned to see a man in the uniform of an army lieutenant holding a broom in the manner of a musket at the ready. The left side of his face was shriveled up and without an eye. He advanced two paces towards me and was jerked to a halt by a shackle attached to his ankle. Dr. Logan took my arm.

'We have taken in a number of lunatics after the war with Bonaparte, officers and other ranks.'

He led me on down the corridor.

'The other ranks are in the pauper wing so you won't be troubled by them. So many paupers now after the war. The country seems to have been near bankrupted by it.'

A few yards further on, he showed me into a room with a barred window that looked out on to unkempt parkland. A large man with the cheerful ruddy face of a farm hand joined us and Dr. Logan introduced him.

'This gentleman is Mr. Bennett., Miss Fanshawe. He'll be your cousin's keeper. You'll look after Mr. Fanshawe properly, won't you, Mr. Bennett?'

'Certainly, sir,' Mr. Bennett said with a smile. I looked around at the bed, the bedside table, the writing desk, and the armchair. Then I saw a coiled chain attached to the floor with an ankle shackle at its end. The sight of it made me nauseous and I had to force myself to speak with a level voice.

'I'll bring Mr. Fanshawe along tomorrow morning. He'll need thick curtains to keep out the daylight as I explained.'

'We'll arrange that for him, Miss Fanshawe.'

'Thank you. He will be sedated with laudanum and blindfolded during the journey and there'll be two men with me to constrain him should that prove necessary.'

***

When I returned to Calthorpe Street, Robert was lying back on his sofa looking worn out.

'How is he?' I asked.

'He's calm. I've dosed him pretty heavily with laudanum. We can hear him mumbling "Askion, Kataskion, Lix, Tetrax, Danameneus," again and again.'

'How did it go with the magistrate?' I asked.

'He was disconcerted by it all as you can imagine. He didn't see any easy to investigate it further but I'll have to attend a post mortem.

He paused and his expression darkened.

'Listen, Sarah. It pains me to say this, but it's important that you're aware of the delusion that led John to throw the kettle at you. The last time I was with him, he asked where the woman was who was trying to kill him. He didn't know your name but he said you were the handmaiden of Ra and you were trying to use candlelight to destroy him.'

'What a thing to believe about me.' I felt my eyes prick with tears.

'It must be terrible for you, Sarah. I'm so sorry.'

Robert asked me about Stepney House.

'It's a very depressing place as you can imagine and I feel terrible about John being confined there but I've no reason to believe it's worse than any other private madhouse.'

I recited Dr. Logan's catalogue of treatments and told Robert about the keeper who would attend John and the room he would be given with its shackle fixed to the floor.

'When can we take him there?'

'Tomorrow morning.'

'We'll need Sam's help.'

Chapter Thirty Eight

MOUNTFORD

Fanshawe was curled up asleep when I rose the next morning and waited for Sarah to come back with a carriage from the stand at Roseberry Avenue. A few minutes later, she arrived followed by Maggie and Sam. I shook Fanshawe awake as gently as I could.

'Listen, Fanshawe, we're going to a temple where you'll be safe from candlelight. I'll cover your eyes during the journey.'

I called to Sam and the two of us helped Fanshawe off the bed. I tied a scarf around his head and we guided him down the stairs and out to the steps leading down to the street. Sarah walked on ahead, ready to help him into the carriage. Sam and Maggie took up the rear. On the third step, Fanshawe slipped, his arms flailing to save himself. I jumped behind him, grabbing hold of him to break his fall. The back of his head slid against my chest, pushing the scarf down. Fanshawe looked into the bright sunlight and saw Sarah silhouetted against it, running towards him.

'No!' he bellowed, his arms thrashing, catching the side of my head and knocking me down. Sam ran down and twisted Fanshawe's arm behind his back, making him shout in pain as he tried to get away from him. By this time, Maggie had run into the house and had come back with the strait-waistcoat, holding it up for her brother to see. Sam put his large hand over Fanshawe's nose and mouth, preventing him from breathing until his body went limp and Maggie and Sarah began to pull the strait-waistcoat over his head. I held up his arms and Maggie pushed them into the sleeves and pulled the jacket down. Sam crossed his arms behind his back and tied the strings together. I tied the scarf back over his face and we walked Fanshawe to the carriage where Sarah was holding the door open. Before we could lift him in, the carriage driver looked down at Sarah.

'I'm doubling the fare for this. You never told me he was a dangerous lunatic and if he causes any damage, you'll have to pay for it.'

***

We found it a wretched business, getting Fanshawe into Stepney House while I kept up a story of temples and priests to get him into the building. Worst of all was leaving him there.

The following day I received a letter from Sarah telling me that on her return to Tavistock Square, a letter from her aunt's physician was awaiting her. Her aunt had suffered a heart attack and was on the point of death. She was to leave for Oxford without delay.

I read the letter with a heavy heart. I had found Sarah such a warm and helpful companion throughout the course of these dreadful events. I wished she could be with me when I was to pay my first visit to Stepney House the next day. Now, as I sat in my armchair with a glass of laudanum before going to bed, I was beginning to realise that my feelings towards her were more than those of a friend. For the first time in my life, I wondered if I was in love.

Chapter Thirty Nine

Stepney House was as depressing a place as I had pictured when Sarah had described it to me and Fanshawe's condition was equally disheartening. He was sitting in darkness on his bed, mumbling incoherently to himself. A thick brown blanket had been nailed over his window and his ankle was chained to the floor. I could get no reaction to my greeting or my attempts at conversation and, after half an hour, I left for home.

Two letters awaited me. One was from a clerk of a coroner's court saying that the inquest into the deaths at Albion House was to be convened in the Hoop and Grapes public house in Aldgate High Street. The other, to my surprise, was from Wesley Fitzgibbon. It subsequently proved to be the only letter I was to receive from a member of the Wigmore Society. It had a kindly tone, expressing great sorrow about what had happened to Villiers, and I felt some guilt about having dismissed him as a rather pompous man without much of a sympathetic disposition. Fitzgibbon had written to say that he would welcome the opportunity to learn more about what had happened and would I care to have a drink with him at his club the following afternoon.

***

'What do you make of it?' Fitzgibbon asked when I had told him my story. 'I mean the idea of Fanshawe's father's voice coming out of him and the disappearance of this priest fellow. Do you consider there might there be a preternatural dimension to it?'

'I don't know. You could argue that science can't disprove the existence of the supernatural. It can only state that there's no evidence that's been made for it so far which hasn't proved susceptible to an alternative rational explanation.'

'What about the disappearance of the priest?'

'I suppose someone could have taken his body out of the chamber, but I can't imagine it. And Fanshawe saying that he had visited him could be one of his fantasies along with all his other delusions.'

'And Josiah's voice coming out of his son's mouth?'

'It could be a hidden part of his unconscious self.'

'You sound as if you're spouting the ideas of that French mesmerist fellow, Devereux, whose work you presented to the society.'

'I believe there's a lot to be said for it.'

'You may be right. Anyway, it would have to be a profoundly evil part of Fanshawe, given what the voice said. Can you believe that of your friend?

'No, I can't.'

Fitzgibbon lifted his glass of brandy and gave me a teasing smile.'

'Of course, as a Christian, I can speak of such matters as the works of the devil, unlike most of you Wigmore Society materialists. Not so?'

'You're right, of course, sir.'

Fitzgibbon's expression changed.

'Actually, Mountford, the truth is, I'm a man of science, just as you are and I'm disturbed by what you've told me. I

335

have to confess I'm trying not to let it shake my belief that we live in a natural universe and God alone controls the laws that govern it.'

'I'm having the same problem, Sir Wesley, apart from a belief in the existence of God.'

'Well, apart from that, I'm glad we're of the same mind. Tell me, is Fanshawe being looked after well at Stepney House? I believe Dr. Logan's a good man and very up to date with his treatments.'

'I can't answer that, I'm afraid. All I can say is that when I visited him yesterday, he just sat on his bed mumbling to himself and didn't acknowledge my presence.'

'What a sad business. I presume there's to be an inquest into the events at Rotherhithe.'

'Next Tuesday, at the Hoop and Grapes, in Aldgate High Street.'

'I'll come along if you're happy for me to do so.'

'Please do. It'll be good to have a friend there. It starts at eleven o'clock.'

'I'll have a word with the coroner if you like to say I'm happy to be a character witness for you.'

'That's very kind of you, sir.'

'Think nothing of it. By the way, have any of the other members written to you?'

'No, they haven't.'

'I think they're too embarrassed, you know. The contemplation of a fellow man of science believing in magic must be rather disconcerting for them.'

We were about to leave when I remembered Sarah's copy of the hieratic script. I handed it to Fitzgibbon and described

Fanshawe's obsessive attachment to it. Fitzgibbon looked at it under his eye-glass.

'It's Egyptian hieratic script isn't it?'

'It is. How do you know, sir?'

'I learned about it from Thomas Young. He is the most brilliant man I have had the good fortune to know. He has made tremendous advances in his studies in all manner of topics in natural philosophy and he has presented papers to the Wigmore Society. He recently decoded the hieratic script on the Rosetta stone but has yet to decode the hieroglyphs. Do you know about that?'

'I've heard about it, sir,' I replied, recalling Ashton saying that some clever fellow had decoded part of the Egyptian text on the stone.

'Would you like me to show your script to him?'

'I would be most grateful, sir.'

***

The bizarre nature of the events that had taken place at Albion House had drawn a large crowd at the inquest, most people having to stand to get a view of the proceedings. Fitzgibbon was seated at the front. The bodies of Dr. Villiers, Shukura and Gilchrist were laid out in the cellar for the jury to examine. Before the proceedings started, the coroner took me aside.

'Mr. Mountford, I must assume that you were mistaken when you made out the dead body in the chamber to have been that of the man called Amon. I have to draw the conclusion that he left the chamber before the explosion took place and as an inquest is an investigation into the cause of a death, his disappearance will not be part of the proceedings.'

337

'I understand, sir', I said, keeping to myself my certainty that Amon hadn't left the chamber. The coroner returned to his seat next to the magistrate to whom I had reported the events at Rotherhithe. Next to him sat a churchman, there most probably to assess whether or not real devilry had been going on.

It was a strange affair. My copy of Villiers's confession was handed round the members of the jury and many of them scratched their heads as they tried to make sense of it. I was the only witness to be deposed as I was the only sane witness to the event. The coroner did call on Fitzgibbon as a character witness at one point and was given a good account of my being an upstanding member of the community. In the end, my story was accepted, Villiers death being an act of suicide and those of the others being caused by acts of murder by Dr. Villiers and the priest.

When the proceedings came to an end, a man weaved his way through the crowd, announcing himself to me as a reporter from the *Observer*, a newspaper that I knew to be radical in its sympathies but which generated its sales through the purveying of gossip and scandal. When the reporter asked me if I would be happy to tell my story to the paper's readers, I told him I had no more to add to what I had said during the inquest. I felt dismayed that the story would soon be disseminated throughout the city both by the *Observer* and the other papers that would pick it up. Fitzgibbon followed me out and took me home in a cab.

Chapter Forty

During my next visit to Stepney House, Dr. Logan told me that Fanshawe had been suffering particularly violent delusions during the previous week and they had tried a new treatment called the bath of surprise which seemed to have a beneficial effect but only for a while. When I asked what it was, Dr. Logan explained that it worked by means of a tank full of cold water with a trap-door above it on which the patient would stand. When the trap door was released the patient would be precipitated into the water.

'The shock of it calmed him for quite a while,' Dr. Logan commented. 'He was terrified that he might be put into it again. However, the following day his delusions returned.'

Dr. Logan could see that I didn't like the sound of it.

'I know it seems harsh, Mr. Mountford, but treatments of this kind have been tried and tested by highly experienced lunacy physicians and they have effected cures on many lunatics. We shouldn't give up on their efficacy in helping Mr. Fanshawe. It's just a question of time. We're now trying another treatment, the spinning chair. It's the creation of Erasmus Darwin. It helps to rearrange the contents of the brain into their right order. We've found it very effective with patients suffering from mania. Mr. Fanshawe is being put into it now. Would you care to see it?'

I didn't like the idea of it any more than the bath of surprise but I agreed and was taken to the treatment room where Fanshawe was being strapped into a chair, shouting obscenities, and pleading for darkness. The chair was attached to a vertical pole fixed to the floor and ceiling in a way that allowed it to rotate, the chair being held a few inches off the floor. Bennett was standing on a platform next to a handle attached to the top of the pole. When Fanshawe was strapped in, Bennett turned the handle and the chair began to spin round.

'We can spin it at a speed of a hundred rotations a minute,' Logan pronounced. 'We've used it on Mr. Fanshawe three times during the last two days. Get it up to full speed!' he called up to Bennett. 'I think five minutes will suffice, this time.'

I ached with pity for the suffering and indignity of my poor mad friend as I looked at the blur of his white face spinning round. When five minutes had passed, Dr. Logan looked at his watch and raised a finger. Bennett stopped turning and climbed down from the platform. When the chair had come to a halt, Fanshawe's head was leaning back and his eyes were closed. Bennett undid the leather straps and put a bowl on his lap. After a few moments, Fanshawe threw himself forward and vomited violently into the bowl until he had emptied the contents of his stomach. When he had finished and was sitting, exhausted, his head hanging down, Dr. Logan turned to Mountford.

'When Miss Fanshawe first came here, I explained that we don't go in for the purging of the bowels, but the cleansing of the system through vomiting after the spinning chair treatment is no bad thing. Now look.'

I turned to watch Bennett lifting Fanshawe up and helping him to the door, Fanshawe's arm over his shoulder.

'You see. He's become quite calm.'

***

Each of my visits rendered me more and more skeptical of the treatment Fanshawe was receiving. On one visit, I found him lying supine on his bed unconscious, his face as pale as death. There was a tourniquet around his upper arm. I spoke his name leaning over him and tapped his shoulder but he didn't respond. Fearing the worst, I put my ear to his mouth and listened for his breath. It was there but only just. It looked as if he had been bled to within an inch of his life. I went to the door and called out for Dr. Logan. Lunatic voices called back from the open doors along the corridor. "Where's the constable!" "Call the king of the fairies, this instant." "Halt. Who goes there?" There was no sane voice to be heard.

'Dr. Logan, Mr. Bennett! Are either of you there?' I called out. The Greek chorus took up the cry.

'Dr. Logan, Mr. Bennett, Dr. Logan, Mr. Bennett.'

I ran down to the refectory which was empty apart from the three men dressed as 18th century aristocrats.

'Do you know the whereabouts of Dr. Logan,' I asked, my voice raised in urgency but trying not to frighten them. One of them looked at me with bulging eyes and raised a finger as if he had the answer, but he lost the thread of his thought and looked down at the table.

I walked to the door at the back of the refectory. It was unlocked and I entered a hall that looked as if it had once been the entry to the servant's quarters. I opened a door at the other end of the hall and began to retch as I breathed in the stench of excrement. I put a handkerchief to my face and walked into a murky room whose feeble light came from two dirty, barred windows. Twelve inmates in rags sat on filthy straw mattresses, nine men and three women, gazing into space. Each had an ankle chained to the floor and their blank stares spoke of the depth of their isolation from the world and from one another. They took no notice of me coming into the room. A small, brown catholic cross with a circle around its centre had been daubed in what looked like excrement on one of the walls. Below it, a woman held a blanket bundled up close to her chest as if it were a baby. A rat crawled out from under her mattress as she sat, rocking back and forth and whispering to herself.

I heard the distant sound of a man raging and Bennett's voice shouting, 'Hold still! Hold still!' coming from an open door to a passageway on the far side of the room. I hurried down the passage past another room in which more wretched creatures were sitting on straw mattresses and found myself in a scullery lined with sinks and cupboards. A young man was sitting on a chair in the middle of the room, his eyes rabid and his arms tied behind his back in a strait-waistcoat. Bennett and another attendant were bending over him, Bennett holding a large metal key with which he kept the man's mouth cranked open, while the other pushed the long spout of a pot deep into his mouth, tipping it down to get its contents to go down his throat. The man's front teeth were broken off and blood and gruel were dribbling down his chin. I was revolted by the sight.

'What's happened to Mr. Fanshawe?' I shouted to Bennett. 'He looks deathly pale. Has Dr. Logan been bleeding him?'

Bennett turned to see me in the doorway.

'Yes, sir. He's taken no more than three pints. He'll be back checking on the patients on the first floor any minute now.'

The man he was feeding was trying to bite his teeth together, growling and gurgling, his lips drawn back in a snarl and Bennett had to concentrate on keeping his mouth open.

'If you'd like to go back to Mr. Fanshawe's floor you'll soon find him. You don't want to be down here sir. I'm only here 'cause we're bit short of attendants today. By the way, have you seen that newspaper?'

Bennett pointed with his free hand to a penny paper lying on a table next to the door.

'I can't read it, but he can sir,' he said as he looked admiringly at the blazing eyes of the man whose mouth he was holding open. 'He's read it to me.'

I looked at the headline.

The Faithful Narrative of
THREE BLACK MAGIC
MURDERS
One by
BEHEADING
in an Egyptian
BURIAL CHAMBER

'That's all about Mr. Fanshawe, isn't it, sir?'

'I'm afraid you're right, Bennett.'

I ran my eye down the piece quickly, repelled by the account of the terrible events that had taken place being turned into entertainment for a scandal-hungry public. I hurried back to Fanshawe's room, my thoughts in disarray;

anxiety about Fanshawe surviving the loss of three pints of blood, repugnance at the sight of force-feeding and outrage that physicians could contemplate with equanimity their treatment of the pauper lunatics in their care.

Back in Fanshawe's darkened room, Dr. Logan stood looking at his semi-conscious form. He told me that he was quite sanguine about his condition.

'I have great experience in the use of blood-letting, Mr. Mountford. The loss of two or three pints can be very beneficial, alleviating the harmful state of excitability from having too much blood circulating around the brain. With those suffering from mania it has a very calming effect. Mr. Fanshawe's brain is being given a much needed rest after his periods of frenzy. I considered using leeches placed around his neck but I didn't think they would draw enough blood.'

Seeing my expression, he put forward a stout defence of Fanshawe's treatment.

'I have to tell you, Mr. Mountford that we do all we can to keep Mr. Famshawe under control. Recently, he's sometimes needed two attendants to deal with him during his violent episodes, usually brought on by candlelight and so on, as you know. Bennett always puts a blindfold on him when he takes him to the refectory but sometimes other patients pull it off before he can stop them. He's alright in here, with the blanket covering the window. He seems to be able to cope with semidarkness and twilight, and even daylight when the sky is heavily clouded but candlelight and sunlight send him into a violent mania. By the way, he frequently talks about a man he calls "Amon." He has a delusion that the man visits him here to remind him of what must happen on the winter solstice.'

344

'It's just one of his delusions,' I replied, not wanting to get into a discussion about what some would regard as a supernatural reappearance of the dead priest.

When I returned to Calthorpe Street, there was a letter for me from Sarah saying that her aunt's funeral had taken place and she would be taking the coach to London in two days' time. She would arrive at the Golden Cross coach office at three o'clock in the afternoon. She very much looked forward to seeing me again but she was greatly distressed at the prospect of seeing John, given the condition in which she would most likely find him.

***

I met Sarah off the coach and took her arm as I told her about my visits to Stepney House.

'It sounds terrible, Robert. Do you think they're doing him any good?'

'I don't know. He's not scratching his face any more. His keeper's a simple man but not cruel as I imagine many such people are.'

Sarah waited for me to continue.

'But he's still mad. He still has delusions about the demonic snake inside him and he still raves when he sees bright light. There's a blanket covering the window of his room and he wears his blindfold when he's taken to the refectory for his meals. Dr. Logan's been bleeding him to the point of fainting in the belief that his mania is caused by an excess of blood around the brain. Three pints! And his blindfold's taken off when he's given his treatments. Dr.

345

Logan says that habituating him to seeing candlelight and sunlight will speed his recovery from insanity.'

'Do you believe he's right?'

'I don't have the knowledge to judge the matter.'

'What treatments are they?'

'Do you really want to know?'

'Yes.'

Sarah was horrified by my descriptions of the bath of surprise and the spinning chair.

'How could they possibly help him, Robert?'

'I don't know.'

When we were in a cab bound for Tavistock Square I felt I should tell her about the penny paper I had seen with its salacious account of what had taken place in the burial chamber. She broke into my description of the piece.

'Please stop, Robert, I don't want to know.'

'I have some other news for you.' I said at length. 'I've found somebody who's going to translate your copy of the hieratic script in John's pocket. He's a friend of Fitzgibbon, one of the members of the Wigmore Society.'

I told her about Thomas Young and the Rosetta stone. Sarah was silent for a moment and then said, 'I wonder what it turns out to mean?' but her tone of voice suggested that she didn't want to know more about that than she did about the penny paper. We were silent for a while and then she said, 'I have something to show you as well. I found one page of a letter behind my aunt's blanket chest that would explain some of her ramblings. It was from a French priest and it must have been written over twenty years ago. I couldn't find any other pages and there was no other letter with it but it tells us what my aunt meant when she talked about Josiah's crimes.'

She took a piece of crumpled writing paper from her bag and handed it to me.

"Dear Madame Fanshawe,

My name is Monseigneur Gerard Vadier. I enclose my English translation of a letter written to me by a man who is an inmate in the Bastille. I hope my knowledge of English is sufficient to make the translation understandable. I am also an inmate because I am a royalist. He is here because of the terrible crimes he has committed. He now wants me to give him absolution. You will see that the letter is a confession of atrocities he was involved with in Paris during the Revolution while he was a follower of an evil man who gave himself the Egyptian name Sobek. You will learn from the letter of the terrible evils which Sobek made his followers carry out. I have now found out that Sobek's birth name was Josiah Fanshawe and that he was an English natural philosopher who once lived in Kidlington. Would I be right in thinking that he was your husband? Perhaps you have seen him since he left Paris. If so, you must guard anyone who knows him against the mesmeric power he has in gathering followers. I very much regret to bring this bad news to you but I thought you should know. You must pray for him and..."

'Isn't it all a terrible business, Robert?' Sarah said when I had read it.

'I know. At least it's a relief to know there wasn't a supernatural element in your aunt's ramblings?'

'I suppose so,' she said, her voice flat. I changed the subject.

'I'm going to see John tomorrow. Do you really want to come with me? You'll find it very distressing.'

'Of course I do, Robert,' she replied sternly.

Chapter Forty One

The housekeeper ushered us into the refectory where Dr. Logan joined us.

'Good morning to you both,' he said, taking a seat and turning to me.

'I'm afraid we have something of a problem, Mr. Mountford. I understand that Mr. Bennett told you about the penny paper that one of the patients read to him. I believe it described what happened at the house in Rotherhithe and it referred to murder and black magic.'

'That's right.'

'Unfortunately, the story has travelled around the other attendants and two days ago, one of them claims he saw Mr. Fanshawe looking at a piece of parchment with magic symbols on it. That night, when the attendant was taking out the slops to the dustbins, he claims he saw Mr. Fanshawe flying in the air outside his window. I don't really know what to make of it but since then, all the talk has been of your cousin being a black magician and Bennett has taken fright, refusing to attend him. I have transferred his duties to a Mr. Alcott who doesn't have any truck with magic and magicians. However, he's not quite as easygoing as Bennett.'

He turned to Sarah.

'Changing the subject, we've been trying an experiment using what we call our tranquility treatment on Mr. Fanshawe. If you'd care to come to the treatment room, I'll show you both.'

After the horrors of the spinning chair and the bath of surprise, I was encouraged by the idea of a treatment that would give John some peace. When we entered the room, Dr. Logan was taken aside by one of the attendants.

'Excuse me a moment,' he said to us. 'The man has been frightened by the black magic story.'

He talked to the attendant quietly while Sarah and I looked around the room. Our eye was caught by the figure of a man seated in an upright chair with a box covering his head. He was bound to the chair by leather straps around his chest, his arms and wrists and his legs. The wooden box on his head was fixed to the top of the chair with a hole cut into its front to enable him to see forward without being able to move his head from side to side. A piece of wood protruded from the base of the chair to which his feet were strapped. His breeches were lowered to his knees and there was a hole in the seat and stool-pan on the floor beneath it.

We looked into the hole in the front of the box. The man's eyes were blazing and there was a gag bound tightly around his mouth, stretching it sideways and making him look like a gargoyle. Behind it a squashed piece of yellow, saliva-soaked material filled his mouth pushing against the back of his front teeth. It took Sarah and me a few moments to realise who it was we were looking at. I was horror-struck and Sarah ran out of the room, her hand covering her mouth. When Dr. Logan saw Sarah hurrying out, he broke off his conversation with the attendant and came over to me.

'Forgive me, Mr. Mountford. Perhaps I shouldn't have brought Miss Fanshawe in here. I'm afraid a madhouse isn't a place for a woman of delicate sensibilities.'

He pointed to Fanshawe.

'This is our tranquilizing chair. It has proved very successful in treating patients suffering from mania.'

'Excuse me,' I said and followed Sarah out of the room where I found her leaning against a wall in the corridor, her head in her hands.

'Go back in there, Robert,' she said. 'Find out how John's coping with all this.'

'This has to come to an end,' I whispered and returned to the treatment room where Dr Logan looked at me with pastoral concern.

'Is Miss Fanshawe going to be alright?

'I hope so.' I said, not being inclined to discuss Sarah's reaction to seeing her beloved John trussed up like a chicken.

'What a pity that such a wonderful contrivance should be upsetting to her, not understanding its curative powers,' Dr. Logan went on. 'The chair controls the flow of blood to the brain by restraining the action of the muscles. It's the invention of Benjamin Rush, a great physician and humanitarian. He was one of the founding fathers of the United States, I'm proud to say.'

He pointed to a wooden stand with a burning candle on top of it placed in front of the chair at a level that Fanshawe could see it through the hole in the front of the box.

'In Mr. Fanshawe's case, we have been experimenting to see if we can habituate him to the sight of candlelight while he's in the chair.

'How long do you keep him in it?'

I tried to keep my sense of horror out of his voice.

'No more than a day.'

'Is the stifling of his ability to speak part of the treatment?' I asked.

'It is. As well as his not being able to move when seeing the candlelight, I want him to learn to be calm by not being able to rail against it.'

'And when will he be unstrapped from the chair?'

Dr Logan took out his watch.

'In an hour or so.'

'Is this the first day he's had this treatment?'

'No, the third.'

I felt my stomach churn.

'And does it seem to be helping?' I asked in disbelief.

'It's too early to say.'

I heard a muffled groan coming from the box, feeling dumbfounded by the cruelty of it all. How in God's name was this supposed to help him? I took a last look at the Fanshawe's trussed up figure before taking my leave. In the corridor, Sarah came up to me with tears in her eyes.

'My dear Sarah, I'm going to take John out of here. I think he could be looked after in his own home. I've been wondering about Maggie's brother, Sam. He needs work and he's got the strength to be a keeper. It would be better than having him tortured in this godforsaken place.'

***

That afternoon, Sarah and I talked to Maggie about Sam attending Fanshawe at his home. Maggie went to see him and returned with the good news that he would be pleased to take on the job.

Chapter Forty Two

During a restless night, I recalled my conversation with Victor Abramov and his account of the tribes in Siberia and Mongolia in which shamans brought back the souls of those from whom they had been stolen by evil spirits. Could Abramov rescue Fanshawe from his demons?

In the morning, I sent note to John Denley and the following day Denley took me to Abramov's rooms in Maiden Lane. Through the dirty windows of the floor above, I could see the thin figures of young seamstresses bent over their work. Abramov welcomed me and I asked if I could consult him about my friend, Fanshawe. Denley excused himself, needing to return to his shop.

Abramov led me along a dark corridor to a large, smoky, book-filled room lit by two candles on a writing desk, the room's only daylight coming from a small window facing a courtyard at the back of the house. We sat down in frayed armchairs and I looked around as I breathed in the musty smell of furnishings steeped in the aroma of Abramov's tobacco.

'Thank you for giving me the opportunity to see you again, Mr. Abramov. I'll try not to take up too much of your time. I found our last meeting most interesting and I would appreciate it if you could help me in a matter which is causing me the gravest concern. You will remember our conversation about the Temple of Apep and the voice of Mr. Fanshawe's father seeming to come out of him?'

'I do, indeed. Tell me, as we are talking about such intimate matters concerning your friend, may I call him by his first name? It's John as I recall.'

'Of course.'

Abramov listened intently as I told him about what had happened in the burial chamber after my kidnapping and seeing Amon's mutilated body after the explosion.

'And it doesn't end there. The day after I took John to my lodging I found him looking at a piece of paper that he hastily pushed into his breeches as soon as he saw me. He was clearly afraid that I might snatch it from him and see what was on it. Then he started mumbling, "It will happen on the day of the winter solstice when the body of Osiris was entombed." When I asked him who had said this to him he said it was the priest, Amon who had visited him that morning. When I went to the chamber again to identity the bodies for the constable, Amon's body had disappeared.'

I took out a document from my greatcoat pocket and handed it to Abramov.

'This is the confession that was delivered to Villiers's wife the day after he died.'

Abramov read it with great concentration. When he had finished it he looked at me intently.

'This is a very dark matter, Mr. Mountford. Tell me how you think I may be able to help you?'

I told him about Fanshawe's subsequent insanity that had resulted in his confinement in a madhouse.

'It's a terrible place, Mr. Abramov. His treatments are like torture. His cousin, Sarah and I have decided to take him out of there and get him home where Sarah can look after him with the help of a male keeper.'

I paused as Abramov held me in a steady gaze.

'I've been thinking about those healers in Siberia you mentioned and the French mesmerist, Devereux, whose work I spoke to you about. Last night I wondered if John could be rescued from his delirium by reaching into his unconscious mind in some way and freeing him from whatever it is that holds him captive.'

'You mean through mesmerism?'

'I mean more than that.'

'You're thinking of shamans?'

'I am.'

Abramov leaned forward in his chair.

'Tell me, what is your attitude to John's belief in what has happened to him?'

'I want to believe it's a delusion.'

'You mean that he believes something to be true that isn't true.'

'Yes.'

'You may remember my recommending that you try to allow for the possibility of there being a supernatural element in what's happened to him.'

'I do. The thought has been going through my mind frequently but I'm still trying to hold on to my belief that John's condition has a natural explanation even though we don't have the knowledge to understand what it is.'

'Interesting that you use the word belief. Tell me, does this belief that nothing exists beyond the natural world mean that the laws of nature cannot be subverted by an act of human will?'

'You mean by a magician?'

'By a magician, for example.'

'That's what my reasoning mind tells me.'

'So tell me how it is that when you mesmerise a patient you can switch off his sensory nervous system by your act of will while you amputate his arm?'

I held up my hands.

'I don't know.'

'When faced with something of which you have no understanding, such as mesmerism, what is the difference between having faith in science coming up with an explanation and faith in there being a supernatural one?'

'You have me there, sir.' I felt beaten.

'Forgive me. I can't help hankering for dialectical arguments with materialists or, in your case, perhaps, an uncertain materialist. Do you know about Keats's notion of negative capability?'

I shook my head.

'He coined the term to describe the acceptance of living with mystery and doubt without reaching for fact or reason in the belief that the truths found in the imagination alone have access to … divine authority.'

'In my case, there is no divinity and I can't help reaching for fact and reason.'

'I can understand that. I'm only posing these thoughts to see how you can help John. Maybe you will be able to use mesmerism to free him from his delusion. And maybe his insanity is a physical condition for which physical treatment is the only answer. Too much blood in the brain and similar nonsense. I'm sure you don't believe that.'

'I don't.'

'Tell me, why did you come to see me knowing that I believe there's likely to be a supernatural dimension to

Fanshawe's delirium? Perhaps you want me to challenge your convictions, to undermine them or, in failing to do so, allow you to return to them. Your predicament is that you are troubled about the outcome you may secretly desire. That may be your veiled excitement at the possibility of discovering the supernatural. It may be as tempting to you as it was to Dr. Villiers.'

I was shocked at the thought and felt goose bumps rise on my arms.

'You see, if you were immune to such a possibility, you wouldn't do yourself any harm mesmerising John and it might have a beneficial effect, although I doubt it. I consider it a sign of your intelligence that you have an open mind despite your trepidation about admitting it. That's why you came to see me.'

'Perhaps you're right,' I admitted, feeling deeply unsettled. I looked up at a crude mask hanging on the wall next to Abramov's desk. It was carved out of wood and painted red around the mouth and eyes. I was stirred by it and it troubled me.

'A shamanic mask,' Abramov said. He pointed to a drum that looked like a very large tambourine but without the jingles hanging on another wall. 'A shaman's drum, which he beats to drive himself into a trance.'

I was silent for a moment as I prepared myself for my next question.

'Could you act as a shaman and cure my friend?'

'I'm afraid not. I used it to heal my daughter who was suffering from the falling sickness. I encountered powerful spirits inside her and I did battle with them, pitching my will against theirs. I experienced terrible states of madness in my

357

efforts to beat them. I did beat them but I was unconscious for two days before I came out of my trance. My daughter was cured but she was no longer able to recognise me and she hasn't been able to do so since. That's the kind of risk that's involved and I've never wanted to undertake such an endeavour again.'

I said nothing, fearful of suggesting another possibility. Abramov picked up my unspoken thought.

'You're wondering if you could undertake a shamanic journey in search of John's soul through the use of mesmerism.' He paused. 'You're very close to John, aren't you?'

'I am, and I'm close to Sarah, who cares for him deeply and is devastated by what's happened to him.'

There was a tremble in my hands as I asked the next question.

'Is your impression of me one that suggests that I might have such a gift and that I could exercise it through the use of mesmerism?'

Abramov waited before answering and I didn't know what answer I wanted to hear.

'The truth is, I believe you have, but I have to remind you of the risks. It will require you to mesmerise yourself as well as John and you will have to lower your level of consciousness until it becomes one with his. To do that, you will have to be open to his beliefs. As I have told you before, it's a very dangerous quest. The shaman is at risk of insanity or even death when he enters the underworld and bargains with the spirits or goes into battle with them. You should think about it very carefully for a day or two and come to see me again. Then we'll talk about it some more.'

***

That night, I dreamt about my sister, Alice. She was standing before me on the drovers' path in the Cairngorms. The wind was blowing through her hair as it had been on the day she died and she was carrying her sketch book and pencils. Her face was deathly pale but her expression was peaceful.

'My darling Alice,' I cried out and began to weep.

'Calm yourself, Robert. I am at peace, my dear brother, and I have something to tell you.'

She held up her sketch book. On it was a hieroglyph of the Egyptian god, Bastet in the form of a cat cutting off the head of the serpent, Apep. I looked up at my sister's pale face.

'Did you draw that, Alice?'

'Yes.'

'Do you know what it represents?'

'I do. Listen to me, dear brother. If you make the journey to save the soul of your friend, I will be there with you. Don't call out for me or try to see me as Orpheus did Eurydice. I will be silent and you may feel alone but I will be there. Have faith in yourself and you will bring back John's soul to him.'

I awoke with a start and a thump of grief, once more living out the memory of looking down at Alice's pale face under the water, her hair drifting above her head in the stream. I sat up and shook my head to bring myself back to full consciousness. What was happening to me? Had I dreamt of Alice and the hieroglyph as an unconscious incentive to go ahead, or was my sister really alive in some unreachable place?

When Sarah next came to my lodgings, I told her what I had learned from Abramov.

'You mustn't do it, Robert. You could end up as mad as John, and the Russian thinks you could even die. Anyway, whatever he believes about souls being stolen by demons, your mind can suffer terrible damage without it having a supernatural source. The lunatics in Stepney House aren't necessarily possessed.'

'You're right, Sarah, but my rationalism has been shaken when I think about what happened in the burial chamber'. I hesitated. 'If I could rescue John...'

'Why do you say that? You're not going to do this, are you?'

'Just think, Sarah. Wouldn't it be wonderful if John could be saved from his lunacy?'

Sarah took a moment to reply.

'I know. I would try to save him myself if I had the ability to do so.'

'So why not me?'

'I couldn't bear to lose both of you.'

My heart missed a beat on hearing myself included with her cousin as someone she deeply cared for.

'I had a dream about my sister, Alice, the night before last.'

I took a sketchbook out of my cupboard. It was the one that Alice had taken with her on the day she died. I opened it at the page on which she had drawn the sketch of the crag before she fell. The drawing was smudged here and there by drops of water that had fallen on it when the villagers had picked up her body from the stream. I handed the book to Sarah.

'This was the last drawing Alice made before she fell into the ravine.'

I told her about my dream and blew out my breath.

'I'm feeling so perturbed, Sarah, being drawn into this nightmare. Abramov told me that if I am to plumb the depths of John's unconscious mind, I will have to be open to his beliefs. Am I able to do that?'

'I don't know, but John is fortunate to be able to count on your determination to help him. You're going to do it, aren't you, Robert?'

Chapter Forty Three

Two days' later, I was outside my lodging about to get into a cab to take me to Abramov's rooms when a boy ran up the steps to my front door. I beckoned him over.

'It's a letter, sir, for a Mr. Mountford.'

'Let me have a look.'

I recognised Fitzgibbon's handwriting.

'Thank you young man, it's for me.'

I climbed into the cab and opened the letter, feeling apprehensive about discovering the meaning of Fanshawe's hieratic script. I was shaken by what I read.

***

'So have you decided to embark on this odyssey?' Abramov asked as we sat down in his rooms in maiden Lane.

'That's what I wanted to talk to you about, sir, but something else has just happened to add to my disquiet.'

'Tell me.'

He rolled a cigarito, waiting for an answer.

'You may remember my telling you that when I took John to my lodging after the explosion in the burial chamber, I found him looking at a piece of parchment with something written on it. He hastily pushed it into his breeches as soon as he saw me.'

Abramov nodded and tapped his temple with a forefinger.

'Didn't you hear him saying something about what was to happen on the day of the winter solstice when the body of Osiris was entombed?'

'Yes. Sarah managed to get the note out of his breeches and copy it while he was asleep. She recognised what was on it as Egyptian hieratic script. Wesley Fitzgibbon, a fellow member of Villiers's Wigmore Society sent it to his friend, Thomas Young, who has been decoding the text of the Rosetta stone. Do you know about that?

Abramov nodded.

'I've just received the translated text. I read it on the way here.'

I handed the letter to Abramov.

Dear Sir Wesley,

Thank you for sending me Mr. Mountford's rather mysterious instruction. I find it most intriguing. I cannot guarantee the total accuracy of my translation but I believe the text to read as follows:

"The child born on the first day of the first month in the season of inundation is to be sacrificed on the night of the winter solstice when Osiris was entombed."

Given my view that the old Coptic calendar, which is known to us, was based on the Ancient Egyptian calendar, the first day of the first month in the season of inundation would be the 19th of July. This year, the winter solstice will take place on the 21st of December. I hope this helps to solve Mr. Mountford's mystery.

Yours truly,
Thomas Young

I waited for Abramov to put the letter down and look at me before speaking.

'I was born on the 19th of July.'

Abramov waited for me to continue.

'I think he's been instructed to kill me.'

'I have to agree that's a possible interpretation.'

'This is horrifying.'

'I am wondering. Perhaps John's father, or the father he holds in his imagination, still has some power over him and has given this instruction in order to overcome Dr. Villiers's ritual to prevent his reincarnation.'

'It all sounds horribly plausible. But what about the instruction? Who would have written it?'

'Perhaps the priest wrote it before the ceremony knowing what was to happen. In any event, I think you should take comfort from the likelihood that the instruction most probably has that power only while John remains in a state of delirium.'

'You mean if I could rescue him from his insanity in some ... some shamanic way, the instruction would be nullified?'

'It's possible.'

My fear was undermining my good intentions.

'I hate to say this but perhaps he should remain in an asylum.'

'I can understand that but, from what I have learned about you, I think you may not forgive yourself. Think of what you were determined to do before you received that letter. You wanted to bring an end to John's terrible suffering and to the suffering of his cousin who is devastated by what is happening to him.'

Abramov finished rolling his cigarito.

'And I think there's a third reason.'

'Yes?'

'It is that you are in love with his cousin.'

I felt my face flush I and was silent for a long moment.

'You are right.' I said at length. 'This is my first experience of such an emotion.'

'Have you told her?'

'Not yet. I'm not ready to find out if my feelings are reciprocated.'

I cleared my throat.

'There's something else, Mr. Abramov.'

I told him about my dream about my sister.

'If I were a rationalist,' Abramov said, having listened to it, 'I would think the dream was most probably an unconscious spur to you to go ahead and rescue your friend from his insanity.'

'Which you would call bringing his soul back to him.'

'You know what I think, Mr. Mountford. Remember what Keats wrote about negative capability, the acceptance of living with mystery and doubt? And remember what I have told you. You must be open to what John believes in order to bring back his soul. Or what you would call his sanity. The fact that you have come back to see me makes me confident that you are willing to be open to your friend's beliefs. Coleridge wrote something about it, calling it the willing suspension of disbelief in which supernatural phenomena are given the appearance of truth so as to bring them to life in the imagination. Your faith needs to be deeper than a faith in poetic imagery but you know that, don't you? And you want to believe in anything that might save John from such terrible suffering.'

'Yes.'

'And you are prepared to use mesmerism to put him and yourself into trance states to try to achieve this?'

'Yes.'

Abramov took a small bottle of amber liquid and a tiny doll made of cotton and ivory from a chest of drawers and handed them to me.

'It is a shamanic doll from Siberia. You won't be using the same techniques as a Siberian shaman but it should offer you some protection. The bottle contains lotus wine with a few drops of snake venom in it. In a small quantity, the venom isn't poisonous but it will have a powerful hallucinatory effect on both of you. Pour half the bottle into each of two glasses. Before you start to mesmerise John, get him to drink the wine in his glass. Do it late at night in your friend's bedchamber with the curtains drawn and the talisman around your neck. He should lie supine on his bed and you should sit in a chair next to it. The room should then be in complete darkness. When he is in a deep trance state, tell him that you're going to undertake a journey to find his soul. Drink the other glass yourself and wait. As the lotus wine takes effect, the progress of your journey will be taken out of your hands. I can't say more than that as I have no way of anticipating what will happen.'

'Should I have Sarah's copy of the hieratic script with me?'

'Yes, I think you should.'

'More importantly, do you think my sister will be with me?'

'I'm sorry, I really have no idea.'

I was in a state of nervous agitation, wondering what would happen in what might be a narcotically induced delusion or the realm of magic.

'Mr. Mountford, I have to ask you again if you are truly committed to this course of action. I've told you before that there are risks to your sanity involved and even greater risks than that, including John's possible threat to your life. Despite what I have said, maybe you think he should remain in an asylum.'

'No, I can't countenance that. I must go ahead with it, Mr. Abramov. Sarah is deeply devoted to him and both of their lives will be blighted if he spends the rest of his life in a madhouse.'

'Very well. You mustn't wait too long. The winter solstice is in six weeks' time.'

I felt a jolt of fear.

'It's not long, is it? Now listen. It may take some time to surrender your consciousness to that of your friend and it will require a journey through regions of your own mind that you have never encountered before. When you reach the heart of John's madness, you will be able to distinguish him and the snake as separate entities. That is when you will come to your most difficult challenge, requiring an extreme act of will. In order to take on the creature you must reinstate your sense of self and dispossess yourself of John's thoughts and feelings, however much you may sympathise with him. It will be a battle of wills. The demon will fight you by trying to keep you inside your friend and denying your separate existence. You will be acutely aware of your friend's suffering as he imagines you trying to tear him apart and he will appear to be fighting with the creature against you. And you must remember that if you lose that battle of wills, the snake may destroy you mentally and, possibly, even physically.'

He paused and looked intently into my eyes.

'I can see the fear in you, Mr. Mountford, but I can also see the determination. When the work is done, John will be sleeping and you will come out of your trance state. Draw back the curtains and leave the room. If all has gone well, he will wake up in the morning freed from the serpent and the fear of light and the instruction in the hieratic script. He will have returned to his old self and he won't remember what happened while he was in his demented state.'

'And if all does not go well?

'I have no way of knowing. It's a risk you will have to accept.

'Including the possibility, that the instruction to kill me remains buried in John's unconscious mind.'

***

Sarah was horrified by my interpretation of the script. She said that if I wanted John to stay in an asylum, she would accept my decision. My answer was 'no.' I was determined to go ahead.

The two of us evicted the hangers-on from Fanshawe's house with Sam's help and released Fanshawe from Stepney House. We offered the post of housekeeper to Sam's sister, Maggie which she gladly accepted. Fanshawe stayed in his bedchamber all day and night with the curtains drawn,

368

mumbling from time to time. As long as he remained in the dark, he didn't behave in any threatening way towards me or Sarah or Sam. Sarah fed him and Sam kept an eye on him. Each day, both Sarah and I felt the 21st of December getting closer. On the 1st of December I decided we should wait no longer. An uneasy Sarah agreed. It was time to try to release Fanshawe's demented mind from whatever it was that possessed it.

Chapter Forty Four

A dim blue half-light permeated Fanshawe's bedchamber when I opened the door. Its source, designed not to disturb him, was a candle in a tall, blue glass vase on top of a chest in the corridor opposite the room's open door. It was eleven o'clock at night, the hour that Abramov had suggested for what felt to me to be an act of exorcism. The room smelled of opium and Fanshawe was sitting at a table eating the porridge that Sarah had brought him.

He put his spoon down and looked warily at me. I was holding a glass of lotus wine.

'What do you want?' he asked in dull, flat tones.

'I've brought you something to give you pleasant dreams, Fanshawe. It's like opium but the dreams last longer.'

'We don't want it.'

'Why not?'

'We don't trust you. You want to separate us but you won't!'

He stood up and lifted up his chair, pointing it at me as a weapon and a shield.

'Keep away from us.'

I backed away towards the open door.

'Sam, I'll need help,' I called out. Sam came into the room and Fanshawe thrust the chair at him to spike him with its legs as he approached. Sam snatched it away from him and dropped it to the floor.

'K..k..keep away from us', Fanshawe stammered, his eyes now bright with fear. Sam grasped one of his hands and twisted his arm behind his back, making him cry out in pain, while I picked up the chair and set it down behind him. Sam forced him down on to it, holding both his arms behind the back of the chair.

'We w...w...won't drink it,' Fanshawe gasped and snapped his mouth shut, his lips pinched together.

Sarah was now in the room. We knew that this might happen and we had agreed that she would pinch Fanshawe's nose closed so that he had to open his mouth to breathe. This she did and Sam tilted the chair back and I poured the liquid into Fanshawe's mouth. With his nose closed, he had no option but to swallow it, coughing some of it up. His eyes darted wildly from Sarah's face to mine. It reminded me of my revulsion at seeing the force feeding at Stepney House. Sam brought the chair upright, holding on to Fanshawe's arms and I knelt down to try to make out his expression in the gloom. After a few seconds, I saw him become wide-eyed, gazing at nothing like a blind man and his body became limp. Sam and I carried him to his bed and laid him down on his back. I drew up a chair next to the bed and I instinctively touched the cotton and ivory talisman around my neck. Sarah brought me the other glass of lotus wine and stood by the open door giving me enough light to use the raised arm technique I had used before to put Fanshawe into a trance. When I had done so, I motioned Sarah to leave the room and shut the door. We were now in total darkness. I began to brush the bridge of Fanshawe's nose with my thumb in slow upward strokes to intensify the trance state. When I was confident of its depth, I picked up the lotus wine, thinking of what Abramov had said to me. "It's a powerful drug, Mountford. It'll take you into another world very quickly. When it does so, let the drug help you to lose your sense of yourself. Try to surrender your mind to John's until it merges with the madness inside him."

I swallowed the potion in one gulp. Within moments, I felt my head bursting and I was falling into darkness. A harsh, metallic whispering voice spoke inside me, the sound resonating in my chest as if it were a cave. Its tone was both ingratiating and threatening.

'You remember the mesmerist who could unlock the secrets in the unconscious minds of his patients? Now you've done something very similar. You've unlocked your own unconscious mind.'

'You mean you are part of me?'

'Yes.'

I felt myself spinning in space.

'You mean I'm talking to myself?'

'Yes, but the truth is much greater than that. You are in the Abyss, and you will go wherever your mind takes you. Of course, if you want to give up the quest for your friend's soul, you only have to wish it.'

I forced myself to ask my next question.

'What do you have to say about the sacrifice on the day of the winter solstice?'

'We have nothing to say about it.'

'Who is to be sacrificed?'

There was a long silence before the voice replied.

'You must remember that you are talking to yourself. Only *you* can have the answer.'

I was convinced that the creature inside me was not part of me. It was a separate, evil entity inside me. The thought brought a picture of my sister to mind and I remembered the words in my dream about her, standing before me on the drovers' path. "Have faith in yourself and you will bring back John's soul to him."

The voice came back.

'You are wondering if Alice is alive, somewhere beyond reach, but you are a materialist and you know in your heart that she is a figment of your imagination.'

Was it true or was the creature trying to keep her ethereal presence away from me? A room appeared below me. It was the operating theatre at Barts Hospital and I was floating below its ceiling, looking down at the girl whose arm had been crushed in the printing press. I heard her scream as she twisted her body to be free of the two assistants who were holding her down. I closed his eyes but it made no difference. I could still see her, her eyes bulging wide before becoming dull in death.

Another dimly lit room appeared. It was my brother's room in Aberdeen and, once again, I was floating below its ceiling. As my eyes focused, I was stunned to see my young brother's dead and decaying body lying on his bed, being eaten by maggots. My mother and father stood next to the bed, my father looking up at me.

'Oh, no. Is it true that he's dead?' I howled.

My father ignored the question.

'You're a wicked man, Robert; a Sabbath-breaker, a non-believer, abandoning the Lord and holding him in contempt while you pursue the profane ideas of the freethinkers.'

'I'm sorry, father.'

'And why did you let your sister fall to her death?'

'I couldn't help it, father. She ran on ahead when I sprained my ankle'.

'Wicked boy.' It was my mother's voice now, reminding me of when I was locked in the cupboard under the stairs. I had stolen a shilling from my father's desk and the palm in which I held the coin was burning hot.

My father spoke again.

'You will learn what it means to be excluded from the sacraments of the church.'

My mother looked up saying 'We have something for you.' She threw a parcel up to me wrapped in a penny paper. I read the headline.

THE FAITHFUL NARRATIVE OF THREE BLACK MAGIC MURDERS BY BEHEADING IN AN EGYPTIAN BURIAL CHAMBER.

I opened the parcel. Inside was the rotting head of Henry Burrows.

'Oh, no,' I roared in terror as I let it go and watched it crash on to the rotting flesh of my brother's chest. The upturned faces of my mother and father stared back, unflinching in their condemnation.

Once again, I was falling into darkness and into a cavern enclosing a huge lake, palely lit by an invisible moon. Its surface was as still as glass. At the water's edge, I noticed the mechanical doll from Sarah's house sitting at its writing table, dipping its pen into the ink well and starting to write, its eyes following the text. The sound of it whirring and clicking echoed in the vast cavern. When it had stopped writing, I picked up the piece of paper and read the words:

'Please help me, Mountford, and swim into the lake.'

Could this be the real Fanshawe. It was the only time that he had used the word, 'me', not 'us' since his descent into madness.

'It means nothing,' the voice rasped. 'Are you sure you want to go on and end your journey in a lunatic asylum?'

At that moment I felt the invisible presence of my sister and it gave me courage.

'If all this is just the creation of my imagination,' I shouted, my voice echoing in the cavernous space, 'I can do what I want. After all I'm a materialist.'

'What a comic case you are.' There was a pause. 'Go ahead.'

I dived into the lake. A flaming torch floated in front of me, guiding me as I swam, the water growing colder. By the time I reached the middle of the lake there were thin slivers of ice on its surface. The torch dropped down below the surface and I followed it down, finding myself swimming along a narrow, downward sloping passage whose walls were covered with ancient Egyptian images and hieroglyphs. The torch was still ahead of me. I waited for the voice inside me to speak.

'You are in the entrance of a tomb in the Valley of the Kings in the hills above the Nile. It was built for Sobek, Egypt's greatest magician. When the king discovered that Sobek's dark power came from the demon, Apep, he wanted to stop the work but he was too afraid to do so. It remains an entrance into the underworld where Sobek awaits you. Do you really want to go there?'

I ignored the question and swam on.

'I'm merging with you, Fanshawe and I'm losing my reason. I'm on the edge of madness, the edge of your madness.'

'We can feel it,' came the response. 'Soon you will have to live in darkness like us for the rest of your life, however short a time that may be.'

'Am I to be sacrificed?' I asked.

There was no response.

'Are you to be the one who performs it?'

Again, silence.

The tunnel opened out into Sobek's burial chamber lit by a solitary candle on the block used for the beheadings. The flagstone floor was awash with blood. The deranged figure of Fanshawe was strapped into his chair, his head drooping forward. I tried to bring to mind Abramov's next instruction but I couldn't remember it. The snake was preventing me from recalling the words.

'Welcome,' the voice said. 'You are with us forever now.'

'No!' I shouted, desperate to remember. Eventually, the words came back to me. "When you reach the heart of John's madness, you will be able to perceive him and the snake as separate entities." I had to challenge the creature.

'Show me your face, Fanshawe, just your face, nobody else's.'

'Very well.'

Fanshawe lifted his head and I saw my own face, my eyes dead and my skin white as in death. I stared in horror as it transmogrified into the head of a shiny, brown, mummified corpse. It was then that I knew my consciousness had merged with Fanshawe's.

'I am inside you now, Fanshawe, and I can feel the snake inside you. You are not conjoined twins. It is a separate evil being and I am going to free you from it.'

Once again I forced myself to think of Abramov's words: "That is when you will come to your most difficult challenge, requiring an extreme act of will. In order to take on the creature you must reinstate your sense of self and dispossess yourself of John's thoughts and feelings, however much you may empathize with him. It will be a battle of wills."

'Show me your face again, Fanshawe.'

This time I saw the face of my friend smiling at me. He seemed to be his old self, looking as cheerful and spirited as when we had first met. Again, the voice spoke inside me.

'Isn't it good to see how contented we are?'

I hardened myself against any sympathy I might feel for Fanshawe, and prepared myself for what I was about to say.

'I have to tell you about an unpleasant part of you, Fanshawe, a part that delights in cruelty. It derives gratification from causing pain and degradation. It enjoys horse-whipping whores while sodomising them. It enjoyed pushing that needle into one of Dr. Pierot's girls? Do you remember? And do you know why?'

The voice inside me whispered, 'You're hurting him you know.' I ignored it.

'Listen, Fanshawe. I'll tell you what Sarah told me. She believes that you were deeply troubled by your father's disappearance, and you hid it away. You were also enraged with him for abandoning you and you hid that away too. Sarah believes your devil-may-care attitude is a mask and those early years of your life are hidden behind it. The truth is that your cruelty is a way of getting the anger with your father out of you without you unconsciously knowing where it comes from.'

I read Fanshawe's lips mouthing the words, 'Please stop, Mountford.'

I waited for a response from the voice inside me and looked at Fanshawe's now vacant features. As I stared at him, Fanshawe's mouth began to open, becoming wider and wider until it stretched right across his face as if it were made of India rubber. Then something began to push its way out of it. It was the head of a snake, its body as thick as a man's arm. When the whole length of it had come out and slithered down his body, it coiled and twisted around on the blood-soaked floor of the burial chamber.

I looked up and saw identical figures of Fanshawe sitting as still as death in all the chairs around the wall of the chamber. Each had the same expression of expectancy, and each had his eyes turned to me.

'Which one do you want to save?' the voice inside me asked.

'None. They are all illusions. I'm here to destroy you.'

'Really? Do you want to cut my head off? This would be difficult for you.'

I watched the snake vanish.

'I have shrunk a little. Do you want to know where I am now?'

I began to retch as I felt the coils of the snake twisting around in my stomach.

'I think you should know that while I'm inside you, you are still inside your friend. You remember what Abramov told you.

378

'You're not inside Fanshawe any more,' I gasped between retches. 'And neither am I. You know that. That's why you're hiding inside me.'

I felt an agonising pain as the snake twisted and turned, pushing against the walls of my stomach. I tensed my diaphragm with all my might to force the creature out of me. When I felt it entering my throat, I pushed my hand deep into my mouth until I felt its head between my forefinger and thumb. Then I pulled it out, hand over hand. It had become the size of an adder. When its head and upper body were free, it twisted upwards and sunk its teeth my neck. I fell to the floor suffused with agony and pulled its head away, holding it by the neck and crawled towards the axe that was resting against the block of wood. With enormous effort, I lifted myself up, picked up the axe and chopped off the snake's head. I hung on to its neck as it twisted and turned, swishing its tail violently. Eventually it fell limp in my hand and I dropped it to the floor.

Chapter Forty Five

SARAH

Sam and I were sitting in the corridor outside John's bedchamber when we heard the sound of a dull thud. It was three o'clock in the morning. I ran to the door.

'We must go in, Sam.'

'Shouldn't we wait, miss?'

'No.'

Sam followed me into the room. Robert was on the floor, lying on his front, one knee bent up and an arm thrown out, fist clenched. I leant over him while Sam went to look at John.

'Mr. Fanshawe's fast asleep, Miss.'

'Oh, my God. Come here, Sam. Robert's not breathing.'

Sam put his ear to Robert's mouth for several seconds and slowly raised his head.

'Failure of the heart, Miss Fanshawe. There's something I can try.'

'Go ahead, Sam. Quickly.'

Sam turned Robert on to his back, tilted his head back and sat astride him. Then, with the heel of one hand placed over the other, he pressed down hard and fast on the centre of his chest more than thirty times, forcing little exhalations of air from John's mouth. He stopped and put his ear next to Fanshawe's mouth, listening for signs of his breath. He shook his head and started pounding again, this time for longer. He listened again.

'He's breathing,' he said, sitting up. He pounded some more and listened again before looking up at Sarah and nodding. He's going to be alright, ma'am.'

'Thank God you were here, Sam.'

Sam put a cushion under Robert's head and covered him with a blanket from the bed.

'How did you know what to do?' I asked.

'I learned it from an Indian surgeon, ma'am. There are lots of times in battle when the heart fails and breathing stops.'

He pointed to the bed.

'Mr. Fanshawe is sleeping peacefully.'

'Sarah,' Robert murmured as he began to regain consciousness. 'What happened?'

'You don't remember?

'The last thing I remember is drinking the lotus wine.'

'You need to rest, Robert. Sam, help me get him to bed.'

The two of us lifted him up and we made our way to a neighbouring room, Robert's arm draped over Sam's shoulder, Sam holding on to his hand to keep him upright. Robert was asleep as soon as his head touched the pillow.

'Is there anything else I can do to help, ma'am? Sam asked when we had returned to John's room.

'No thank you. You deserve a medal for saving Robert's life. Now get some rest. I'm going to sleep on the sofa in here. I want to be here when John wakes up.

'D'you think he'll wake up sane, ma'am?'

I don't know and I daren't let myself hope.

***

381

I woke when the Temple Church struck five o'clock. I went to the window and parted the curtains for a moment. Dawn was breaking and the sky was blue. It would be a sunny day. What would John do when he saw it? I lay down on the sofa and waited, listening to the sound of John's breathing. Occasionally he made a hoarse grunting sound and pulled the blankets over his shoulder before returning to a state of deep sleep. An hour later, Robert walked unsteadily into the room, looking pale, his hair in disarray, and dropped down into an armchair. He turned to me, his expression dazed and vacant.

'Are you alright,' I asked, deeply worried about his state of mind after whatever it was that he had gone through during his trance.

'I think so,' he replied at length. 'How is John?'

'He's sleeping peacefully. We'll just have to wait and see what happens when he wakes up.'

'You've opened the curtains. Does that mean you're optimistic?'

'I'm trying to be.'

'Why was I on the floor in here?'

'That's how Sam and I found you. I thought you were dead. Your heart had stopped and you weren't breathing. Sam banged on your chest until your heart started up and you began to breathe again. He'd learned how to do it from an Indian surgeon in his regiment. He saved your life, Robert.'

'I've never heard of that before. Thank God for Sam.'

Robert was staring before him, lost in his own world of thought.

'Do you remember what happened during your trance, Robert?'

'No. All I can remember is drinking the lotus wine and lying on the floor looking up at you.'

I looked at the bright morning through the parted curtains. There was another grunt from Fanshawe but this time it was the sound of waking. I sat by the bed, looking down at his half closed, slowly waking eyes. It seemed to take him a while to focus on the image in front of him.

'Sarah, you poor thing. You look worn out.'

He looked at the bright early morning sky and back at me. He smiled and I began to cry.

'What's happened? Are you all right?' he asked, stroking the tears from my cheeks.

I kissed him on the forehead and dropped down next to him, sliding an arm under his back and clasping my hands together around him, resting my head on his chest and listening to the sound of his breathing.

Chapter Forty Six

Sam and I stayed on at the house to look after John. Robert returned to Calthorpe Street. His visits to Lincoln's Inn were mostly confined to the evenings after work. He was suffering from his own loss of memory and for a week, he could recall nothing of what had happened in his trance state. Eventually, jumbled and partial recollections of it emerged like pieces of a jigsaw in recurring dreams and nightmares that sometimes made him fear for his soundness of mind. The following month, he received a letter from his mother telling him that his brother had died. The funeral had taken place the previous week and his body had been buried in St Nicholas Churchyard.

***

It took over six weeks for John to regain something of his old self. During that time, he began to put together a picture of what had happened to him, but it was full of gaps and disconnected fragments of memory. He asked after Caroline and she visited him at Robert's request. She was clearly dismayed by his debilitated condition and she found it difficult to deal with his confused state of mind. What we could see but John couldn't was that her world too had been turned upside down and her spirit crushed by what had happened. She had never fully regained her strength after her operation and she appeared to be lost and alone in her widowhood. She didn't offer to make another visit when Robert accompanied her back to her house and he didn't press her to do so. She told him she had made her lady's maid, Janet, her companion.

***

Both John and I wanted Robert to take one of the rooms in Lincoln's Inn so that the three of us could be together, partly for John's sake and partly, in my mind, for Robert's. He needed some care too and I didn't like the idea of him being alone in Calthorpe Street after everything that had happened to him. However, we knew that an unmarried and unrelated young man and woman living under the same roof could endanger my reputation. I didn't really mind but Robert did. As a result, with the regular payments that John was still giving him, Robert acquired a lodging nearby in Portugal Street.

During the evenings that Robert spent at Lincoln's Inn, John would talk to him about what he remembered, and Robert would contribute his own memory of the times when they were together during John's delirium. John had no recollection of the Egyptian hieratic script that he had guarded so carefully or of Robert's shamanic voyage in search of the cause of his madness. He never asked Robert to prompt his memory and Robert never offered to do so, being acutely aware of the fragility of John's restored sanity.

John had frequent spells of palpitation, dizziness and nausea and for some time he was too frightened to leave the house. Nevertheless, his reason had been restored and he was able to tolerate sunlight and candlelight. He remembered being in the abyss in Albion House and candlelight became essential to him at night. It was as if, being freed from his conjoined demon, he had returned to the fear of darkness that had overwhelmed him in there. Now, he had to have a candle in his room in order to sleep at night.

He slept a great deal, both at night and during the day and, from time to time, he would lose his memory of where he was. On occasion he would have sudden 'waking nightmares' that could be triggered by anything from the sight of an object or the sound of a voice. The moment they struck, they became alive inside him and he would cower and whimper, staring at some invisible threat and holding up his hands to protect himself. Luckily, none of these apparitions contained the delusion that I was an enemy out to destroy him or that he had instructions to kill Robert. When Robert or I was in his company during these episodes we would draw him out of his panic by reminding him where he was and telling him that he was safe.

At the beginning of December, what had been a windy, rain-soaked autumn became a cold, bright, sunny winter. John was still sleeping a good deal and his mind was hazy when he was awake. Nevertheless, he had become calm and his waking nightmares had faded. A time came when Robert and I felt he was strong enough for his memory to be prompted about the gaps in his recollection of what had happened to him. They began with the Egyptian hieratic script.

'Do you remember this?' I asked, handing him my copy of the note.

John studied it closely before looking up to the ceiling as if searching for a memory of it. He looked at it again.

'It looks a bit like Egyptian hieroglyphics, doesn't it?'

'You don't remember it?'

'No,' he replied sleepily.

'It's a copy of a note written on parchment that you kept in a pocket in your breeches. You didn't want Robert or me to see it.'

'Really? What on earth could I have been thinking of?'

He stood up slowly with a grunt and felt in his pockets.

'There's nothing here. I'll look in my room.'

'Not now, John. The important thing is that you don't remember it.'

John dropped back into his armchair.

'What does it say?' he asked looking at Robert.

'I had it translated by a scholar who decoded the Egyptian hieratic script on the Rosetta stone', Robert said and I tensed as he picked up the letter and read out the translation. "The child born on the first day of the first month in the season of inundation is to be sacrificed on the day of the winter solstice when the body of Osiris was entombed." According to Thomas Young, the first month in the Egyptian season of inundation is called Thoth and the first day in the month is the 19th of July.

Fanshawe looked bemused.

'It doesn't make any sense to me. Does it to you?'

'Robert was born on the 19th of July,' I said.

Fanshawe turned to Robert, looking bewildered.

'Are you thinking that you might be the intended sacrifice?'

'That's one way of interpreting it.'

Fanshawe closed his eyes tight for a long moment, shaking his head slowly from side to side. When he opened them he looked at Robert, trying to focus his thoughts.

'I don't understand, Mountford. Are you saying that I kept the note because I 'm supposed to be the one to carry it out?'

'I'm sorry, John. We feared that the instruction might have been given to you when you were in your deranged state of mind while all this was going on. I've talked to a scholar who has considerable knowledge of esoteric matters and he said that if I were to succeed in returning your sanity, he thinks that the instruction would no longer have any power over you.'

'It's strange to hear you delving into the world of esoteric thought, Mountford. I don't know what to make of any of it but you have my undying thanks for what you have done. You have saved me from all that horror. If your scholar is right, we need give it no further thought.'

'You're right, Fanshawe.'

***

It was half past eleven on the evening of the 21st of December. Robert and I were sitting in John's drawing room. John had gone to bed quite early. During the evening, we had both wondered what he would do but, now that he was asleep, we felt confident that nothing would happen. John hadn't remembered what the date was and we hadn't reminded him. He had shown no aggression towards Robert on his arrival at Lincoln's Inn that day and he didn't behave oddly in any way in his presence.

Robert and I tried to retain our skepticism about the whole business during the evening but we decided to wait until midnight passed before Robert returned to Portugal Street.

There was a knock on the door and Sam came into the room.

'Mr. Fanshawe's making a curious noise, sir.'

Robert began to rise from his chair but I stopped him.

'I'll go up with Sam. I don't want him deciding to attack you.'

When I entered the bedchamber, John was crying out, tossing and turning, his eyes closed. As soon as he heard footsteps, he sat bolt upright, eyes wide open, holding up his arm in front of his face as if to ward off an assault from some invisible force at the end of the bed.

'John, John,' I called to him, shaking his shoulder. He continued to stare ahead of him so I stood in front of him in the space that seemed to be occupied by the creature in his imagination and I looked into his eyes, calling out to him again and again to make the apparition give way to my real living corporeal presence.

'Sarah,' he said at last, shaking badly and holding his arms out to me. I came round to the side of the bed and hugged him.

'What were you dreaming about, John?'

He squeezed his eyes tight shut.

'I don't want to tell you.'

We were both silent for a long moment before he spoke again.

'Amon was in the room. Under one arm he was holding a bell jar with the skeleton of a snake curled up inside it. I had seen it before among the curiosities in the Egyptian Hall in Piccadilly. Now the skeleton was alive, twisting and turning. Amon handed me the piece of parchment you told me about and lifted the bell jar off its base. He dropped the snake on to my lap, telling me it was a horned sand viper from the western desert. He told me to hold it by the neck. A young girl holding a sketchbook appeared and tried to take the skeleton from me, but Amon struck her and she fell. Then he took me down to the drawing room where Robert was stoking the fire. Amon stood behind me and told me to push the snake's fangs into the back of Robert's neck. This I did and he fell to the floor.

I was horrified. Had John returned to a state of dementia? I tried to comfort him.

'What a terrible nightmare, John. But it's over now.'

I picked up a glass of laudanum from the bedside table.

'Drink this.'

He swallowed it in one go.

Shall I ask Robert to come up to see you?

'Not yet, Sarah. I feel too distressed about the dream.

He fell back on to the pillows and I held his hand. Within moments, he was in a deep sleep.

Would my beloved John wake up deranged? I couldn't bear the thought. I recalled what Robert had told me about the work of the Marquis de Puysegur and the mind keeping secrets from itself. If John's instruction had been to kill Robert on the day of the winter Solstice, perhaps John had held it in his unconscious mind and it had been reawakened on this night in his sleep. Whatever the reason for it, I thought about the distress it would cause Robert to hear about it. I let go of John's hand, preparing myself for what I had to tell Robert. As I stood up, I looked at John's other hand. It was bunched up and a piece of parchment was protruding from between his thumb and forefinger. Oh God,

I thought. He had found the hieratic text. I took it from him without waking him.

When I entered the drawing room I saw Robert lying on the floor, one knee bent up and an arm thrown out, just as it had been when he had come out of his trance state after rescuing John's sanity.

'Robert, oh no, dear Robert! Oh God!' I cried out. 'Sam!' I shouted at the top of my voice. 'Save him, Sam!'

Sam ran into the room moments later. Once again, he put his ear to Robert's mouth for several seconds and slowly raised his head, saying nothing and not looking at me. He turned Robert on to his back as he had done before. Once again, he sat astride him and pressed down hard and fast on the centre of his chest forcing air from Robert's mouth. He stopped and put his ear next to his mouth and listened. He felt his pulse. He started pounding again, this time for longer. He listened again and kept going, pounding and listening and feeling for his pulse. I knew it would do no good. Sam stood up as I knelt on the floor and stroked Robert's hair. I had lost my beloved Robert and I was devastated. Sam looked down at me.

'What a terrible thing, miss.'

He hesitated before he spoke again.

'Shall I waken Mr. Fanshawe, miss?'

My body was trembling as I shook my head and managed to whisper, 'No, Sam. Just leave me with Robert.'

As Sam left the room, I lay down and put my arms around the man I had loved more than I had known. I stayed there throughout the night, weeping uncontrollably.

Chapter Forty Seven

As I would have expected, when John awoke the following morning, he was devastated by the news. Robert had been the only true friend he had ever had and his death left him in a state of shock and bereavement. I soon discovered that John had no recollection of his dream or the hieratic script and the significance of the instructions it contained. It was going to be a terrible burden for me not to share my unwilling belief in there being a supernatural cause to Robert's death and that John had unknowingly played a part in it. However, I knew it would destroy him and I steeled myself to keep that secret, allowing him to remain in the belief that Robert had died of a heart attack. Meanwhile, I raged at the satanic magician who had brought about Robert's death.

John had become a shadow of his former self. He rose late in the morning and retired early to bed. He no longer took any pleasure in the amusements of his old London life and he immersed himself in books for most of the day. I wanted to return to Kidlington and it didn't take long for me to persuade him to sell the house in Lincoln's Inn and to come back there with me. The housekeeper there was old and becoming increasingly infirm so we decided to bring Sam and Maggie with us to help look after the house.

Chapter Forty Eight

EGYPT – THE WESTERN DESERT NEAR LUXOR
1851

It was early evening when the travelers reached the Theban Hills, glowing red in the light of the setting sun. Twelve camels made up the caravan, ten of them ridden by Egyptians and two by Arab-speaking English travellers in their middle years, having been romantically drawn to the country many times by its mysterious past. All were dressed in brown robes and turbans. The leader sat upright staring into the distance. The other men leant forward, tired after their month-long journey down the Nile from Cairo to Luxor by dahabiya, followed by this trek across the desert.

They addressed the leader as Sefu. He was the young son of a wealthy merchant, no more than thirty years old, but he carried himself with great authority. He had collected his group of adherents in Cairo by performing for four days as a story-teller, recounting wondrous tales of ancient Egypt outside the hanging church in the old city. At the end of each day's performance he selected a few members of his audience, those who were most captivated by his tales and who would best suit his purpose. He told them that, if they were to return at sunrise on the day of the new moon, he would take them to the Valley of the Kings where he would show them the power of ancient Egyptian magic. His proviso was that they must not to ask him what was to happen there. They must wait until he chose to tell them. His drawing power was such that all the men he had selected returned on the day of the new moon. The younger men were excited like children. The older Egyptians were more reserved, given the Islamic faith that their forebears had adopted, but they were deeply curious. The English travellers were aroused by the thought of tales of ancient Egypt that they would bring home with them.

Only the Englishmen had visited the Valley of the Kings before and had been led round the famous tombs of the Pharaohs dug out of the eastern valley. Sefu led the caravan up a track into the western valley where only two tombs had been discovered.

The camels had difficulty with the steepness of the ascent and the crumbly stones underfoot. The riders dismounted and Sefu gave the reins of his camel to one of the men. He walked on ahead as they pulled their animals up the slope. Sefu led them into a cleft in the hillside that had a pile of stones at its end. Under his instruction, they lifted away the stones that they could carry before tying ropes around the larger stones and attaching them to the bridles of the two strongest camels. Then they beat the creatures' sides with sticks and shouted at them, the camels letting out deep mournful groans as they pulled. When four large stones had been pulled away, the entrance to a tomb became visible. Sefu took a box of Lucifer matches from under his cloak and handed it to one of the men who went round lighting the oil lamps that the men took from their saddle bags.

They followed Sefu into the entrance where steps led down to a downward sloping corridor. The lanterns threw the men's animated shadows on to white-plastered walls that were covered in wall-paintings and hieroglyphs. Some of the paintings were of animals, others of human figures with the heads of crocodiles, falcons and dogs. Along the ceiling was painted the endless, undulating form of a serpent. At the end of the corridor the image of the snake continued its progress across the ceiling of an antechamber and into another doorway. Sefu led the men through it into a huge chamber whose circular wall and domed ceiling were painted black. There were no hieroglyphs and there was only one image in the centre of its ceiling, that of the snake's head. A large triangle was painted in gold on the flags of the floor, its three points touching the base of the wall. In the middle of the floor stood a sarcophagus whose sides were etched with depictions of the twisting bodies of Egyptian hooded cobras. Sephu stood at its head and instructed the men to lift off its lid. With enormous effort, they managed to do so and to lift the lid of the anthropoid coffin beneath it. The mummified body inside was tightly wrapped in strips of linen, brown with age, bound with leather straps. The head was covered by a mask, its face painted gold with large white eyes outlined in black. Above it was a headdress that took the form of four red serpents. Around the mummy were the skeletons of seven snakes.

Sefu put his hand into the bag he was carrying and took out a coiling hooded cobra. All the men stood back as he placed it next to the mummy and ordered the lid of the coffin and of the sarcophagus to be replaced. When it was done, he took a glass and a bottle of liquid from his bag and walked over to each man, pouring a little of it into the glass and instructing him to drink it. The young men gulped it down and the older Egyptians drank it more cautiously. The Englishmen looked at each other as if to say, 'well, here goes, old chap,' and tossed the liquid back. It was a mixture of wine and snake venom and within moments they all started to hallucinate, descending into a state of terror in which they saw themselves surrounded by the paintings of the men with animal heads brought to life. Sefu then commanded them to swear an oath of allegiance to him which, if broken, would render them insane. Under the influence of the snake venom, they all did so without question, their gaze fixed upon him as his pale blue eyes glinted like ice in the light of the lanterns. At that point he told them that they were standing in the tomb of Sobek, Ancient Egypt's greatest magician who lived 3000 years ago under the rule of Ramesses II. He then proclaimed himself to be Sobek's eighth incarnation.

Lightning Source UK Ltd.
Milton Keynes UK
UKOW05f0056070913

216712UK00005B/500/P